What Readers Are Saying about Karen Kingsbury's Books

Karen's book *Oceans Apart* changed my life. She has an amazing gift of bringing a reader into her stories. I can only pray she never stops writing.

Susan L.

Everyone should have the opportunity to read or listen to a book by Karen Kingsbury. It should be in the *Bill of Rights*.

Rachel S.

I want to thank Karen Kingsbury for what she is doing with the power of her storytelling—touching hearts like mine and letting God use her to change the world for Him.

Brittney N.

Karen Kingsbury's books are filled with the unshakable, remarkable, miraculous fact that God's grace is greater than our suffering. There are no words for Ms. Kingsbury's writing.

Wendie K.

Because I loaned these books to my mother, she BECAME a Christian! Thank you for a richer life here and in heaven!

Jennifer E.

When I read my first Karen Kingsbury book, I couldn't stop.... I read thirteen more in one summer!

Jamie B.

I have never read anything so uplifting and entertaining. I'm shocked as I read each new release because it's always better than the last one.

Bonnie S.

I am unable to put your books down, and I plan to read many more of them. What a wonderful spiritual message I find in each one!

Rhonda T.

I love the way Karen Kingsbury writes, and the topics she chooses to write about! Thank you so much for sharing your talent with us, your readers!

Barbara S.

My husband is equally hooked on your books. It is a family affair for us now! Can't wait for the next one.

Angie

I can't even begin to tell you what your books mean to me.... Thank you for your wonderful books and the way they touch my life again and again.

Martje L.

Every time our school buys your next new book, everybody goes crazy trying to read it first!

Roxanne

Recently I made an effort to find GOOD Christian writers, and I've hit the jackpot with Karen Kingsbury!

Linda

When Karen Kingsbury calls her books "Life-Changing Fiction™," she's merely telling the unvarnished truth. I'm still sorting through the changes in my life that have come from reading just a few of her books!

Robert M.

I must admit that I wish I was a much slower reader ... or you were a much faster writer. Either way, I can't seem to get enough of Karen Kingsbury's books!

Jillian B.

I was offered $50 one time in the airport for the fourth book in the Redemption Series. The lady's husband just couldn't understand why I wasn't interested in selling it. Through sharing Karen's books with my friends, many have decided that contemporary Christian fiction is the next best thing to the Bible. Thank you so much, Karen. It is truly a God-thing that you write the way you do.

Sue Ellen H.

Karen Kingsbury's books have made me see things in ways that I had never thought about before. I have to force myself to put them down and come up for air!

Tabitha H.

I have read many of Karen's books and I cry with every one. I feel like I actually know the people in the story, and my heart goes out to all of them when something happens!

Kathy N.

Wow, what an amazing author Karen Kingsbury is! Her stories are so heart-wrenching ... I can't wait until the next book comes out.... Karen, please don't ever lay your pen down.

Nancy T.

Karen Kingsbury's words leap off the page.... I just finished a new series last night and once again she has touched me beyond compare!

Kendra S.

Other Life-Changing Fiction™ by Karen Kingsbury

9/11 Series
One Tuesday Morning
Beyond Tuesday Morning
Every Now and Then

Lost Love Series
Even Now
Ever After
Every Now and Then

Above the Line Series
Above the Line: Take One
Above the Line: Take Two
Above the Line: Take Three
Above the Line: Take Four (summer 2010)

Stand-Alone Titles
Oceans Apart
Between Sundays
This Side of Heaven
When Joy Came to Stay
On Every Side
Divine
Like Dandelion Dust
Where Yesterday Lives
Shades of Blue

Redemption Series
Redemption
Remember
Return
Rejoice
Reunion

Firstborn Series
Fame
Forgiven
Found
Family
Forever

Sunrise Series
Sunrise
Summer
Someday
Sunset

Red Glove Series
Gideon's Gift
Maggie's Miracle
Sarah's Song
Hannah's Hope

Forever Faithful Series
Waiting for Morning
Moment of Weakness
Halfway to Forever

Women of Faith Fiction Series
A Time to Dance
A Time to Embrace

Cody Gunner Series
A Thousand Tomorrows
Just Beyond the Clouds

Children's Titles
Let Me Hold You Longer
Let's Go on a Mommy Date
We Believe in Christmas
Let's Go Have a Daddy Day (spring 2009)

Miracle Collections
A Treasury of Christmas Miracles
A Treasury of Miracles for Women
A Treasury of Miracles for Teens
A Treasury of Miracles for Friends
A Treasury of Adoption Miracles

Gift Books
Stay Close Little Girl
Be Safe Little Boy
Forever Young: Ten Gifts of Faith for the Graduate

www.KarenKingsbury.com

ABOVE THE LINE SERIES

Take Three

ZONDERVAN.com/
AUTHORTRACKER
follow your favorite authors

ZONDERVAN

Take Three

This title is also available as a Zondervan ebook.
Visit www.zondervan.com/ebooks.

This title is also available in a Zondervan audio edition.
Visit www.zondervan.fm.

Requests for information should be addressed to:

Zondervan, *Grand Rapids, Michigan 49530*

Library of Congress Cataloging-in-Publication Data

Kingsbury, Karen.
Take three / Karen Kingsbury.
p. cm.-(Above the line series ; bk. 3)
ISBN 978-0-310-32201-6 (hardcover, jacketed)
1. Motion picture producers and directors—Fiction. I. Title.
PS3561.I4873T365 2010b
813'.54—dc22—dc21 2010001895

Published in association with the literary agency of Alive Communications, Inc., 7680 Goddard Street, Suite 200, Colorado Springs, CO 80920. www.alivecommunications.com

Interior design: Michelle Espinoza

Printed in the United States of America

---

10 11 12 13 14 15 /DCI/ 21 20 19 18 17 16 15 14 13 12 11 10 9 8 7 6 5 4 3 2 1

Dedication

To Donald, my Prince Charming …

How I rejoice to see you coaching again, sharing your gift of teaching and your uncanny basketball ability with another generation of kids—and best yet, now our boys are part of the mix. Can you believe it? Josh, one of the leading rushers in our area in his freshman year? Sean catching everything thrown to him? And Tyler tearing up the basketball court? You and our boys, making memories together. Isn't this what we always dreamed of? I love sitting back this time and letting you and God figure it out. I'll always be here—cheering for you and the team from the bleachers. But God's taught me a thing or two about being a coach's wife. He's so good that way. It's fitting that you would find varsity coaching again now—after twenty years of marriage. Hard to believe that as you read this, our twentieth anniversary has come and gone. I look at you and I still see the blond, blue-eyed guy who would ride his bike to my house and read the Bible with me before a movie date. You stuck with me back then and you stand by me now—when I need you more than ever. I love you, my husband, my best friend, my Prince Charming. Stay with me, by my side, and let's watch our children take wing, savoring every memory and each day gone by. Always and always … The ride is breathtakingly beautiful, my love. I pray it lasts far into our twilight years. Until then, I'll enjoy not always knowing where I end and you begin. I love you always and forever.

To Kelsey, my precious daughter …

You are twenty now, a young woman, and my heart soars with joy when I see all that you are, all you've become. I'll never forget your tears that last night when you were still nineteen. Not tears of sorrow or fear for the future. But quiet, pensive tears because your childhood is truly behind you. I remember what you said: "Mom, I've loved being your little girl, and I've loved being a part of this family. I can't imagine how leaving it all behind one day soon will be somehow better." My sweet, sweet girl. Remember that God walks with us every step of this life, and for those who love Him, the best is always yet to be. This year is a precious one for us because you're still home, attending junior college and spending nearly every day studying, preparing, readying for the future. When you're not dancing or singing, you're helping with the business and ministry of Life-Changing Fiction™—so we have many precious hours together. I know this time is short and won't last, but I'm enjoying it so much. I know that come some bright fall morning you'll be going to Los Angeles to finish college, and you will grow and become all that God desires of you. Meanwhile, you will always have a place here with us. Of course we pray you'll fall in love and find that special young man who will love God more than you, and who will treasure your innocence and integrity, your passion and purity. But even as you find him, you'll never really leave our family. Rather you will add to it, honey. You'll always be our little girl, Kelsey. And you'll always be part of this family. Forever and always. I'm so proud of the strength you're finding in this, your twenty-first year. You are beautiful inside and out, and I am more convinced than ever that God has great, wonderful plans for you. Take your talents and go find your platform for Him! In the meantime, we'll leave the porch light on. I love you, sweetheart.

To Tyler, my lasting song . . .

What a tremendous year of growth for you, my precious son. You put aside the stage for now and focused on becoming the young man God wants you to be. In the process you have become convinced that you'd like to be a Christian artist—writing and singing songs for His glory. You'll never know how proud that makes me and your dad. We love our evenings when your homework is finished and you head into the piano room. The chords blend together as you create, and your golden voice fills our home. How blessed we are that your music is the soundtrack of our life. And yet I know that the song will only last so long. You are nearing the end of your junior year already. One more school year and you'll be off to college. One more trip for back-to-school supplies, one more homecoming, one more basketball season, one more prom. I'm holding onto every precious moment, with everything I have. These are the bittersweet years, when the end is all too clearly in sight. And yet, like Kelsey, you will always be a part of our lives here, Ty. You'll excel in the coming year, growing in your talents and convictions, I'm sure. And the deep and lasting relationships you've begun here in your childhood will remain. Thank you for the hours of joy you bring our family, and as you head into a year of lasts, I promise to stop and listen a little longer when I hear you singing. I'm proud of you, Ty. I'm proud of your talent and your compassion for people and your place in our family. However your dreams unfold, I'll be in the front row to watch them happen. Hold on to Jesus, son. I love you.

To Sean, my happy sunshine ...

What a thrill it was watching you take on varsity football, this, your freshman year of high school. You were concerned going in, and that's understandable. "What if I can't play as well as the older guys?" you asked me. "What if I can't tackle?" We prayed and believed and then, right before the season started, you did something I'll always remember. You came to me and asked if I could find custom wristbands for the team. "I want them to say Philippians 4:13," you told me. You'd seen the University of Florida's Timmy Tebow donning that verse on his eye black before each game, and now you wanted to have a similar show of faith. A week passed and another, and every few days you asked until finally I set everything aside and ordered them for the whole team. I'll never see that verse without seeing the sincerity in your eyes, the desperation, almost, that if you were going to play football, you needed to always remind yourself of the truth. You can do everything through Christ who gives you strength. And you can, Sean. You proved that this year by being the team's leading receiver. Oh, and one of the best tacklers on the team. You remain a bright sunbeam, bringing warmth to everyone around you. And now you are an example of faith as well. I'm proud of you, Sean. I love you so much. I pray God will use your dependence on Him to always make a difference in the lives around you. You're a precious gift, son. Keep smiling and keep seeking God's best for your life.

To Josh, my tenderhearted perfectionist . . .

The weeks of this past school year have flown by, and you have grown right along with them, my precious son. So many memories will remind me of your first year of high school, but some will always stand out. The week, for instance, when you first appeared in the paper as one of the area's top leading rushers. The next game someone on the sidelines commented on your talents, and in your quiet, humble way, you simply pointed up and said, "It's all because of God." So young, and yet such a leader already. Another memory I'll hold tight to is the time you attended a youth rally at your Christian school. A few girls from the public middle school attended and spotted you. They walked up and made a face at you. "You go to this Christian school," they sneered. "Yes," you answered. "So what's that mean, you're a goody good?" Rather than be intimidated or feel the need to impress them, you smiled and nodded. "That's right. I want to be a goody good." More than all your touchdowns and more than your great grades, I'm proud of your character, son. Hold tight to that. With great talent comes great temptation, and I'm sure the years ahead will prove that. I have no doubt that someday we will see your name in headlines and that—if God allows it—you'll make it to the pros. You're that good, and everyone around you says so. Now flash back to that single moment in a broken-down Haitian orphanage. There I was meeting Sean and EJ for the first time when you walked up, reached up with your small fingers and brushed back my bangs, and said, "Hi, Mommy. I love you." It might've taken six months, but I knew as you said those words that you belonged with us. The picture becomes clearer all the time. Keep being a leader on the field and off. One day people will say, "Hmmm. Karen Kingsbury? Isn't she Josh's mom?" I can't wait for the day. You have an unlimited future ahead of you, Josh, and I'll forever be cheering on the sidelines. Keep God first in your life. I love you always.

To EJ, my chosen one . . .

Here you are in the last few months of eighth grade, and I can barely recognize the social academic leader you've become. We worried that moving you to the Christian school with one year left in junior high might hurt you. Maybe you'd have trouble making new friends or adjusting. I think you worried too. But look at what you've become in this one short school year! You are one of our top students, and you're inviting a different set of friends over every weekend. I compare that to your utter silence back at the public schools and I can only celebrate and thank God that this was the best decision we've ever made for you. But even beyond your grades and your natural way of leading your peers in the right path, we are blessed to have you in our family for so many reasons. You are wonderful with our pets—always the first to feed them and pet them and look out for them—and you are a willing worker when it comes to chores. Besides all that, you make us laugh—oftentimes right out loud. I've always believed that getting through life's little difficulties and challenges requires a lot of laughter—and I thank you for bringing that to our home. You're a wonderful boy, son, a child with such potential. I'm amazed because you're so talented in so many ways, but all of them pale in comparison to your desire to truly live for the Lord. I'm praying you'll have a strong passion to use your gifts for God as you enter high school in the fall. Because EJ, God has great plans for you, and we want to be the first to congratulate you as you work to discover those. Thanks for your giving heart, EJ. I love you so.

To Austin, my miracle boy ...

Here it is, baseball season again—your very last in Little League. Funny how life goes so fast. We signed you up to play T-ball, and once in a while on hot summer days when you were playing, we'd gaze at the far end of the park, at the field where the big kids played. It was hard to picture you ever getting that big, because that seemed like forever away. So many stages and levels of baseball between T-Ball and the end of Little League. But now, precious son, you're there. One more season, one more All-Stars, and someday soon, one final at-bat in Little League. Your very last. You're an amazing athlete, Austin, defying the odds and proving again and again that you are our miracle boy. I'm sure you'll play baseball again in one of the older leagues or for your high school one day soon. But for now, I will gladly relinquish the role of author and speaker and simply sit in the stands and keep score for your team. Little League mom for one more season. I'm grateful you take your sports so seriously, but even more than that, I'm blessed that you take your role as a Christian so seriously. The other day we were driving somewhere and you said that your friend Karter made an observation. "Austin," he said, "I think you're going to grow up to be just exactly like your dad." You shared that story proudly and beamed at us from the backseat. And up in the front seat, your dad had tears in his eyes. Yes, Austin, you are growing up to be like your daddy. There could be no greater compliment, because your dad is the most amazing man. The bittersweet of knowing that every morning you stand a little taller is juxtaposed with the joy of knowing that Karter is right. You're a little more like your dad every day. I've said it before, and it's true. Heaven has windows, and I'm convinced Papa's still cheering for you, son. Especially this season. As you soar toward your teenage years, please don't forget that or him. You're my youngest, my last, Austin. I'm holding on to every moment, for sure. Thanks for giving me so many wonderful reasons to treasure today. I thank God for you, for the miracle of your life. I love you, Austin.

And to God Almighty, the Author of Life, who has—for now—blessed me with these.

Acknowledgments

No book comes together without a great and talented team of people making it happen. For that reason, a special thanks to my friends at Zondervan who combined efforts to make *Take Three* all it could be. A special thanks to my dedicated editor, Sue Brower, and to my brilliant publicist Karen Campbell, and to Karwyn Bursma, whose creative marketing is unrivaled in the publishing business.

Also, thanks to my amazing agent, Rick Christian, president of Alive Communications. Rick, you've always believed only the best for me. When we talk about the highest possible goals, you see them as doable, reachable. You are a brilliant manager of my career, and I thank God for you. But even with all you do for my ministry of writing, I am doubly grateful for your encouragement and prayers. Every time I finish a book, you send me a letter that deserves to be framed, and when something big happens, yours is the first call I receive. Thank you for that. But even more, the fact that you and Debbie are praying for me and my family keeps me confident every morning that God will continue to breathe life into the stories in my heart. Thank you for being so much more than a brilliant agent.

A special thank-you to my husband, who puts up with me on deadline and doesn't mind driving through Taco Bell after a baseball game if I've been editing all day. This wild ride wouldn't be possible without you, Donald. Your love keeps me writing; your prayers keep me believing that God has a plan in this ministry of Life-Changing Fiction™. And thanks for the hours you put in working with the guestbook entries on my website. It's a full-time job, and I am grateful for your concern for my reader friends. I look forward to that time every day when you read through the entries, sharing them with me and releasing them to the public, lifting up the prayer requests. Thank you, honey, and thanks to all my kids, who pull together, bringing me iced green tea, and understanding my sometimes crazy schedule. I love that you know you're still first, before any deadline.

Thank you also to my mom, Anne Kingsbury, and to my sisters, Tricia, Sue, and Lynne. Mom, you are amazing as my assistant—working day and night sorting through the mail from my readers. I appreciate you more than you'll ever know.

Tricia, you are the best executive assistant I could ever hope to have. I treasure your loyalty and honesty, the way you include me in every decision and the daily exciting website changes. My site has been a different place since you stepped in, and the hits have grown tenfold. Along the way, the readers have so much more to help them in their faith, so much more than a story. Please know that I pray for God's blessings on you always, for your dedication to helping me in this season of writing, and for your wonderful son, Andrew. And aren't we having such a good time too? God works all things to the good!

Sue, I believe you should've been a counselor! From your home far from mine, you get batches of reader letters every day, and you diligently answer them using God's wisdom and His Word. When readers get a response from "Karen's sister Susan," I hope they know how carefully you've prayed for them and for the responses you give. Thank you for truly loving what you do, Sue. You're gifted with people, and I'm blessed to have you aboard.

A special thanks also to Will Montgomery, my manager. In the beginning, I was terrified to venture into the business of selling my books at events. First, I never wanted to profit from selling my books, and second, because I would never have the time to handle such details. More recently, I've been driven to alter my speaking events so that I can be home more often on the weekends. Through it all, you've been creative and hardworking, always ahead of me with ideas of how to continue marketing this ministry of fiction while still putting my family first. With a mission statement that reads, "To love and serve the readers," you have helped me supply books and free gifts to tens of thousands of readers at events across the country. More than that, you've become my friend, a very valuable part of this team. You are loyal and kind and fiercely protective of me, my family, and the work God has me doing. Thank you for everything you've done, and continue to do.

Thanks too, to Olga Kalachik, my office assistant, who helps organize my supplies and storage areas, and who prepares our home for the marketing events and research gatherings that take place here on a regular basis. I appreciate all you're doing to make sure I have time to write. You're wonderful, Olga, and I pray God continues to bless you and your precious family.

I also want to thank my friends at Extraordinary Women—Roy Morgan, Tim and Julie Clinton, Beth Cleveland, Charles Billingsley, Angela Thomas, Matthew West, Chonda Pierce, and so many others. How wonderful to be a part of what God is doing through all of you. Thank you for including me in your family.

Thanks also to my forever friends and family, the ones who have been there and continue to be there. Your love has been a tangible source of comfort, pulling us through the tough times and making us know how very blessed we are to have you in our lives.

And the greatest thanks to God. The gift is Yours. I pray I might use it for years to come in a way that will bring You honor and glory.

Forever in Fiction

Whenever I receive the completed paperwork for a Forever in Fiction winner, I read through the details of the life being honored in fiction — whether the person is alive or dead — and I am touched by the real-life stories that come my way.

That was especially true for seven-year-old Annalee Sullivan — or Annie, as her family and friends call her. Blonde, blue-eyed little Annie suffered a brain injury at three years old due to an undiagnosed case of Addison's Disease. The incident caused her to lose the ability to walk, talk, eat, and sing. Today she has a developmental age of just twelve months old. Even still, Annie is sweet and happy. She wears her pretty hair in a ponytail and always wants a colorful ribbon to hold it back. Despite her injury, Annie expresses a desire to go to heaven one day — a place where she will run and play and gaze at the stars the way she once did. Forever in Fiction was purchased by a number of people at the Annie Sullivan Auction in Bothel, Washington. Annie's friends and church family raised nearly ten thousand dollars for her continued medical care and support. In return, you will find Annie in the pages of this book. I chose to make Annie a famous child actress — one who can do all the things Annie loved doing before her injury. I pray that those who love little Annie will be honored by her placement in *Take Three*, where she will be Forever in Fiction.

Also in *Take Three*, you will find the Kunzmann family. Felix Kunzmann, 44, and his family are citizens of Switzerland, where Felix is a banking executive and his active, young family loves and serves the Lord. Felix won Forever in Fiction on my annual ebay auction. The recipient of this year's ebay auction was our local

Christian Youth Theater—the inspiration for my Christian Kids Theater that first appeared in the Firstborn Series.

Felix's winning bid was nearly $4,000. But he sent a check for $13,000 to CYT. His explanation? He told me that if I believed in a charitable cause, he could believe in it. He had one request. Could I please make his whole family Forever in Fiction, if possible? As it turned out, the fit was perfect for *Take Three*. The Kunzmann family plays a family visiting the United States for a year while the dad takes part in an American banking project. In Indianapolis they play a crucial counseling-type role in the life of Andi Ellison. Felix, thank you for your generosity and for helping me think outside the box when it comes to Forever in Fiction™.

In addition to his banking expertise, Felix is known among his family and friends as a man very much in love with his wife. He met her at age ten at a Christian Scout camp, and he knew from the moment he saw her that one day he would marry her. But it took a little longer to convince Lucia. Seven years later he began to turn her head, and Felix still remembers their first kiss. Today Lucia remains a devoted follower of Jesus, and she oversees the lives of their three children. The Kunzmanns have a big house with lots of activities for kids, and an open door to the teens in their area who need to know someone cares for them. Lucia is taking counseling courses so she can better help teens and married couples. Their children are Marco, 17; Kenny, 15; and Nathalie, 13. Like their parents, the Kunzmann kids do Christian Scouts. They also love soccer, music, and being available to hang out with the kids who frequently visit their house. Felix, I hope you see yourself and your family in *Take Three*, and I hope you are honored to know that the five of you will now be Forever in Fiction.

For those of you who are not familiar with Forever in Fiction™, it is my way of involving you, the readers, in my stories, while raising money for charities. To date, Forever in Fiction has raised more than $100,000 at charity auctions across the country. Obviously, I am only able to donate a limited number of these each year. For that reason, I have set a fairly high minimum bid on this package so that the maximum funds are raised for charities.

If you are interested in having a Forever in Fiction™ package donated to your auction, contact my assistant, Tricia Kingsbury, at Kingsburydesk@aol.com. Please write *Forever in Fiction* in the subject line.

Take Three

One

Andi was sick of lying to herself.

After her first night with Taz, the two of them spent most of the next week in each other's arms. But then he began making strange excuses and standing her up. He was working on another film, he told her. Something that would take up most of his summer. It wasn't until one afternoon when she was walking from the library to the cafeteria that she saw Taz arm in arm with a petite brunette. Andi was almost certain she recognized the girl, and as they came closer, she knew where she'd seen her. The brunette had been part of the ensemble in *Scrooge*.

Which could only mean one thing. She was Taz's new actress, his new project. He was probably telling her that true beauty came from using her body as art, or something like that. Andi watched the way the girl gazed at him, how she laughed and giggled and walked close to his arm. The picture burned an image in her mind and tortured her late at night.

As the truth dawned on her, Andi could think only one thing: Bailey's warning had been right after all. Now Andi had no one but herself to blame. She was a fool, and her heart was broken in half. She couldn't eat or sleep, and she felt nauseous nearly every morning, drowning in the heartache of all she'd given up, all she'd lost to a guy who had played her for a fool.

Taz was a fraud. Everything he'd told her had been a lie, and once Andi admitted that much to herself, she knew she could move on. She was still devastated, but at least she wasn't waiting for his call while he was out sleeping with someone else.

The next lie was harder to handle, the one she'd been telling herself. The lie that the physical changes in her body could all be explained by a broken heart. The headaches and nausea, the vomiting some mornings. Her symptoms were too strong to be merely a physical manifestation of heartache. Finally, on the last day of May she drove to the local pharmacy and bought something she had never planned to need until well after she was married.

A pregnancy test.

She took it home, read the directions, and then drew a deep and steadying breath. In two minutes she'd have the results.

Results that—whatever they were—would change the rest of her life.

BAILEY GRABBED HER BROTHER'S DUFFEL BAG from the hall closet and raced back to her bedroom. Fifteen minutes until she had to be on the road, headed to Lake Monroe for the Campus Crusade retreat. She'd been waiting months for this weekend, but her history test for her summer course at Indiana University had run late and now she was scrambling. She felt frantic as she grabbed a pair of jeans, a few T-shirts, and a hooded sweatshirt. She looked around her room, and her eyes fell on a framed photo of her and Tim. For an instant she didn't move or breathe or remember what she was doing. Why did the picture bug her? It was taken on opening night of *Scrooge* last winter, she and Tim both dressed in their costumes. But something about his eyes weren't right, like she was any other fan, lucky to have her picture taken with him. He was her boyfriend, but his expression would've been the same if she wasn't in the picture at all.

"Focus." She turned her attention back to the bag and picked up where she left off. Socks, her Bible, the journal her mom gave her for the trip. Half a dozen other necessities and she zipped the top. Tim was attending the retreat for sure, which was good. They needed to talk. Bailey hoped time alone at the campsite would bring them closer to God and each other—something to help her remember why she was dating him when her heart couldn't stop thinking about Cody Coleman.

A sad sigh slipped through her lips as she slung the duffel bag over her shoulder. Cody wouldn't be there this weekend. He had plans with his mom, last Bailey heard. Just as well. Cody never seemed to want more than a friendship with her, but when Bailey was near him she could barely remember Tim's name. That had to mean something, right? She and Cody were closer now than they'd been for a while. They texted sometimes, and once in a while they even talked on the phone. Tim said he didn't mind this and was confident in who he was and with his place in Bailey's life.

Even if privately Bailey had doubts.

Bailey breathed deep and steadied her heart. Forget about the guys. This weekend was about time alone with God and her friends from Cru. Her ringtone went off just as she left her room. The caller ID told her it was Tim, and she smiled. He was a great guy, really. If it weren't for Cody, she'd probably be wondering whether Tim was maybe the one she could spend her life with. Her crush on Tim had lasted since she was a sophomore in high school, and now that they'd been dating for more than a year, she should've been the happiest girl on the Indiana campus.

She slid her phone open. "Hey!" She kept her tone upbeat. "Don't tell me you're already there!"

"Hey," his voice told her something was wrong. "I've got strep throat. A hundred and two fever. I'm a wreck."

"No." Disappointment came over her. She'd pictured taking walks with Tim during free time at the retreat, learning more about his dreams for the future. Maybe getting past her uncertainty and finding a stronger connection with him. "Did you go to the doctor?"

"We just got back. I'm in bed all weekend. Doc says no going out, no visitors, and to take all my antibiotics. I guess it's really contagious."

"That's terrible." Bailey flopped onto her bed. As sorry as she was about how this changed the feel of the retreat, she felt worse for him. "Okay. Well get some rest and take care of yourself. I'll call you Monday."

"Okay." He sounded defeated. "I'll pray for you."

"You too."

They hung up and Bailey slumped over her knees. Maybe she wouldn't go after all. There was a chance of rain, so how much fun would that be? Stuck in a cabin with a bunch of girls she didn't know that well, trying to stay dry all weekend. She sighed, but as she did she caught a glimpse of the sky. A sliver of blue between the clouds. The school year was wrapping up and classes this week had been tougher than she expected. She was worried about a couple upcoming finals. Between that and the New York audition she was hoping for in August, she needed this time. Needed to be close to God to prepare for whatever the next season in life held.

"Fine," she spoke the word out loud, as if God were standing there watching her. Which He was, in a way. "I'll go, Lord. And You go with me, okay?" She couldn't think of a single time when she'd gone to a church camp or retreat or listened to a sermon and not come home with something special, some way that the Lord had proved the time well spent.

This retreat would be no different. Maybe she'd get closer to the girls in her Bible study. They had plans to start up again in the fall, and next term maybe they would become closer friends outside Cru. She knew some of the girls had to be struggling the way Andi was—with the campus party life or guys who wanted more than they were willing to give. Their struggles were the same ones Bailey faced—uncertainty about life and their futures, and it helped to talk to each other. But so far the meetings had netted little more than a surface discussion about the weekly Bible passage. Maybe if she led the way and talked about her struggles, the tone of the meetings would change.

She gathered her bag, lifted it up onto her shoulder again, and tucked her sleeping bag and pillow under her other arm. When she reached the bottom of the stairs, her mom was sitting next to Ricky, helping him with his math.

"Okay, so if Susie has five horse stickers, Claire has three cat stickers, and Edward has four dog stickers, what is the average number of stickers they each have? That's the question."

Bailey smiled as she set her things down. She remembered those days, when the most difficult thing about life was figuring out how many stickers Edward had. She put her arm around Ricky's shoulders. "How's it going, bud?"

"Pretty good." He tapped his pencil on his paper and flashed her a crooked grin. "I hate word problems."

"I know." She shared a look with her mom. "I must've been the worst Flanigan kid at word problems, wouldn't you say?"

"You and Connor." Her mom laughed. "I had to use drawings and apples and oranges, sometimes full-on dramas just to get the problem to click in your head."

"Good news, bud," she kissed Ricky on the cheek. "If you don't major in math, you'll be finished with it after your first quarter in college." She pressed her fist in the air and did a little dance. "The way I'm finished with it."

"That's forever away." Ricky sighed and stared once more at the math paper.

Their mother's smile softened. "Not forever, buddy. I would slow life down if I could. You're my last little guy to go through Mrs. Ebner's word problems." She patted Ricky's hand. "We can take our time."

Ricky groaned and laughed at the same time. "As long as I finish before dinner. Me and Dad wanna play catch."

With Tim not going on the retreat, Bailey was no longer in a hurry. She would get there eventually, but she loved this—time around her family. The older she got, the more every weekend at home, every summer, felt precious. As if she could feel time pulling her toward a grown-up life. Whatever that might be.

"Where's Dad?"

"Meetings in the city. The team's excited about next season."

A smile lifted Bailey's spirits. That was the beauty of sports, the joy of having a coach for a father. Every season was full of hope and expectation. It kept life entertaining and full of possibility. "We'll have to take in a few days of summer camp."

"A few?" Ricky shook his head. "No, sir. I'm going as many days as I can. Dad says their new running back is the fastest guy he's ever seen." He puffed out his chest. "Other than me, of course."

They all laughed, and Bailey asked about the other boys.

"No homework." Jenny stood and got cups of water for herself and Ricky. "They're on a bike ride with Connor."

"Oh." Bailey took a seat at the kitchen bar. "I have that Campus Crusade retreat at Lake Monroe, but I'll wait till they come back. I haven't talked to Connor in two days. The other boys either."

"They're doing great. I can't believe how tall Connor's getting."

"Is he doing CKT's summer camp?"

"He said he'd like to focus more on football this summer." Jenny took a long sip of her water. "I'm proud of him. It isn't easy to switch gears."

"Definitely not." Bailey pictured her younger brother, her best friend. In the end, he was bound to be a better singer than a tackler, but he was willing to try new things. She loved that about him. Her mom returned to helping Ricky, and after five minutes, the other boys trudged through the back door.

"I can't believe it; I mean you could've been killed." Shawn was talking fast, his words running together. "That was the craziest thing I've ever seen."

Their mom was immediately on her feet. "Who could've been killed?"

"BJ." Shawn let out a long breath, as if he'd been holding it in the whole ride back. "It was a northern copperhead, Mom. I swear. I studied that snake this year, and it was exactly the same."

"Yep." BJ flexed his biceps. "I'm a hero. I saved all our lives."

"No, he was crazy, I swear." Shawn was adamant.

Jenny held up her hand. "Will someone start at the beginning? Please."

"We were riding off-road," Justin stepped forward, "through that field at the end of the street, just up from the stream. And all of a sudden, this snake crossed our path. Connor went around him, but BJ was next and he ran right over him, right across the middle of him."

BJ let his arms fall to his side. "I didn't really mean to, Mom. It just sort of happened."

"So we got off our bikes and looked at him, and sure enough," Shawn still looked stunned. "It was a northern copperhead. Same spade-shaped head, same puffy body. I'd know that snake anywhere."

Bailey walked up and listened to the conversation. In no time, their mom took control. "You should've gone around him, BJ. You need to respect snakes and keep your distance. Especially if it's poisonous."

"Yeah, you don't run right over them." Shawn waved at his brother and then flashed nervous eyes at their mom. "He could've been killed, Mom. I swear."

"And Connor, as for you ... you rode around the snake, but maybe you should've stopped and told your brothers about the danger."

"I didn't know it was a copperhead."

"Still, you were the first to come across it. Next time, pull over and stop. Make sure your brothers follow your lead."

The whole drama was resolved in a matter of minutes, but Bailey shuddered at the way it might've played out. What if Connor had been bitten, or one of her other brothers? For that matter, what if there were copperhead snakes lurking near the cabins on the far side of Lake Monroe? She tried not to think about it as she said her good-byes. Certainly God would protect her from the wrath of the northern copperhead.

Her mom hugged her before she left. "I'm sorry about Tim. But God has a reason for you to be out there this weekend." She put her hand alongside Bailey's face. "You're my sweet girl, Bailey. I love you so much." She kissed her daughter's cheek. "I can't wait to hear about it when you get home."

Bailey hugged her mom for a long time, and as she walked to her car and started out, she kept thinking about her family, how much she loved them, and how a single snake encounter could've cost one of her brothers his life. She felt sick as she reached the main road. *Don't think about it*, she told herself. *Focus on what's ahead.*

The drive to the campground took longer than Bailey expected, and she found herself scanning the side of the road for snakes. Just in case. Maybe there was a copperhead infestation happening in the hills around Bloomington. If so, at the first possible chance, she would head back home. She could have a retreat in her own bedroom.

She pulled up at the camp as a few girls from her Bible study arrived. They checked in with Daniel—the retreat leader—and received their cabin assignments. Bailey felt her spirits lighten. Most of the girls from her small group were rooming with her. "Watch out for copperheads," Bailey allowed a half grin as they carried their sleeping bags and pillows to their cabin. Theirs was the one closest to the common area. "My brothers were nearly killed by one earlier."

They unpacked and were lying on their bunks talking about the weekend, when they heard the sound of a whistle, followed by a megaphone announcement. "Everyone report to the fire pit."

Not until they filed out and took their spots around a roaring campfire did Bailey look across the circle and see Cody. Her brow raised and she had to stop herself from getting up and going to him. Instead she locked eyes with him and showed her surprise with her expression. He wasn't supposed to be here, right? "You're here," she mouthed the words silently.

He smiled, his eyes lingering on hers. Whatever had happened, he'd explain later.

For now they needed to focus on Daniel. He explained that he hoped they would accomplish two goals while out in the woods that weekend. First, he had prayed they would all come away closer to Jesus, closer to the faith that bound them. And second, he hoped they would be closer with each other. He picked up a large stick and poked at the fire for a minute. As he did, he separated a few pieces of burning wood from the rest of the blaze.

"College life is a lot like this fire. Professors, class agendas, clubs, friends … there's a bunch of things that will try to separate you from the fire of faith. And once you're separated," he poked at the lone pieces again and everyone watched, the realization clear. The flame around those pieces had already gone out. "Once you're separated, you can grow cold pretty fast. Especially on a college campus." Then, with one more push of his stick, he moved the once-burning pieces of wood back to the fire. Immediately the flames circled them and they began to burn once more. "We have to stay in the fire, friends. And what better way to do that than by building friendships through Cru."

Bailey thought of the cooling pieces of wood, at the way the glow from the fire faded entirely in a matter of seconds. Andi was like that. She'd come to Indiana University so strong—the daughter of missionaries, after all. But her doubts and curiosity had taken her in all the wrong directions. And toward Taz, which wasn't a wise direction at all. These days Andi was distant and gone most of the time. When Bailey tried to talk seriously with her, Andi always had a class or a study group to get to. Bailey's heart hurt for her friend. She should be here now, a part of the retreat.

She blinked and looked up, and without trying, her eyes found Cody's again. A memory came to mind, she and her family at Cedar Point in Ohio one summer vacation when she was in middle school. A new roller coaster had just opened, and Bailey and Connor couldn't wait to try it. They rode it four times that day, and every time they reached the long downhill, for a few thrilling seconds, her heart flew to her throat, and she felt dizzy and free and beyond wonderful.

The same way she felt now.

She turned her attention to Daniel again. The roller coaster feeling was gone, but her heart was pounding. *God, what's happening? Cody wasn't supposed to be here, and now … why these feelings? Don't let me get distracted, please.* Daniel handed out a list of duties for the weekend. Each cabin would be responsible for cooking one meal and for cleaning up after another. Working as a team would be part of the fun, for sure. Daniel asked them to check the schedules, and with the girls gathered around her, Bailey pointed out that they were responsible for tonight's dinner. No matter how much she wanted to talk to Cody, the conversation would have to wait. Daniel went over the rest of the itinerary, and Bailey was glad to see that he'd included many hours of solitary time, chances when they could get to know each other or take time alone with God.

"The times with an asterisk are intended as silent times, moments when no one should be talking. Sometimes with God, it's important that we listen. Doesn't matter if you stay close by or find a bluff overlooking the water. Just don't talk." He grinned at Bailey and the girls on either side of her. "Of course, that might be harder for some Cru kids than others."

"Hey," Bailey was quick to tease him back, but then she immediately covered her mouth with her hands.

"See. Talking just comes easier for some of us."

Again Cody caught her eye and they shared a quiet laugh. If anyone knew about Bailey's ability to talk, it was Cody. He'd practically been another brother back when he lived with her family. The laughter faded, and a few guys threw more wood on the fire as Daniel dismissed them and gave out final directions for the night. "Bailey, your group should start dinner."

"We're on it," Bailey moved with the group toward a canopy covering a series of picnic tables and a camp stove setup. "Best burritos ever, coming up." She glanced over her shoulder and walked a little slower so Cody could catch up.

He wore jeans and a soft blue plaid button-down shirt layered over a white T-shirt. Bailey tried not to notice, but there was no denying the fact—he looked so handsome.

"Hey," he brushed his elbow against hers as he came alongside her, his voice low. "We'll talk later." He nodded toward the camp stove. "You're busy."

"Your mom?" Bailey let the other girls get ahead of them.

His smile faded. "It's a long story."

"Later." Again their eyes held. "I'm glad you're here."

"Me too." He glanced at the girls unloading coolers and pulling large pans from a box. Then he gave her a wary look. "Good luck on the burritos."

"Hey!" He was teasing her, but only because he knew her that well. "My cooking's gotten better. Seriously."

"Hmmm." He nodded, his expression one of mock doubt. "You mean you got over your fear of turning on the stove? Even for boiling water?"

"I wasn't that bad." She was laughing quietly now, because he was right. She used to have Connor cook Cream of Wheat for her because she was afraid of the stove. "I can even cook frozen lasagna now."

"Wow ..." his eyes danced, but he backed further away, his eyes on the girls again. "Go work. We'll talk after dinner."

She waited a few seconds, then hurried to join her team. Already the girls had lit the stove and were warming up the precooked ground beef in an oversized pan. They divided up the tasks, taking turns grating cheese and lettuce, and stirring the meat. Bailey put herself in charge of heating the tortillas.

While they worked, Bailey kept looking up and discretely finding Cody. He was working with the guys in his cabin, collecting wood from the campsite and stacking it near the fire. The muscles in his back flexed every time he bent down for another armful, and Bailey struggled to focus on the dinner.

"Don't know how much good the wood will do us," one of the girls sighed as she cut tomatoes and put them into a bowl. "If it rains, we'll be sitting around a bunch of soggy logs."

"Actually, the latest reports say the rain won't come till next week."

Another girl smiled big. "Which is why I'm here. I'm not a big fan of camping in the rain."

Bailey was glad to hear the updated weather report. They still would have had fun in the rain, but it would have limited the time they could spend outdoors. Either way, this weekend was bound to make Cody and her stronger friends. She could already feel that much. Even if they didn't quite find the sort of connection they'd shared all those yesterdays ago.

One of the girls came up beside her. "You're quiet." She glanced at the pan of warmed tortillas and used her hand to feel for heat. "What're you thinking about?"

"Life." She shifted the pan and turned down the heat. "And how glad I am that I didn't let a northern copperhead snake stop me from being here this weekend."

They both laughed, and Bailey promised to tell the story about the snake later, when they were all tucked in their sleeping bags, safe from whatever creepy crawly things might come out at night.

The meal took very little time to pull together, and the guys had two oversized piles of wood collected by the time Daniel called everyone to a double row of picnic tables. "Thank You for the food, God, and thanks for the dry weather. We really appreciate it." Daniel raised his fork. "Amen!"

Already Bailey could feel herself relax, feel the tension from the past week and her upcoming finals slipping away. She and Cody exchanged glances now and then, but Bailey sat with the girls around the fire and talked about the tests ahead and the grades they were expecting. A few of them, like Bailey, were taking classes, but the rest of them were going home in a few weeks or sticking around for summer jobs.

"You're lucky you live here," one of them told Bailey. "I'd be up at this lake all the time."

She thought about that, how living close to a place like Lake Monroe made it easier to take it for granted. Maybe after the retreat she could talk Andi into coming up here. Whatever it took to help her find the truth once more. She looked across the fire and watched Cody talking to a group of guys. With Daniel in charge, she and Cody might not have much time to talk alone. That was okay, really. She had a boyfriend, after all. This trip was about seeking God and finding direction for the days ahead.

And these days she needed that more than anything else.

Two

THE LOS ANGELES FILM FESTIVAL HAD been under way for three days, and Keith Ellison couldn't believe how well things were going. They'd put the Brandon Paul issue aside for now, but what they'd learned was encouraging. Despite a recent press release, the young heartthrob had never agreed to participate in an NTM original film with a storyline so much like *Unlocked.* The bestselling novel was the basis for the next movie Keith and his friend Chase Ryan were set to make, and Brandon Paul wanted to star in the picture. His agent and Luke Baxter—lawyer for Jeremiah Productions—were working behind the scenes putting big pressure on NTM to print a retraction.

Chase and Keith had both made up their minds, that no matter what stance NTM took when the discussions were complete, they wanted to work with a different studio. The buzz around town was that an announcement could come any day with NTM's retraction about the proposed film and Brandon Paul's decision to do the *Unlocked* picture with Jeremiah Productions.

Major studios were courting them like a high school prom queen, and now they were thirty minutes from the red carpet premiere of *The Last Letter*. Keith, Lisa, Chase, and Kendall were staying in hotel a mile away from the festival.

"Can you fix my bowtie?" Keith was in Chase's room. He stepped out of the bathroom. "It won't stay straight."

"Shouldn't Lisa do this?" Chase laughed. "No, seriously, come here. I'll fix it." He met his friend halfway and tweaked the back of the bowtie so that the front straightened out and stayed that way. "Where is she anyway?"

"Curling her hair. She won't make us late, but she'll be done with fifteen seconds to spare." Keith checked his look and visibly relaxed a little. He'd been praying for weeks about this event, and now it was here. "Can you believe this? Our first premiere just half an hour away?"

Chase smiled. "Makes me wonder how my feet are still on the ground." He slipped on his shoes and adjusted his pant legs. "I keep thinking back to all we've gone through, back when this day looked like it'd never come."

"Then God brought Ben Adams to the rescue." Keith grinned. "He'll be here, right?"

"He's in the lobby with Kendall. I stopped down to check on our ride and they were already there." He paused. "Kendall looks stunning. Made me remember what a big deal this is."

Keith studied his friend, and a hint of concern flashed across his heart. Chase and Kendall had gotten closer lately. Nothing overt, but Keith had seen a subtle joining of their hearts. Her tendency to stand next to Chase or the quiet way they had of sharing a quick conversation apart from the group. Keith hoped it was nothing to worry about, but he had to wonder. Chase's wife, Kelly, wasn't here, and the fact that Chase noticed how Kendall looked was a little unsettling. Keith made a mental note to watch his friends closely tonight. They had to stay above the line, or everything they'd prayed to accomplish would be nothing more than a mockery of their faith and their character.

"Five minutes til we need to leave for the red carpet!" Chase grinned. "This is the most amazing feeling."

Keith felt his heartbeat pick up. It was really about to happen, the first showing of their movie on a big screen. Two rows were reserved for cast—which had come in its entirety. The rest were for the public. After the showing, there would be a question-and-answer session with Keith and Chase and the cast.

The only one missing was Kelly.

Chase seemed to read his mind. "I called her."

"Kelly?"

"She feels fine, but Macy still has a fever. Doctor thinks it's the swine flu." He grimaced. "I should be there. Kelly's being strong, but she needs me."

"The timing's terrible."

"Even if Macy were fine, Molly had a doctor's appointment for her arm, and this is the last week of preschool." A sigh crossed his lips. "It just didn't work out."

Keith leaned against the hotel dresser and crossed his arms. "Lisa talked to Kelly this morning. Ever since the women's conference, she's like a new person. I've seen it too."

"She is." Chase smiled and it reached deep into his eyes. He was serious now, less flip. "She's happier and more at peace. It's like God worked some complete transformation in her soul all in one day. Or maybe He'd been working it all along and the conference was the final step." He smoothed his hands over his jacket. "I'll call her again. As soon as the premiere's over."

"Good." Keith felt himself relax. "I like knowing the two of you are okay. I can't imagine all this, gaining so much ground, and then losing ourselves. I can't imagine it for either of us."

Keith hoped Chase understood what he was getting at. It was possible to lose themselves and their marriages, their goals of serving God. It was possible because it had happened to other Christians in the public eye. Just because they loved the Lord and their wives, and even though they wanted to make movies with a message, they would always need to be on guard against a fall. They might as well have targets on their backs, and knowing so was half the battle. The bigger their names got in Hollywood, the more they needed to keep an eye on each other, to keep accountable to the highest standard.

"You ready?" Keith took a step toward the door and gave Chase a hearty pat on the back.

"Ready."

Suddenly, Keith wasn't sure whether to laugh or cry. This was a moment they had dreamed about since their days in the jungle. He swallowed hard. "Let's find the rest of our team."

Down in the lobby they met up with Kendall and her father, Ben. Luke was caught up in a conversation with one of the heads from MGM studios, and he joined them a minute later. Ben had arranged for a limo, and it was waiting to take them to the theater. Fitting for a red carpet affair.

"Our carriage awaits." Kendall's eyes sparkled. She wore a long black dress accented with brilliant sequins.

Keith watched Chase, how he lingered a little longer at Kendall's side. He was wondering how to talk to Chase about his concerns when Lisa walked up. She also looked beautiful, so much like their daughter, Andi. Lisa wore a navy pantsuit with flowing sleeves—very Hollywood chic. The six of them headed for the limo, and Chase was the last one to step inside, right after Kendall. Now that they were alone together, Keith wanted to pray. "This is a big night. If God wants us to make an impact in this city, it'll start here."

The others agreed, and in the little time they had on the short trip, they held hands and asked for God's blessing on the night, that the actors would feel God's presence in the work they'd accomplished, and that the audience would be changed by the film. In addition, they asked the Lord for continued favor from the media and for the *Unlocked* project, still being discussed behind the scenes. They dedicated the night to God and uttered a round of amens just as the limo pulled up in front of the red carpet.

Outside, a wall of paparazzi lined either side of the stretch of red. Keith had to put his hand on the cool metal of the limo door before he actually believed what he was seeing. The media had turned out in droves to celebrate their premiere, to see for themselves the film everyone was talking about.

As soon as he opened the door and stepped out, the cameras began clicking. Hundreds of them, thousands. So this was how it felt. The sensation was heady and intoxicating, but Keith stuffed it. *This isn't about us*, he told himself. *Ignore it*. But the cameras kept clicking, and Keith was conscious of every move he made. Every move his team made. He looked back at Chase just as he was helping Kendall from the limo. Keith winced, unwittingly. He wished he could freeze the moment and tell Chase to distance himself from Kendall before another camera caught their picture. But there was nothing he could do. Every camera was capturing Chase, his hand wrapped around Kendall's as she exited the limo.

Keith looked away, intent on smiling for the cameras and giving the accurate appearance that all was well. They moved along the red carpet as a group, and immediately someone yelled out from the sea of reporters. "Your wife's stunning, Chase. What's her name?"

"My wife's home with our girls," he yelled back. He took a step away from Kendall, but no matter where he turned, she was only inches away. Cameras were pointed at them from every angle.

Another photographer shouted, "Chase, Keith … pose with your wives!"

"Chase, Keith … over here!" The shouts continued at a frenzied pace.

"One more over here."

"Get together in a group! That's it, smile. Hold it … and another this way."

The voices blurred, the camera flashes so steady and constant that Keith wondered if his eyes would ever be the same. When the reporters asked them to form a group, there was no getting around the natural way of things. Keith and Lisa, Chase and Kendall. Luke and Ben off to the side, giving the team of producers their moment. Again the question flew at them. "Keith, your wife's Lisa, right?" a reporter yelled.

"And what about you, Chase? Introduce us to your wife."

There was no point trying to clear up the mess. As many times as Chase might yell that his wife was at home, his voice was drowned out by the paparazzi. They would simply have to make sure the mainstream reporters got it right later. Otherwise the pictures from the event would identify Kendall as Chase's wife. Something bound to hurt Kelly.

But once they were inside, Keith was distracted from thinking about Chase and Kendall as he stared at the scene playing out. Here was the entire cast of *The Last Letter*, a reunion Chase had longed for, and here the Lord was giving it to them. The faithfulness of God was beyond anything Keith could grasp.

The mingling time ended twenty minutes later as everyone took their seats in the theater and the lights dimmed. Keith noticed that Chase sat between him and Luke—almost as if he was unaware of Kendall or how things had looked earlier. Keith hoped the reporters took note. The theater went dark, and the movie came to life. From the opening scene, the audience was gripped. They laughed where they were supposed to laugh, and when Jake Olson read the last letter from his father, people around the dark theater weren't merely crying.

Some of them were quietly weeping.

Keith knew every line of the movie backwards and forwards. He'd helped create it and his work in the editing room had helped bring it to life. Now he watched the actors and the audience and checked for the reaction among the reporters who'd been invited to the premiere.

When it was over, he had the thrilling sense that once again the movie was better than anyone expected. The festival director was Liam Montgomery, a tuxedoed black man who was one of the top movie reviewers in Hollywood. His write-up of an independent film could make or break the picture's theatrical release. With audience members still wiping their eyes and blowing their noses, Liam moved to the front of the theater and summoned the actors and producers. As Keith and Chase arrived at the front, Liam held out his hand toward them. "The producers, ladies and gentlemen."

With that, the crowd spontaneously rose to their feet and the applause from earlier grew and built into a rousing ovation. Keith blinked back tears. He was torn between trying to believe this was happening and wishing Kelly was here to share the moment with Chase. Once the cast was lined up, the questions began. People wanted to know if the emotion they saw on the screen was evident on the set, and whether there had been any difficulties filming the movie.

"I can take that one," Keith reached for the microphone. He laughed as he exchanged a look with everyone up front. "The list of problems would last longer than the film. So we'll just say we had a lot of help from God in making this movie."

He watched to see the crowd's reaction at the mention of God, but no one bolted from their seat or stood up and chastised them. They were Christians. People seemed to understand that, and they liked them anyway.

A lady stood in the back row, and Liam called on her. "Go ahead. You'll have to yell so we can hear you."

The woman had no trouble raising her voice loud enough for the entire theater to hear her. "There was a powerful message of redemption in this film." She hesitated, choked by her own emotions. "I've been cut off from my father for ten years, and after seeing this film … I'll call him as soon as I get home. Was that your intention when you made this film? That it would motivate people to make amends with those they love?"

Again Keith felt a lump in his throat. He reached for the microphone, and then changed his mind and passed it to Chase.

His friend cleared his throat, clearly struck by the same wave of emotion. "Well, actually, yes." He smiled back at Keith. "Our goal was that this movie might be life-changing. That people would find their way back to their families and lost loved ones, and even back to faith in God."

Keith took the microphone. "That was our intent from the beginning and it remains our intent now. We're shameless about it."

Throughout the audience people smiled and nodded, appreciating the fresh newness of watching a movie and being more than just entertained. Many of them were clearly changed in the process, and they apparently liked how that felt.

Before the question-and-answer time ended, Keith remembered the confusion about Kendall being Chase's wife. He took the microphone and smiled. "One more thing," he kept his tone casual. "I'd like to introduce the people who've helped make this movie possible." He gestured toward the audience. "Ben Adams, and his daughter, Kendall."

The two stood and offered a brief wave. Keith clapped, leading the audience in a polite applause for the father-daughter team.

"Also, our wives, Lisa Ellison," Keith waited until Lisa stood and received her applause, "and Kelly Ryan, who is home tonight with their two daughters."

Next, Liam made the announcement they'd been waiting for. The committee had made its decision. *The Last Letter* was indeed best film of the festival, and Jake Olson, best actor. In addition, Chase Ryan was awarded the top director award, meaning their film had raked up more honors than any other at the festival.

"I must say," Liam waved his hand toward Chase and Keith. "It's been a long time since we've been touched by a film this powerful. I think this is the beginning of a long and accomplished career in movie-making for both of you." He grinned. "My review will be in next week's paper."

Again the room burst into applause, and Keith shared a look with Chase. God was making it happen. Everything was panning out just like they'd prayed it might. *Thank You, Jesus ... thank You for this.* Keith said the silent prayer as he pointed upward, his eyes lifted to the ceiling. This was all because of God, nothing more. The experience was so great, the reality was overwhelming. God was winning, and if they continued to follow Him through filmmaking, He would win again and again and again. That's why he needed to talk to Chase later. Not only that, but he needed to talk to Andi, find out why she'd been so quiet, so withdrawn lately.

Only then could he be sure they were doing all they could to follow God now, the way they'd followed Him when they first began.

Three

By the time dinner was ready, more Cru kids had shown up and the camp bustled with conversation and activity. In one corner a few kids played the guitar, warming up for the worship time around the campfire later. While they ate, Bailey could feel Cody's presence like a physical touch. A couple times she glanced over her shoulder at him, and once she caught him looking too. He still hadn't explained what had happened with his mother.

One of the other guys' cabins had clean-up that night, so when they finished dinner, Bailey and her group of girls went to their cabin and made up their beds. They still had most of the hour before the worship time, and some of the girls wanted to make phone calls or write in their journals. Bailey made a quick call to her parents and then headed out to the fire pit. Cody was there, one of a group of guys gathering still more wood. He smiled at her and moved one more armful closer to the pit before taking the spot beside her.

She could feel his warmth even though their bodies weren't touching. "Okay, so talk to me." She kept her voice low. This wasn't the place for a deep conversation. That wouldn't happen until they were alone. But she still wondered why his plans had changed. "You were supposed to have dinner with your mom."

His expression cooled. "She forgot." He leaned over his knees and kept his eyes from hers. He wasn't angry, but there was no denying the hurt in his voice. "It's a long story. I'll tell you later." He stood and stretched. "I have to get my bunk made up."

She was on her feet too. Her heart felt like it had slipped down to her socks. "Umm ... okay."

He took a few steps toward his cabin, then stopped and turned. A long sigh rattled above the sound of the whisper of leaves overhead. "I'm sorry." He raked his fingers through his hair and stared off at the early evening sky for a moment. "It's not your fault." He looked at her, his eyes deep, more open to her. "If you have time ... meet me at my cabin. Ten minutes?"

She nodded and shrugged a little. What was going on? All of a sudden she was shy around him. *You're crazy*, she told herself. *You've known Cody forever.* She turned back to her cabin and found the other girls preoccupied. When she was sure none of them were looking to talk to her, she wandered back outside, down the path toward Cody's cabin. She saw him long before she reached his little log building. He was sitting on a tree stump, staring at the lake, his shoulders broad and muscled.

She stopped and watched him, the familiar way he held his head, the way the fading sunlight illuminated his profile. What was he thinking, sitting there like that? Was he worried about his mom, or a new girl in his life? Or maybe he was merely taking in God's beauty. She almost didn't want to disturb him, but then—as if he could read her mind—he looked her way and smiled. "Hey."

The path was smooth, but she watched her step anyway. Just in case some critter might cross in front of her. She was much more of a hotel girl, more comfortable at the Doubletree with samples of lotion and shampoo, than here in the woods. But she could appreciate both, and she was glad she'd come. Even with the threat of copperhead snakes.

She reached him and grinned. "I didn't want to interrupt."

For a second she thought he might tell her what he'd been thinking about, but then he set his jaw and his smile stayed guarded. "I'm glad you did." He pointed to a path that led closer to the lake. "Wanna take a walk?"

"Sure." They set out slowly side-by-side, and suddenly Bailey laughed out loud. "I just remembered something funny."

"Which thing?" He hooked his thumbs in his jean pockets and chuckled a little. The way he always did around her. "Something funny's always happening when you're around."

"Hey." She pretended to be hurt. "I'm not sure that's a compliment."

"It is." His eyes danced and he looked straight ahead again. "Believe me, it is."

"Well, okay … remember when we were at the beach with my family, on the other side of the lake? We took a walk and you challenged me to a race."

"Me?" He stopped and pointed to himself. "That was you, Missy. You're the one who wanted to race."

"Anyway," she kept walking, undaunted. "I got about ten steps and I twisted my ankle. You had to practically carry me back to the picnic tables."

"The summer before I shipped out."

"Right." She allowed her laughter to fade softly, mingling with the evening summer breeze. They turned a corner and were out of view of the campsite. The lake spread out before them, but still they walked on. Up ahead, the lake side of the path was bordered by a rocky outcropping, and when they reached it, they climbed onto the top and sat together. Cody seemed careful to allow space between them. For a while they were quiet, watching the lake, taking in the beauty around them. Bailey could've spent the next half hour sitting there in silence. If Cody didn't want to talk, that was fine. It was enough simply to be with God, to be with him.

He broke the silence first. "My mom met some guy." He drew a slow breath and frowned. "I'm not sure about him. I was sort of hoping she'd meet someone at church, but she met him at the health club."

"They're out tonight?"

"Yeah. She said she forgot about our dinner. Then she said it didn't matter. She didn't want me to miss the retreat on her account."

"That was nice."

"I guess." He leaned back on both hands. "I worry about her."

"I know."

"It's like that with an addict. Relapse is always possible."

They were quiet for a while, and Bailey thought about Cody's world. She could always count on her parents. That wasn't true for him. She lifted her chin and filled her lungs with the sweet-smelling air. "I forget how great it feels to be out here."

"That's why I came." He looked intently at her. "To really pray about this coaching idea and what else lies ahead for me."

Bailey felt her heart warm, despite the cool stone beneath her. Even with his concerns for his mom, Cody's future seemed to be taking shape. He was finishing school soon and his desire was to coach at Clear Creek High. His life was a living miracle, every aspect. "I still pray for you all the time." Again she felt shy. "Every day, actually."

His eyes grew deeper, the connection between them as close as she shared with any of her brothers, but different. More intimate. "The way I still pray for you." He faced the water again. "Speaking of which, what happened to Tim? I thought he was going to be here."

"He got sick. Strep throat."

"Oooh." Cody frowned. "That's too bad."

"Yeah."

Cody was quiet for a long moment. In the distance there was the shrill haunting cry of an eagle, swooping low over the water. The sun had already gone down, and dusk was settling across the lake. "You and Tim," Cody said finally. "You're still serious, aren't you?"

She sighed. He never quite understood that she had loved him first, that if he'd come back from Iraq and declared his love for her, she would've moved on from Tim long ago.

"Sorry." Cody faced her. "You don't have to answer."

"No, it's fine." She folded her arms in front of her and pulled one foot up onto the rock. "Things are the same."

"Your dad said you and Tim are auditioning in New York this summer."

"In August." She shrugged. "It's something I've always wanted to do."

"They'll love you."

His compliment touched her, and she smiled despite the confusion clouding her soul. "I don't know. Last time I was there, the city didn't have the same appeal." She looked out at the water, at the way the breeze sent ripples across the width of the lake. "New York's crazy. Constant noise and strange smells, people living on top of each other. You have to look straight up to see the sky."

"Hmm." Cody gave a single shake of his head and narrowed his eyes. "Not my style."

"Definitely not." This time her smile felt sad. If she wound up in New York, that would be the end for her and Cody. Distance would have the final say. "My dad can't stand it either." The conversation was easy, without the walls she'd felt between the two of them for so much of the last school year. "When we go to New York, we shop, sightsee, go to the theater. We stay three days and then we're gone. But that's not how it would be if I lived there." She looked at him. "I'd be commuting in on a bridge or by subway, walking fast and afraid of getting accosted. I'd pay high rent for a small apartment and have almost no fresh air." The sky was nearly dark, but in the dim light that remained, a pair of eagles drifted up from the branches of a nearby pine. A breeze brushed against her face, and for a few seconds she closed her eyes. When she opened them, she smiled. "No moments like this."

"What about Tim?" Cody seemed guarded when he talked about Tim. "How does he feel about the city?"

"He loves it. I think he could live there for the next five years. Maybe forever. He really wants to perform."

"Are there churches in Manhattan?"

"A few." She uttered a sad laugh. "But Broadway's a long way from the Bible Belt." They talked for a few minutes about a church not far from Times Square. "If I lived there, I guess I'd go there."

Again Cody was quiet. Their hour was almost up, and they needed to get back soon. Besides, if it got too dark they could be in trouble. Neither of them had brought a flashlight. "So you really think it could happen, huh? You and Tim, performing on Broadway, living in New York City?" His smile was more guarded now.

"I guess." She'd longed for the chance to perform professionally since her early days with Christian Kids Theater. But here, with the crisp lake air around them, and Cody by her side, her dreams were no longer clear. "What about you?" She hadn't asked for a long time, and now she wanted to know. Even if she was afraid of his answer. "Any girls in your life?"

"Me?" A quiet laugh rattled around in his chest. "Definitely not. God's still making me into the guy I need to be. I want that before I want a girlfriend."

His answer left her starry-eyed.

"I'm saving my heart for her." His eyes shone as he looked at her. "Really."

"I'm impressed. Not many guys are willing to talk about something like that."

"Yeah, well. She'll be worth the wait." He looked out at the water again. "Whoever she is."

For the craziest moment, Bailey wondered if she might ever be that girl, the one Cody was saving his heart for. But she dismissed the idea as soon as it came. She had a boyfriend. She could hardly think about loving the friend beside her when she had just finished talking about possibly building a life with Tim in New York City.

"What are you thinking?" Again Cody seemed to read her mind.

"Nothing." Her smile faded. "Nothing I can tell *you* anyway." She stood, brushed the sand off her shorts, and kicked at his tennis shoe. She hopped off the rock and onto the path. "I'd say let's race back, but I can't afford another sprained ankle."

Again he laughed. He stepped on the path beside her. "That's just one of the things I love about you, Bailey. You make me laugh."

"Same with you."

"Can I tell you something?" They were facing each other, maybe a little too close. He took a slight step back, keeping distance between them.

"Sure." She tapped his foot again. "You can tell me anything, Cody Coleman."

"Okay, now don't weird out on me or think I'm trying to get between you and Tim or anything."

"Go on." She giggled. "At this rate you'll never spit it out."

He turned so they were both facing the lake, side by side. He crossed his arms and clenched his jaw, his eyes set straight ahead. Whatever he wanted to say, he was struggling. Finally he turned to her again and she watched his guard fall a little. "I'm glad we … I don't know, I'm glad we found this again." He hesitated. "I thank God every day for you. For your family and your friendship."

Bailey tilted her head and let her eyes get lost in his. The moon was making its way into the sky and it shone on his face. Whatever else the future held, she'd remember this moment as long as she lived. She didn't want it to end. Without wondering whether it was right or wrong, she put her arms around his neck and hugged him. "That means the world, Cody." The hug lasted longer than usual, and it took her breath. "I'm glad you told me." She pulled back and felt her eyes start to dance. "Okay, my turn."

He studied her, and there in the moonlight he almost looked like he had feelings for her. Feelings more than friendship. His voice was low and soft against her heart. "Go on."

She could feel her expression growing more serious, deeper. "I was so mad at you last fall, when you wouldn't talk to me." She gently touched her fingers to the side of his face. "I thought in all our lives we'd never have a day like this again."

"I was worried about it."

"But here we are." She eased her hands back to her sides, keeping her behavior appropriate. "That's why God's so amazing. He knows how to fix things, even after we make a mess of them."

"Exactly." He reached out his hand. "Come on; it'll be pitch dark in a few minutes."

She took his hand and felt the thrill of his touch all the way to her toes. Once they were on a steadier part of the path again she drew her fingers from his and kept the conversation light. But her heart was beating so hard she wondered if he would say something about the sound. Holding hands with Tim never made her feel like this, which was why she definitely couldn't hold hands with Cody now, here. She wasn't ready to analyze what that meant or what it said about her relationship with Tim. Better simply to keep her distance where Cody was concerned. Besides, he was holding out body and soul for the girl of his dreams. She didn't want to get in the way of that, even if a part of her desperately wished she were that girl.

On the way back, Cody told her about a bear sighting in the woods not far from the campsite.

"Great." She was about to tell him the story of her little brother BJ and the northern copperhead he rode his bike over, when her foot settled on something soft and slithery. She screamed and fell all at the same time, her ankle giving way beneath her as she dropped. She had no idea how Cody moved so fast or how in the dim light he was able to catch her, but the next thing she knew, she was in his arms, clinging to his neck. She pointed down at the ground. "There's a snake, Cody! Be careful."

He set her down a few feet away and went back to the spot where she'd felt the snake. Using the toe of his shoe, he pressed around and came up with something long and bendable. "This, you mean?"

He brought it closer and she stifled another scream. "Don't, Cody! It could be poisonous. Shawn says copperheads are all around this lake."

"Well," he held his hands out so she could see exactly what had frightened her. "This branch is definitely not part of the copperhead family. I promise."

Bailey straightened and stared at the thing Cody was holding. "A branch? You've gotta be kidding. I could feel it moving."

"It's a young branch. A little more flexible than some." He tossed it off the path and grinned at her. "You probably scared it to death."

She tested her ankle, but it was fine, and suddenly she pictured herself stepping on the branch and practically jumping into Cody's arms. She burst into laughter again and had to hold onto Cody's waist as they walked. Otherwise she would've fallen to the ground, unable to breathe.

The other campers already had flashlights out, and as they reached base camp, everyone wanted to know what was so funny. Bailey told her snake story, but when she reached the part about stepping on the branch, she cracked up again and Cody had to finish for her.

It was like that throughout the weekend. She had hours of solitude with the Lord, times when she could pray about the direction God had for her life, and whether New York City was something she really wanted. Other hours she and the girls talked, and still others, when she and Cody sat alone, rebuilding their friendship. Always their time together ended in laughter, except for once — the last night of the retreat.

That night, with the moon a little more than a thumbnail of light overhead, they sat by the fire until everyone else had turned in. They talked about Cody's mother and Bailey's family and Cody's dream to help kids the way Bailey's parents had helped him. They sat close together, neither of them seeming to mind when their knees touched a time or two.

Before they turned in, Cody held out his hands to her. "Pray with me, Bailey. Will you?"

She didn't hesitate. She slipped her fingers into his and together they bowed their heads. She started the prayer, the way she'd seen her mom and dad pray together so many times over the years. "Dear Lord, this time away has been so good for us, for the friendships that have grown stronger and for the way You feel closer than ever." She paused, working to focus. "Thank You for Cody and his friendship. Please, Lord, keep the two of us close to You, and let Cody know how much he means to me."

It was Cody's turn, and he gave her fingers a subtle squeeze as he started. "God, You know how I feel about Bailey," he hesitated for a moment, as if his feelings for her weren't something he was willing to actually put into words. "I begged You for a second chance at her friendship, and now here we are. Copperhead snake branches and all." They both shared a couple seconds of quiet laughter, the sound of the fire crackling a few feet away. When he had control again, he finished. "Lord, I ask that You protect what we've found on the far side of Lake Monroe this weekend. Life is too short to waste on half-hearted connections and meaningless run-throughs. Now I feel closer to Bailey than ever before, and I'm blessed for the fact.

"People could live all their lives and never have a friend like Bailey Flanigan. So thank You, Lord. And I pray for her audition coming up. If You want her to live in New York, to perform there and be part of maybe a revival taking place in that city, then throw open the doors for her this August. Let her stand out and let her get a role in a Broadway play." He paused, and there was no hiding the sadness that had crept into his voice. "But only if it's Your will, Father. Otherwise, shut the door. Then she'll know which way You're leading her. In Jesus' name, amen."

Bailey didn't want to let go of his hands, but slowly he let go first. She had lost her breath somewhere around the part about half-hearted connections and meaningless run-throughs, and when he asked God to let her go to New York only if it was His will, she felt her heart go into a rhythm she didn't recognize. She swallowed hard, trying to find a way to set her world back on its axis.

But as they stood and shared a long hug, and as he walked her to her cabin and they said good night, Bailey was breathing normally again. She was dating Tim, and until that changed, she couldn't let herself have feelings for Cody beyond the ones they'd found here at camp. She lay in her bed in her sleeping bag for a long time, looking out the window at a brilliant spread of stars.

God had met her in this place, in a number of ways. She felt ready to take her finals, ready to take on the challenges of the summer, ready for her audition. And she felt certain about one thing. She didn't want to settle for an existence of half-hearted connections and meaningless run-throughs. Not with Cody or Tim or God Himself.

And after this weekend, settling for anything less than God's best wasn't even an option.

Four

Chase was grateful the premiere was almost over. The night seemed to last forever, and he could hardly wait to talk to Kelly, to see how she and the girls were doing. He'd been caught off guard earlier in the limo at the start of the night. He could barely focus on their prayer because of Kendall's hand in his. And so his prayer had been a personal one. *God, thank You for bringing Kendall and her father to us at a time when we were ready to close shop and quit. We're here at the top of a mountain that belongs only to You. Please ... don't let me forget our mission ...*

Keith was looking at him, which could only mean one thing. A question had come his way. He shot his friend a desperate look, one Keith must've read immediately.

"As a director," Keith spoke into the microphone, showing none of the concern he must've been feeling, "what was the most difficult part of making this movie?"

Chase nodded and took the mic. "The actors made it easy on me, really. The hardest part was making sure the intensity of their emotions came across in every scene."

"You pulled it off!" a person from the middle row shouted. "Great job, Chase!"

He nodded, humbled. How could this be happening, the audience so taken by a film they almost couldn't make? This moment, this realization that God was opening the floodgates was more than he could fully comprehend. He only wished Kelly were here to share it with him.

Finally the question-and-answer session ended, and as they filed out of the theater and into the lobby, as one person after another congratulated them, Chase's emotions shifted from exultation to something quite disturbing: Fear. Because the higher God took them, the more difficult the expectations. How were they going to top this moment? Chase swallowed hard and kept his attention on the moment at hand. *Don't be ridiculous*, he told himself.

He put his inner dialogue to rest and focused on the numerous executives in attendance from every major movie studio. Everyone wanted to talk to the up-and-coming producers from Jeremiah Productions—Chase or Keith, Luke or Ben. From across the room, Chase noticed that even Kendall was brought into a number of conversations by executives anxious for a chance. He admired her professionalism and ability to hold her own with Hollywood's movers and shakers.

"Where'd you get your experience?" a vice president from one of the top studios caught up with Chase at the food table. "Your work as a director ... it's amazing. Impeccable."

"We had training from some of the best college professors in LA before leaving the U.S. for mission work," Chase said. He tried to sound modest, but he couldn't fight an overwhelming desire to impress the man. He gave the guy an unassuming smile. "It's God's gift, but a highlight of this experience has been winning at the festival."

"You deserve it." The man nodded appreciatively. "It's uncanny, having the ability to produce and direct a film of this caliber, with virtually no experience." He shook his head, as if he couldn't quite get over Chase's talent. "Our team wants to work something out with you and Keith. For this film or the next. You're exactly the kind of team we want to work with."

They exchanged business cards and the conversation ended, but it was followed by another dozen like it. At the end of two hours, Chase felt the strangest sensation that he'd missed out. Not in making the movie, but because he hadn't really enjoyed what God had given them this night. He'd been tempted by Kendall, flattered by movie execs, and he'd spent much of the night regretting that he couldn't be with Kelly when she needed him back home.

Before the end of the night, Luke Baxter brought them a preliminary offer from American Pictures. The offer was beyond anything any of them had ever imagined: ten million dollars for *The Last Letter.* The figure was eight million more than any of them had hoped to get up front. In addition, the studio was still willing to front half the publicity and advertising money. Luke was giddy over the proposal. "They want a full theatrical release, a thousand screens across America."

Keith looked at him, and his eyes said everything he clearly couldn't put into words. He came to Chase and hugged him hard, the way two friends embrace after surviving a war together. As Keith released him, Chase looked across the room. Kendall and Ben were having what looked like a serious conversation in the opposite corner of the lobby.

Keith and Luke were going on about God's mercy and grace, His perfect timing, and how they would have the freedom to make more movies with the commitment from American Pictures. They were still celebrating, when Luke's cell phone rang. He checked the caller ID and his eyes lit up. "NTM." The last guests were gone by then, but Luke distanced himself from the group as he answered.

Kendall and her father must've finished their conversation, because they crossed the lobby and joined Chase and Keith. Kendall looked weary, her eyes darker than Chase had ever seen them. "What's all the excitement for?"

"We've got an offer!" Keith stepped up and hugged Ben Adams. "American Pictures wants to give us ten million for a theatrical release!"

Chase kept his attention on Keith and Ben. He could've been wrong, but Ben's enthusiasm seemed tempered, somehow. He would have to ask him about it later. Luke returned to them a few minutes later. As he reached them, a grin spread across his face. "It's happened!"

"What?" Chase couldn't imagine anything else tonight. Already he was dizzy from everything he was feeling.

Keith moved in close to Chase so they could hear, and Luke gave each of them a strong pat on their backs. "NTM is printing a retraction tomorrow. I guess they got pressure from Brandon's agent that he'd pull out of his existing contract Monday if they didn't run something taking back the story."

Chase wished he had something to hold onto, but since there was nothing, he put his hand on Keith's shoulder and grabbed tight. Wasn't this what they'd prayed for? Wasn't it what Keith had believed could happen, and what Kendall was absolutely convinced would take place? That NTM would back down and Hollywood's top young actor, Brandon Paul, could actually star in their next film?

Luke was going on about how NTM never does this, and how the news release would state that failed communication was to blame for their retraction. Chase wanted to be sure he understood. "What exactly does this mean for *Unlocked*?"

This time Luke leaned his head back and laughed out loud. "It means you and Brandon Paul can take this deal to whatever studio you'd like. Sounds like American Pictures might be your first stop. Either way, NTM is so worried about losing Brandon, they're even willing to let him film this movie before he fulfills his agreement with them. As long as he doesn't pull out of his contract."

When Ben and Kendall got up to speed about the latest developments, Ben directed everyone to hold hands one more time. "We've taken time to ask God for His blessing," Ben's voice was scratchy, thick with emotion. "Now it's time to thank Him."

Chase studied the older man. He seemed deeply emotional, maybe because of his earlier talk with Kendall. The conversation had been very private and seemed more intense than was fitting for a night like this. Chase wondered if Kendall's dad was warning her to keep her distance from Chase, reminding her that Chase was married. He hoped not. He'd be mortified if his errant thoughts were that obvious.

This time Keith was between him and Kendall as they linked hands and bowed their heads. This time the profound nature of the moment spilled into their prayer and they went on for ten minutes while each of them took turns praising God for His direction and wisdom, and thanking Him for the premiere and the way it was received, and the way it was already working to change lives for His glory, and finally for the deal with American Pictures and the breakthrough with Brandon Paul and their next film.

As they finally climbed into the waiting limo and drove across town to their hotel, Chase was positive he'd never felt like this before. He wasn't tired, and when Kendall asked him if he wanted to join her for a cup of coffee in the lobby, he agreed before he could remember a single reason why he shouldn't. Keith and Lisa went off to their room, and Luke to his—clearly assuming everyone was turning in, and Kendall's father set off for home.

And like that, Chase and Kendall were alone.

They chose a table tucked into the corner of the lobby, near a roaring fire and out of sight from the main traffic at the front desk. She put her elbows on the table and leaned in close, her eyes imploring him. "Before we talk, I need to apologize." She held his gaze. "That was awkward, on the red carpet. People thinking we were ... you know, married." She rushed ahead, her voice rich with regret. "I had no idea ... I mean, I would've walked five feet behind you if I'd known."

She seemed anxious for him to find her innocent in the situation, and Chase did so immediately. He clasped his hands around hers and squeezed gently before letting go. "Don't worry about it. You did nothing wrong."

Her remorse eased a bit, and something in her eyes made him feel uneasy. Did her expression hold a hint of desire, or were his own feelings shading the way she came across in a moment like this?

"Still." She blinked, and the desire — if there'd been desire — was gone completely. "It was awkward, and I apologize. Please tell Kelly it was one of those crazy moments. Neither of us meant anything by it."

Again Chase swallowed hard, and he moved his hands out onto the table again. For the next half hour he forgot about his promise to call Kelly. Instead, he and Kendall replayed every moment of the amazing night, the red carpet and the premiere, the reaction from the audience, and the telltale questions that followed. Through it all, their hands touched at times, and once their faces were so close Chase could imagine kissing her. He didn't want the moment to end. This was only the beginning, right? The start of all they would accomplish together as a team — Keith and him and Kendall and Ben. Luke working out the details.

Finally, she blinked twice, as if she was only just realizing how they might've looked together, how they'd been acting. She blinked twice and withdrew her hands to her lap. The color in her cheeks deepened. "Chase. I didn't only want to talk about the premiere ... or Brandon Paul." She looked away, as if the eye contact between them had become too much for her.

Only then did Chase notice that her fingers were trembling. She looked up and her eyes were deep with agony. Whatever was coming, it wasn't good. He felt his heart skip a beat and then pound into a faster rhythm.

Kendall lifted her eyes. "My dad asked me something tonight that shocked me. He wanted to know if I was falling for you."

"What?" Chase's heart slammed against his chest and he felt suddenly clammy. Had things between them become so obvious that Ben had picked up on it? When neither of them had even hinted at the possibility until tonight? "I can apologize to him if he thinks—"

"Chase." She peered at him through teary eyes, her heart clearly anguished. "I'm finished with Jeremiah Productions. I've loved every minute, but now ... my dad made it clear tonight. I need to move on. There's too much at stake."

"You can't quit." He rose halfway out of his seat, shocked and angry, embarrassed at the implied accusation from Kendall's father. "We didn't do anything wrong. We were on the same team, Kendall. We were bound to get close. We were ..."

His words trailed off and Kendall said nothing, only stared at him, deep into his eyes, and the message was beyond clear. He could lie to himself, but he couldn't lie to her. She must've known every time he'd been moved by her, every time he'd found her interesting or alluring. The proof was all over her face.

Chase studied her, unable to completely process the finality of what was happening. A few minutes ago they'd been celebrating, right? But the whole time Kendall had been harboring her father's warning, holding back about the fact that this wasn't only their greatest night as a team—it was their last.

Suddenly like a tsunami overtaking him, the truth hit. Never mind that he hadn't acted on his private wanderings. He had unwittingly given Kendall a piece of his heart. In doing so he had gone against God and Kelly and everything he believed in. Even if only in thought. This was God's answer to the half-hearted prayers he'd uttered off and on through the night. He couldn't possibly be a filmmaker looking to touch the world with God's message of hope and redemption if he was having feelings for someone other than his wife. And now the decision about how to handle himself around Kendall had been made for him. His hands suddenly felt uncomfortable on the table and he lowered them to his knees. "How soon?"

"Monday." Shame filled her eyes. "I'm sorry, Chase. It wasn't only you."

And like that, the second wave hit. He wasn't the only one entertaining wrong thoughts. This new truth was both flattering and horrifying at the same time. He couldn't possibly ask her to stay now. They'd avoided a disaster, but clearly the only option was to split ways. He didn't say anything, because there was nothing to say. Her admission had said it all.

She sat a little straighter, more composed than before. "Life is made up of seasons. My dad used to say that." No smile lifted the corners of her mouth. The sadness in her eyes was all-encompassing. "Maybe some other season I'll be back."

All Chase could think about was Kelly, and how badly he wanted to call her. "It's late."

They took the elevator up, and her floor was before his. As the door opened, she stepped out quickly without a hug or any physical contact. She waved. "Keep in touch."

"We will." He got out the words just as the door shut, and like that he was alone with his raging emotions. Guilt for his earlier thoughts, and shock over the news about Ben Adams. Relief because he no longer had to worry about Kendall.

But he still had to worry.

What flaw in his faith and commitment to Kelly had allowed him to take even a few steps down the path of infidelity? He was still buzzing from the shock when he reached his room and flipped on the TV. *Entertainment Tonight* was showing highlights from the premiere, but the thrill was overshadowed by the obvious impression the images gave off. He and Kendall looked like they were together, and Chase could only admit the obvious.

He had stood at the brink of disaster, toes over the edge of a cliff from which there would've been no return, nothing but certain destruction. The thought hit him like a freight train as he flipped off the television and stared at the darkened screen. There would be other women with every stage of filmmaking, actresses and casting agents and directors. People drawn to the success of

Jeremiah Productions. If he could so easily let his feelings get out of hand for Kendall, what about the next woman to come along? Or the one after that?

He lowered his head to his hands. *God, I need Your help. What's the answer? I don't care about the fame, but what if I can't handle the temptations? What if I mess up?* He squeezed his eyes shut and tried to picture his wife—his amazing wife—back home with their two daughters. Trusting him, believing in him. Needing him. And what about his little girls—Molly and Macy.

Marketing *The Last Letter*, planning and filming their next picture. All of it would take more time away from home. Already he'd missed much of the past year—time he wouldn't get back again. *Help me, God. Show me what You want me to do. Please, Lord.*

Suddenly he remembered the words Keith had said earlier, how easy it would be to win the world for Christ through film, and meanwhile lose themselves. Chase stood and walked to the bathroom, gripped the granite countertop, and stared at himself in the mirror. *I need an answer, God. Please show me how to survive this.*

Back in his bedroom he found the framed photo of Kelly and the girls, the one he took on road trips. His heart hurt as he picked it up and stared at the faces he loved. How close had he come tonight to falling? Slowly and with an ache in his chest, Chase dropped back to the bed, the picture still clutched in his hands. "No, God … please no," his words were an anguished whisper. "I don't want to fail. I need Your protection." He couldn't have even a hint of impropriety. Not now or ever. "Show me the way, please."

When his desperate prayer was over, he struggled to his feet and realized how strange this night had been—the highest of highs and the lowest of lows. He was not going to make films for God only to lose his marriage along the way. He knew what he had to do, and he strode purposefully to his laptop, opened it, and set it on the small desk.

With a series of clicks he ordered a dozen long-stemmed roses sent to Kelly at their home address. On the note card he directed them to write only this: "We won big tonight, but it was not the same without you. I love you more than you know. Chase."

He scheduled the roses to be delivered the next day, and then he made the call he should've made an hour ago. Kelly had never sounded more glad to hear from him, more absolutely trusting. The girls were in bed, of course, and she'd been waiting for his call. Macy's fever was down, and Kelly thought she had turned the corner and was recovering from the flu. Chase savored every word that came across the line. Her voice was like an oasis, an embrace that brought a physical comfort, one that soothed every rough, jagged part of his heart.

"I prayed for you," she said. "Tell me everything."

Guilt sliced through his soul because he couldn't tell her everything. Not the part about his temptations and struggles or how the reporters thought Kendall was his wife or how even Ben Adams had been concerned that Chase and Kendall might have an attraction to each other. Kelly didn't deserve those details. Instead he told her everything else. About the paparazzi and the enormous crowd outside the theater, the packed house, and the representatives from every studio in Hollywood.

"Honey, that's amazing." She released a quiet squeal. "It's everything I asked God about."

He finished by telling her about the offer from American Pictures and the news that NTM had retracted their earlier announcement about Brandon Paul. "I keep thinking I'm going to wake up and the whole thing will be one wonderful dream." He closed his eyes and massaged his brow. He hated this, feeling like a phony. He didn't deserve any part of what was happening around him. Least of all, the loving woman waiting back home for him. He kept his tone appropriately upbeat. "It doesn't feel real."

"But it is. Because God's doing this, Chase." Her love, her support, warmed her words and touched him deeply. She paused, and passion filled her voice. "I only wish I were there with you."

They talked a while longer, and before their conversation ended, Kelly remembered one last thing. "Check your email. I forgot to tell you, but Pastor Hastings called. I guess he sent you something. Said it was time sensitive."

"About the movie?"

"He didn't say." Kelly didn't sound too concerned about the message. "I'm so proud of you, Chase. I love you so much."

Again Chase felt sick about what could've happened. He swallowed hard. "I love you too, baby. I can't wait to see you."

"This is just the beginning."

"Exactly." *The beginning of what?* Chase wondered. A sick feeling wrapped its arms around him. "I miss you."

"You too. It's so good to hear your voice."

As the call ended, Chase set the phone down on the end table and stared at the plain beige wall across from him. If this was the beginning, then did that mean he'd face a life of temptation and terrible guilt? Years of being away from home and spending long days on the road? He felt weary and lifeless, and more than anything he wanted to be home with Kelly and the girls. He remembered the email, and he stood slowly, like a man twice his age.

Why would Pastor Hastings email him? The man was in his seventies, a respected teacher known throughout the area for his wisdom and Bible knowledge. Their church was made up of several leaders and thousands of members, but Chase doubted the main pastor had a clue about the movie industry or what Chase was working on. He opened his Mac, waited the few seconds while it sprang to life, and opened his mailbox. The email from the pastor was near the top. The subject line read "Opportunity."

Had the pastor come across local investors? Chase clicked the email open and saw that it was brief. Only a few lines. He narrowed his eyes, confused, and began reading.

Dear Chase,

I want to make you aware of a recent opportunity. Our youth pastor has unexpectedly moved back to New Jersey because of a family crisis. Our team met this morning and prayed about a replacement candidate, and your name quickly rose to the top of our list. We are aware of your previous experience and your education in ministry. I understand that your new ventures have taken you away much of the time. Therefore, this may not be something you're interested in pursuing. But then again, it might bring you closer to home and the role of raising your young daughters.

Please do not feel pressured to take the position. Either way our team would appreciate a response at your soonest convenience. Until then we are praying for your thoughtful consideration.

Because of Him,
Pastor Joseph Hastings

Chase stared at the email and then read it over again three times. If he thought he was dreaming before, this was the clincher. Pastor Hastings was asking him to be youth pastor at their church? A youth pastor, when already Chase had committed to making movies, to producing and directing? Did no one at the church know how much success they were having in Hollywood?

The email was still shouting at him, so Chase closed it and shut down his computer. Why in the world would his name rise to the top of the list of candidates capable of leading the church's youth? Sure he was trained in ministry, and he'd served as an ordained pastor on the mission fields. But still ... a youth pastor? He thought back, remembering a decade ago before filmmaking became a part of his life. For a brief season his dream had been youth ministry. But Pastor Hastings couldn't have known that.

Chase dismissed the thought and turned his heart once more to the Lord. *God, I have no idea why Pastor Hastings sent me that email, but help me turn him down gently. In the meantime, I need an answer about the future, God.* Chase rolled onto his back, restless. He sighed out loud, grabbed a pillow, and pulled it to his chest. He needed a way to handle times like tonight, a stronger spirit, a greater resolve. Whatever it took so he could survive this season of filmmaking and still come out the man he was before this crazy ride started. He stared at the ceiling, restless and unsure. God had given him a warning tonight. Now Chase could only believe that if God had helped him survive a night of temptation, He would show him how to survive a lifetime of it.

He wasn't going to let the devil tempt him with Kendall or anyone else. This was God's mission field, not a Hollywood playground. He wouldn't fail his wife or his faith or his family. Chase was surer about that than he was about his next breath. And with that certainty, he was finally able to drift off to sleep dreaming about the only woman he would ever love.

His precious wife, Kelly.

Five

Andi had her test results. Most of the night she'd been staring at the white plastic stick, her pulse fast and irregular, her mouth dry, panic coursing through her. One minute she'd lie on her bed crying her eyes out, and the next she'd pace her room, frantic, desperate for a way out. There was none.

She was pregnant with Taz's child. There was no hiding from the fact any longer.

This new reality had been a part of her for several hours, but the shock was still decimating its way through her, tearing apart her soul and screaming at her for all the ways she'd failed. Andi looked at the clock and saw it was nearly two in the morning. She pulled herself out of bed, and in a rush, a wave of nausea dragged her down. As fast as she could move, she hurried to the bathroom and fell to her knees at the edge of the toilet. For the third time that night, she dry-heaved into the cold porcelain bowl, gasping for air between convulsions.

She hadn't eaten all night, so nothing came up. Nothing but the reality that her life was never going to be the same again. Her stomach twisted and turned until Andi wondered if she might collapse there on the bathroom floor. It was like her body was rebelling, the way she had rebelled against God and her family, against the wisdom of her roommate, Bailey, and her deceased friend, Rachel Baugher.

The wave passed, though her stomach still hurt desperately. She rocked back on her heels and hung her head. Maybe if she threw up enough times the pregnancy would go away. She clung to the toilet and tried to steady herself. But the room rocked and tilted and she didn't dare move.

Like she'd done countless times that night, she thought again about her lack of options. In the moments after she had her news she made a desperate call to Taz. *Stupid*, she told herself now. What good could he possibly do now that she was pregnant? Did she really expect him to take the news with kindness and compassion? Come to her and promise to stay by her side? Did she think he'd offer to marry her and make a life with her and their child?

Her attempt to reach him never even got that far. A girl answered his phone, and in the background she could hear Taz scolding her to hang up. "That's my phone," he hissed at her. Then the line went dead. Andi vowed it was the last time she would call him. Her next call had been to her parents, not that she was about to tell them her news. Rather, she wanted to hear their voices, to know that the safe world of hope and truth in Christ still existed somewhere.

But her father didn't answer his cell, and when her mom picked up, what sounded like a loud celebration in the background made it impossible for her to hear. "Andi," her mom shouted above the noise, "everyone loved the film! Your father and I are so happy, sweetheart. Wish you were here."

"Mom ... I don't feel good."

The noise on the other end grew louder. "What? Andi, can you speak up? Is everything okay?"

"Yes." She practically yelled her response, tears streaming down her face. "Go celebrate, Mama. I'm fine."

"Okay. Talk to you tomorrow. I love you, honey!"

And with that she was alone again, sitting in her room, the walls closing in around her. The room stopped spinning and Andi opened her eyes. She was weak and drenched in sweat and her stomachache spread through her whole body. She moved slowly to the bathroom and looked at herself in the mirror, but all she could see was Taz. She covered her face and shook her head. How could she have believed someone so opposed to God, someone so dangerous? What possessed her to agree with him, that nudity in film meant quality movie-making? The idea was disgusting. Or that sleeping with him was some sick form of art?

She shuddered and grabbed the toilet again. The memory of his sickly suggestive words choked her, made it hard for her to draw a breath. With everything in her she had known Taz was wrong for her, but she'd ignored every sound, godly thought that crossed her mind back then. How could she have let herself fall so fully, so thoroughly? She would give anything to be the old Andi again. To be Bailey Flanigan — sure of her convictions, confident in her faith. If only Bailey were here right now, maybe Andi could tell her the truth about being pregnant. But Bailey was at the Cru retreat — where Andi might've been if she hadn't chosen her own ways. And Rachel was with Jesus in heaven — where she couldn't do Andi a single bit of good.

What would it matter anyway? She could stand in the Indiana University commons and tell the whole student body she was pregnant. No amount of sympathy or understanding could change the fact. Taz's baby was growing inside her. She was no longer a virgin, no longer the sweet Andi Ellison, innocent daughter of missionaries, no longer a young girl with the world ahead of her. She had given up her innocence without a fight, and now she'd be better off dead.

For the first time in her life she understood why someone might want to die. If her heart stopped right now, her parents would never know the truth. She wouldn't have to go through life with the knowledge that she'd broken her promise to God and ruined her future. She swallowed hard and leaned closer to the cool white rim. In a violent rush, another series of dry heaves shook her body and made it almost impossible to breathe.

The room slowly stopped spinning and Andi opened her eyes tentatively. She was weak and drenched in sweat, but she needed to rest, even just a little. Her body shook as she planted her feet on the floor and dragged herself up.

Halfway to her bed she caught a glimpse of Rachel, smiling at her from the framed photo that still hung on the wall near the window. Andi had always felt sorry for Rachel, saving herself for the right guy, believing in God's plans for her life only to be snuffed out in a car accident far too soon. Rachel's death convinced Andi that God was unfair at best. If anyone deserved a rich, full life it was Rachel Baugher. But now, betrayed by her body and certain that her future was ruined, Rachel seemed like the lucky one. Safe in heaven, walking with Jesus, free of the confusion and hurt of this world. Rachel had hoped for an abundant life, and God had given her that, after all.

Just not the way any of them had expected.

She fell into bed and curled up on her side. Lying there, her heart raced, her lungs refused to work correctly, and Andi could only see two options, two ways out of her current nightmare. She could kill herself. First she'd have to find a way, and then she'd have to have the guts to pull it off. Pills maybe, or she could suffocate herself somehow. Her problems would be over, but what about her parents? What about Bailey? The people who knew her would suffer the aftereffects of her suicide for years. Maybe forever.

The idea made her feel more sick than before, and from the pit of her stomach a slow anger began to churn within her. Why should she kill herself? Why put her family through that sort of heartache and pain? This wasn't their fault, and it wasn't hers either. Taz was to blame for this mess she was in. He'd known about her faith and conviction, but he'd led her down the path of destruction anyway. He could've chosen any girl, but he chose her. This nightmare was his fault.

Which led her to her other conclusion: She would put Taz out of her mind and have the baby on her own, love the baby with every day of her life from this point on. She would be the sort of mother her own mom had been to her, even if she never had a man to help her.

Andi rolled onto her back and stared at the ceiling. She would move to California, live with her parents in San Jose. Her mom would help her know what to do, how to take care of the baby without the help of a husband. When to change the baby's diapers, when a cry meant the baby was hungry or tired or sick. And when the baby was a few months old, Andi would go back to school. When she had her degree she would make a great life for the two of them. She and her baby.

As soon as she had a plan, she put her hands protectively over her stomach and felt herself drifting off, dreaming about the days ahead and the life she would choose to live, not for herself. But for her baby. Andi felt fresh tears in her eyes. She had done everything wrong when it came to love, made every wrong choice and believed every wrong thing Taz had ever told her.

But this ... this she would do right.

Six

Keith took a shaky breath as he parked deep in the cement garage beneath Delta Talent Agency's enormous Century City building. He looked at the clock on his dashboard. Nine-twenty. Ten minutes before the biggest meeting he'd ever taken—the one where Brandon Paul and his management team would sign a preliminary deal locking the young heartthrob as star of their film, *Unlocked.* Luke Baxter, their attorney, was joining Keith here with the paperwork, and by all indications the meeting was a matter of formality. Brandon wanted to make the picture, and his team wanted to keep Brandon happy. The deal shouldn't take more than half an hour to discuss and then they could celebrate the signatures. But Keith had never been more nervous in all his life for one reason.

Something was wrong with Chase.

It was Friday in a week that had been marked by some of the biggest meetings the team of Jeremiah Productions had ever taken part in. Three meetings with various brass at American Pictures, each of them fine-tuning the process of seeing *The Last Letter* released to the big screen. A key lunch with the author of *Unlocked* and her agent, and now this crucial session with Brandon Paul. And Chase had missed them all.

His phone call had come last weekend, hours before they were scheduled to fly out. "I need to be home," Chase had said. He was adamant, and unwilling to talk about the reasons. "Look, Keith, I'm sorry. It's not something I can talk about. Tell everyone I'll explain later. I can't be on the road this week. I just can't."

Of course Keith had pressed him, asked whether Macy's flu had gotten worse or whether something was wrong with Kelly. But Chase only sighed. "We can talk when you get back. Right now I need you to do one thing for me."

"What?" Keith was desperate. He wanted to shake Chase and bring him to his senses. Whatever the crisis at home, it could wait. These meetings were what they'd worked the past year to achieve. Keith hadn't felt this confused since he and Chase had dreamed up the idea of making movies back on the mission field. "What do you want me to do?"

"Pray for me. I've got a lot to think through."

Even now that the week of meetings had come and gone, Keith couldn't understand what his friend meant by that. A lot to think through? They were at the top of their game. What could Chase possibly have to think through now? It was one thing to doubt their direction back when the funds weren't available and everything about the production of *The Last Letter* seemed to be falling apart. But now? When they had a lucrative offer from American Pictures on the table and they were this close to a serious deal with Brandon Paul? Chase should've been thrilled to hit the road this week.

Keith glanced at the clock again. It was time. He climbed out of his car and felt the suffocating stillness of the underground garage. What was it about being in one of these parking structures? He shook off the strange feeling and made his way to the elevator. Three minutes later he met up with Luke Baxter in the lobby of DTA's lucrative firm. If a person didn't know the talent agency was top in the business, they would certainly figure it out by entering the firm's front doors. Granite and crystal, marble and plush carpet marked every inch of the place.

"This is it," Luke grinned. "We can make our own press announcement when we're finished here. Once Brandon is officially linked to the project, everything else will come together." Luke sorted through his paperwork. "Everything's very clear-cut at this point. We'll work out the finer details of the contract later."

Keith nodded, trying to feel enthusiastic. What if something really was wrong with Kelly? Or maybe one of the girls was sick with something worse than the flu and Chase wasn't ready to talk about it. What choices could he possibly need to make that would take a week of prayer and thought? He stared out the window, only dimly aware of Luke and his enthusiasm.

"Hey," Luke touched his shoulder. "You all right?"

"Huh?" Keith turned to his attorney. "Sorry." He allowed an uncomfortable pause. "Thinking about Chase."

Luke's expression showed his frustration. "He should be here. The two of you are a team."

"Exactly."

"Have you heard from him, why he missed this week?"

"Nothing." Keith shrugged. "I can only figure it's something with his family. Maybe he needed a week to regroup."

"Let's hope so. This is too big a project to handle alone. Besides, Chase is your director. I'm not sure where you'd be without him."

Keith didn't want to think about it, and at the moment he didn't have to. The receptionist invited them back to the meeting room, and they sat around a stunning burl wood table that looked like a piece of artwork. Luke and Keith had only just taken their seats when Brandon breezed in followed by five members of his management team and his agent from DTA.

"Hello, gentlemen." The lead DTA guy was Jacque Ruse, a Frenchman with a high-powered charisma that made Keith feel out of his league. But Luke was up for the challenge.

He stood and shook Ruse's hand. "Luke Baxter, attorney for Jeremiah Productions."

"Pleasure." Ruse moved quickly to Keith. "And the talk of the town — Keith Ellison, I presume."

Keith's heart felt like it would give out, but he hid the fact. He stood and shook hands with the man, and then moved down the table, greeting Brandon Paul. *God, what are we doing here? Can this really be us? Having a meeting like this and preparing to make a film with a star like Brandon Paul? Help me feel able, God. Please.*

Introductions and small talk lasted another five minutes, and during that time Keith snuck a few long looks at Brandon. His eyes looked a little bloodshot, and he had the hint of crow's feet around the corners of his eyes. Not a big deal if the guy was in his forties. But Brandon was only twenty-four. The physical signs were one more reason to worry. Lately, the paparazzi had talked about Brandon becoming a party boy. Once, a month ago, Keith had called Dayne Matthews — who had been at least as famous as Brandon Paul a few years ago — and asked about the young actor.

"You can't trust everything you read in the rags," Dayne had advised. "But if they're catching photos of Brandon partying, there's probably some truth to it."

Now Keith had to wonder, and again he wished Chase were here. They didn't need Brandon Paul, really. Yes, he was a huge actor, and yes he had gone to the author of *Unlocked* practically begging to play the lead. But if Brandon brought a tainted image to the film, or if he embarrassed them, the fallout could hurt Jeremiah Productions more than it might ever help.

As the meeting got under way, Ruse talked about the supporting cast. He pulled out a sheet of notes and grinned at the people around the table. "Great news just in from our children's division. The script calls for Brandon to have a younger sister, someone who is instrumental in helping bring the character out of his prison of autism." He passed out copies of a single headshot of a pretty young girl with shining blue eyes. "This is Annalee Sullivan. She's seven years old and by all accounts one of the fastest rising child stars in the business. Her agent says if Brandon's the lead, she definitely wants the part of his sister." He pointed to a few bullet points on the child's resume. "She goes by Annie Sullivan, and she loves to sing and dance. I imagine she might even sing a partial song in the movie." He winked at Brandon. "Talk about your heart-grabbers."

"Mmhmm." Brandon was texting, his entire focus on his phone.

"Right." Ruse chuckled. No one from DTA seemed bothered by Brandon's lack of focus. He was still something of a kid himself. At least that's what his team had called him a time or two.

Keith had a sense that whatever Brandon wanted, he got. Who was going to tell him what to do when he was the biggest box office draw around? Besides, Keith didn't have to be sold on Annie Sullivan. He knew who she was. The idea that she would co-star in *Unlocked* was only one more unbelievable development. He nodded at Luke and then at Ruse. "We'd love to work with Annie. She'd make a very believable sister for Brandon."

"Definitely." Brandon looked up from his phone. "Annie's great. I'll have to bring my A-game or the kid'll leave me in the dust."

The conversation shifted to other co-stars, and with each successive role Keith had to work to contain his excitement. He and Chase had talked about what it would mean to investors and creative types to have Brandon Paul. But he hadn't imagined they'd be able to round up such a star-studded cast. The film would easily be one of the most talked about of the year.

So why isn't Chase here, God? I need him. Keith hid his concern about his friend, and Chase's name came up just once toward the end of the meeting. Ruse handed a stack of documents to Brandon, and on the star's other side one of the team presented the actor with a pen. "Time to make it official." Ruse's face was a perpetual grin. "The lawyers can hammer out the rest later."

Brandon took the papers and read through none of it. His trust of his team was complete. "Where do I sign?"

The DTA executive on his right side pointed to a number of lines and Brandon easily signed everywhere he was told. While that was happening, Ruse focused an intense look at Keith. "I understand Chase has some family matter at home?"

Keith was caught off guard, but he rebounded quickly. "Uh ... yes, he's home this week. I expect to meet with him tomorrow and get him up to speed on all this."

"Good." Ruse tapped the table a few times. He was the antithesis of laid back. "Chase is a vital part of the team. We'll want to meet with both of you next week to set production dates, line up a director of photography, nail down a director. All the important pieces."

"Definitely." Keith figured Luke must've told Ruse about Chase's family issue. The explanation was honest and it bought Keith time. He would thank Luke later. He could hardly tell Ruse that he had no idea what was going on with Chase or that he could barely get him to talk on the phone.

The meeting was over, and Brandon stood first, reaching across the table and shaking both Keith's and Luke's hands. "This film is gonna rock! I'm already Twittering about it. Got a couple million followers. They can't wait to see it!" He flashed a sideways peace sign on his way toward the conference room door. "Got another meeting down the hall. Later, guys."

His team lingered a little longer, and Ruse was the last to leave. He set up specific meeting times with Luke, hours of discussion that would bring Keith back to LA for most of the next three weeks. Whatever Chase was working through at home, Keith hoped he had the details resolved. Things were picking up speed.

There was a chance they'd film *Unlocked* in Bloomington, Indiana, of all places. The state offered great tax incentives to filmmakers, and already Keith and Chase were connected with caterers and the technical staff needed to pull off a major motion picture. Either way, they wouldn't be home for a long time at this rate. Maybe this week at home would give Chase added energy and enthusiasm so he'd be ready for the race ahead.

Keith and Luke discussed a few more legalities in the lobby before Keith headed down the elevator three floors into the parking structure. He was halfway to his car when the ground began to move. It was an earthquake, Keith was certain. He'd lived through his share of temblors and now there was no denying the telltale signs — the way the lights swung above him and the noise of creaking cement and rebar.

He grabbed hold of the nearest cement post as the swaying strengthened. Was this only the beginning? Would the layers of rock and steel begin to collapse around him, crushing him? *God, be with me.* He braced himself, knowing there was nothing he could do if the intensity increased. But instead, gradually, the shaking stopped.

At that point he realized he wasn't alone. Half a dozen other business men and women sprang into action as the building stilled. All of them including Keith hurried into their cars and exited the structure as quickly as they could. Once out on the street, Keith turned on the radio in time to hear the announcement. A five-point-six earthquake had rocked the San Andreas Fault in an area ten miles east of San Bernardino. Aftershocks were expected.

Keith felt slightly sick to his stomach as he pulled onto the 101 and headed north toward home. If the earthquake had been worse, he and the others in the garage wouldn't have stood a chance. The weight of the building would've pancaked the garage structure, burying them so far beneath cement and steel, no one would've found their bodies.

He was still thanking God for sparing him when his cell phone rang. He glanced at it and saw it was Chase. The traffic was heavy, mostly stop and go. Typical for a Friday. He answered the phone with his bluetooth and kept both hands on the wheel. "Hello?"

"Did you feel it?" Chase sounded more relaxed than he had in months.

"Definitely." A chill passed over Keith's arms. "I was in the parking structure beneath DTA. Scary, man. Seriously."

"I bet." Chase's voice fell away, and for an uncomfortable moment there was silence between them. "Hey, what time are you home?"

"Depends on the traffic. Hopefully by six."

"Hmmm. Sort of late."

Keith wanted to scream at his friend. Whatever was going on, he wanted to know. Even if it meant talking at midnight. "What's on your mind?"

"I want to get together. Tonight, if you're up for it." Again Chase sounded easygoing, as if he didn't have a care in the world.

"Of course I'm up for it. Whatever time I get home." Keith worked to keep frustration from his voice. "Can you tell me what's happening here, Chase? You're killing me."

The pause on the other end was deafening. "It's not something I can discuss on the phone, Keith. Please understand. It's taken all week to work through this."

Keith held his breath and focused on the snarled traffic ahead. "Fine. I'll call you when I'm ten minutes from home. I'll tell Lisa to expect you."

"Great." Another awkward silence. "How did the meeting go?"

"Amazing. Jacque Ruse asked about you. He expects you to be at the next round of planning sessions. We're scheduled out for the next three weeks."

"Right. Okay, we'll talk about that." In the background there was the sound of little girl laughter. "Listen Keith, I gotta run. Call me."

The phone call ended and Keith ripped the bluetooth headset from his ear. He tossed it on the seat beside him and clenched his jaw. What was Chase doing? And why so cryptic about his past week? Keith gripped the wheel with an intensity that defined the moment, and then he slowly eased off. What was happening to their team? On the surface everything looked beyond amazing, like God was answering their prayers in ways they never could've imagined. But beneath the surface there were fault lines that rivaled the San Andreas.

Brandon Paul was certainly one of those. The kid was a huge box office draw, yes, but what about the red eyes and crow's feet? If he was partying, then anything could happen. They could sink millions into *Unlocked* only to have him turn up in the tabloids caught red-handed in a drug bust. Or overdosed on the streets of Hollywood like a number of other stars who'd gotten trapped by partying and wild living. He could get some girl pregnant or find himself in any number of uncompromising situations—all of which could bring the movie to its knees and impact Jeremiah Productions for all time.

Then there was the situation with Chase—whatever it was. Keith wanted to believe tonight's conversation would be nothing more than common courtesy, Chase's way of telling Keith how badly he'd needed time with his family. Now that his head was clear he was ready to move forward, fully committed. But he had the strange, sinking feeling Chase was coming over tonight not to apologize for a missed week of work, but to call it quits.

Now, in the middle of everything great and wonderful.

Keith could hardly stand the drive home, through hours of life-sucking LA traffic and long stretches of the 5 freeway toward San Jose. Even so, he made better time than he expected. It was only four thirty when he entered the city limits and called Chase. Again his friend sounded calm and deliberate, and again Keith was convinced something was very, very wrong. Never mind that they were on the brink of everything they'd ever dreamed, and forget the fact that God seemed to be opening doors faster than they could walk through them. As he pulled into his driveway, Keith had the feeling he was standing in the underground parking structure once again, the walls and ceiling beams shaking overhead.

Everything about his life as a producer about to collapse in around him.

Seven

Cody was finished with his last final and hoping for a few hours with his mother. This new boyfriend she'd been seeing had Cody worried more than any time since her release from prison. Once an addict, there was always the temptation to fall again, and if this guy dabbled in any sort of drugs, his mother could lose everything because of him.

He drove across town and pulled up in front of her small house. A few weeks ago he'd convinced his mother to give him a key—though she'd been reluctant at first. "I'm fine, Cody. You don't need to check up on me."

His concerns about her relapsing couldn't be the reason for his wanting a way into her house, otherwise she would never agree to it. Instead he came at it from another angle. "You live alone. What if you fell and broke your leg and couldn't get up? Anyone who lives alone should have someone looking out for them. Whatever age they are."

His mother's expression had softened. "You really care, don't you?"

"Yes, Mom. You know I do." Since then Cody had kept her house key with him in anticipation of moments like this. He walked up her uneven sidewalk and knocked on the door. While he waited, he noticed that her front yard was littered with weeds, the edges uneven and the flowerbeds forgotten and untended. His mother waited tables at a diner near the campus. She probably had no time for gardening. He chided himself for not helping her with the work sooner.

"Mom," he knocked again, louder this time. When no one answered, he used the key. The house smelled the same—lavender with a hint of Marlboro. Cody suspected she still snuck a smoke now and then. The first thing he saw was an ashtray on the kitchen counter. Frustration shot through him, but he tried to temper it. Better cigarettes than pot. As long as she stayed sober. He raised his voice. "Mom?"

She worked the morning shift and normally she'd be home by four o'clock, watching *General Hospital*, which she recorded every day. She loved the new chief of staff on the show—a Christian guy who'd starred in soaps for years. The show was a good distraction for her. At least until she met her latest guy friend. Now, when she should've been home watching her soap, the house was empty. He thought about leaving, but curiosity got the better of him. She wouldn't want him snooping around, but how else could he be sure she was doing okay? He knew nothing about this new boyfriend of hers. And who else besides him would care if she were falling off the wagon?

He tiptoed into the kitchen and the sound of a cat's meow caught him off guard, made him lurch a little. "Shadow ... where's Mom?"

The black cat slinked around the corner and rubbed against Cody's left ankle. He couldn't feel it, since that was his prosthetic lower leg. Strange, he thought. How little he even thought about the fact that his left leg wasn't like his right one. He moved into the kitchen and peered into the fridge. No sign of alcohol or anything amiss. Still he had a strange feeling, like she was hiding something. Not telling him everything the way she had since her release.

He opened the cupboard beneath her kitchen sink and pulled out her white plastic trash bin. The top layer was rumpled paper towels and an empty cat food can. Cody almost pushed it back beneath the sink and assured himself everything was fine. He was only victim to his overactive imagination. But instead he dug past the paper towels and dirty can, and there near the bottom he saw something that made his heart stop cold.

Buried there were two Miller Lite bottles and a few half-pieces of plastic straws. His heart jolted back into action, pounding in double time. What was this? His mother was drinking again? She couldn't be drinking. She was an alcoholic, just like him. Every other time in her past when she started drinking, drugs weren't far off. And when she started doing drugs, she had no way of stopping.

He remembered something she'd told him when she got out of prison last time. "Don't ever let me start again, Cody. Please."

"I won't. Not ever."

"It'll kill me next time. If I start again they'll either take me out in a hearse or a squad car, and this time I won't be coming home."

She was right. Drugs had gotten her in trouble with the law too many times. She had a record as long as his arm, because whenever she used drugs she also dealt. Her way of supporting her habit. If she got caught dealing again they would lock her up and throw away the key for a decade. Fifteen years, maybe. It was that bad.

He could hear her now, if she walked in and saw him digging through her trash. *Come on, Cody, what's a couple beers? A girl needs to relax, right?*

But not when the girl was an addict. The Miller Lite bottles were a terrible sign, proof that she was indeed falling—maybe harder than it seemed. Shadow rubbed against his leg again and meowed loudly. Cody felt adrenaline rush through his veins as he peered at the other suspicious items sitting next to the beer bottles. The half-cut straws. He'd seen his mom when she was using, and the straws terrified him. Sure, some people cut straws in half and used them for coffee stirrers. But not his mother. The only time she'd ever used straws like that was when she was doing cocaine. The shorter straws worked as the preferred way to snort the cocaine. Less waste along the inside of the straw.

He straightened and braced himself against the kitchen counter. *Dear God, please, no. Don't let this be happening. Let there be some other explanation. Please.* He replaced the top layer of trash and had just situated the bin back beneath the sink when he heard his mother's laugh and the sound of the door opening. He took a few quick steps from the sink and swept Shadow into his arms.

His mother wasn't alone. The guy with her must've been the man she was seeing. He looked as shocked as Cody's mother to see him standing there in the kitchen. Cody smiled, desperate to cover up the guilt he felt for checking up on her. "Hi! Thought I'd stop in and see how your day was going."

The laughter on his mother's lips faded and she slowly set her purse down on a chair in the living room, her eyes never leaving his. "You came in—when I wasn't home?"

"This here's your mother's property, boy." The man looked like a biker. Sleeveless T-shirt, tattoos everywhere, a bushy dark beard. He glared at Cody as if he were an eight-year-old caught stealing quarters from his mother's coin box. "How long you been here?"

Cody wanted to tell the guy it was none of his business. But he didn't want the scene to turn ugly. Instead he focused his attention on his mother. "I thought you'd be home. I was worried about you."

"I didn't work today." She reached for the man's arm. "Benny and I spent the day at the lake." She smiled at him. "Fishing, right, Tiger?"

"All morning." The man winked at her.

Tiger? Cody resisted the impulse to ask his mother if she'd lost her mind. The last thing she needed was a guy like this character. For a long moment, the three of them stood staring at each other in what felt like a face-off. Finally Cody set the cat down and cleared his throat. "Mom, I'd like to talk to you." He shot a look at Benny. "Alone, if that's okay."

His mother looked nervous; there was no denying the fact. She uttered an anxious-sounding laugh and patted "Tiger" on his soft, oversized shoulder tattoo. "Go on into the TV room. I'll be right back."

Benny glared at Cody, but he did as he was told. Cody watched until the man was out of sight; then he grabbed his keys and walked out onto the front porch. His mother followed, and Cody was quick to shut the door behind her.

"Who's *he*?" Cody's tone hid none of his anger and concern. "Looks like you picked him up at some bar."

"He's a Harley guy." She sounded defensive, but her eyes still looked nervous. She kept glancing back toward the house. "Don't judge people by the way they look, Cody. You're a Christian. You should know better."

"I went through your trash." Cody had no reason to lie to her now. If she was falling, she should know he was on to her. "You're drinking beer, Mom? Is that the kind of influence he has on you?"

"Cody Coleman," she put her hands on her hips. "How dare you go through my things. I didn't give you a key so you could spy on me."

"I didn't plan on it. But you weren't home, so I came in. Figured I love you enough ... I had the right to look."

"You're worried about nothing." She blinked a few times, faster than usual, and her mouth sounded dry. "The beers were Benny's. I'm clean."

He wanted to ask about the straws, but he knew she'd have an answer. Also, if she were doing cocaine again he'd know soon enough. He'd rather come around unannounced over the next few weeks and try to catch her in the act. That way she'd have to agree to get help. "Mom, what's this guy got? I thought you were gonna find a church. Get into a Bible study."

"I tried that." Again she glanced back at the house. "Church people are … I don't know, Cody. So different. Benny understands me."

"What about your new life?" He hated this, having to grill her about her personal decisions, but his heart hurt at the thought of her throwing away her sobriety. "How does Benny fit into that?"

"I'm not sure." She stared at her feet and began wringing her hands. "I have to go. Benny'll wonder what's happening."

"Benny should be working."

"He has a job." She lifted her chin, indignant. "He's a mechanic." She took a step back toward the door. "Things are a little slow right now, that's all. Gives us more time together."

Cody studied her for several seconds. "Okay. If that's what you want to believe." He hugged her. This close he was almost certain he could smell alcohol on her skin. It repulsed him, the way alcohol always did ever since the time he nearly died drinking, back when he was in high school. Again he saw no point in saying something about it to her. If she was drinking again, clearly she wasn't going to tell Cody. He drew back and searched her eyes. "I love you, Mom. I want you to make it this time." He was caught off guard by a wave of emotion too strong to fight. "I just …" His voice cracked and he looked off at the place where the maple trees met with the blue sky overhead. He found her eyes again. "I want it so bad."

She put her hands on his shoulders and gave them a strong squeeze. "I want it too, son. I'm okay. Really." She glanced back once more. "I'd tell you."

He nodded, knowing she was only saying the words because they were what both of them wanted to believe. But as he walked away, as he reached his car where he'd parked down the street and drove off, tears blurred his vision. A block away from his mom's house, he pulled over and pressed his fists to his eyes. She wasn't okay; he could feel it. Benny was trouble, and his mom wouldn't tell him if she was struggling or falling. Not until she admitted it through the bars of a prison or a room in the ICU.

God, please show me how to help her. Get this guy out of her life, and let her desire be for You. Only with You will she beat this addiction, God. I know that, because … because I'm the same way. I love her, God. I don't want to lose her. She's all I have.

You have me, son. Never forget that. Do not be afraid, for you are not alone. Not ever.

The voice echoed across his soul, and Cody wiped his eyes, regaining control. He heard the voice of God in his heart once in a while. But never this clearly. A verse flashed through his mind, one they'd focused on at the Cru retreat last weekend. *Be strong and courageous. Do not be terrified; do not be discouraged, for the Lord your God will be with you wherever you go.* It was from Joshua 1:8-9, and Cody felt it ring true alone in his car. His mother wasn't all he had. He had the Lord, certainly. And God had given him a second family long ago when he'd needed one most.

The Flanigan family.

Bailey might have a boyfriend, but that didn't mean he was any less welcome at the Flanigan home. He clenched his teeth, wrestling with his emotions. He hadn't been by in far too long. His classes had been tougher than usual, and now that finals were over, and in light of his concerns for his mother, he suddenly wanted to be with the Flanigans as badly as he wanted his next breath.

He flipped a U-turn, and ten minutes later he was pulling up the long driveway that marked the Flanigans' enormous house. Any time of the year the place was beautiful—beige with substantial white trim and a heavily defined black roof, wrapped halfway around with a covered porch that looked like something out of a storybook. He pulled his car up in the circle and stared at the front entrance. How many times had he walked through that door without giving his life here a second thought? As if he might be a part of this family forever.

Now he was grateful any time he found his way back. He still thought of Bailey's brothers like his own, and her father—her father was one of the most special people in Cody's whole life. No one would ever be a dad to him like Jim Flanigan. The man still coached the Indianapolis Colts, and they were in the middle of summer camp. But once in a while he was home on Friday for the weekend. That's what Bailey had told him.

He climbed out of his car and hoped this was one of those times.

Bailey Flanigan pushed the shopping cart next to her mother through their local supermarket. They were out of practically everything, so they each pushed a cart. Her mom was slightly distracted, trying to remember what they needed. Even still she was able to catch up on Bailey's life the way they so easily did when they were together.

"Have you heard from Andi?"

"Not much." Bailey frowned as she reached for the produce display. "Four packs of blueberries?"

"Make it six. The boys go through them faster in the summer."

Bailey grabbed six and tossed them into her cart. "It's like she's avoiding me."

"The whole Taz thing?"

"Right. I mean, Mom, you know how hard I tried. The guy was so bad for her. Now he's broken her heart and she's more closed off than ever."

"Maybe she should move in with us. Skip the whole dorm scene."

"I'd love that." Bailey had thought about the possibility before. Andi had not turned out to be the friend she had hoped for, but here at her parents' house they might still become close.

They moved down the frozen food aisle to the produce section. "You think she'd be open to it?"

"Not really." Bailey wanted to be honest with her mom and herself. "She won't talk to me. I have no reason to think she'd want to live with us."

"That's too bad."

"It is. She needs a friend now, especially since she and Taz are broken up." Bailey grabbed three bunches of bananas and put them next to the blueberries. "Sometimes I wonder what she's thinking, why she's so distant."

"Guilt, maybe."

"Maybe."

"That's sad."

"It is. I can't find a way to get through to her."

Bailey's mom filled a plastic bag with vine-ripened tomatoes and another one with cilantro. Every summer she cut up fresh pico de gallo and kept it in a container in the fridge. They ate it on everything from fish to turkey sandwiches. "Tell me about your finals."

"I did okay." Bailey wrinkled her nose. "I'm a little worried about my statistics class. The questions she gave us weren't on the study sheet." They talked about the grades Bailey expected from the semester and the courses she would take in the fall. They were almost to the checkstand when her mom gave her a knowing look. "So ... how's Tim?"

Bailey sighed, and she realized she was always doing that. Sighing when someone mentioned Tim. That had to be a problem, right? "I keep asking myself why I stay with him. I mean, he's nice and we have a lot of the same interests."

"He comes from a good family."

"Yes." Bailey pushed her cart more slowly. "But so do a lot of guys. That doesn't mean I should date them."

Her mom hesitated, her eyes more on Bailey than what was in front of her. She almost sideswiped a cart being pushed by a little gray-haired old lady. "Sorry." Jenny covered her mouth, embarrassed. Then she and Bailey swapped a quiet laugh. "I have to watch where I'm going."

"We both do."

This time her mom kept her eyes straight ahead. "Why, then, Bailey? Why date him?"

Bailey had thought about the question every night for what felt like months. "I guess because I spent so long crushing on him back when we were in CKT." Her heart sank a little as they reached the check stand. "He's easy to be with, likeable. He shares my faith. That, and because he's the only guy in my life. No one else is interested."

Jenny began unloading her cart, but she raised one eyebrow and flashed Bailey a kind look. "That isn't true."

"It is." She let the disappointment sound in her voice. She had no walls where her mother was concerned. The older she got, the more her mom was her best friend. "If Cody liked me, he'd say so. He's waiting for his dream girl. He told me so."

Jenny nodded slowly and didn't say more on the topic. They finished unloading the carts, and Bailey allowed herself to get lost in thought just a little. This was the sort of night when she would've loved nothing more than to ask Cody over to her parents' house. They were planning to watch a football movie—*Remember the Titans*. And before that, her mom was going to make the famous Baxter Enchilada Casserole—the recipe she got from Ashley Baxter Blake years ago. They'd probably even play a round of Pictionary before the night was over. Cody would love a night like that. Tim was still recovering from being sick, but even so, she couldn't call Cody and ask him over. So she did the only thing she could do.

She prayed that wherever Cody was, he'd know how much she cared. And that someday—if he really had feelings for her the way her mother believed—he would make his intentions clear.

Until then, nothing would ever change between them.

Ricky met Cody at the Flanigan front door, a football in his hands. "Cody!"

"Wow, look at you." Cody jogged up the front steps and hugged the youngest Flanigan boy. "You must've grown a foot!"

Ricky beamed. "I think I did."

"You must be almost as tall as your brothers."

"Taller than Shawn and almost as tall as Justin." He stuck his chest out. "Dad thinks I'm gonna be six-five."

Cody stifled a quiet laugh. "Could be, buddy. You're the biggest twelve-year-old I've ever seen. That's for sure."

"Yeah, and guess what? I'm playing quarterback next year for the seventh grade team. Isn't that great?"

"Wow. That's great, Ricky. You'll be amazing."

Ricky led the way back into the house. "You have to come see my games."

They walked down an open hallway toward the kitchen. Every time he was back, Cody wished he never would've left. But joining the service was the best thing for him—no matter the personal cost. The army was paying for his college education, and he had done his part to defend his country. He didn't regret that for a single moment.

The kitchen was empty, but through a wall of windows Cody spotted Jim out back, an acre from the house tossing a football with Justin, Shawn, BJ, and Connor. All the Flanigan boys played football—though Connor, at seventeen, would rather spend an evening writing music at the family piano than watching a Monday Night game on ESPN.

"Come play with us," Ricky grinned as he tossed the ball to Cody. "Now we can go three-on-three!"

That's what he loved about the Flanigan boys. It didn't matter if he'd been gone for weeks or months. They treated him like family, like his presence here was as natural as if he'd never left. He wanted to ask Ricky how his heart was doing, and whether he'd had any more rhythm issues. But it didn't seem like the time. Plus, if he was planning on playing football next year for his middle school, he must be doing well. Cody was glad. He worried about the youngest Flanigan boy.

"Come on!" Ricky tried again as he was halfway out the back door. He cupped his hands around his mouth. "Cody's here," he shouted. "Game time!"

Cody looked around, listening for anyone else in the house. Bailey had moved home before summer classes started. He wondered if she was home now, but he didn't hear her. He hadn't come to play football, but now the idea sounded great. He still worked out every day, pushing himself on his prosthetic lower left leg so that now he could run and swim and bike better than before his war injury. Today he wore jeans and tennis shoes. As he jogged out to join Jim and the Flanigan boys, Cody was pleased that he didn't have even the slightest limp.

"Cody!" Jim held his hand high, his face taken up by a smile as genuine as the Bloomington sky. "Great to see you!"

"You're gonna play, right?" BJ ran up to him first, breathless. "We've needed a sixth guy all afternoon."

Cody laughed. "I'm in."

The game was wildly competitive for a backyard contest, but then that was always how the Flanigan kids played. Like the Super Bowl was on the line with every play. Ricky was the worst—calling fouls and arguing over yardage gained and whether a first down really was a first down. In the end, Cody won with a team of Justin and Connor. Ricky hung his head as they walked back to the house, but only for a minute. "I was terrible today."

"Hey," Jim roughed up his son's blond hair and gave him a somewhat stern look. "None of that. Someone has to lose. You all played well."

Ricky looked like he might disagree, but then he stopped short with a reluctant smile. "Okay."

They were almost to the house, when Jim stopped short. He put his hands on his waist, still catching his breath. "You boys go in and see if your mom and Bailey are home. See if they need help bringing in the groceries or getting dinner ready."

Not one of the kids argued. Instead they walked off as a group, already letting the intensity of the competition go. Justin slung his arm around Ricky's back. "You looked great today. We got lucky, that's all."

"A win's a win." They grinned at each other and a minute later they were all inside.

Cody watched, amazed. This family was exactly how he wanted his family to be one day. The kids truly were friends. Cody grabbed a full breath and exhaled slowly. The sun was in his eyes as he squinted at Jim. "How long did it take for them to get that close? After you adopted, I mean?"

"Adopting was a family decision." Jim held the football. He tossed it in the air and easily caught it, his eyes never leaving Cody's. "We all promised not to feel sorry for our new boys from Haiti. That way they would have the same love, the same expectations as our biological kids." He shrugged. "That and a lot of prayer. I can't remember a time when these kids weren't all as close as they are right now."

"I guess I never asked much about it when I lived here." Cody shaded his eyes. "Too caught up in myself."

"You had a lot going on."

Cody hadn't planned on having time alone with Jim, but now that they were here together, it only made sense to share what was on his mind. His breathing was back to normal, his body cooled off from the game. "You have a minute? To talk, I mean?"

"Sure." Jim didn't hesitate. Here was one of the most powerful pro football coaches in the country with a whole houseful of kids on one of his only days off. But there wasn't even a hesitation about whether he had time for Cody. That was Jim Flanigan. He threw a short spiral pass and the football landed near the back door. Then he nodded to Cody to follow him. "Let's walk. I want to see how the path through the woods is doing. Sometimes it gets overgrown during the spring."

Cody fell in beside him. "I've been thinking a lot about my future, what I want to do with my life."

"I'm glad." Jim grinned at him. "That's half the battle, putting a little thought into it. So many kids never even do that." Jim kept the pace slow, his focus entirely on Cody. In the distance a woodpecker's tap-tap-tap echoed through the woods, but otherwise there wasn't a sound. Not even a breeze to rustle the new summer leaves. "So ... what have you come up with?"

He narrowed his eyes, looking at the blue beyond the tree branches. "I keep remembering something you told me a long time ago when I still lived here. You said life isn't a dress rehearsal, and it's important to find joy in the short time you have."

"Yes." Jim nodded slowly. "I tell that to all my kids."

"You said joy comes first from knowing the Lord, from having a personal relationship with Jesus."

"Definitely."

The path ahead looked like it needed work, but there was room to pass. "Second, you said joy comes from your family. So it's more important who you marry than what you do for a living."

"True." His smile was easy. "Jobs come and go."

"Right." Cody could remember the conversation like it had just happened. Jim Flanigan had given him more direction in life than anyone he knew. "And you said joy came from having as little debt as possible. Living within your means."

"Very important."

"Finally, you told me that a joyful life was one where you loved your line of work."

"Absolutely." Jim breathed in deep and took in the beauty around them. "You'll never be sorry if you spend a lifetime doing what you love. No matter how much money you make."

"Exactly." Cody loved this, talking to Jim. "I've thought about being an EMT, and I've thought about going to law school. Being a big-shot prosecutor. Like the guys on TV." He chuckled, and Jim did the same. "Drive a nice car, live in a nice house. That sort of thing."

Jim tilted his head and raised his brow, his laughter giving way to a warning. "Stuff can be a trap. Jenny married me believing I'd be a penniless high school teacher. Both of us were okay with that."

"Right, which is what I've been thinking lately." He stopped and faced Jim. "I think I want to coach football. Make a living at it." He felt vulnerable sharing his feelings, not sure if Jim would think him crazy for even thinking he could coach. But before he could explain himself more fully, Jim was nodding in agreement.

"I've watched you around the game, around our kids. I think you'd be a natural, Cody. If you want to coach, then coach. Volunteer for Clear Creek High. If you hate it, move on to something else. But if you never try, you could miss a lifetime of doing something you might truly enjoy."

"Really?" With every word Jim uttered, Cody felt his heart soar. "Even for this coming season?"

"Of course. You're young. Younger than I was when I started coaching. There's no better time to try it than now. It could change your life."

Cody felt a thrill rush through him. Was it possible? Could he be coaching at Clear Creek as soon as fall? He stood a little straighter and suddenly he felt more excited about his future than he had all year. They walked a little further and Jim shifted the conversation. "How's your faith, Cody? You staying close to Jesus?"

"Definitely." He told Jim about the Cru retreat, how he'd enjoyed focused time to read his Bible and pray about God's direction for his life. "That's partly why I wanted to talk to you. The

Lord made it clear at the retreat that I needed to try coaching. It's something inside me."

"That's how it felt for me too." Jim grinned and patted Cody on the back. "I'm glad you stopped by." They turned around and headed back to the house. "Bailey was on the retreat."

"Yes." Cody never liked talking about Bailey with her family. He wasn't sure how they felt about Tim Reed, but he was her boyfriend. All of them knew that. "She and I talked. It was nice. Being together like that."

Jim slowed his pace, his attention more fully on Cody. "She cares a great deal for you." He looked like he might say something more, but he stopped himself. "Probably more than you know."

"I ... I like hearing that." Cody wanted to say more too. He wanted to ask if Bailey cared so much, then why was she dating Tim. But that wasn't a conversation he could have with her father. And the last thing Cody wanted was any awkwardness between them. Instead he shifted the conversation again. "Pray for my mom, will you? She's acting funny. I'm worried about her."

Concern clouded Jim's eyes. "She's still clean?"

"I'm not sure. The guy she's dating, the way she seems nervous all the time. I think she's about to fall." He studied the ground for a few seconds. "There's nothing I can do to stop her, but I'd like to try."

Jim nodded, understanding. "I'll tell Jenny. We'll pray." He put his arm around Cody's shoulders. "Let us know if there's anything we can do."

"I will." Cody felt his emotions gather in his throat, a combination of the way Jim treated him like a son, and the certainty that his mother was about to suffer yet another crisis. He was so grateful for the Flanigans, for this time with Jim. As they reached the house, Cody hugged Jim hard. "Thanks. For letting me talk."

"Stay for dinner." Jim gathered the football and reached for the back door handle. "I'll call Ryan Taylor. See if he could use another assistant through summer league."

Cody could hardly believe it. "You don't have to do that."

"I want to. You're here all summer, right?" His smile was kind, compassionate.

"I am."

"Okay, then. You might as well be on a football field."

Cody grinned, again grateful. He hadn't imagined Jim would make a phone call this quickly. Ryan Taylor had been the assistant at Clear Creek High when Cody played there, back when Jim was the head coach. It was a position he'd taken after his first retirement from the NFL. But when the Colts hired Jim, Ryan took over at the high school. Cody followed Jim into the house.

The scene was happy chaos inside—typical Flanigan stuff. Bailey and Jenny were unloading grocery bags while a tag team of Flanigan boys carried in one armload after another. Jenny spotted him first. "Cody! The boys said you were here!" She blew at a wisp of hair in her eyes. "You'd think we were stocking up for a month."

Bailey exchanged a look with him then. She mouthed a quiet hi, her eyes sparkling in the sunlight streaming through the window. "The checker always gives us a funny look." She pulled five oversized packs of eggs from a single bag. "'You must run a daycare,' they say, or sometimes it's, 'What in the world are you doing with all these eggs!'" Bailey giggled and put her hand on her mother's shoulder. "What did we figure it was each week?"

"A hundred and eight eggs every seven days." Jenny laughed. "Unless we have extra kids on the weekend. Then it's more."

"It was more when I lived here." Cody moved into the kitchen and started unloading one of the bags lined across the counter. They worked together, while Jenny whipped up the great-smelling enchilada casserole and popped it into the oven. When the groceries were unloaded and the mess from two dozen plastic bags was cleaned up, when toilet paper had been taken to each of the Flanigans' nine bathrooms, and cleaning supplies had been distributed to the same, Cody motioned for Bailey to follow him into the piano room.

She did, and he was quick with his question. "I should've asked." He studied her, looking for signs that she might be upset he was here. "Is Tim coming by tonight? I mean ... it's Friday."

"No. He's going to bed early." Her eyes had a way of seeing to the very core of his being. "Still recovering."

"Oh." Cody nodded, hiding how happy that made him. "So ... I can hang out?"

"Of course." She hugged him quickly, impulsively. "I love when you're here. It's like ... I don't know." She drew back, searching his eyes. "Like old times."

He wanted to say that he felt the same way, that this was where he felt most at home and that she was the only girl he'd want to spend Friday night with as long as he lived. But he didn't say so then or while they were sharing stories around the dinner table or later when they played Pictionary. As usual, Bailey kept them laughing through the game.

The word was *cadaver* and Bailey was drawing for Cody and Ricky. She started with something that looked like a boot, then she carefully added the detail of a spiky thing near the ankle.

"What's that?" Ricky snapped his fingers, frustrated that he couldn't think of the word. He was as competitive around the game table as he was playing football.

Across from them, Bailey's brothers and her parents were snickering. None of them were drawing, so they all watched Bailey's attempt at the illustration. Cody knew where Ricky was headed with his guess so he quickly shouted out what had to be the answer. "Spur, cowboy spurs."

Bailey shook her head, but she motioned that they were close. This time she drew a very pointed arrow aimed directly at the spur-like thing. Her efforts lasted another ten seconds before time was up. She groaned out loud and threw her hands in the air. "I drew it perfectly."

The laughter from across the table was getting louder. Everyone but Bailey's team had already seen the card.

Bailey gave them a silly look as if she were offended, then she held up the picture so Cody and Ricky could see it better. She pointed to the object attached to the ankle of the boot. "It's right there. Cadaver. Clear as day."

Cody looked at Jim and Jenny, both of whom shrugged. At the same time Justin and BJ fell onto the floor laughing. "Seriously?" Cody shifted his attention to Bailey. "The word's cadaver?"

"Wow." Ricky smacked himself on the forehead. "Even I know what a cadaver is." He was half laughing, half frustrated. "Really, Dad? Can't she be on *your* team?"

"What?" Bailey studied her drawing. "That's not a cadaver?"

Jenny was the first one to have sympathy on her. "A cadaver's a dead body, honey. Not something you attach to your boot."

"Unless," Cody laughed out loud, "unless you're in the wild west, dragging a dead body out of town on your boot."

Bailey frowned at the photo. "A dead body? Seriously?"

"Cadaver!" Ricky had given up getting any points for the round. He patted his sister on the back as if he felt sorry for her. "Don't you ever see those police shows? They're always talking about some cadaver or another. No one ever says anything about boots."

Even Bailey laughed this time, and the night continued with all three teams close until the very end, when Jenny, BJ, and Connor won. "Just because Connor's the best drawer in the family." Ricky shrugged, careful not to get down because of the loss. "At least we get to watch the best movie ever."

They did that, too, celebrating with the Titans and wiping tears at the end when one of the star players was killed in a car accident. It was a night unlike any Cody had experienced for far too long. He wanted to say he'd be back every Friday, but that wasn't possible. Instead he savored the memories they'd made that night since he couldn't know when he'd have another chance like this one.

Before he left, Jim found him at the kitchen sink getting water. "I talked to Ryan before the movie. He said he'd love to have you. They'll be out on the field at three o'clock Monday if you can make it."

Cody remembered just a blink ago when he was one of the players suiting up for summer practices, dreaming of the fall ahead. Now he'd be dreaming up plays and play-breakers. He couldn't wipe the grin from his face if he wanted to. "He doesn't mind?"

"He's glad. He said he could use a quarterback coach." Jim patted Cody on the shoulder. "You were one of the best at Clear Creek High."

The compliment was the perfect ending to a perfect night. They talked a few more minutes about Ryan's coaching style and how Cody would be wise to watch a lot at first. When they were finished, Bailey walked him to the front door. He nudged his elbow against hers as they walked down the hallway. "Glad you're not going into forensics."

"Maybe I should." She cast teasing eyes at him. "At least now I know what to call a dead body."

"And what not to call a set of spurs."

"Right." She laughed out loud. "That too."

They reached the door, and Cody had to fight an overwhelming urge to kiss her. Was this what it would be like dating her? Being part of the Flanigan family night after night? He couldn't imagine anything better. But as soon as the thought crossed his mind, it was tempered by the greater reality. Bailey had made her choice—at least for now. And he wasn't that guy.

"I had fun tonight." He slipped his hands in his back pockets and took a step closer to the door.

"Me too." Bailey came closer. "You should come over more often."

He wanted to ask her about Tim. What would her boyfriend think of Cody hanging out with her family on a Friday night? But it was pointless. Nothing about Bailey and Tim made sense, so asking her about him would only confuse him more. Instead he smiled. "We'll see." He tried to back away without hugging her. The nearness of her was more than he could take—especially after being with her all night.

But she closed the distance and put her arms around his neck. Her hug lasted longer than any she'd given him since they'd found their friendship again. "Come back, Cody," she whispered near his ear. "I need you. We all do." She eased away, but only far enough so she could look into his eyes.

With her this close, he could feel her kiss on his lips, imagine what it would be like with her in his embrace. But before he lost all control, he gritted his teeth and slipped free of her grasp. "I'll try." He worked to keep his expression even. "I need you guys too." He stepped out onto the porch and gave her a single last wave. "See ya, Bailey."

She didn't answer him, not until he reached his car. As he opened the door, he heard her say, "You don't get it, do you?"

He stopped and turned toward her. "What?"

"Nothing." She crossed her arms in front of her and moved back into her house. "Bye, Cody."

He waved again, climbed into his car, and drove slowly down the driveway. What a great night. His game with the boys, and his great talk with Jim. The fact that Ryan Taylor wanted him on the field Monday afternoon. Laughing with Bailey. The apartment he shared with his three roommates would feel lonely indeed after so many hours with the Flanigans. The night was perfect. He pictured Tim Reed waiting at home for Bailey.

Okay, almost perfect.

The closer he got to home, the less he thought about the night and the more he thought about Bailey's last words. What could she possibly have meant? *You don't get it*? She was wrong if that's what she'd really said. Of course he got it. No matter how wonderful their time together, or how well he fit with her family, Bailey had a boyfriend. Period.

What else was there to understand?

Nine

CHASE STEADIED HIS NERVES AS HE drove the few miles from his house to the Ellisons'. He was dreading the next few hours and excited about them all the same. He'd never felt more right about anything in his life.

Once he got home after the premiere, once he walked through the door, the strangest thing happened. Kelly and the girls were in the backyard, so they didn't hear him come in. He set down his bags and walked to the back of the house. He stood at the kitchen sink and watched them through an open window, listened to their happy laughter, really studied them.

Kelly was taking turns pushing Molly and Macy on the swings, and all three of them giggled and talked as they played together. As Molly's swing slowed down, she reached back and took hold of Kelly's hand. "You're the best mommy in the whole world."

"And you're the best little Molly." Kelly kissed the top of their daughter's head.

"That means I'm the best Macy, right Mommy?" Their blonde little one leaned back, grinning at Kelly. She still looked pale, but clearly she was feeling better. "Right?"

"Of course." She kissed Macy's head next. "You're both the best daughters ever."

"And don't forget about Daddy." Molly looked from her mother to her sister. "He's the best daddy too."

Chase strained closer, wanting to hear every word.

"Yes." Kelly set one hand on each girl's shoulder. "Daddy loves you very much."

That's when it happened. Macy said something she might not have meant, but something Chase was convinced he was supposed to hear. Her smile fell away and she looked truly sad. Scared even. "Sometimes ... I forget what Daddy looks like."

The comment almost dropped Chase to his knees. His four-year-old daughter sometimes forgot what he looked like? Was that what making movies was doing to his family? He stood breathless, watching the scene play out.

"Honey," Kelly was quick to his defense. "You know what Daddy looks like. He's home almost every weekend."

"But he's busy when he's home." Molly's expression fell too. She reached out and took hold of her sister's hand. "On the 'puter." She looked at Macy. "Sometimes I forget his voice."

Chase felt a piercing shock, and sudden tears gathered in the corner of his eyes. Molly too? She was six this year. If she couldn't remember how he sounded, then he was doing something wrong. There was instantly no doubt in his mind. Kelly told the girls they could video chat with their daddy more often. "Then you won't forget so easily."

Chase had heard enough.

Standing there in the kitchen the answer was suddenly so loud it might as well have been blared through a loudspeaker right in his face. Pastor Hastings and his team had believed Chase to be at the top of a list of candidates to replace the youth pastor. Not because the team was unaware of his work in Hollywood. To the contrary. Because they were very well aware of his work, and the way it had taken him away from home week after week after week. Perhaps the email wasn't something to be dismissed as a crazy idea, but rather God throwing him a life rope.

Before his little girls didn't know him anymore.

Chase wiped at his eyes and moved to the back patio door. His heart was heavy, but a bright ray of light shone through the shadows that had gathered there. He opened the door just as his girls turned to see him.

"Daddy!" They cried out his name at the same time, flying off the swings and into his arms. Kelly walked up more slowly, her eyes warm and full of love. She wasn't angry with him or disappointed. She would defend his work in Hollywood even when their daughters were painfully honest about the cost.

But in that moment he knew something as clearly as he knew his name. His days of leaving his family were over. Someone else could help Keith change the world through the power of film. His mission field was here with his wife and daughters. As a youth pastor, he would be around them all the time. Kelly could teach Sunday school, maybe help out at the church office in future years when the girls were at school.

Most of all they could be a family again — something he hadn't realized he'd given up until now. That night in their bedroom he told Kelly what he'd seen when he came home, what he'd heard. And what he planned to do. "I'm not going back to Hollywood next week," he told her. "I want to be home, Kelly. I've been praying for an answer about how to handle the time away and God gave me one. It couldn't be any clearer."

She shook her head, not believing his words at first. Then a hesitant smile grew until it filled her face. "I never ... never would've asked you to give this up," she told him. "But I've been praying too. I want you home so badly, Chase. Someone will make those movies. God will find the right person." She hugged him for a long time. "I remember when we first got married, how you wanted to teach kids about God."

"I figured the mission field was God's answer to that desire." He kissed her, a kiss that shared the promise of all that suddenly lay before them. "Until now." He would've thought he'd have more angst about the situation. That he'd feel at least a little torn. Instead he felt nothing but peace. He stroked Kelly's hair and he thought about what his daughters had said. "You know what's scary?"

She looked into his eyes, loving him. "What?"

"I had forgotten what they sounded like too. Their little voices, the way they laugh." A shiver ran down his arms, and the image of Kendall flashed in his mind. "I almost lost it all, Kelly." He pressed the side of his face to hers. "Thank God I came home when I did." He breathed in deep and laughed out loud. As he did he swung Kelly around. "You know how I feel?"

"How?" she laughed like she hadn't since he started working with Keith.

"Like life is just beginning for us." He let his smile drop off a bit. "I'm sorry, Kel. I didn't know how much time it would take and I ... I hurt you in the process." He put his hand on her cheek. "Forgive me?"

"I have." She leaned in and tenderly kissed him, letting her lips linger as if to convince him. "I forgave you a long time ago. I knew if any change would come, it would have to come from God, not me." She smiled and her eyes lit up the way they'd done when she was a new bride. "And now it has."

He could hardly wait for morning to call Pastor Hastings. That call, too, had confirmed everything he now felt about his future. "I've prayed about your offer," he told the man. "I'd like to accept the position. I think it'll be good for me and my family."

"I expected your call." The pastor was a serious sort, and his tone now showed not a bit of surprise over Chase's acceptance. "God told me you needed this change."

Chase choked up, and he coughed to find his voice again. "The funny thing is, a long time ago it was my dream to be a youth pastor."

"Yes." There was a smile in the pastor's voice. "God told me that too." He paused. They talked about getting Chase's ordination papers in order, and Pastor Hastings grinned. "When would you like to start?"

Chase's mind raced. He could hardly start the job while Keith was taking meetings in LA, assuming Chase would be back at it come Monday. "Can I have a week?"

"Of course." Pastor Hastings was almost matter-of-fact about the news. "I'll share your acceptance with the team." His tone warmed. "We're excited to have you aboard, Chase."

"Yes, sir." Chase's mind raced. Was he really doing this? Changing directions so completely when everything in Hollywood was going so well? He blinked, clearing his mind. "I'm excited too." He thought about telling the news to Keith. He was excited and terrified at the same time. His friend would certainly struggle to understand any of this.

The next part was the best of all—telling the girls. Sunday before church, Chase helped Kelly make scrambled eggs and slice up fresh fruit. Over the meal, Chase set his napkin down and grinned at his precious daughters. "I have news for you."

"I know." Molly looked nervous. "You're leaving tomorrow, right?"

Chase swapped a long smile with Kelly, and under the table he reached for her hand. He turned his attention back to Molly. "No sweetheart, I'm not leaving."

Macy clapped her hands together. "You're staying home an extra day! Goody, Daddy. We can play hide-and-go-seek, okay?"

Chase and Kelly laughed. "Yes, sweetie. We can play hide-and-seek as much as you like." He reached across the table with his free hand and covered Macy's fingers with his own. "Daddy's not going away anymore, honey."

Molly's mouth fell open, and Macy tilted her head, clearly confused. Molly's question came first. "But ... you have to be in Lollywood for the movies, right?"

He smiled, but he bit his lip. This was a serious moment, and he needed his girls to understand the change about to take place in their lives. "I'm not going to make movies anymore."

"So you can stay home and play with us?" Macy's eyes lit up.

"Sort of." Chase couldn't contain his excitement. As crazy and uncertain as the change might seem to anyone else, he had not one bit of regret over this decision. "Daddy's going to work at church. Teaching the kids."

Molly was on her feet now, her eyes so wide they could see the whites all the way around them. "If you work here, you can tuck me in at night!"

Peace and joy spread through him, assuring him he would look back on this time decades from now and know—absolutely know—it was a gift from God. "That's right, baby. Daddy's going to be here every night to tuck you in."

She danced in circles around the dining room. "Daddy's staying home ... Daddy's staying home ... my daddy's staying home!"

Macy joined her then, grabbing hold of her sister's hands and dancing with her. "Yay! Daddy's staying home!"

Kelly was laughing and crying at the same time, dabbing at her tears as she watched their girls celebrate. Chase stood and helped Kelly to her feet, holding her close, rocking her to the sound of their daughters' laughing and singing and dancing.

"It's the best thing I've ever done." He whispered to her. Then he kissed her softly. "My girls will never have to wonder what I look like again."

"There's just one thing left to do." Kelly framed his face with her hands, and a ripple of concern crossed her otherwise joyful face.

"What's that?" Chase was so happy, so sure this was the miraculous answer he'd prayed for; he couldn't imagine what might cause Kelly any concern at all.

She hesitated, studying him. "You have to tell Keith."

The memory faded, and a ripple of fear stirred the otherwise calm waters in his soul. Because now that's exactly what he was going to do. Kelly offered to come, but Chase asked her to stay home with the girls. He had joined forces with Keith in Jeremiah Productions. Now it would be his responsibility to tell Keith he was moving on. When he wasn't playing hide-and-seek or taking the girls to the park and the zoo, Chase had prayed all week that his friend would understand. That their friendship could survive his decision to leave.

Chase turned onto Keith's street, drove past four houses, and parked. His stomach was in his throat by the time he reached the front door. *God, give me Your peace. Help Keith understand I'm not crazy, that this is the best thing I can do for my family. Please, God ...*

My son, anyone who knows the good he ought to do and doesn't do it, sins. Go forward now and do what you know to do.

The answer that resonated through him came from something he'd heard from Pastor Hastings halfway through the week. They'd talked several times since Chase's acceptance. Chase had a feeling they were going to be close friends, that the older man would become an important mentor to him and his family.

He knocked and waited. Scripture was clear about the list of sins, choices people made that separated them from God. But something sometimes overlooked was the admonition from James, chapter four, where God reminded people that sin was also knowing the good one was supposed to do, and not doing it. Chase was convinced without a doubt of the good he was supposed to do. He was being called back to his family, to a life of leading the kids of their church. Back to his first calling, really. If he didn't respond, he would be in error. Certainly Keith would understand that.

His thoughts were still racing as Keith opened the door. He looked tired and worn down. "Come in."

Chase followed him and saw that Lisa was already sitting in the living room. She, too, looked concerned. Clearly the two of them were expecting bad news. The whole room felt weighted by a layer of awkward tension. "Lisa …" He nodded at her.

"Hello, Chase." She stood briefly. "Can I get you water? Coffee?"

Keith took the seat next to his wife and crossed his arms. He didn't look angry. Just confused.

"No, thanks." Clearly Chase had let too much time go by without explaining himself. They couldn't go another moment with things feeling this strange between them. He felt sorry for the pain he was about to cause. With a heavy heart he sat opposite the two of them and leaned his forearms on his knees. "Let's start by praying. Would that be okay?"

"Sure." Keith looked at Lisa and then back at him. His tone was kind, despite his clear frustration. "We have no idea what's coming, buddy. You go ahead."

Chase closed his eyes and gripped his hands together. "Dear God, You've brought us here for an important meeting. We ask that Your Spirit of mercy and grace fall on this place, on each of us. That understanding would reign and love would prevail. Thank You for my great friends, Lord. Be with them and with me this night. In Your name, amen."

A quiet round of amens followed, and in the silence afterward, Chase grabbed onto God's strength. The time had come for him to explain himself. "A strange thing happened at the premiere." He decided to downplay the temptation from that night, and focus instead on his family. After all, that had been what caused him to make the change. He drew a long breath, steadying his voice. "There we were," he looked at Keith, "top of our game. But at the end of the night I felt like someone I didn't recognize. For a lot of reasons, I guess."

He told them about asking God for a way to reckon his family life with his life as a producer and director, and when he told them about seeing the footage of him and Kendall on the red carpet, an understanding filled Keith's eyes. As if from that point on he could see where Chase was headed. Chase continued, telling them about coming home and hearing his little girls talk about not remembering what he looked like, what he sounded like.

Lisa's eyes got teary during that part, and she looped her arm through Keith's. Chase wondered if she was thinking about their daughter, Andi. Sure she was in college, but how often were they able to talk to her or visit? The movie business took all their time.

"I guess that's when I knew," he sat straighter, his eyes on Keith's, imploring him to understand. He had to be very clear here. "I'm finished making movies, Keith. I've been offered a position at church." He shrugged, his eyes intent and unwavering. "I'm staying home with my family. It's what God's calling me to do."

Keith looked amazed and shocked and dizzy, like if he tried to stand he might topple over. But he didn't look angry. He was quiet for a long time before he raised his brow and allowed a soft chuckle. "I saw this coming, really I did." He looked at Lisa. "If I can be honest, I thought you and Kendall were getting a little too close."

His friend's admission brought with it another burst of shame, another confirmation that he was making the right move. "She's moving on. She told me so, but you're right. I was out of God's will in a lot of areas."

"We talked about you that night back in our room, how we were worried about you being away from Kelly and the girls." He breathed in deep, like he was trying to find his balance again. "But not for a minute did I expect this."

"I know." Chase couldn't help but offer a weak smile. The joy inside him was that great. "That's the best part. I didn't expect it either. But God did. He had this plan all along; I really have to believe that."

"I'm not sure where that leaves us—Jeremiah Productions, I mean." Keith looked at Lisa, and his eyes filled with a fear that was uncommon for him. For a moment it seemed he might recite all the company had going on—the great news about the theatrical release and American Pictures, the deal with Brandon Paul, and the potential success of that next film. "You and Kendall, both gone."

Chase waited, and for a few moments the silence became uncomfortable again.

Then Keith exhaled slowly and turned his eyes back to Chase. "God will show us what to do. Luke Baxter can draw up paperwork releasing you. But the bottom line is already clear. Whatever happens with Jeremiah Productions, it no longer concerns you."

Of all the things Keith could say, this touched Chase most of all. By acknowledging that Chase wasn't responsible for the trouble he'd caused or how Keith would move forward from here, he was releasing Chase. Releasing him with a full heart. For a long time none of them said anything. Keith folded his hands and looked at the floor for nearly a minute. When he lifted his face, there were tears in his eyes. "I've loved every minute of this journey. Even the scary times." His voice was strained. "I couldn't have done it without you, buddy."

For the first time since he'd made his decision, Chase fully registered that there was indeed a loss here, a loss that paled in comparison with the gift he was gaining. But a loss all the same. He stood and helped Keith to his feet, and the two of them hugged. Not the victory hug from the premiere night. But a hug that said no matter how difficult this moment was, the two of them would remain friends. "I'm sorry," Chase could barely speak the words. "God wants me to do this. I have no choice."

"I know." He sniffed hard and drew back, wiping the back of his hand beneath his eyes. Lisa was quietly crying on the couch, her hand to her mouth as she watched the two men. Keith nodded, still struggling. "I will pray for you and your new ministry every day. I promise you that."

Relief flooded Chase's heart. He put his hand on his friend's shoulder. "And I'll pray for you."

There were a thousand unanswered questions. How would Keith proceed alone, and how quickly could someone fill Chase's spot? But all that mattered here and now was that Keith understood, and he did so with a love and grace that didn't surprise Chase. It was one more answer to prayer, and Chase expected nothing less from their gracious God. The men hugged one more time and as Keith took his spot beside Lisa again, he laughed to break the sadness in the room.

"I don't have to ask this, but ... you know what you're walking away from, right?"

"I know." Chase chuckled a few times and shook his head. "Kelly's asked me more than once if I hit my head on the way home from LA last weekend. No one walks away from all you've got going on, Keith."

His friend seemed to note the way Chase distanced himself from the company, how he referred to the work of Jeremiah Productions as what Keith had going on, no longer the two of them. Keith nodded slowly. "I guess it's not about what you're walking away from." He smiled and put his arm around Lisa. "It's about what you're walking toward."

"Those sweet babies." Lisa's voice caught. "You're doing the right thing, Chase. I didn't see this coming. Not now with so much going on." She smiled and her sincerity rang with every word. "But you're doing the right thing."

"Thank you." Chase finally leaned back in his seat, able to relax. "I will always be here for the two of you. Anything I can do from my home, I'm happy to help out. And I believe God will bring someone along, someone who will be better for Jeremiah Productions than I ever could've been."

Keith raised one eyebrow. "Let's not get carried away."

They all laughed, and the conversation shifted away from work. As it did, there was nothing left to talk about. The two of them were no longer a team, no longer ready to take on the world of filmmaking in an attempt to change the culture. The dreams they'd believed in back on the mission fields of Indonesia had changed for Chase, and some sorrow colored the moment the way it was bound to.

Even so, Chase drove home with a smile in his heart, and when he walked through the front door, he found Kelly curled up on the sofa reading. "The girls are in bed," she whispered. "How did it go?"

"Perfectly. God met us there." He motioned that he'd tell her more later. First he needed to find his girls. He tiptoed down the hall and into the bedroom they shared, and he stood over them, watching the way their little bodies breathed so peacefully. He had almost lost this, the chance to watch them grow, to pray over them every night. But God had spared him, and now one thing was absolutely certain.

He wasn't going to miss another moment.

Ten

KEITH NO LONGER HAD TO WONDER what it would feel like to be trapped beneath thirty floors of rebar and cement. The moment his friend shut the door behind him, as soon as Keith and Lisa were alone in their silent living room, a weight like nothing he'd ever felt hit him square on the shoulders, dropping him to the edge of the sofa.

"Honey?" Lisa took the spot beside him. Her face was masked in worry, and she put one hand on his shoulder. "It's okay. God will show us a way out."

The pain of losing Chase now, when he needed him most, was so strong he struggled to breathe, struggled even to believe the events of the last hour had actually happened. Chase was gone. Their team was broken up, and now anything was possible. Every contract on the table was in jeopardy. "I ... I'm not sure what to do." He stood and crossed the room. He wouldn't cry or raise his voice or fall apart. God would get him through this the way He'd gotten them through so many other situations.

If only Keith could figure out what to do next.

He crossed the room to the front window and stared out at the dark night. Not even the hint of a moon lit the ground outside, and Keith found that fitting. He was suddenly headed a hundred miles an hour into the thickest fog he'd ever seen. No idea what the next minute might hold, let alone tomorrow.

"Keith ..." Lisa stood and came to him. "Talk to me." She put her hand gently on his shoulder. "What're you thinking?"

He looked back at her. "It might be over. Without Chase, every contract could be cancelled. That's how it works."

Lisa didn't look surprised. She nodded slowly. "Okay. So you walk away from Hollywood."

Her words had a strangely calming effect on him. His life in Hollywood had gotten so complicated that he rarely considered the obvious. He could walk away from it tomorrow—as long as his investors were taken care of. Because he could only do so much, and if American Pictures wanted to pull out, if Brandon Paul no longer wanted to work with him, then so be it.

He leaned his head against hers and remembered a sermon a year ago, something he'd forgotten until now. "Remember what Pastor Hastings said awhile back?" Keith's voice held a calm that he still didn't quite feel. "He said sometimes life gets too complicated to figure it out on your own. When that happens, God has to do the figuring."

"Mmm." Lisa eased her arm around his waist and pressed her body close to him. "I remember."

"And while God does the figuring, there's only one thing we can do."

He felt Lisa smile. "The next thing."

"Right. We just do the next thing and let God reveal the bigger answers." They were quiet, clinging to each other and to the certainty that God would see them through. Even if it was impossible to see the way out from here. Keith peered into the darkness. Chase had a right to follow God's plan for his life, even if that plan had seemingly come out of nowhere. It wasn't like Chase had a contract to fulfill. They were only now signing deals with American Pictures and DTA, with Brandon Paul and the author of *Unlocked*. They had yet to contact new investors about the publicity and advertising budget for their theatrical release of *The Last Letter*.

Legally, Chase was free and clear, and Keith could do nothing but release him with complete understanding. Keith sighed, feeling the heaviness around him again. Tomorrow he would need to call Luke Baxter and tell him. Luke would have ideas, someone in the industry who might be interested in filling Chase's position. But what about their vision? Making movies that could change the world? Would anyone else work as passionately to that end as Chase Ryan?

"Don't." Lisa whispered against his face.

He looked at her, loving her. "Don't what?"

"Don't borrow trouble from tomorrow." She kissed him on his cheek, her eyes never leaving his. "Do the next thing."

"Hmmm." His heart filled with gratitude for the strength of the woman beside him. She had been this way when he married her, and her resolve had helped him through their time in Indonesia. Now here she was again, her tender wisdom helping him believe that God hadn't abandoned them, that His plans were still good. He touched his fingers to her face, lost in her. "The next thing, huh?"

"Yes."

He shrugged, at a loss. "And what's that?"

"We call our daughter, read our Bibles, and go to sleep."

"Are you sure that's the next—" The phone rang before he could finish his sentence. He looked at the clock on the wall. It was just after seven, which meant it was ten o'clock in Bloomington. "Maybe that's her." The situation with Chase had distracted him much of the week, but now he was reminded about Andi. They'd talked to her just a few times since last weekend, and with each call she sounded more distant, distracted. Keith pointed toward the phone. "There it is ... the next thing."

Lisa smiled, and her unwavering joy relieved the pressure weighing on him. He moved to the phone and picked up the receiver. "Hello?"

"Keith, hey it's Dayne Matthews. I'm not calling too late, am I?"

"No, not at all." Keith wrinkled his brow, baffled. Dayne Matthews had never called him at home. The two hadn't talked since they were in Bloomington a year ago filming. He mouthed to Lisa that the caller was Dayne Matthews.

Her eyes grew wide, and she moved slowly to the nearest chair.

"Do you have a minute?" Dayne sounded excited, practically bursting with whatever he'd called about. "I mean, if this is a good time?"

"It's fine." Keith returned to his place by the window and leaned against the adjacent wall. "What's on your mind?"

"Well," he chuckled, as if he wasn't sure where to begin. "I've been following your work—you and Chase. I read earlier today about your premiere and the offer from American Pictures. The whole Brandon Paul deal that must be coming together based on the retraction from NTM." Dayne sounded impressed. "God's doing amazing work through you two, which got me thinking."

Dayne went on to say that he'd been away from movies for a long time—several years. "CKT is running itself. We have wonderful directors and people handling the office. The kids' theater group doesn't need Katy and me like it used to."

Keith felt his heart speed up. Where was Dayne going?

"What I'm saying is, Katy and I talked about it and we'd like to be a part of Jeremiah Productions. Sophie is old enough to travel, but too young for school. Katy and I could take her with us, spend time on the set. Help with the productions somehow or with the publicity and advertising."

Keith's head started to spin. He turned his back to the window and rested against it, his eyes closed. How was this happening? And was Dayne really proposing what it sounded like? Keith forced himself to concentrate.

"We'd like to invest as well. We and some friends of mine from Hollywood. We really believe in what you're doing." He paused but only for a second or two. "Of course, we wouldn't want you or Chase to feel like we were taking over. You might not have room for us, and that's fine. It's just ... we talked about it all day, and I couldn't go to sleep without calling you and Chase to see if—"

"Dayne." Keith shot a disbelieving look at Lisa. Then he uttered a single awestruck laugh. "There is no Chase."

A long silence filled the line. "What?"

"There's no Chase. He resigned from Jeremiah Productions an hour ago."

Now it was Dayne's turn to be overcome with disbelief. "Because ... because of some problem?"

"Yes. His family needs him. His girls are in preschool. They can't travel with him." Keith moved to the chair across from Lisa. He needed to sit down. "They need to be home and he needs to be on the road." He pictured Chase's young daughters. "They were forgetting what he looked like."

"This just happened?" Dayne was obviously confused. "Now? When you're on the verge of making history with Jeremiah Productions?"

"Yeah." Keith sucked in a long breath, but it didn't help. He was still dizzy, still too shocked to fully grasp what was happening. "But Chase had no doubts. Our church staff offered him a position as youth pastor, and he accepted." Another chuckle came from him. "Lisa and I were just reminding each other that God still had a plan for Jeremiah Productions. That everything wasn't really going to fall apart. We just couldn't see what was next."

Gradually Dayne must've understood. "Until now?"

"Yes." Keith reached for Lisa's hand, and he saw understanding dawn in her eyes. "Until now."

"Dear God, thank You." Lisa bowed her head, her whispered prayer little more than a breath. She must've heard some of Dayne's side of the conversation and pieced together what was happening.

"Well, then." Dayne's quiet laughter bridged the distance in the pause that followed. "I guess there's just one more question ..."

"When can you start?"

They talked a few minutes more, and Keith promised to make a trip to Bloomington to talk about details. "But before that, how would you feel about taking meetings with me over the next few weeks? As my co-producer."

"This is crazy." Dayne's laugh was full now, his enthusiasm clear over the phone lines. "Just tell me when and where."

"Your brother Luke can rearrange things, fit the meetings into the next couple weeks, but we're needed out there pretty much all that time."

"Hmmm." Dayne thought for a moment. "I have an idea." He went on to explain that he still had friends in real estate outside Los Angeles. "They handle corporate rentals too." Dayne agreed to make a few phone calls and line up a house on the beach—something with enough room for both their wives and little Sophie. "That way they can have a vacation while we're taking care of business."

Keith's mind raced. Dayne would have to get up to speed very quickly. They would likely need another few hours on the phone tomorrow, but Dayne seemed certain he could have a place rented by Monday. They could fly in then and hit the ground full speed. What Dayne didn't know in background information and contract details he would learn. Until then, his name would raise the visibility and credibility of Jeremiah Productions to an even higher level.

The phone call finally ended and Keith stared at his wife, speechless.

"Am I understanding this right?" She came to him and knelt at his side, her hand alongside his face. "Dayne Matthews just called and asked if he could work with Jeremiah Productions?"

"Umm ... Yes." A single laugh slipped from Keith and he lifted his hands, still stunned. "I think so." He looked around and then put both his hands on her shoulders. "I'm not dreaming, right?"

"No." They giggled, giddy over the unbelievable turn of

events. "You're walking in faith." She looped her arms around his neck and hugged him close.

As long as they lived they would remember this day. It was as if a sudden storm had come upon them and threatened to capsize their boat, threatened to destroy them and all they'd worked for. But then Jesus Himself had calmed the wind and the waves with a single phone call. Dayne Matthews, wanting to be a part of Jeremiah Productions. Minutes after Chase had stepped down. Only God could've done this, and Keith stood, helping Lisa to her feet as well.

The reality was sinking in and Keith let out a victory shout as he threw his arms around his wife. They weren't done making movies. God had a plan better than anything they could've come up with. Chase was going home to be with his family, and Keith would have the chance to work with one of the top names in Hollywood. A man who had seen the ugliest side of Hollywood, but who still believed that God could use the power of film.

"Keith!" Lisa pushed back and sucked in a quick gasp. "I have an idea!"

He laughed again. "I'm not sure I can take much more."

"No, this is perfect." She backed away and paced a few steps, her hand to her forehead. "Dayne lives in Bloomington."

"Yes." Keith wasn't sure where Lisa was headed with this, but he loved her enthusiasm.

"Andi will be there for another three years, right?"

"At least." He caught a glimpse of what she might be thinking. "You're saying we—"

"We move there! We can be closer to Andi, and you and Dayne will be better able to work together."

Keith nodded, letting the idea sink in. "Wouldn't it make more sense for everyone to move to LA?"

"Dayne won't want that." Lisa was adamant. "Neither would we. And LA would be the worst place for Andi. She's had trouble staying grounded in Indiana."

Her excitement was contagious. "We could rent a place in LA when we need to be there, and do most of our filming in Bloomington. Or somewhere close by."

"Exactly." Lisa raised her fist in the air and let out a joyous cry. "This just keeps getting better."

Keith realized then how much he'd missed his Andi. She wasn't young like Chase's daughters, but she was still their little girl. On the mission field they'd shared every day together for years. Never mind that she was an adult now. She was floundering —they all knew that much. And now they could be together again.

The receiver was still on the sofa where Keith had placed it after the call from Dayne. Now Lisa raced over and grabbed it. "Let's call her. She won't believe everything that's happened."

Keith thought about telling his wife that maybe they should wait. They shouldn't get Andi excited that her parents were moving closer unless they were sure. "Shouldn't we pray about it first?"

"Keith. God's the one who dropped this in our laps." Her smile lit the room, but she set the phone down on the arm of the sofa. "Okay, fine. Let's pray."

Again, laughter filled Keith's throat and he nodded at his wife. "You do it."

She took his hands and closed her eyes. "Dear Lord, thank You for making the answers so clear. Please let the pieces fall in place quickly. In Jesus' name, amen." She opened her eyes. "Let's call Andi."

Again they laughed together, reveling in God's goodness and the certainty of His plans for the next season of their lives. They called Andi twice that night, but both times the call went to her voicemail. Keith frowned. "I hope she's not out with that Taz guy. He's not good for her."

"She's not." Lisa stared at the phone and then at Keith. "They stopped seeing each other a month ago."

"Good."

"She's probably out with Bailey. She'll call us back when she gets in."

Keith was pensive for a moment, his mind lost on their only daughter. "She needs us." He looked at Lisa. "Maybe more than we know."

"Which leads us to the next thing." Lisa's smile was tender, her enthusiasm tempered some in light of their daughter.

Keith kissed her, this time slow and full on the lips. "What's the next thing, Mrs. Ellison?"

"That's easy." Her smile reached her eyes once more. "We need to list our house."

Eleven

Life had become a sudden and complete whirlwind overnight, but Dayne couldn't have been happier. Katy was completely on board with his idea—though the speed with which it was happening had taken them both by surprise. The next morning Dayne shared an early conversation with Keith, called his California realtor to secure a beach house for Monday morning, and on Sunday he and Katy and Sophie headed to church.

The ten o'clock service was where all the Baxters met every Sunday morning. Dayne and Katy arrived early, and before the service began, Dayne found his father in the lobby. "Hey, Dad," he couldn't stop grinning. "We need to talk."

"I still love that." His father smiled. "Hearing you call me Dad."

Dayne slipped his arm around his father's shoulders. "I still love saying it." He took a step back and glanced toward the front door. He didn't want to get caught in a conversation with anyone else before he told his dad what was happening. "Can we do a Baxter dinner tonight? Katy and I need to talk to the whole family."

"Really?" John raised an eyebrow. "Is Sophie getting a baby brother?"

"No, no." Dayne laughed. "Nothing like that. But it's still big. We're flying out to Los Angeles in the morning."

"The three of you?"

"Yes. We have a lot to talk about." People were filing in, and Kari and Ryan and their kids were walking up, their kids chattering as they came. Dayne kept his eyes on his dad. "Dinner tonight?"

"Sure. I'll invite the rest." His dad looked happy to oblige. "Five o'clock?"

"Perfect." Dayne hugged his dad again and then hurried back into the sanctuary to join Katy. Sophie was asleep in her arms. Dayne leaned down and kissed his baby daughter's forehead. Then he did the same to Katy. "We're on for tonight."

"I can't believe how much we have to do." She giggled quietly. "You're a crazy man, Dayne. But what's life without an adventure?"

He took the seat beside her. "Think of it as a mission trip."

Pastor Mark spoke that morning on answering the call. Time and again, Jesus presented people with the chance to follow Him, and when people truly believed Him, they set down what they were doing that very moment and followed. Dayne listened intently, and beside him he felt Katy squeeze his hand.

"The point," Pastor Mark said, "is that we need to be listening. When God calls us, it's time to act—whatever He's asking us to do. We should have our yes on the table at all times."

Dayne smiled to himself throughout the hour. The sermon seemed written specifically for him. Clearly God was working in all this. The words from Scripture that morning were further proof. When church ended, the Baxters gathered in the foyer and John invited everyone for dinner. Brooke and Peter had to cancel plans with friends, but they didn't think it would be a problem. Everyone else was free.

"Looks like we'll all be there." John smiled at his kids and their families. Then he winked at Cole, Ashley's son. "I bet there are still tadpoles in the pond."

"Really?" Cole was eleven now, but he still loved spending time at the pond with his grandpa. He nudged his brother. "You hear that, Devin? We better get there first."

Landon gave his wife a questioning look. "What do you think, Ash? We can get there at four, maybe?"

"Yeah, because you're the biggest kid of all." Her eyes held an endless sort of love for him. "That's fine. I'll help Elaine with dinner. You and my dad and the boys can do your pond thing."

The plan was set and everyone headed out. Katy talked the whole way home about what to pack, but in the end she didn't put together much. Just enough clothes to get through a week. The house they were renting had a washer and dryer. And they could always shop if they needed something.

Time flew, and hours later when they pulled up at the Baxter house, Dayne was amazed at all they'd accomplished. "Who would've thought so much could change in a single weekend?" He cut the engine and let his head fall back against the seat.

"It's a little hard to believe, still. I mean, the idea of Chase stepping down now?" Katy reached back and took hold of Sophie's little hand. "Not that I blame him. Our kids are only little for so long."

"I wouldn't do this if you and Soph couldn't come with me." He looked back at his daughter. "I can't believe you're already two, right little one?"

"A'most two!" Sophie giggled and rocked forward in her car seat, pointing to the big farmhouse. "See Papa, Daddy?"

"Yes, baby. We're going to see Papa." Dayne opened his door, but he stayed seated. "No matter what happens, I don't want to move away." He looked at the Baxter house and a rush of memories flooded his heart. "This is where our family is; it's home."

Relief lifted Katy's expression. "We haven't talked about it, but I feel the same way. A few weeks in LA is one thing, but this … the Baxter family? I couldn't walk away now."

"Not after all it took to find them."

"Exactly."

They climbed out, and Dayne unbuckled Sophie's car seat. She was running now, and Dayne watched her go as he set her down.

"Papa!" Her hair was as blonde as Katy's, as blonde as her big cousin, Cole. She had Katy's fine features, but her eyes were the same as most of the Baxter kids. Baxter blue, they called it.

As they walked in the side door, Cole and Devin came through the front with Landon and Dayne's dad in tow. "Papa was right!" Cole's enthusiasm never dimmed. "The best of the season!" He had a small fishbowl, and swimming inside were a number of tadpoles.

"Wonderful." Ashley stepped out of the kitchen, a spatula in her hand. She directed it at Cole. "They stay in the laundry room this time."

"Aw, Mom. They hate the laundry room." Cole peered in at them, and next to him, Devin did the same. "They like people. Tadpoles are social."

"They are." Dayne took a few steps toward Cole and squinted at the glass bowl. "I read that tadpoles are more social than dogs."

Laughter came from the kitchen. "Come on, Dayne." Katy was washing her hands at the sink. "No one's that good an actor!"

The conversation continued as first Kari and Ryan and their three kids, then Brooke and Peter and their two girls, and finally Erin and Sam and their four daughters all arrived. By then, Luke's wife Reagan and their two kids had been there most of the afternoon. With Luke doing business in LA more often, Reagan liked spending Sundays at the Baxter house.

Dayne found a kickball in the garage and set the cousins up outside. The three littlest girls were too small to play, so they sat on the porch steps and watched. Sophie, and Ashley's youngest—Janessa Faith, along with Kari's little one—three-year-old Annie.

But that still left twelve cousins suddenly engaged in a wild, rule-free game of kickball. "I'm captain," Cole announced. "Everyone line up and we'll pick teams."

"No! I'm captain." Tommy stuck out his chest. "I pick Maddie!"

Cole gave his younger cousin a patient look. "We can both be captains."

"And I'm on Tommy's team." Maddie high-fived Tommy. "We can beat Cole any day." She smiled sweetly at Cole. "You know it's true."

Cole surveyed the kids on the line and pointed at his strapping younger brother. "I pick Devin."

Dayne chuckled quietly from the porch steps. He loved times like this, and he sat by the little girls for a few minutes. He especially loved watching Hayley run with the other kids. Hayley was nine this summer, and her disabilities were almost too slight to notice. Dayne hadn't known his family back when Hayley had nearly died in a drowning in their family pool. But he'd heard stories from Brooke and Peter and the other Baxters. Hayley's doctors had given her only a slim chance at life back then, certain she'd never leave her bed if she survived. Every day was a miracle for Hayley, proof that God would forever have the final word.

Ashley stepped outside and took the spot beside him. Dayne was close to all his sisters, but he and Ashley would always have a special bond. She was the one who had pursued him the hardest, the sister who first figured out that Dayne was part of the Baxter family. "Hi, there."

"Hi." He had to talk loud to be heard above the kids.

"You coach?"

"Referee."

"Good luck." She laughed and hugged her knees to her chest. After a while she smiled at him. "It's hard to imagine heaven any better than this."

Dayne nodded, and he understood even more why Chase had to back out of Jeremiah Productions. He couldn't imagine a day when Sophie might forget what he looked like or no longer remember the sound of his voice. He thought about telling Ashley, but he decided to wait. The story was too long to tell twice. He smiled at his sister. "What's new?"

"We have tadpoles." Ashley grinned. "But that's not really new." She angled her face. "Landon's been promoted at the station, and I'm working on a new painting. The Baxter house with a bunch of blonde kids playing out front. Too many to count."

"Sounds perfect." He remembered the loss their family had suffered a few years ago when Ashley's baby, Sarah, had died hours after birth. She and Brooke had opened a crisis pregnancy center in honor of the infant. "How's Sarah's House?"

"Great." Ashley's eyes told him she was glad he'd asked, glad people still remembered little Sarah. "Every week girls are coming in. Only God knows how many babies have been saved because of the work taking place there."

Dayne was about to ask how Cole was doing in baseball. He'd made All-Stars, Dayne knew that much. But Elaine opened the door and called out, "Dinner! Everyone wash up!"

They filed in, and somehow through the craziness of so many kids and a dozen conversations, they wound up seated at two long tables in the Baxter dining room. Dayne was practically bursting with his and Katy's news, but he waited while the others talked. Sam's company was laying off, but he'd been told late last week that his position was safe. "We're grateful," Erin said. She looked beyond relieved. "Sam and I don't want to move again."

"I'd switch jobs first." He smiled at the faces around the table. "What we have here, it's too special to walk away from again."

Dayne knew their story, how they'd lived in Texas for several years. Now that they were here, Dayne had to agree. The family wouldn't be the same without them.

The conversation shifted to Brooke and Peter, and the way their medical practices were growing. "I think the recession must be lifting. Bloomington seems to be adding new families all the time."

"It's a great place to live!" Landon raised his glass of water and grinned at Ashley. "Right, honey?"

"As long as there are no fires." She gave him a wary smile. "I'm ready for you to run the department. Then you can keep your uniform clean."

They all murmured their agreement. The times when Landon had been injured in serious fires were before Dayne had come into the family. But the chance always remained. It reminded Dayne to pray for his brother-in-law every day. He needed absolute protection in his line of work.

The conversation was slowing when Reagan put down her fork and looked around the table. "I have some news. Luke asked for your prayers for us."

Concern showed on their father's face. "He's traveling a lot lately."

Dayne wondered if this was his segue. Maybe Luke wanted prayers because of the changes taking place with Jeremiah Productions. In addition to handling Dayne's business, Luke was now almost entirely working with Keith's production company. Dayne could barely contain his news.

"We're fine." Reagan's eyes warmed. "It's just ... we're thinking of adopting again. Maybe from the U.S. this time. I talked to Luke earlier today and he asked you to pray. He'll be home in a few weeks. We might start the process then."

"Reagan, that's great!" Ashley was sitting beside her. She reached out and took hold of her sister-in-law's hand. "We'll all pray."

"Can you make this one a boy, please?" Cole sat up straighter. "We need more boy cousins."

"They're talking about a baby." Landon put an arm around their oldest son. "I don't think cousin kickball will be a part of his or her life for quite a while."

"Ya," Cole looked disappointed. "I guess you're right."

They all laughed, and Reagan promised to keep them posted. The time had come, and Dayne couldn't keep the news a secret a moment longer. Besides, his father was watching him, waiting for whatever it was he'd called the dinner for. Dayne set his napkin down and grinned, first at Katy, then at the others. "Katy and I are taking Sophie to Los Angeles tomorrow."

"For Disneyland?" Tommy jumped out of his seat. "Daddy's taking me and Malin to Disneyland this summer, right Mommy?" He spun around and stared at Reagan, then spun back to the group again, eyes big. "Disneyland's the happiest place on earth."

Reagan helped Tommy back to his seat. Dayne waited for the commotion to die down. "No, not for Disneyland, not this time." He winked at his young nephew. "But maybe we'll join you later this summer!"

Cole whispered something to Ashley, but she held her finger to her lips and whispered, "Later." Then she turned to Dayne. "Is this business, then?"

"Yes." He grinned. "I'm joining Keith Ellison as the newest producer with Jeremiah Productions." His family leaned in closer, listening to every word while Dayne explained how Chase had stepped down, and how at the same time he and Katy had felt God calling them into moviemaking. "The timing is perfect. Katy and Sophie can travel with me when we need to be in LA. Otherwise we can work from here."

His father nodded thoughtfully. "Sounds fantastic."

"I talked to Keith this morning. He and Lisa are listing their house and moving here to Bloomington. We want to film as many movies in Indiana as possible." He held his hands out to the rest of the group. "That way we don't have to give up this."

"And Keith and Lisa can be closer to their daughter." Ashley sat back in her seat, beaming over Dayne's news. "That's wonderful. Congratulations!"

Peter asked if Dayne would consider acting in one of the Jeremiah Productions films. "Not yet." He remembered how crazy his life had been back when he was in two or three movies a year. He shared a knowing look with Katy. "God would have to make that very clear."

"When will the media know?" Elaine's question was a good one.

Dayne imagined the public attention just ahead of them. There would be major interest in him joining forces with one of the most talked about new producers in town. Especially since Jeremiah Productions was clearly a Christian-based company. "Luke's releasing a statement to the press tomorrow. I imagine we'll have interviews pretty quickly after that."

Reagan exhaled hard, as if she'd been holding her breath. "Luke told me before we came over." She smiled at Dayne. "If you didn't say something soon, I was going to tell them myself."

Their father expressed his gratitude that Luke and Dayne would once again be working closely together. "And it's great you and Katy and Sophie can do this together. When you have to be on the road," he patted Dayne's shoulder. "I'm very happy for you. For all of you."

By the time everyone left, the whole family was excited about the future of Jeremiah Productions, and Maddie had announced that she planned to star in one of the movies. Just as soon as she finished middle school. Dayne was still smiling when he and Katy and Sophie piled into their SUV and headed home. They were packed, but there was still one thing Dayne wanted to do before they turned in for the night.

Back at their lake house, they tucked Sophie into bed and Dayne took Katy's hand. "Come with me," he whispered.

She followed him down the hallway, through the dining room, and out onto the back porch. The stars were bright against the dark sky, and in the distance the soft cry of an owl carried across the lake. They stood beside each other against the porch railing, staring out across the sloped hillside toward the water.

"Everything's happened so fast." Dayne slipped his arm around Katy's shoulders and held her close. "I guess I didn't want to set off for Hollywood tomorrow without making a few things clear."

Katy smiled up at him. She didn't seem worried. Rather her eyes told him she completely trusted his lead in this new venture. She looked straight ahead again and rested her head on his chest. "Tell me."

"It's been awhile, and time ... well, time's healed a lot of the wounds from the past." He paused, choosing his words carefully. "But I want you to know I remember what making movies cost us when we first started out."

"Hmmm." She nodded. "You were nearly killed."

"Yes." He still had occasional aches and stiffness from the car accident that almost took his life. The paparazzi had been so intense that day, they'd run him off the road, straight into an oncoming truck. He spent weeks in a coma, and months of rehabilitation before he could come home to Bloomington to marry Katy. "The accident, and the lies the rags printed every week. Pretty tough times."

"They were."

A light breeze rolled up from the shore, brushing Katy's hair against Dayne's cheek. "I promise you, Katy, it won't be like that this time. We'll only be in LA on occasion. You and Sophie will be safe at our rented house, and the paparazzi will be more concerned with Brandon Paul than me."

She smiled again. "You can't promise that."

He lifted his eyes to the starry sky above. She was right, and that frustrated him. "I'm married with a baby now. I'm boring by the world's standards."

A light laugh slipped between her lips. "Hardly." She leaned up and kissed him softly. "You've never been more handsome."

"What I'm trying to say is—"

"Shhh." She held her finger to his lips. "I trust you, Dayne. That's all that matters. We won't be in LA any longer than we have to, and no matter what anyone says about you or me or our family, we know the truth." She paused, looking deep into his eyes. "We have God and we have each other. What you're doing by joining Jeremiah Productions is mission work. It's what God's calling you to do, and I'm in complete support." Her unwavering love lifted the corners of her lips again. "It'll be an adventure."

"And if it gets too crazy?" He wanted her to know he didn't have all the answers. "What then?"

"That's easy. If God releases us, we do what Chase did. We walk away. This time maybe forever."

He allowed himself to get lost in her eyes, in her smile. "I love you, Katy Matthews."

"I love you too. I always will."

Her words eased the question marks that had popped up in his heart throughout the day. He wanted her to know she came first, and that he'd never put her or Sophie in danger by taking his spot in the public eye again. But he should've known that this would be her response. She was his other half, his best friend. She had stood by him before, and she would stand by him now.

No matter how wild the adventure they were about to begin.

Twelve

BAILEY WAS PACKING UP THE LAST of her things she'd left in her dorm room, when she came across a program for *Scrooge*—the show she and Tim and Andi had starred in last winter. She opened it and looked closely at their photos. The show had been Andi's first, and yet she'd easily sung like an angel and won the lead female role. Bailey studied her roommate's eyes. She'd been full of joy and light back then, innocence shining from her face. Everything she was missing now, since she'd dated Taz.

Ever since the conversation with her mom in the market that day, Bailey had wondered about having Andi live with them. She was willing to make it work, if Andi would consider it. But Bailey guessed Andi wouldn't agree to move in. She was different now, and Bailey had a pretty good idea why. She hadn't said so, but Bailey's guess was that Andi had slept with Taz, that they'd gone too far, and that her compromise of her beliefs had something to do with why they'd broken up. Bailey would've loved the chance to show Andi she didn't judge her. But they hadn't shared a conversation in weeks.

She opened a desk drawer and pulled out a stack of old papers and notepads. Nothing much worth saving, but Bailey wanted to go through it all the same. Somewhere in this mess was a letter from Tim—and she had precious few of those. She pulled up a trash can and began sorting. Halfway through the stack, she heard someone at the door and turned to see Andi walk in. She was carrying an armload of boxes, and Bailey jumped to help her.

"Give me those." She took the stack, while Andi closed the door behind her.

"Thanks." She looked gaunt and withdrawn. "I thought I was going to drop them all on my way here."

Bailey waited until her friend caught her breath. "You … moving in with the girls from your humanities class?"

"No." Andi dropped to the edge of her bed. "A lot's happened since we last talked."

"Yeah." Bailey didn't mention that she'd tried to call half a dozen times. She didn't want to make Andi feel bad. As long as her friend knew she was here for her. "So what's new?"

"I'm staying here for another few weeks. After that I'm moving in with my parents."

Bailey was shocked. "You're moving to California?"

"No." She smiled, but it stopped short of her eyes. "They're moving here." Andi crossed her arms in front of her. "You remember Chase Ryan, the guy who worked with my dad?"

"Of course. Everyone says the movie's amazing. The one we we're in." Their parts were small—featured extra roles, nothing more. But still, Bailey definitely remembered Chase.

"So anyway, Chase quit. He's staying home with his family. I guess the same day my dad got the news, Dayne Matthews called and said he'd like to work with Jeremiah Productions."

"Really?" Bailey was thrilled with this development, happy for Chase and certain that Dayne would be an asset for the production company. "So your parents are moving here?"

"Right. So they can work with Dayne and film in Bloomington. They already have a renter for their house. And a place to stay when they need to be in LA."

Bailey studied her roommate and wondered why she wasn't more enthused. "That's great. I mean, it'll be wonderful having your family here." She hesitated. "Right?"

Andi stood and slowly crossed the room to the photo of Rachel on the wall by the window. "I guess." She turned and crossed her arms again. "I'm different now. I've done some things I'm not so proud of."

"They still love you." Andi's answer stirred concern and sympathy in Bailey. "You know the truth. Even if you made a few bad choices this past year."

"How would you understand?" Andi cocked her head, defiant the way she'd been most of the time lately. "Your life's been perfect since the day you were born, Bailey Flanigan. It's easy for you to talk about being a Christian."

She wanted to argue, tell Andi that her life had not been easy. She'd been ignored by the girls in high school, and the guy she really loved had no interest in her. But she had a feeling her answer would sound laughable to Andi, so she kept quiet.

"Never mind." Andi returned to her bed and moved the stack of boxes to a corner of the room. "It's not your fault." She pulled her iPod from her purse and slipped her ear buds in. "I'm taking a nap."

Bailey's mouth hung open as Andi stretched out on her comforter and rolled onto her side facing the wall. She had to try one more time, no matter how Andi treated her. Something must be very wrong for her to act this way. She stood and moved to the edge of Andi's bed. Then she put her hand on her friend's shoulder. "Andi?"

She uttered a tired sigh, and slipped the ear buds loose. "What?"

"Don't be mad … but is something wrong? I mean, really wrong?"

Andi rolled over just enough to meet Bailey's eyes. For a long moment it seemed she might say something, maybe share whatever was at the root of her obvious pain. But a darkness clouded her eyes and she gave a quick shake of her head. "I'm fine." She turned back toward the wall. "Don't worry about me."

Bailey stared at her for another few seconds before returning to her own bed and resuming her sorting. Something was definitely wrong, but whatever it was, her roommate didn't want to talk. Bailey had tried, but she couldn't force a conversation. A few minutes passed in awkward silence, when Bailey's cell phone rang. She glanced at the small window and saw it was Tim. The two of them hadn't talked much this past week. He was taking dance and voice at a local studio, getting ready for their August audition.

"Hello?"

"Hey. I'm on campus. What're you doing?" He sounded happy and interested in her—the way he hadn't sounded for a long time.

"Packing. Where are you?"

"The cafeteria. Come have coffee with me?"

Bailey stared at Andi's back and didn't hesitate. Maybe when she returned to their room, Andi would feel more like talking. This strange tension between them reminded Bailey of the way her friends in high school had turned against her—all because they could no longer relate to Bailey. Too pure, they'd tell her. Too much a goody-good. Was that how Andi saw her now? As she left the dorm, she prayed for her roommate, that God would break through the walls she'd built around her heart. And that whatever was wrong, Bailey might somehow be part of the solution.

Then, without looking back, she closed the door behind her.

ANDI WAITED UNTIL THE DOOR WAS shut before she let her tears come. She figured she was four weeks pregnant now—four weeks at least—and still she'd told no one. When Bailey asked her what was wrong, she almost broke down and explained everything. But she stopped herself for one reason.

Bailey would never understand.

And by now, Andi's plan to raise her baby with the help of her parents had crumbled like a sand castle at high tide. She had planned to move to California, but now her parents were moving here. Her father would be working with Dayne Matthews now, so everything about their lives would suddenly be very public. Bloomington was a small town, and if she moved home, alone and pregnant, everyone would blame her parents. People would think the Christian faith of the family at the helm of Jeremiah Productions was nothing more than a joke. The press had made a media circus out of other public figures whose conservative Christian kids had gotten pregnant. Her story would be no different.

She couldn't do that to her parents. No way.

So now she'd begun to entertain an entirely different plan, a terrible, gut-wrenching option. One that haunted her day and night, but one that sometimes seemed the only way out.

Either way, she needed to see a doctor. The trouble was money. The clinics she'd called wanted money up front for an appointment, more than she had. Finally Andi had scanned the local Yellow Pages until she found a small ad that said, "Sarah's House—Crisis Pregnancy Center. Free ultrasounds."

Andi didn't know the difference between a clinic and a crisis pregnancy center, but free was free. She had an appointment to be seen at the center tomorrow. After that she'd have her ultrasound and she'd know for sure how far along she was. And then she would face her options. If there were any.

But there was a problem.

She couldn't stop thinking about the baby. Abortions had been so foreign to her that after she found out she was pregnant, after she stopped freaking out and throwing up that first night, she looked up everything she could find on the internet. Some websites said very little about the process of the abortion except to reassure young women that the procedure was their choice, and that "only through an abortion could an unexpected pregnancy truly be resolved."

But other sites showed pictures of aborted babies, graphic pictures that turned Andi's stomach and made her feel like a monster for even considering such a thing. But what were her choices? She couldn't tell her parents now that they were moving here, and unless death mercifully claimed her in the next few weeks, abortion might be her only answer. And the longer she waited, the worse the situation would be.

She could hardly tell Bailey. Her roommate wouldn't consider sleeping with her boyfriend, let alone looking twice at a guy like Taz. Andi covered her stomach with her hands. How could she have gotten pregnant? Why would God have let a baby start to grow inside her? Andi felt the sting of still more tears, and she shut her eyes tight. If God loved her, he never would've let this happen.

Slowly she sat up and opened the drawer of the nightstand beside her bed. There on top was an old copy of the Bloomington paper, and on the front page was a photo of Katy and Dayne—taken back when they first met, when they worked on a movie together. They looked like they were in Arizona, or on some desert scene. Dayne was clearly caught up in the moment, and Katy was smiling at him.

Wasn't that all she ever wanted? Taz was supposed to be like Dayne Matthews, and she was supposed to be like Katy Hart—the way Katy had been back when this picture was taken. Andi stared at the photo, studying it.

Why couldn't that be her? Smiling and beautiful and sure that all of life would turn out okay? Back before she started dating Taz and hacked her hair off and dyed it dark, people would sometimes tell her she looked like Katy Hart Matthews. Her long blonde hair and tan skin, the way she lit up a room or brought a scene to life. But Taz ... Taz never was anything like Dayne. He'd made a mockery of God and her faith. Andi was at fault from the beginning for not seeing that he was the wrong guy for her.

Because of that, she would never be part of a scene like the one on the front page of the paper. What Katy and Dayne shared, she would never know. Whether she had an abortion or not. She tucked the newspaper back in the drawer and lay down on her side again. Bailey would come back soon enough, and she wanted to be asleep when that happened. Her friend meant well, but they no longer had anything in common. If anyone had a chance at living the storybook life of Katy and Dayne, it was Bailey Flanigan. She didn't want to talk to Bailey or her parents ever again. The three of them made her feel cheap and guilty and dirty.

Andi closed her eyes, and gradually an idea came to her, another way out. What if she moved away? She could board a bus and head for Indianapolis and start her own life. That way she could still have her baby, find a life for just the two of them. That way she wouldn't embarrass her parents and herself. She could move where no one knew her name or who her parents were. She could make a way for herself, and her parents would have to let her go. She was an adult, after all.

The longer she thought about the idea, the better it seemed. She needed out before her parents got here. She could tell them she was taking a few classes at the campus an hour away in Indianapolis, staying with students there. And in time that's just what she would do. Certainly she could find a room for rent, and once the baby was born, she could find a job. But then … who would hire her? And who would watch her baby? How could she finish school if she was working full-time and raising a child? Her head hurt, and every option seemed unimaginable. She closed her eyes and let sleep catch her. The answers would come in time. Until then she only wanted two things: Sleep.

And distance from Bailey Flanigan.

BAILEY SPOTTED TIM WAITING FOR HER outside the cafeteria. He had two coffees and he'd found a table surrounded by shady trees. The afternoon was warm and blue and summer was bursting all around them. Tim stood and hugged her as she walked up. "You look beautiful."

"Really?" His comment caught her off guard. "That's sweet."

"It's true." They sat down opposite each other, and he pulled a piece of paper from his pocket and slid it across to her. "I found out more about New York. They're holding two separate auditions. Non-equity first, then equity."

"Hmmm." Bailey looked at the paper. It was a copy of two different *Back Stage* ads. "I'm not sure how that works."

"I wasn't either, so I called. Equity, well that's for Broadway people in the union. Anyone can go, but there's a good chance we won't get seen. We'd be last on the list after everyone in the union."

"And the non-equity?"

"Like it says, that audition is for newcomers, people trying to break in. The good news is they'll look at everyone." He hesitated and made a face. "Bad news? Only a few people will be picked for next year's shows. If that."

The odds sounded astronomically against them. But before she could say so, she remembered her father's words from a few weeks ago. *Bailey, believe in yourself. You're a beautiful singer and dancer. Someone has to be the next Broadway star—it might as well be you!*

She nodded at Tim. "So which should we go to?"

"I'm leaning toward the non-equity audition." He was holding another copy of the paper, and now he pursed his lips, concentrating on the information. "They'll be looking for someone to wow them. Also, that audition comes first. If it doesn't go well, we could always go back for the equity call."

Bailey wanted to feel more enthused, but something caught

her eye, and she turned in time to see Cody Coleman walk up. Her heart sank, and she felt her cheeks grow instantly hot. Tim followed her stare and saw who had caught her attention. He stayed seated and nodded in Cody's direction. "Cody." His enthusiasm fell off by half. "How are you?"

"Good." Cody acknowledged Tim, but he quickly turned his attention back to Bailey. "Did you see Katy and Dayne on the front page?"

"I did. Dayne's going to be great as a producer."

"And their plans for Bloomington?" Cody seemed to try to include Tim in the conversation, but Tim looked distracted. Cody again focused on Bailey. "They could make it the Hollywood of the Midwest."

Bailey's heart thudded in her throat. What was happening to her? Here she was sitting with a boy who cared deeply for her and still Cody took her breath away.

Cody looked at Tim and then back at Bailey. "What're you guys up to?"

"Talking about our New York audition." Tim had never been arrogant or condescending. But right now he sounded like he was both. "Privately, if you don't mind."

Cody hesitated, and Bailey watched a quick flash of anger burn in his eyes. It passed quickly. "Sure." The muscles in his jaw clenched a few times, but he nodded, taking a step back. "It's cool." He waved casually and began walking away. "See ya."

"Later." Tim sounded glad Cody was leaving.

"Bye." Bailey was too caught off guard to say anything else. She wanted to ask whether things were okay with Cody's mom. But clearly this wasn't the time. She would call him later. When Cody was out of earshot, Bailey turned frustrated eyes toward Tim. "That was rude."

"What?" He produced a blank expression. "We're busy here, Bailey. I have voice in ten minutes."

"So, you could've been cordial."

"I was." He rolled his eyes. "Come on, Bailey. The guy practically stalks you. He spends more time with you than I do."

There it was. Bailey had wondered, and now she knew. Tim had seemed a little frustrated that Cody had hung out with the Flanigans last weekend, but the incident had passed. Until now.

Tim's expression softened. He stretched his arm across the table and took hold of Bailey's fingers. "I'm sorry. Really. He shouldn't bug me."

Bailey resisted her desire to turn and watch Cody walk away. She couldn't do that, not now. She needed to focus on her boyfriend, needed to figure out why he even was her boyfriend. "You don't have to worry about Cody. He doesn't see me that way."

Tim watched her for a long time, studying her. "What about you? How do you see him?"

Bailey wished she could smile and come up with a confident answer, something about how Tim shouldn't be ridiculous because she could never see Cody as more than a good friend or a brother. But that would be a lie, so she studied the table instead.

"Bailey ... look at me." He waited, his tone patient this time.

She lifted her eyes, not sure what to say. Was this the conversation they needed to have, the one she'd been thinking about for months now? Was it finally time they break things off and figure out life on their own? At least for a while? "Tim ... I don't know."

"It's okay." He should've been hurt or angry, because her silence was admitting the obvious. She had feelings for Cody. There was no denying that now, not for either of them. But instead Tim only looked straight to her heart. "I understand you're feeling confused. I've been busy, focused on finals and New York, sick with strep throat. I haven't been the boyfriend you deserve. I'm sorry for that."

Bailey felt dizzy. Why was he saying this? Couldn't he see how torn she was?

"I want you to know something." His attention was completely on her, his eyes shining with feelings he rarely expressed. "I love you. I'll never love any girl like I love you. And whatever happens in New York, wherever the next few years take us, I'm going to marry you someday."

"Tim, I—"

"I understand." He gave her hand a tender squeeze. "Of course you have feelings for Cody. He's been part of your family longer than me." Tim seemed to gather his determination. "I need to treat you better. Then you'd have no doubts."

He stood and came to her, easing her to her feet. "We're perfect together. Our families and our passion for the stage." He grinned and he looked more striking than he had in a long time. "We grew up with the same values and standards, Bailey. A guy like Cody Coleman?" Tim was trying to explain himself, but he was coming off arrogant again. "He could never be your type." Tim brushed her cheek with his fingers. "Of course we'll marry someday. Until then, I'll be patient about Cody. I know he's a friend." Tim kissed her forehead softly.

Bailey wanted to feel swept off her feet. She swallowed, unable to swim in this sea of emotions. "I ... I don't know."

Tim looked at the time on his cell phone. "I gotta go." He touched her face, her hair. "Forgive me, okay? No one matters to me more than you."

"Okay." Bailey didn't know what else to say. Tim hugged her, and then in a blur of motion he gathered his things and hurried off toward the parking lot.

Bailey dropped back to the chair and stared at her coffee. What in the world had just happened? Tim had basically told her he wasn't threatened by Cody Coleman, and that he had every intention of marrying her. More than that, he'd dismissed any feelings she might have for Cody as little more than brotherly, because Tim—not Cody—had more in common with her. Their families and their pasts, their future interests.

It was a moment that should've swept Bailey off her feet, but it left her feeling swept under the table. Who but Tim Reed could say such romantic things and still come across unbearably self-righteous? As if she didn't have a say in the situation at all. She covered her face with her hands and sat there, unmoving. Tim was absolutely wrong. The two of them were not destined to get married or share a future or even go on another date together.

He talked about her as if she were a neglected pet. A little more interest on his part and he'd be back in her good graces, the object of her devotion once more. She took a sip of coffee and sat back in her chair. How dare he treat Cody like that? She grabbed her cell phone from her bag and called Cody. It rang three times before his voicemail picked up. Bailey didn't leave a message. She wanted to apologize for not being more vocal when Tim was rude to him, but she couldn't do that on a recording.

For a long time she sat there, sipping her coffee and replaying the conversation with Tim, the awkward scene with Cody. As much as she disliked Tim for the way he'd acted, she disliked herself more. She'd doubted her feelings for Tim, and now she needed to make herself clear on the matter. She could no longer be his girlfriend. Whatever that meant for her and Cody was irrelevant. Tim was becoming someone she no longer wanted to spend time with.

She would talk to her mom about her feelings tonight. After that it was time to let Tim know. Then he could move on and find a girl who would be right for him. She had no idea who that girl might be, but she suddenly and certainly knew one thing.

It wasn't her.

Thirteen

ASHLEY BAXTER HURRIED AROUND THE KITCHEN with Janessa on her hip. Brooke wasn't able to make her shift at Sarah's House, which meant Ashley needed to be there. An appointment was coming in, a girl Brooke was worried about. Apparently she'd already contacted an abortion clinic.

The day had already been planned. Janessa would nap in an hour and Ashley would work on her latest painting. But that was the thrill of life. Rarely did things go exactly according to a schedule. Landon had the day off, but he'd been lost beneath their family van for the past half hour, changing the oil, and he had a list of things to do around the house after that. Ashley didn't have the heart to tell him he needed to watch Janessa. Whatever Ashley did that day, Janessa could come along.

She rinsed the dishes in the sink with one hand and loaded them into the dishwasher.

"Down." Janessa stretched toward the floor, both hands outreached.

"Not yet." Ashley kissed her daughter's cheek. "The floor has to dry. Otherwise your sockies will get wet."

Janessa whimpered. "Down, Mama."

Ashley searched for a distraction and found one in the plastic spoon standing in the jar by the stove. She grabbed it and handed it to her daughter. "Here, Nessa, play with this."

Immediately, Janessa put the spoon into her mouth. She was almost two, and she was teething like crazy. Cutting her back molars. The spoon made her happy, and Ashley was able to go back to the dishes. She was still working over the sink when she felt someone come up behind her.

"Has anyone told you," Landon's voice was soft against her ear, "you have the most beautiful hair?"

Ashley stopped and leaned back against him, feeling the warmth of his body, the definition in his chest. "Not lately."

"Well, you do." He nuzzled her neck. "Someone should tell you more often." He grabbed a paper towel and wiped a few grease spots off his forehead. "One oil change completed."

"Thanks." She took the paper towel from him and tossed it in the trash. "You spoil me."

At the same time Janessa bopped Landon on the head with the plastic spoon. "Oops." Ashley laughed a little. "Sorry." She took the spoon from their little girl and set her down on the floor. "All dry. You can run around now."

Janessa giggled and hurried across the floor and back again, thrilled to be free.

"You're painting, right?" Landon poured a glass of water and leaned against the counter, clearly admiring her.

"Not anymore." She loaded the last of the dishes and gave him a lopsided grin. "Brooke needs me at the clinic. Something came up and she can't be there." Ashley had taken a night class and learned how to operate the ultrasound machine. That way they could meet the needs of more girls, and maybe play a part in saving more babies. "I guess someone's coming in. Brooke said she sounded really upset."

Landon stooped down and swept Janessa into his arms. The little girl's laughter sounded like silvery wind chimes. Ashley stopped what she was doing and watched the two of them together. She would never take for granted a minute of her time with Janessa Faith. After losing Sarah, Janessa was an unexpected gift. The daughter Ashley felt sure she'd never have. She was doted on by everyone in the family—her brothers and her daddy most of all.

Janessa's laughter rang through the kitchen again. "Daddy ... down!"

"Okay, little wanderer." He kissed her head and set her back on the floor.

She ran into the living room and found her pacifier on the table. They'd been trying to break her of it, but this close to nap-time neither of them was going to take it from her. She popped it in her mouth and sat down on the kitchen floor, her back against Landon's legs. He looked down at her and tousled her wispy brown hair. "She looks just like you, Ash."

"That's what my dad says."

"It's true." He met her eyes, and the moment took on a deeper feel to it. "You and your mother. Her expressions sometimes remind me of your mom."

Ashley dried her hands and hung the dish towel back on the stove. As she did, she studied their daughter. "I see it too. I think Mom must be very proud of her. From her window in heaven."

"She must be proud of all her grandkids. They're growing up so fast." He eased his leg free of Janessa and circled his arms around Ashley's waist. "I'll watch her. I can do the work around here later."

"That's okay. She can come with me. I might stop by Sunset Hills."

"They'd love her." His smile made him look boyish, the way he'd looked when she first met him. "Sounds like you have it figured out."

They talked for a few more minutes, and then Landon returned to the garage. Ashley cleaned up and found Janessa's shoes. A few minutes later they were headed for Sunset Hills. Halfway there, Ashley made an impulsive turn and took a side trip to the cemetery. It was a beautiful day, the sort where she liked to stop and place flowers on the two graves that mattered most to her.

She parked as close as she could and then helped Janessa out of her car seat. Holding her daughter's small hand, they crossed the quiet street to an empty field. Wild flowers grew there this time of year, and she gathered two small bundles.

"Pretty!" Janessa delicately touched the tips of the flowers. "Pretty flowers, Mama."

"Yes, baby. They are pretty."

They walked back to the cemetery, staying at Janessa's little-girl pace. When they reached the grave markers, Ashley bent down and put one handful of flowers on each. Then she dusted off the names. Elizabeth Baxter, and Sarah Blake. Her precious mother and firstborn daughter.

Ashley didn't come here often, and never had she come with Janessa. But between the warm sunshiny morning and the happy heart of her two-year-old, it was impossible to feel very sad. At least her mom and daughter were together, waiting for the rest of the family to join them.

She didn't linger, but rather lifted Janessa onto her hip and prayed out loud. "God, thank You for giving us time to remember." Then she lifted her eyes to the blue sky. "Tell my mom and little Sarah we miss them. We always will."

Janessa couldn't possibly understand what was happening, let alone where they were. But she rested her head on Ashley's shoulder and stuck her fingers in her mouth. As if she somehow knew there was something sacred about the moment. Ashley nuzzled her cheek against Janessa's and walked her back to the van. One day she would explain to Janessa about her grandmother and her sister—how their deaths had come too early. But how the number of days in their lives hadn't mattered nearly as much as the life in their days.

The rich, beautiful, unforgettable life.

Keith and Lisa were driving across country, stunned at the speed in which God had helped them wrap up details back in San Jose. They'd listed their house the day after Dayne Matthews had called, and the next day they heard from a couple at church about a family who needed a house to rent. They worked out all the details and would either sell their house later or continue to rent it out. Dayne had been kind enough to agree to take on a few of the meetings for Jeremiah Productions so Keith could drive out to Indiana with Lisa. When Keith and Lisa traveled back to LA, they would stay in the leased beach house with the Matthews family. God was helping them to work it all out.

Chase and Kelly and several families from church had helped them pack and load up the moving van, and now they were only a day's drive from Bloomington. Keith glanced at his wife, asleep beside him. He focused on the road and remembered the way Chase stayed around, helping until the very end.

Kelly was talking to Lisa in the house when Keith and his friend loaded the last few boxes. Chase dusted off his hands and stood back, looking at Keith. "I guess I still can't believe it. We dreamed about making movies together for so long."

It only figured that the reality was bound to hit Chase eventually. He'd made his decision based on God's leading, but the changes had happened so fast, there'd been almost no time to acknowledge all they were losing along the way. Keith came closer and patted his friend's shoulder. "We were good together."

"We were."

Keith wasn't sure what to say. This was a more final good-bye than they'd first expected. He'd be in Bloomington or in LA, but he and Lisa would have no reason to return to San Jose. It could be a very long time before their two families were together once more. Before Keith and Chase shared a moment like this again. "How's it going?" He grinned at Chase in the waning afternoon light. "The youth pastor job?"

"I think I'm going to love it." Chase shrugged. "I'm already learning so much about the kids."

"The church kids or yours?" Keith's question was pointed, filled with a depth of understanding. He wanted Chase to know just how fully his decision made sense to him.

"Both. I know Molly's favorite songs now, and how Macy likes her pancakes smothered in peanut butter." He chuckled. "No danger of them forgetting my voice now. We sing together every morning."

Keith nodded slowly. He would miss this friend. They'd been together through so much — the years of mission work, the season of dreaming about making movies, and their push through the maze of Hollywood. "You made the right choice. Really."

"I know." His voice caught in his throat. He hesitated, then he hugged Keith hard, holding him for a long time before letting go. "I'll miss you, buddy. As right as this choice is, I want you to know I'll miss you."

Now Keith stared at the road ahead. He was glad for that final scene, the chance to have closure with Chase. There was no undoing all they'd been through. The memories would last, even as they moved into this next season of life. As they did, Keith would pray for his friend, the same way he was sure Chase would pray for him.

Beside him, Lisa stirred and blinked her eyes open. "Mmmm. That was a good nap."

"For me too." He smiled at her.

"Want me to drive?" Her eyes were apologetic. "I haven't really done my share."

Keith laughed. "You haven't driven."

"That's what I mean."

"Don't worry about it." He patted her knee. "It's enough having you with me." The truck was a twenty-four-footer, and they were pulling their family sedan behind them. Lisa was nervous about driving the rig, and Keith didn't blame her. "Have you heard from Andi?"

"This morning. She knows we'll be there tomorrow." Worry creased Lisa's forehead. "I asked her how she was doing, like I always do. She says she's fine, but she's not. I think she's worried about something."

"Maybe it's her grades. Did you ask how she finished?"

"Mostly A's, a few B's—at least as far as she can tell." Lisa looked out the window, quiet for a while. "I keep wondering if she could be depressed." She turned back to Keith. "That happens to college kids sometimes."

"I don't know." He kept his eyes on the road. "Andi's always been one of the happiest kids I know. Her smile's the first thing people notice about her."

"Before." Lisa's voice was proof of her heavy heart for their daughter. "It's like she's a different person. This move is the best thing we could've done. I can't get there soon enough."

"Every time I pray for her, I feel an urgency. Like she's not telling us something."

"I feel it too."

Frustration welled up inside Keith. "It makes me wish we were closer. I feel so helpless out here on the road. Like maybe she needs us now. Today." He reached for Lisa's hand. "I want to help her, however I can."

They rode in silence for a minute or so. "There's one thing we can do."

Keith nodded. His wife was right. There was nothing small or limiting about praying for their daughter. It was the one thing they could most certainly do for her. Keith drew a long breath. "Dear Lord, You know our Andi. You know what she's going through and why she doesn't sound like herself lately. We ask that even this very minute You might be with her. Comfort her and remind her of the truth. Place people in her path who will point her back to You. In Your name, amen."

"Amen."

They stayed quiet after that. There wasn't much to say where Andi was concerned. Not until they saw her in person and figured out what was going on, why she sounded so different. In the meantime, they needed to keep praying.

The urgency in Keith's heart was constant proof.

Fourteen

ASHLEY STILL HAD AN HOUR BEFORE the appointment at Sarah's House.

This would be the perfect day to take Janessa by the Sunset Hills Adult Care Home. She hadn't been by the old place in far too long. Only Burt and Helen remained from among the Alzheimer's patients Ashley had once cared for at the four-bedroom assisted living home. Her favorite patient had been Irvel, a gentle woman who had cared very much for Ashley. It was Irvel who had commented so often about Ashley's hair, how beautiful it was. Ashley smiled at the memory. The kind woman's comments weren't so much because Ashley's hair was really all that beautiful. But because Irvel wanted something kind to say, and the comment about her hair always seemed to be the first thing that came to her mind. Five times an hour, most days.

The stop at Sunset Hills was just what Ashley needed. Burt was doing better than ever. He seemed to remember her, and Ashley introduced him to Janessa. She was shy around the older people, but she waved her fingers at Burt and he did the same in return, tears filling his eyes. Babies were a rarity at Sunset Hills.

Helen was awake too. She had a scowl on her face as Ashley entered the kitchen, and she was complaining about something swimming in her coffee. The girl working that morning gave Ashley a knowing look. Nothing was swimming in Helen's coffee.

Ashley introduced herself, and the girl did the same. "Helen has her good days," she told Ashley when they were in the next room. "She loves when her daughter stops by."

"Her daughter?" Ashley's heart leapt at the news. "She still remembers her?"

"Yes." The girl smiled. "Her name's Sue."

"I know. I ... I've met her several times." There was no point rehashing the story of how Sue had come to see her mother for years, and how always Helen would yell at her to leave, not believing she was really Sue, and demanding to know what the middle-aged woman had done with her real daughter.

Not until Ashley finally understood that Helen was expecting Sue to be a teenager still, were they able to gently, carefully bridge the gap between Helen's memory and the reality. Ashley had been there the day the breakthrough happened, when Helen finally understood that her daughter Sue was, in fact, a middle-aged woman now. That Helen still remembered Sue was enough to make Ashley's day. She stopped in the kitchen before she left and bid Helen good-bye. Janessa did the same.

Helen shook her head, her face a mask of disgust. "Your baby's pretty." She jerked her thumb toward her coffee. "But there's something swimming in my drink. No one will help me."

"I'll help you." The girl on duty walked up with a fresh cup of coffee. She replaced the perfectly fine one and smiled at Helen. "There you go. Nothing swimming."

Ashley was glad Cole wasn't with them. Her son would've inevitably launched into a talk about his tadpoles, and how they were swimming in their fishbowl. That would've really put Helen over the edge. Ashley thanked the girl for letting her and Janessa stop in. She said a final farewell to Burt and the two of them were on their way.

She reached Sarah's House well before the appointment. Janessa toddled around the waiting area while Ashley went over the notes in the schedule book. Brooke had written in the margins that she suspected an abortion was in order for the girl about to come in. She'd given her age as nineteen, and her name as Andi.

Whether that was her real name or not, Ashley couldn't be sure. Many girls facing a crisis pregnancy were reluctant to share their real identity.

In the time left, she and Janessa sat at a table and colored. Janessa was just starting to like drawing, and her pictures were still faint and unrecognizable. But Ashley wondered whether her daughter might follow in her footsteps, maybe become an artist creating memorable designs on canvas someday.

They were still sitting together coloring a picture of a rainbow and a flower when the front door opened. Ashley stood, but before she could welcome the young woman standing out front, she felt her breath catch in her throat. She knew this girl. She'd seen her before—on the set of the movie filmed in Bloomington last year. This was the producer's daughter, right?

"Andi?"

Fear iced the girl's expression and she shook her head, taking a single step back. "I'm ... I'm afraid I have the wrong ..."

"Andi." Ashley tried to still her pounding heart. The girl obviously recognized her too. "It's okay. Our work here is confidential."

Andi's face had lost color. She looked like she might be sick, but she took a slow step forward and clutched her purse to her stomach. "You ... you know Bailey Flanigan, right?"

"I do." Ashley wasn't sure how much to tell her. The less, the better. She racked her mind, trying to remember what she knew about the producer's daughter. Her parents had been missionaries in Indonesia. That much she remembered. If the girl was pregnant now, then no wonder she looked terrified. "I met you on the movie set last summer."

Andi nodded, and again she looked like she might pass out. Janessa jumped up from the table then and ran to the girl. The toddler stopped short and flashed her a grin, then she waved.

"Hi!"

"Hi." Andi sat down primly on the edge of a waiting room chair.

"Mama!" Janessa turned suddenly shy and ran, giggling, into Ashley's arms. Ashley lifted her up onto her hip. She pulled the pacifier from her diaper bag and handed it to Janessa. Her daughter stuck it in her mouth and instantly cradled her head against Ashley's shoulder. "It's almost naptime." Ashley smiled at Andi. "She'll be asleep in a few minutes."

Andi didn't look interested. She kept her eyes on her lap and nodded absently. "No one ..." she lifted her eyes to Ashley. "No one knows about this. I don't want anyone to know."

"I understand." She came slowly toward Andi and took the chair opposite her. Janessa stayed quiet, her head still on Ashley's shoulder. "This is a crisis pregnancy center, Andi. Do you know what that is?"

"I read the ad." She ran her tongue over her lower lip. Clearly she was scared to death. "You give free ultrasounds. I know that."

"We're a Christian center." Ashley wanted to be kind, but she also wanted to be very clear. "Our goal is to show you the truth, that your unborn baby is a very real little person, a life. From there we pray that every frightened girl like yourself who comes through the door might make a decision to go through with her pregnancy. Whether she gives up her baby for adoption or chooses to raise the baby herself."

Andi's shoulders tensed up. She covered her face with one hand and waited a long time before she looked up again. "I ... I'm not sure what to do." A number of emotions flickered across her face—frustration and anger, and most of all, desperation. "Do you know my parents?"

"I met them briefly, but I don't know them." She handed Andi a clipboard. "Here. We need you to fill this out before the ultrasound, okay?"

The girl still looked like she might bolt. But she took the paperwork and a pen and quietly filled out the form. There was so much Ashley wanted to say. She had her own story to share, her own personal understanding of the value of life. But right now Andi wouldn't hear her anyway. She was too caught up in the nightmare happening to her. Ashley tried another tactic instead.

Andi handed the paperwork back, and Ashley looked it over. "Are you ready for the ultrasound?"

"Yes, please." She looked like she might run out of the center at any moment. "I need to know how ... how far along I am."

Ashley knew what that might mean. Abortion clinics would want that information, and testing at other clinics wouldn't be free. If Andi hadn't planned on getting pregnant, she probably had no idea how many weeks pregnant she was. She stood and smiled at Andi, willing the girl to feel safe and protected. "Follow me. We'll get started, okay?"

Ashley led her to a changing room and told her she could leave on her jeans as long as she unzipped them. "Put the gown on open in the front, and tie it loosely. I'll meet you in the examination room."

Andi was shaking, so scared she seemed barely able to move, let alone respond. Ashley was still holding Janessa, who had fallen asleep. There was a crib in the exam room, so she laid her daughter there and turned on the ultrasound machine. The whole time her heart broke for Andi and the decisions she was facing. *Dear God, this is why we opened the center. For girls like Andi. Please, Father, let Your Spirit fill this room. Let her feel Your supernatural peace so that she can truly grasp the reality of the life inside her, so she can hear the words You give me to say. I can't do this, Lord. This is beyond me. Please spare this little one. Both the baby and the precious young mother.*

You will not have to fight this battle, my daughter. Stand firm and see the deliverance I will give you.

Ashley felt the response soothe the wrinkles in her soul.

Thank You, God. I will stand firm. Help me stand firm. She loved the picture the Lord had given her. Ashley was a fighter—she always had been. But in a time like this, the battle wasn't hers. It was God's alone. The reality eased her anxiety and helped her know that the Lord was in control.

Andi knocked on the door, and Ashley opened it. The machine was warmed up and ready. "Lie down on the table. Try to get comfortable." Ashley remembered the music. A donor had given them a portable stereo system with six CDs of calming Christian songs, music by Jeremy Camp and Matthew West, Britt Nicole and Mandisa and NewSong. Music about life and peace and hope and grace. While Andi eased herself up onto the table, Ashley hit the Play button and adjusted the volume.

The gentle refrains of Mandisa's song "Voice of a Savior" quietly filled the room.

Andi sniffed, and a single tear slid down the side of her face. "I love this song."

"Me too." Ashley smiled. She checked once more on Janessa asleep in the crib across the room. Then she returned to Andi's side. Already the girl had pushed her jeans down and exposed her stomach. Ashley took a bottle of warm gel and dispensed enough across Andi's belly for the machine to work. "This won't take long."

In the lobby, she heard the sound of the door opening again. A retired nurse worked the day shift at the front desk. The door to the examination room was still open. "Is that you, Betty?"

"It is. You're working with the first appointment?"

Ashley turned compassionate eyes to the college girl on the table. "Yes. We're just getting started."

Betty appeared at the door with a clipboard. She wasn't trained in ultrasounds, but she would register the results. She stood a few feet away and waited.

Ashley took the wand of the machine and began working

it slowly across Andi's stomach. The machine made a series of sounds, and in no time she settled the probe over an area just beneath Andi's belly button. At the same time, a rhythmic wooshing sound filled the room, pulsing in an unmistakable pattern.

Andi drew a soft gasp. "That's ..."

"The baby's heartbeat." Ashley never tired of this, catching the first sounds of new life. Tears gathered in her eyes, but she blinked them away, smiling. "Your baby's heart sounds very healthy, Andi."

The girl craned her neck forward, peering at the screen. "Can I see it?"

Ashley adjusted the probe a little more until a tiny pulsating picture could be seen at the center of the screen. "There it is." She pointed to the image. "That's your baby's heart." She moved her finger along a curved area adjacent to the baby's beating heart. "That's the spine. Can you see that?"

"Yes. I ... I didn't think it would be so clear."

"It is. Your baby's a little miracle. Already growing and becoming." Ashley kept her tone kind and tender. The music added to the emotion of the moment and she thanked God again for the wonder of the ultrasound machine. Anyone could tell a pregnant woman her body contained nothing more than a mass of tissues. But ultrasounds were different. The pictures, the sounds ... the images didn't lie. A baby was growing inside Andi, no question.

"How far along am I?"

"Let's see." Ashley was new at this, but she captured a few pictures of the unborn baby and clicked a few buttons. The machine computed the age of the fetus. "Looks like you're ten weeks. Maybe ten and a half."

"Ten weeks?" Andi looked shocked at the news. Her face grew ashen again and she turned away from the images. "Can ... I be done now?"

"Of course."

Betty made a few notations on the clipboard, and she handed Andi a clean towel.

Ashley turned off the machine and wiped down the wand. "Go ahead and dry off, then you can get dressed in the changing room. Let's meet back here in a few minutes."

"Thank you." Andi's voice was almost inaudible. She pulled the gown tight around herself as she took the towel and left for the changing room.

When she was gone, Betty exchanged a sad look with Ashley. "She's so scared."

"I know." They were whispering. "Pray, Betty."

"I am." Her eyes softened. "I have been the whole time."

Betty caught the printout from the ultrasound and finished filling in the chart. She was back at her desk by the time Andi returned to the examination area. There was a sofa in the far corner, next to the crib where Janessa was sleeping. Ashley led Andi there, and they sat on opposite ends. Andi kept her eyes focused intently on her hands.

Give me the words, please God. "I've been in your seat, Andi. People make mistakes."

Andi kept her face downturned, but she lifted her eyes to Ashley's. "You were pregnant before ... when you weren't married?"

"Yes." Ashley felt a surge of joy. Andi was willing to listen. "I was in France, about your age. I'd left home and I wanted to make my own way. Live by my own rules." Ashley didn't know anything about Andi's story, how she'd gotten into this situation or who the guy might be. But she could sense Andi listening a little more intently. "I began dating a famous painter, and after a few months I wound up pregnant." She paused, still ashamed of the details. "He was a married man. He told me he wasn't about to leave his wife, and he gave me the address of an abortion clinic in Paris."

"You ... had an abortion?" Andi crossed her arms tight across her stomach. She looked small and frail, completely overwhelmed by her situation.

"I didn't." Ashley would forever be grateful for her answer. She pictured her precious Cole. "I got as far as the waiting room, and I couldn't do it. I didn't know what to do, but I was sure of one thing. My baby wasn't to blame for my actions."

Quiet tears slipped from Andi's eyes and trickled down her face. Ashley handed her a tissue and continued. "Do you know my family?"

Andi sniffed. "The ... the Baxters?"

"Yes." Ashley felt the heaviness of those long ago days. "I came home alone and pregnant. No one in my family had ever done anything like that. I felt like the worst person in the world."

"What did your parents say?"

"They were disappointed." It was important to keep the details real. "But they welcomed me home, and when Cole was born, they loved him with all the love they had to give." Ashley pictured her mother, caring for little Cole, teaching Ashley how to be a mommy. "There are lots of grandkids in our family today. But I think my mom always loved Cole the best. Because he didn't have the easiest start."

Andi sniffed again. "I don't know how my parents will react. They're busy. A baby would ... it would make life hard for them. In their line of work." She shook her head, fear gathering around her again.

"There are options." Again Ashley didn't want to be pushy. But it was important Andi have all the information before she left. Ashley reached for a folder on the table next to the couch. Then she stood and collected a few photos from the printer. She tucked them into the folder and handed it to Andi. "Take this. Pictures of your baby, and other information about adoption—both closed and open. Ways you can connect with a private Christian agency and even choose your baby's adoptive parents."

Andi looked terrified at the thought. She took the folder and struggled to her feet. "Thank you. For your time." For a quick moment she looked at Janessa sleeping in the crib. Then she took a few steps toward the door. "I ... I have to go."

Ashley walked her to the door, praying that Andi would stop, that she'd stay and talk a little longer. But nothing would stop her this time. She thanked Ashley once more and practically ran from the clinic. Ashley felt the disappointment settle in around her heart.

Be with her, God. Save her baby's life. Please, Lord.

"I have a feeling about this one." Betty smiled sadly from her place behind the desk. "That God has a very special plan for both of them. The mother and the baby."

"Me too." Ashley sighed. "I just wish she would've stayed."

Only then did she look more closely at Andi's paperwork. She'd put her name as Andi Smith, and the address and phone number were clearly made up. Ashley could reach her if she needed to. She could get the girl's information from Jenny and Bailey Flanigan. Without giving away anything, of course.

But she hoped she wouldn't need to do that. Andi had the material she needed to choose life. Now Ashley could only stand firm and pray.

And let God Himself fight the battle for the life of Andi's baby.

Fifteen

Cody stood next to Ryan Taylor and listened as the head coach shouted orders to the lineman.

"Get low," Coach Taylor strode closer and leaned down, eye level to the lineman. "That's not low enough. You have to get lower, men." He put himself on the line and got down so low he looked like he was sitting in an invisible chair. "This is low. Can you see this?" He straightened. "Now get low." He walked the line, analyzing their efforts. "I know this is summer, but that doesn't mean we give half an effort. What we do in June will determine who we'll be in October."

Cody soaked in every word, every piece of advice. He loved everything about being at Clear Creek High this week. He'd been given a playbook, and already he had memorized most of it. Coaching was a whole new world to him, and the lessons he was learning were enough to convince him he was right about his suspicions. He loved being out here. Already he was sure that he wanted nothing more than to be a coach. Like Ryan Taylor.

Like Jim Flanigan.

This week of practice had been good for him in another way too. It had taken his mind off Bailey and the strange incident with her and Tim at the school cafeteria the other day. Cody crossed his arms and kept his feet shoulder-width apart—the way he'd seen the other coaches stand for as far back as he could remember playing. It felt amazing to be on this side of the game, but this week he was supposed to spend his time watching.

"There," Ryan yelled—mostly so he could be heard across

the field. Coach Taylor was not one of those coaches who ruled by fear. "That's getting low. Everyone look at McCoy. See that? Get low like that. All your power comes from the explosion off the line, and that only happens if you're low."

Cody blinked, and the action before him blurred. Instead he was back on campus, spotting Bailey and Tim and deciding to stop by for a quick hello. Cody couldn't lie to himself. It hurt, seeing her with him. Especially when Cody and Bailey had been together so often lately. Almost like Tim was some imaginary boyfriend who didn't really exist in Bailey's world. But seeing them that afternoon was painful proof.

You told her you'd be her friend, he reminded himself. *Now's your chance to prove it.* With that he'd altered his course across the mall so he'd walk past their table. Bailey seemed surprised to see him. She blushed as soon as he walked up—whatever that meant. But before she could say anything, Tim's attitude kicked in. It wasn't just that he seemed bothered by Cody's interruption. He seemed condescending. Like he thought he was better than Cody. Or that maybe Cody was wasting their time. Cody was already getting the point when Tim made his blunt comment, about how he and Bailey wanted to talk about their auditions alone.

In his younger football-playing, high school partying days, Cody would've solved the problem with a single blow to Tim Reed's face. And he was sorely tempted in that moment. But in the same instant, he realized there was no point. If Tim wanted to be a jerk, if that was the kind of guy he was becoming, then so be it. He was the guy Bailey had chosen, after all. If she wanted to be with a guy like that, then fine.

Bailey had tried to call him three times since then, but each time he let the call go. What could she possibly want to say? That she was sorry for sitting by while Tim treated him like some lower class citizen? That she still wasn't sure she wanted to be serious with Tim? He was sick of her explanations, no matter how much fun he had with her. She had chosen Tim. Now let her spend her time with him.

A whistle blew. "Take five, men. Get some water and get back here." Ryan Taylor jogged easily over to the other coaches and motioned for Cody to join them. "During the season we'll have a line coach working with the guys. But they need to understand their importance on the line. Everything fails or succeeds based on that, absolutely everything."

The other coaches agreed, and Ryan dismissed them for the five minutes. Only Cody stayed. "I love this. I'm soaking it all in, Coach. Thanks so much for having me."

"I'm watching you. The times I have you working with our quarterbacks. You're a natural, Cody." Ryan grinned at him. "I've already thanked Jim for sending you out here." They walked together toward the water cooler. "Seems like yesterday you were out there yourself."

"It's been three years. Amazing how time goes."

"Gets worse as you get older." Ryan squinted at the empty field. "A blink ago I was out there playing pro ball." He patted his still flat stomach. "Now I couldn't run a series of forty-yard dashes to save my life."

"I think you could." Cody laughed. He loved the camaraderie he was finding with Coach Taylor. "You're in better shape than most of the kids out there."

"Now you sound like Kari."

Cody grinned and helped himself to a few quick gulps of water. He knew a little of Coach Taylor's story. Pretty sensational stuff. He and Kari Baxter had dated when they were in high school, but then Ryan had gone off to a big college to play football and she had gone on to work as a fashion model. On one fateful college football Saturday, Ryan suffered an injury that nearly paralyzed him. Kari and her dad, John Baxter, rushed to his side, but somehow Kari came away from the hospital believing Ryan had fallen in love with someone else. A year later she married someone else, but the guy had an affair and wound up getting shot and killed by some lunatic stalker guy on the IU campus.

After that, Ryan and Kari found each other again, and a few years later the two of them married. Ryan left pro football five or six years ago and moved to Bloomington so Kari could be near her family. That's how he wound up coaching at Clear Creek High.

Coach Taylor's story had resonated with Cody since Bailey had shared it with him. Maybe because he could relate to Ryan's patience, the way he'd kept his love for Kari all those years. The way he was willing to be her friend after she lost her husband. Even if that's all he ever was to her. It made him think of his friendship with Bailey.

But there was a difference.

Kari Baxter had been convinced Ryan loved someone else. Bailey knew better. How much clearer could Cody possibly be? He had sat on that rock overlooking the lake at the Cru retreat and told her he wasn't dating because he was waiting for that one special girl. She couldn't possibly think he meant anyone but her, right?

He finished his paper cup of water, crumpled it, and threw it in the trash. They had another hour before practice was over. Action was about to start up again when Connor came up to him. Connor was playing tight end and backup quarterback for Clear Creek next year. Already he was impressing the coaches with his speed and agility. He had his father's build, and even if football wasn't his first love, he was bound to start next fall.

Connor grinned at him. "Think Coach wants us to stay low?"

Cody laughed so hard he spit his water on the grass. "Way to listen, Flanigan."

"I try." He chuckled hard as he walked off. His younger brothers

—Justin and Shawn—were both freshmen with a shot at making varsity. They were fast and strong, and they could jump a mile in the air, hanging there until the football landed in their hands.

On the next set of plays, Coach Taylor placed Shawn at wide receiver and ran three plays at him. Each time Shawn soared off the ground, snatched the ball from the sky, and scored a touchdown. No one could touch him. Cody was on the sidelines with Connor and the rest of the team, and all of them whooped and hollered at Shawn Flanigan's impressive showing.

"Yep," Connor raised his fist in the air. "That's my brother. We might as well be twins. Two peas in a pod."

Everyone laughed and hit Connor on the back. The Flanigan boys always had fun talking as if they were blood related. Once when Cody lived with them, Connor brought a girl to the house. As they walked into the kitchen, Cody was sitting on one side of the bar, Shawn and Justin on the other. Connor introduced Cody as an adopted member of the family, but with Shawn and Justin he said simply, "These are my brothers."

The girl hesitated, then she gave Connor a skeptical look. "Your brothers?"

Connor didn't skip a beat. He wrinkled his brow, walked up to Shawn, and held his white arm next to his brother's black one. "What, you think he's not my brother 'cause he's a little tanner than me?"

It was the same thing here. Connor's Haitian brothers might out-perform him on the football field, but that only gave Connor another reason to claim them as his brothers. The Flanigan family had a love that could laugh through anything, a love that knew no color barriers or resentment.

When practice was over, Connor rounded up Cody and his younger brothers. "Bailey called. Her roommate Andi needs our help." Connor checked his cell phone. "I guess Andi's parents pulled into town this morning with their moving van." Connor flexed his arms. "At least she knew who to call."

They all laughed, and Cody agreed to join them. The only thing he needed to do tonight was check on his mother. She was still hanging out with Benny the Tiger, much to Cody's dismay. He liked to stop by unexpectedly, in case he might find her at a time when she needed him.

He drove the boys in his car, and they pulled up at the address Bailey had given them in time to see her park across the street. For a long few seconds, Cody's eyes met hers and neither of them made a move to get out of their cars.

"Uh ... it's okay if we get out, right?" Connor tapped Cody's shoulder. He and Shawn were in the back seat. "You and Bailey can look at each other later."

"Hey ... be nice." Cody leaned back and playfully punched the oldest Flanigan boy. But as he got out, he avoided looking at Bailey again. He hadn't thought much about what he would feel seeing her here. This was the first time they'd been together since the Tim incident.

Jim Flanigan must've been off this afternoon, because he was already there, along with John Baxter and Ashley and Landon Blake. Ryan Taylor was pulling up too. The Flanigan boys ran to be with their dad, and Cody took his time locking his car. As he did, Bailey approached him, her voice softer than usual. "Hey."

"Hey." Cody turned to face her, but he kept his guard up, leaning against his car, his hands in his shorts pockets. He never felt self-conscious about his prosthetic leg, but for some reason here, he did. He wasn't sure Bailey had seen him in shorts since his injury. He thought about glancing down, trying to imagine how it might've looked to someone who hadn't seen it before. He wore a knee brace to bridge the look of his real leg and the artificial lower limb, and with the socks and his shoes matching, most people would have to look hard to tell the difference.

Maybe it was the way Tim had treated him. Whatever it was, the leg or Bailey's boyfriend, Cody felt inadequate standing there. Awkward, like he didn't belong in her life—even as her friend. She was looking hard at him, searching his eyes. "You haven't answered my calls."

He shrugged one shoulder. "I've been busy."

"No." Bailey knew him better. "That's not true. You're mad about the Tim thing." She released a frustrated breath and paced a few steps away, then back again. "He was a jerk that day. I called so I could apologize for him."

Cody stayed chill, determined that she wouldn't see the hurt he'd felt then or now. "No big deal." He tried a smile, but it fell short. "Don't worry about it, Bailey. If there's an apology made, it should come from him." He pointed his thumb over his right shoulder. "There's work to do. Talk to you later." And with that, he side-stepped her and headed for the guys clustered at the back of the moving van.

After the first few loads, he was setting a box down in the back bedroom when Bailey showed up at the doorway. He smiled politely at her and tried to walk around her, but she wouldn't move. "Don't do this. Please."

He felt his shoulders sink, and a sigh died on his lips. "Do what?"

"Punish me for the way he acted." Bailey's voice was quiet, so none of the others would hear her. But the passion in her tone was loud and clear. "He was rude and I told him so."

Cody stared at her, disbelieving what he was hearing. "You told him he was rude?"

"Yes." She sounded indignant. "He was rude, and I wanted him to know it."

Normally Cody kept his comments about Tim and Bailey to himself. The last thing he wanted was to push her away from a guy she still clearly wanted to date. And she was still seeing him.

She had to be. How else could he read that? But here, he felt a desperate need to comment. "You're in love with the guy, right?" He refused to get angry. Instead he used his softest voice so she wouldn't feel cornered.

She hesitated, her lips parted. "I need to talk to him ... I think it's over between us."

"You think?" He dropped his tone to a more passionate hiss. "You just told me yourself, he was rude. And for the record, you were right. He was rude and condescending and arrogant." A laugh came from him, but it held not even a little humor. "And this is the guy you've been dating?" He stared at her, unable to stop himself. "Can I tell you something, Bailey?"

She didn't seem to have any way to fight back. Instead she hung her head. When she looked up, tears pooled in her eyes.

"You don't look happy when you're with him."

"I told you, I'm going to talk to him. Our schedules haven't worked out."

"That's it." Cody held up his hands and let them fall to his sides again. "I have to get back to work." He tried to walk past her, hoping she would step aside so he could pass.

Instead, she put her hands on his shoulders. "Please, Cody," her voice was strained, her eyes pleading with him. "Don't do this. My relationship with Tim has nothing to do with you and me. Don't be mad."

"Why?" He hated his tone, but he was too hurt to sound any softer. Carefully he moved her hands from his shoulders and slid past her. "You have Tim if you need someone to talk to." And with that he walked fast down the hall and back outside to the moving truck. He wasn't sure where Bailey went, or whether she stayed to help Mrs. Ellison inside the house. Either way, he didn't see her again.

No matter how many times he tried to convince himself, he knew he was wrong. He had no right getting mad at Bailey, just because of his own hurt. The way he saw it, she should've known how he was feeling about Tim. But that didn't mean he wanted to fight with her. It certainly didn't mean he wanted distance between them. But that's exactly what he'd created by being so harsh back in the house.

He was trying to decide whether to find her and apologize, when his cell phone sounded from his pocket. His ringtone was the hit song by Matthew West—"The Motions." Every time his phone rang it reminded him of the truth—he didn't want to live his life going through the motions. He wanted to live every moment for Christ. Whatever the cost. He wished he would've heard his ringtone before his earlier exchange with Bailey.

The call was from his mother's house, so he moved a few yards away from the others and answered it. "Hello? Mom?"

"Cody?" Her voice sounded slurred. "Can y'come over? I don't feel so good."

"I'm on my way." He was halfway to his car by the time the call ended. He yelled to Coach Taylor, who was just coming out for another load. "Something's come up. Gotta run."

"See you tomorrow." Coach waved. "Keep memorizing the playbook."

Cody slid into his car, started the engine, and sped off. Whatever was going on between him and Bailey, it would have to wait. Right now he needed to get to his mother's house, and the whole way he could only thank God for the obvious. No matter what his mother had done, she wasn't where she thought she'd be when she fell off the wagon. She wasn't in a hearse or in the back of a squad car.

Not yet anyway.

BAILEY COULDN'T BELIEVE CODY WOULD LEAVE without saying good-bye. He must've been much more upset than she knew, but she couldn't give the matter much attention because almost as soon as Cody left, Andi walked into the house. Bailey went to her, happy to be part of the moving crew. But from the moment she saw Andi's face, Bailey felt the mood in the house change. Andi looked distant and lost, nothing like the girl she'd been when they first met.

"Hi." Bailey kept her tone tempered. Her friend's mood didn't call for anything too upbeat. "You okay?"

"Fine." Andi's voice was as lifeless as her eyes. She set a bag of cleaning supplies on the kitchen counter and turned to Bailey. "Thanks for being here. Your family too."

Mrs. Ellison walked into the room then, but she stopped short when she saw Andi. "Sweetheart ... what's wrong?"

Andi tried to smile. "I don't feel good." She clutched her stomach, and anyone could see the dark circles beneath her eyes.

Andi's mother came to her, worry lining her face. "Do you have a fever?" She kissed her daughter's forehead. "Hmmm. No." She stood back and assessed Andi. "What are your symptoms?"

Bailey felt awkward, like she should go back to helping with the move. But she wasn't sure if it might be more rude to leave, so she stayed still, quietly watching.

"I'm just tired." Andi shivered a little. "Maybe if I take a nap."

"I don't like this." Her mom's concern seemed stronger than before. "You were in bed by six last night, and you slept in this morning." She ran her hand along Andi's arm. "Maybe it's mono. That happens to lots of college kids. Especially their first year."

The idea seemed possible. Bailey had heard of others in their dorm battling mono.

"I'm fine. Just run down."

"I don't know." Mrs. Ellison circled her arms around Andi and swayed with her. "I hate seeing you like this."

Andi pulled back and tried another smile. "I'm fine. I'll feel better tomorrow."

Her mom hesitated, searching Andi's eyes. But then she smiled with the sort of deep compassion only a mother could muster. "Go sleep. We'll see how you feel in a few hours."

Andi hugged her mom and then turned toward the hallway. She was almost out of sight when she must've remembered Bailey, because she stopped and looked back. "Sorry. I guess I'm out of it."

"That's okay." As much as the idea of mono seemed plausible, Bailey had the feeling once more that something else was responsible for the change in Andi. She smiled at her friend anyway. "Hope you feel better."

"Thanks." Then without another word or even a slight hesitation, she was gone.

Mrs. Ellison waited until she heard Andi shut her new bedroom door before she released a desperate-sounding sigh. She braced herself against the kitchen counter and hung her head for a long moment. When she looked up, she focused grief-stricken eyes at Bailey. "Do you see it? How different she is?"

Bailey wasn't sure how much she should say, but she could certainly agree about the change in Andi. "Definitely." She kept her voice low. "I see it, for sure."

"We were worried about her before we arrived. But seeing her this morning ... she's thin and withdrawn, her dark hair and the dark circles under her eyes. It's like she's an entirely different girl." She massaged her temples. "I've been praying constantly, but I have no answers, no idea what to do." Andi's mom looked intently at Bailey, a pleading sort of look. "Please, tell me what you know. Is she drinking again? Taking drugs?"

"Well ..." Again Bailey wasn't sure it was her place to say much. But then she thought about the friendship she shared with her mother. The best thing for Andi would be a closer relationship with her mom. If she could tell the woman anything that might help, then she would be doing Andi a favor. She gathered her thoughts and hoped Andi wouldn't feel betrayed by anything she might say. She wanted to be a friend more than anything.

"Please, Bailey ... whatever you know."

"Okay, well ..." Bailey looked once back toward the hallway. Andi couldn't hear them, she was sure of that. She moved closer to Andi's mom and leaned on the opposite side of the counter. "I don't think she's drinking. I mean, she might be. But I never smell alcohol around her or see it in the dorm." She hesitated. "She changed a lot when she started seeing Taz. But this depression she's in, that started after they broke up."

"He was bad for her. We knew that, but there was nothing we could do to stop her from seeing him."

"Yes, ma'am."

"So this Taz ..." Mrs. Ellison seemed to dread whatever she was about to ask. But she pushed ahead anyway. "Do you think he and Andi were physical?"

Bailey bit her lip. She wanted to stick to the facts, but she thought maybe Andi's mom should know her suspicions. "I don't know. He's seeing someone else now. But when they were dating, Taz did a film with her and ... I think there might have been some nudity. He told Andi to think of the film as art, and the body as the paint."

"Dear, God ... no." The woman seemed to age ten years in as many seconds. Her hands trembled as she held them to her mouth. "What has she done?"

"I asked her what was wrong. I've tried lots of times. She always tells me she's fine." Bailey pictured the last time, when Andi wouldn't even look at her. "Can you take her to a doctor?"

"I've brought it up three times since we pulled in. She doesn't want to go."

Bailey's heart hurt for her friend. "If there's anything I can do, please ... let me know."

"My sweet Andi." She groaned. "How could this happen?"

"I'm sorry. I wish ... I wish I had more to tell you. I've been at home more often this last semester. I missed my family, and ... well ... Andi didn't seem to want me around. She stopped going to Campus Crusade, and she didn't want to talk about her faith. She just seemed, I don't know, different."

"She is." Mrs. Ellison reached across the counter and patted Bailey's hand. "You go on with the others, Bailey. But pray for her, will you? She's our only child, and I won't stand by while she slips away."

"I'll pray, yes ma'am. Again, I'm sorry." Bailey bid the woman good-bye and joined the others outside. The minute she was back out in the sunshine, she felt like she could breathe again. The tension inside the house was that thick. Even then the sadness of the situation remained. Bailey remembered Andi once saying she needed to experience life. Real life. But now her choices had darkened everything about her world and her existence. Her eyes no longer shone with life. That was the saddest, scariest part about this new Andi.

The life she had tried to find looked a whole lot more like death.

Sixteen

Lisa was finished being passive. It was their third day in Bloomington, and Andi's behavior was terrifying her. When Andi wasn't sleeping, she was slipping out of the house and taking off for hours at a time without a word to either her or Keith. When she'd return, she'd act despondent and nonplussed, as if it were perfectly normal to come and go without checking in.

This morning Lisa had woken to a quiet house, tiptoed back to Andi's room, and peeked in to find her gone again. Fear and sorrow twisted around her heart as she leaned on Andi's bedroom door frame. *What's happening, Lord ... what's going on with her? And why can't we reach her? I know You're here, and I know You care ... so why is this happening?*

Faith without works is dead, my daughter ... you must take action ...

The answer was quick and clear, and it seemed to come straight from God. Faith without works was dead ... that was a Bible verse from James. But what action was she supposed to take?

She walked back down the hallway, collected her well-worn Bible from the desk in their new office, and sat at the dining room table. As she thumbed through the book, sunlight streamed through the window and splashed rays of hope across the pages. She knew exactly where she was headed—the same place she turned as a missionary when she'd reached the end of herself, when the walls were closing in and defeat seemed certain.

1 Chronicles 28:20. She reached it quickly and ran her thumb

over the oft-read section. *Be strong and courageous, and do the work. Do not be afraid or discouraged, for the Lord God, my God, is with you. He will not fail you or forsake you ...*

God was with her. That's what she needed to remember. The Lord knew the battle they were fighting for Andi, and He knew what needed to happen next. She and Keith needed to stay in the fight, they needed to take action somehow and stay courageous. Even when fear over the changes in Andi threatened to consume them. Lisa picked up the phone and made an appointment with a Christian counselor she'd read about in the local Yellow Pages. Then she waited for Keith to wake up.

A few minutes later she heard him in the kitchen making coffee. "Morning, honey."

"Morning."

"I'm in here."

He crossed the kitchen and leaned into the dining room. "Hi." His half smile warmed the chilly space between them. "Where's Andi?"

"Gone again."

He exhaled long and slowly and rubbed the back of his neck. "We need to talk to her."

"Bring the coffee in here when it's ready." Lisa could feel the fight building inside her, the one for her daughter's life. "I booked her an appointment with the Christian counselor I told you about."

Keith held her eyes for a long few seconds. "We'll get through this."

"We will."

As Keith returned to the coffee, Lisa leaned back in her seat and stared out the window at the small fenced yard. Had they really left their house and moved across country in a matter of days? And what about the other changes they'd gone through? Chase done with making movies ... Dayne Matthews jumping in as Keith's new co-producer and ministry partner … everything was happening so fast Lisa could barely see for the dizziness she sometimes felt.

She closed her eyes and breathed in slowly. God was in this; even when life felt crazy, God was in the details for those who loved Him. Dayne was proof. He was a perfect fit for Keith, savvy to the industry and with a name that brought instant respect and open doors. Thankfully, Dayne and Katy had been able to stay on in LA for the last few business meetings pertaining to the release of *The Last Letter* and the pre-production for *Unlocked*. Keith had been there for most of the appointments, but then their San Jose house they'd found renters for their so quickly. Since then life had been a crazy race. Professional movers packed up their house, and they were on the road to Bloomington.

So Dayne Matthews was definitely proof God was still providing. Even so Keith needed a week to help catch Dayne up to speed on the history of Jeremiah Productions and all that went on during the filming of *The Last Letter*, all that was at stake with *Unlocked*. Dayne and his family were flying home from LA this weekend, and early next week Brandon Paul was coming here to meet them. Brandon was happy for the trip. Something about needing a break from Hollywood and wanting to clear his head.

As great as Bloomington was, Lisa couldn't imagine staying here very long. They were renting—a one-year lease. A good call, really. It would allow Keith to work closely with Dayne Matthews and film *Unlocked*. Most of all it had brought them to Andi. But she and Keith had a feeling this wasn't home. Not for any of them. They were missionaries, and the fields God had given them were the ripe ones of Hollywood. It was fine for Dayne to live here and commute, but Lisa had a feeling she and Keith would wind up in Los Angeles.

When that happened, she wanted Andi with them.

From the moment they saw their daughter, Lisa and Keith

knew something was terribly wrong. Lisa guessed Andi was on drugs, and maybe she was. But she'd looked through her daughter's things when Andi was out and found nothing to support the notion. Whatever the reason, the changes were drastic. A year ago Andi was the happiest teenage girl Lisa and Keith knew. Now she seemed trapped in a full-blown case of depression with all the accompanying symptoms. Exhaustion, a lack of interest in life, no appetite, despondency. Lisa stared at her open Bible. Of course there was the other unthinkable possibility, the one Lisa hated to consider.

Andi might be pregnant with Taz's baby.

Whatever was wrong, when Andi came home this time—from wherever she'd gone that morning—she and Keith would sit her down and explain as kindly as they could what they were about to do.

Keith joined her with two cups of coffee. He gave her the one with cream and took the seat opposite her. "I've been praying all morning. I hope she'll at least agree to the appointment."

"She will." Lisa had to believe her daughter wasn't so far gone that she'd defy them to their faces. "The woman's a Christian counselor. That shouldn't feel threatening."

Keith held his coffee up to his face and closed his eyes. He looked weary and worn out. "Tell me more about what Bailey said." He blinked and stared at her, as if he were hoping for a different answer this time.

"Just that the change happened when she started dating this Taz character. But she got worse after they broke up."

"How could a complete stranger convince her to take off her clothes?" Anger simmered in Keith's tone. "That's not how we raised her."

"Honey," Lisa felt compassion for her daughter, even if she didn't understand her decisions. "I think that was the point. She wanted to be different."

"Is this because of the movies? Because we chose Bailey and not her for that extra role?"

"Keith, don't." She took hold of his hand across the table. "We could both blame ourselves. That isn't the point. We have to deal with where she's at now."

"What about ..." his voice broke and he looked at the ceiling for a few seconds. A quick shake of his head and he struggled to find control again. "What if she's pregnant? We have to help her, Lisa. We can't just ... you know, take her to some shrink and hope for the best." He waved his hand toward the front door. "She could be out there having an abortion right now."

Lisa had thought about that. Last night she'd gone into Andi's room and found her curled up beneath the covers before it was dark out. She'd sat on the bed beside her daughter and smoothed her hand over her newly dark short hair. "Baby, tell me ... whatever it is, just tell me."

But Andi only reached out her hand and took hold of Lisa's.

"Really, honey," Lisa kept her voice as kind and nonjudgmental as possible. She prayed her daughter would hear the love of God with every word. "You can tell me anything. Trust me, Andi, please, sweetheart."

"I'm sorry." She muttered without once even turning to look at Lisa. "I'm just tired."

Keith set his coffee down. "Have you seen her eat since we've been home?"

"A bowl of oatmeal yesterday. That's about it."

"Maybe that's where she is now—having breakfast with the guy. Maybe she's running off with him."

"No." Lisa was convinced that wasn't the case. Andi wouldn't have come home at all if Taz still had that kind of control over her. "Bailey says he's seeing someone else."

Keith pursed his lips, seething with anger toward the guy and whatever he'd done to exact such a change in their daughter. But before he could say anything else, they heard the front door open. "Andi?" Keith was on his feet.

"Careful," Lisa whispered. Her look warned him to go easy. She wasn't a minor; she could leave anytime and never come back. It happened with grown kids all the time.

With a quick nod, Keith mouthed that it would be okay. Then he stepped into the entryway. "Andi ..."

"Hi." She walked into the dining room with Keith at her side. As soon as she saw Lisa, she stopped and looked from one of them to the other. "Am I in trouble?"

"We're worried about you." Lisa felt like she was walking a tightrope. She couldn't sound like a martyr or a victim, but she had to get her point across. "As long as you're living with us, you need to tell us where you're going. When you'll be home."

"Okay." Andi set her backpack down. "I wasn't sure you were awake. I went to school and talked to a counselor. I'm thinking about moving to Indianapolis for the summer. So I can take classes at IU's Indianapolis campus."

Nothing Andi said lately added up, and this was no exception. Lisa tried to keep her expression even. "Honey ... don't they offer summer classes here?"

Andi looked nervously from Keith back to Lisa. "Yes, but ... three of my friends from theater are spending the summer in the city. They already have an apartment there, and they said I can live with them." She paused, but when neither Lisa nor Keith said anything, she rushed on. "Plus there's an acting coach there; she's offering us discounted classes, and Mom, you said so yourself, I can't expect to walk into an audition and get a part just because my dad's a producer. Not without training." Andi grabbed a quick breath. "Oh, and the Indianapolis campus has a stronger art department—that's what the counselor told me this morning. I need three art courses to complete my general ed and the pre-reqs for my major."

Andi went on about exactly which art classes she wanted to take, and Lisa listened, skeptical. Her daughter's explanation reminded her of an incident in Indonesia when Andi brought a painted vase home from the village women's craft table. Lisa had a feeling her daughter didn't have permission to take the item, but when she asked about it Andi rattled off a long explanation. It was the first time Lisa had caught her in a lie, and now Andi's tone, the look in her eyes, was the very same. Struggling to create an explanation where in all honesty there was none.

When she finished, Keith looked at Andi for a long time. His eyes told her that clearly he was concerned. "Sounds like your mind's made up."

"It is." Andi was practically breathless from the monologue, but she seemed about to slip back into her new, more sedate personality. She was still standing near the dining room table, but she slouched back against the wall. "I'm driving there Friday to get things settled."

It was already Thursday, so the idea of Andi leaving so soon stirred instant anxiety in Lisa's heart. If they were going to help her, they didn't have much time. "Can I ask, honey, how you're planning to pay for a summer in Indianapolis?"

Andi's hesitation was just long enough for Lisa to be sure. Her daughter clearly hadn't thought about this part of her plan. "I can get a job. I might do some acting too. The coach might have some leads. I was hoping you would help out like you do during the regular school year."

Lisa figured this wasn't the time to explain that expenses would begin the minute she arrived. No one would let her share an apartment without paying rent. Then there would be meals and gas and a number of other costs. She looked at Keith, and his eyes told her it was time to move on, get to the point.

Keith took the lead. He sucked in a long, steadying breath. "Sit down, sweetheart. Your mother and I need to talk to you."

Again Andi looked from him to Lisa and back again. "About what?"

"Just sit down." Keith was struggling to stay patient. "Please, Andi."

She slowly pulled out the seat at the head of the table, putting her between the two of them. Lisa closed her eyes for a few seconds. *Give us the words, Lord. We don't want to turn her away. Please.*

"In the few days since we've been here, your mom and I have seen a drastic change in you, honey." Keith kept his words slow and measured. He sat back and folded his hands on the table. "Something's clearly wrong and we've made you an appointment with—"

"Dad! I told you, I'm fine!" Panic pierced Andi's eyes. She made a sound that was part frustration, part fearful defiance. "Just because I'm tired? Do you know how many college students are tired after finals?" With a quick, jerky motion, she ran her fingers through her bangs, struggling. "I don't need a doctor; I need to catch my breath."

Keith waited a long moment after Andi's interruption before trying again. "What I was saying," his voice was calmer than before, "is that we've made an appointment for you to see a Christian counselor." He looked at Lisa. "It's at one this afternoon, right?"

"Right." Lisa felt tears in her eyes. She was sitting close enough that she put her hand on Andi's shoulder. "Honey, you need to talk to someone. We think maybe you're dealing with some depression."

Lisa expected Andi to fight back about this, too, but she didn't. She slumped in her chair and laid her arms on the table, defeated. "So like, an hour with a counselor? That's what you want me to do?"

"Yes." Keith's tone said that the matter wasn't open to

debate. "If there's something going on, maybe she can help you talk through it." His expression softened. "Sweetheart, we love you, but you're scaring us."

"You were always so happy, Andi." Lisa hoped her daughter could see the concern in her eyes. "You lit up every room you ever entered. And now ... now we don't know how to find that in you again."

"You've only been home three days." Her words were practically mumbled, and she wouldn't make eye contact with them.

"This has been going on longer than that." Keith put his hand on Andi's other shoulder. "We want you to get help, baby. That's all."

For most of the brief talk, Lisa had been praying and now she begged God that Andi would understand. She watched her daughter, wondering how they could possibly feel so distant from each other. For a moment she thought Andi might argue, or worse—refuse to go. Instead she looked long at both of them and slowly nodded. "Fine." She stood and again fear tinged her voice. "I don't think it'll help, but I'll go." She started toward the hallway. "I'll be in my room until then."

When she was gone, Lisa looked at Keith. "What do you think?"

"You want to know?" Keith's shoulders hunched forward a little. He looked like he might break down. "I feel like I'm losing my little girl." He looked out the window, clearly struggling with his composure. "Like someone took my daughter and replaced her with a stranger ... someone I don't even know."

Tears blurred Lisa's vision. "Maybe ... we've been too busy."

"Of course we've been too busy." Keith raised his voice, but then shook his head, clearly frustrated with himself. "I'm sorry. It's not your fault." He shaded his eyes with his hand, and when he looked up, the desperation in his eyes was evident. "What am I doing, Lisa? Spending my days making *movies*?" He seemed to almost spit out the last word. "I have this big dream to change the world with film, but at what cost?" He waved his hand toward the hallway. "At the cost of losing Andi? Because if that's the cost, I'll be like Chase and quit. I can't do it."

Lisa wanted to say something wise and compassionate, a Scripture or bit of advice that would calm her husband and give him hope that he didn't need to quit making movies in order to reach their daughter. But the words wouldn't come. "Maybe we'll know more after today."

Keith nodded. "I'll go with you to the appointment." He stood and pulled Lisa into his arms. "But I mean it. I'll turn the whole thing over to Dayne if that's what it takes. I can't stand by and watch her slip away."

They held onto each other for several minutes, both in silence and in prayer for their daughter. As they got ready for the appointment, Lisa thought about what her husband had said, and she agreed. If they had to leave moviemaking, so be it. They needed to do whatever they could to reach their daughter, to help her become the young woman she'd been before this year at school.

Now Lisa could only pray it wasn't too late.

Seventeen

ANDI SAT RIGIDLY, SILENTLY BETWEEN HER parents in a nondescript chair in the stuffy lobby of the Bloomington Christian Counseling Center and tried to imagine how she'd let herself get into this situation. Had she really gotten into a car with her parents and willingly come here? When she'd lied to her parents every few hours since they'd arrived in Bloomington?

Nausea welled inside her and made her wonder if she'd survive the hour. This visit was a waste of their time and money, and Andi felt terrible for agreeing to it. But maybe if she gave the right answers and got through the hour, her parents would stop worrying about her. She needed an abortion clinic, not a counseling center. She'd made up her mind. And until then she couldn't begin to figure out who she'd been back in the fall or whether she even wanted to find her way back to that girl. But none of that was her parents' fault, so that's why she was here.

A kind-faced older woman stepped into the lobby and smiled at them. "Andi Ellison?"

A moment of disbelief consumed her as she rose to her feet. Was this really happening? Her mother squeezed her hand and whispered, "We love you."

Andi nodded absently and then followed the woman to a room halfway down a carpeted hallway. "Caroline will be right with you," the kind woman smiled, and then she was gone.

This would be the perfect time to run. Andi looked around the room, but there was no door. Just the one that led back to the hallway, and there would be no way past the woman at the front desk. She reminded herself to breathe as she looked around the room. It was inviting, with a small fireplace and two comfortable leather chairs facing each other. A framed water feature hung on one wall, and on the other was an enormous aquarium situated on a table that seemed custom-built for it. A painting hung over the fireplace with the Scripture, "Cast your cares on Him, for He cares for you." The entire room exuded a peace Andi had forgotten about.

She sat in one of the leather chairs and a minute later another woman entered the room, this one trim and neatly dressed, maybe in her mid-thirties. "Andi, hello." She held out her hand. "I'm Caroline. I'm a counselor."

Andi nodded and shook the woman's hand. "Hello." *You're a fraud, Andi Ellison*, she told herself. *Stop wasting everyone's time. This woman can't help you.* She forced the voices in her head to cease so she could carry on a conversation.

The woman was calm and in no hurry to get to the reasons behind Andi's supposed depression. She asked about Andi's year at Indiana University and what sort of things she'd been involved in. Against her will, Andi found the woman easy to talk to. Because she was a stranger, not someone emotionally invested in Andi's right or wrong choices, the answers came easily.

"What about guys?" Caroline's smile didn't hold a hint of judgment. "Did you date anyone special this year?"

The question caught her heart off guard. Anyone special? Someone like Cody Coleman or Tim Reed? Sure, Andi had met guys like that, but she hadn't dated them. "I ... uh ... I haven't met a lot of special guys. Not really special."

"But you met some?"

"I guess. My roommate has a couple special guys in her life." Andi hadn't cried since the days after she learned she was pregnant. But here when she hadn't expected to feel anything, she was realizing something she hadn't before. Her voice fell. "I think I forgot what special really meant."

"Hmmm. Yes, that happens sometimes."

"I did date someone, to answer your question." She looked down at her knees. "He was a film major."

"I see." Caroline still maintained an absolutely kind tone. "Did you think he was a special guy at first?"

Did she? Andi blinked and a few tears dropped to her lap. No, she hadn't thought Taz was special, not if she was honest with herself. Dangerous and charismatic, bold and daring. Risky, certainly. She shook her head, working to find her voice. "No … not special. He was … he was different from the guys I was supposed to date. He complimented me and told me he'd never met anyone so beautiful."

"I see." Caroline paused. "Do you remember, Andi … what you were hoping to get out of dating this guy?"

Hoping to get? She stared at her knees again. "My friend Rachel was killed in a car accident."

Caroline sat back, her eyes tender and patient, waiting for Andi to explain herself.

"What I mean is," Andi sniffed. "Rachel was waiting for a special guy, someone … strong in his faith. The kind of guy you marry. But … she died before …" A swell of tears caught Andi off guard.

A box of tissues sat on a small coffee table between the two leather chairs. Caroline slid it closer to Andi. "It's okay. We have time."

Andi nodded and took a few tissues. What was she doing, spilling everything to this woman? And how come she'd agreed to an appointment with a counselor before she'd thought through this stuff? "I think … I dated Taz because he was different. He was dangerous." She dabbed her nose and held the tissues tight in her hand. "I wanted to live like everyone else. Not have to wait for someone special."

"The way Rachel waited."

"Right." Andi hadn't hurt this much over losing Rachel in a very long time. But the pain was as real and raw now as it had been the day she got the news. "Rachel lived for God." She gave a sad shrug. "Where did it get her?"

"Where do you think it got her?"

Andi thought for a moment. The answer was obvious, but she hadn't really voiced it. "I think she's in heaven, if that's what you mean." Andi looked at Caroline through bleary eyes. "You're saying she's in heaven because she lived right?"

"No." Caroline smiled, her patience and understanding limitless. "She's in heaven because Jesus died on the cross for her salvation, and she trusted Him for eternal life." Caroline paused. "So why did Rachel live right when she was here on earth?"

"Because ..." Andi hadn't worked through this part before. "Because she loved God, and she wanted to. Rachel wanted to live right."

"So tell me, Andi ... was Rachel an unhappy girl?"

New tears sprang to Andi's eyes and she pictured Rachel Baugher, the bigger-than-life kindness she had for everyone she met, the way her eyes and her smile could warm a person on the coldest day of the year. She took another tissue and pressed it to her eyes as she shook her head again. "Rachel loved her family and her friends. She loved school and helping people. She loved me." A small sob came from her and she hesitated until she had more control. "Rachel was one of the happiest people I ever knew. Just like my roommate this year."

Caroline nodded slowly, her sad smile filled with a wisdom that made it easy to believe she cared. "Your roommate?"

"Bailey." Andi stood and crossed the room, dropping the damp tissues in a trash can near the door. When she returned, she sat down and met Caroline's gaze again. "Bailey's the same way. She wants to live right."

"And she's happy?"

"Very happy." There was no need for the counselor to draw conclusions. Andi was drawing them for herself. Rachel and Bailey stayed away from parties and wild guys. They didn't drink or pose nude for some stupid student picture, and they certainly would never trade their virginity for a month of craziness. Yet they were happy, their lives filled with love and peace and laughter — the way Andi's had once been. Meanwhile, Andi was unable to get out of bed, practically drugged with the desire to sleep, and unable to remember even how it felt to smile. She was pregnant and afraid and unwilling to tell her parents the truth.

"Are you happy now?" Caroline kept all sarcasm from her voice, as if she truly wasn't sure what Andi's answer would be even after all she'd said.

It wasn't a question Andi had given much thought to, but the answer was ludicrously simply. "No." She made a sound that was more cry than laugh. "I'm not happy."

They talked a little longer about Taz and the way he'd treated her. Every sentence was excruciating for Andi, since she knew now that he had only used her. He'd gotten what he wanted from her and dumped her like moldy remains of yesterday's roses. Caroline never quite asked her if she was pregnant, but she did ask how Andi was feeling now. "Are you able to move on? Or do you feel somehow trapped by your time with Taz?"

Andi hesitated. This was the line she wasn't willing to cross. "I'm working on it."

"Okay, that's a start." Caroline leaned over her knees, her voice slightly more intense than before. "Who's helping you?"

"Helping me?"

"Yes. Andi, when you have something to work through, it's important to have guidelines or rules. Time-tested wisdom that will help you make healthy choices as you go." Caroline reached for a worn leather Bible next to her chair. "A starting place, of course, is Scripture. When you're not happy, one great way to help yourself is to line up your actions with the truth of the Bible."

"Yes." *After my abortion*, Andi told herself.

"Is there someone you trust ... someone you could share your thoughts with, someone you could present your plan to, so that together you could see if that plan measures up with God's Word?"

Her parents, of course. And Bailey. Maybe Bailey's mother. But if she told any of them the truth—that she was pregnant and planning to have an abortion—the truth in God's Word would prevent her from getting the only sort of help she needed right now. And she couldn't embarrass her parents now, not with all of Bloomington excited about their arrival, their plans for making movies in the city. She'd heard her father talking the other night to Dayne Matthews. They were worried that Brandon Paul's partying could hurt the film and Jeremiah Productions. She could only imagine what her pregnancy would do to them.

Andi looked at her watch. She needed to get out of here. They would only talk in circles on this issue. She cleared her throat. "Yes. I have people I can talk to."

"Good." Caroline was quiet for a moment. "Andi, your mother's concerned that you might be pregnant. Is that something you're concerned about?"

What? Her mother suspected that? Andi swallowed hard and shook her head, recovering as quickly as she could. "No. No, I'm not concerned about that." Andi felt the slightest bit of relief. She'd told the truth, right? She wasn't concerned about being pregnant. She already *knew* she was pregnant. After her abortion next week, she wouldn't be concerned about that either.

Caroline wasn't about to call her a liar or ask her a second time. Instead she slid to the edge of her seat, her eyes shining with an even deeper compassion than before. "I'm here, Andi. Your parents know how to reach me. You can come back next week or more often, if you'd like. The important thing is that you have a chance to process how you're feeling." She kept her pace unrushed. "I want you to go home and think about the things you told me. About Rachel and Bailey and the guys they like to date. About how happy they are, and about why they're happy." Caroline smiled. "You have wonderful parents who love you. They've raised you with the truth, is that right?"

"Yes, ma'am." Andi's heart was beating harder than before. She couldn't wait to leave.

"That's right. You know the answers, Andi. I'm just here to help you remember them."

Andi thanked the counselor. "Am I done?"

"For today." Caroline hesitated. "Would you mind if I talked to your parents to fill them in on a little of our conversation? They just want to make sure you're okay. I don't have to talk to them if you'd rather I didn't."

"Um … sure, you can talk to them." Andi figured that if the counselor talked to her parents, they might stop worrying about her. She signed a form stating that Caroline could discuss their session, thanked the counselor again, and headed down the hall to the lobby. But with every step, her heart beat faster. What was this about talking to her parents? Did Caroline know Andi was lying, that she really was pregnant? Or would she tell her parents to take Andi immediately to a doctor's office for a pregnancy test? Andi wouldn't do it. She couldn't. She tried to stand a little taller, look a little more composed. That way her mom and dad would think they'd spent their money wisely and that Andi was on her way back to being the girl they remembered her being.

Her parents were on their feet as soon as she walked through the door. They didn't rush toward her, but their eyes were filled with questions and hope. Her mom spoke first. "How did it go?"

"Good." Andi remembered to smile, at least a little. "Her name's Caroline. She wants to talk to you before we go."

"I'm proud of you, honey." Her dad kissed her cheek. "I know it wasn't easy for you to come here. But sometimes we need a little help."

Andi's heart raced, but she forced herself to look happier than before. "Thanks, Daddy. That means a lot." She watched her parents walk down the hall and she took her same seat in the lobby. This time her knees were shaking. What sort of person was she, lying to her parents, pretending a session with a Christian counselor had cured her problems? She was the worst possible daughter. If she could walk across the street and have the abortion now, she would. Because then she could start figuring out who she was going to be from that point forward. She could hardly be the old Andi, the untainted, innocent Andi. That girl was gone forever. Now she was a used-up coward, a person unfit to be a mother or a daughter. She had walked away from God and her parents and her upbringing, and every time she opened her mouth she spoke nothing but lies. But at least she wasn't going to shame her parents. Not by having a baby.

Andi thought about her time with Caroline. There was one thing she'd learned from her time with the counselor, a truth that would stay with her forever. Rachel and Bailey had special guys in their lives, of course that much she already knew. But today she finally figured out why no special guys had sought after her. The answer was simple, and it brought with it a sting of tears.

Special guys wanted special girls.

Eighteen

BAILEY HAD BEEN LOOKING FORWARD TO this night since summer began. It was the third week of June, and the Clear Creek High School football team was having its annual Cross-Town Scrimmage, against their rivals from Bloomington. The contest was a tradition in the community, and today it would also be the first time Bailey could watch her younger brothers Shawn and Justin play alongside Connor. The first time she could watch Cody on the sidelines, coaching.

Coach Taylor had worked out the timing of the scrimmage so that Bailey's dad could be there, and now he and her mom were in the front seat of the family Suburban, and Bailey, BJ, and Ricky were in the back as they headed to the field. She and Tim still hadn't gotten together — Tim's schedule had been full as he prepared for their upcoming audition. Bailey hated the thought of breaking up with him, so she didn't care if it took a little longer to make it happen.

But when they had talked, Tim had been kind again. The arrogance from a few weeks ago was gone. His thoughtfulness when they talked the last few times made her wonder if she was supposed to break up with him, after all. Especially when she and Cody were still not back to what they'd been at the Cru retreat. Maybe she could talk to Cody today after the scrimmage. Even if they only had a few minutes.

"Dad, you think Cody's gonna be a good coach?" Ricky sat in the middle. He leaned forward, his eyes big. "Connor said he's helping a lot."

Bailey's dad grinned in the rearview mirror. "Coach Taylor says he's a natural."

"Yeah, because all that time he's spent around you." BJ patted their dad's shoulder. "Every time you watched films, Cody would sit next to you. Remember, Dad?"

"He did do that a lot." Bailey's mom shifted so she could see the rest of the family.

Bailey remembered dozens of times like that, Saturday mornings when Cody lived with them and she'd wake up to find him sitting next to her dad, the two of them watching game film on the family computer. Sometimes Bailey would stop and take in the scene, completely unnoticed because the guys were so caught up in watching and re-watching the images on the screen. She didn't say so now, but she always figured more than the football talk, Cody enjoyed sitting next to her dad, because for a few minutes he could feel what it was like to have a father.

"I miss Cody living with us." Ricky settled back in his seat. "He should move in again."

The heat in Bailey's cheeks told her she was better off staying quiet about that possibility. The feelings in her heart stirred up a familiar guilt and confusion that she still hadn't found a way to deal with.

"You think he could, Dad? Huh?" Ricky was relentless once he hit on an idea. "That'd be perfect. He could work with Connor and Shawn and Justin all the time, and just think how good Clear Creek would be then!"

"He's always welcome." Bailey's mom smiled back at Ricky.

"But he's doing well on his own." Their dad's voice told them he wasn't opposed to the idea, but he wanted what was truly best for Cody. "He's a successful young man, and part of that is being self-sufficient."

Self-sufficient. Bailey liked the way that sounded when it came to Cody. She liked thinking of him more man than boy, moving into his future a different guy because of the time her parents had invested in him. And she loved that he was coaching football.

"Tim's coming to the game, right?" BJ looked at her.

"Who?" Bailey blinked and her thoughts cleared quickly. "Oh, Tim. Um ... I don't think so."

BJ was thirteen this summer, not a kid anymore. He looked at Bailey for a long time, as if to say her response was more than a little strange. Tim was her boyfriend, after all.

"I like Tim for you," Ricky grinned at her. "I just like Cody better."

A grin spread across BJ's face and he winked at their younger brother. "I think Bailey feels the same way."

"Okay, okay." Their mom turned around, her expression part smile, part warning. "Enough. Cody's a friend to all of us."

"Exactly." Bailey worked to muster up a lighthearted look for BJ. She couldn't let anyone see how the remark had hit her heart dead center. "Cody's our friend, buddy. Don't let your imagination get ahead of you."

"It wasn't my idea." BJ reached over and gave Ricky's knee a friendly squeeze. "Ricky brought it up."

"I think he likes Bailey." Ricky shrugged. "I'm just saying."

Bailey worked to slow her racing heart. What if he did have feelings for her? What if he were only waiting for her to figure out how to break things off with Tim, and then he would declare that she had been the girl for him all along? She stared out the window as Clear Creek High School came into view. But all she could see was Cody standing on her porch the day he came home from Iraq, telling her she should date Tim Reed, that he was the right sort of guy for her. How was she supposed to take that except the way she had ever since then? Cody didn't have feelings for her that way.

They parked and spilled out, grabbing blankets and water

bottles from the back of the Suburban. The Friday afternoon was warm and clear and blue, perfect for a summer scrimmage. Bailey's mom came up alongside her as they crossed the field. "Ricky didn't mean anything."

Bailey loved this, how her mom knew what she was thinking and feeling before they shared a word about it. "I know."

"I thought Cody would be around more now that he's coaching the boys."

"He's mad at me." Bailey slowed her pace, her eyes on the coaches lined up along the sidelines half a field away. "Over the whole Tim thing at the cafeteria a few weeks ago."

"Still?"

"I don't know what else it could be."

Her mom was quiet, keeping pace with her. "Maybe it's hard for him to be your friend."

"Because of Tim?" Bailey couldn't understand that. "I really don't see Tim that much. I mean, he's busy with voice lessons and acting classes, getting ready for the New York audition."

Bailey's mom slowed and breathed in deeply, her eyes on the distant blue sky. "Not because of Tim." She paused and looked straight to Bailey's heart. "Because he's in love with you."

Over the years Bailey's mom had thought this about Cody before—though she didn't always like the idea—and often Bailey agreed with her. Even if thinking so was a secret the two of them alone shared. But now Bailey shook her head. "He's not, Mom. Maybe before, but not since he's been home."

She raised an eyebrow and angled her head, as if she couldn't quite agree with Bailey. "I watched you that day when he came home from the war, the way he looked at you." She smiled and her expression said she wasn't going to push the subject. "I know what I saw."

Bailey sighed. They were almost to the bleachers, and she could see Cody standing next to Coach Taylor. He looked tall and confident. A couple players ran up and asked him something, and Cody put a hand on one of their shoulders. Whatever advice he was giving, he looked intense. Like this was more than a summer scrimmage with the cross-town rival. She glanced at her mother. "I need to end things with Tim, right? Don't you think?"

"It's more about what you think." Her mom's tone was genuine. "Tim's a great guy."

"He is."

They reached the bleachers and spread out a couple blankets on a bench near the top. Bailey's mom was quiet while she waited for Bailey to continue.

Bailey took the spot beside her mom and opened her water bottle. "I go back and forth about whether Tim and I should be together. You know? I mean nothing's really bad between us."

Her mom narrowed her eyes and looked out at the players on the field. "I hope, honey, that if you stay with Tim, one day you'll be able to say more than, 'nothing's bad.'"

Bailey allowed a feeble laugh. "I didn't mean it like that."

Her mom looked over her shoulder. "Oh," she stood and smiled. "Hi Tim."

Bailey felt her heart skip a beat as she whipped around and saw Tim make his way up the bleachers toward them. He hadn't heard what she'd said, right? The guilt inside her swelled and she quickly patted the spot beside her. "You came!"

He wore khaki shorts and a nice T-shirt, a little too dressed for an afternoon summer football game. He gave Bailey a quick hug and nodded his hello to Bailey's mom. "I had my headshots taken this morning. My mom found a photographer from Indianapolis. She drove in today for the shoot."

"Oh." Bailey wasn't sure what to say. "I guess I need a headshot too. Before August anyway."

"Yeah, sorry. On the way here I thought I should've told you. We could've split the cost and done the shoot together."

"Don't worry about it." Bailey squinted at the field. She reached into her purse, pulled out her sunglasses, and slipped them into place. "Looks like it's about to start." Bailey kept a few inches between her and Tim. Why did she feel so frustrated with him? He needed a headshot, right? That was part of the audition, bringing an eight-by-ten glossy. Bailey hadn't thought much about the picture or the audition, but she figured she could get it done by their neighbor—a woman who did photography from her house. Tim just seemed a little over the top. Way more involved in the audition than she was.

So why did that frustrate her?

Bailey stared at the guys on the field. Maybe because this was the most passion she'd seen in Tim Reed since he won the part of Scrooge last fall. It was an enthusiasm Bailey hadn't seen him express about anything else. Not about his faith or his relationship with her or his education. Which was fine. Bailey sniffed in a gulp of fresh air and sat straighter, with more of an attitude. Maybe Tim just bugged her. She didn't like how she felt, but she couldn't stop herself.

Just as the game was getting started, Coach Taylor's wife, Kari, and their three kids arrived with Ashley and Landon Blake and their three. Landon was in his firefighting uniform, and Bailey glanced back and saw his fire truck in the parking lot. His partner looked like he was sitting in the rig, on the phone. They must've been on call—a slow fire day in Bloomington. As the group walked up, Bailey saw that they were happy and relaxed. Their laughter added to the sounds of the afternoon. Bailey was grateful for the distraction. "Hey guys ..." She waved at them. "Sit by us!"

Ashley hurried up the bleachers and hugged Bailey and then Tim. "We sure miss you guys at CKT. I'm still painting sets, but the new kids aren't the same." She sat with her family in front of Bailey and Tim. "Well, here we are. It wouldn't be summer without the Cross-Town Scrimmage!"

Jenny leaned forward and gave Ashley a quick hug. "I'm glad you're all here."

"Wouldn't miss it." Kari shaded her eyes and stared at the field. "My husband thinks this is the Super Bowl. It might as well be for how much preparation went into it."

They all laughed, and after a few minutes the game began. Like every year, it was a close contest, with four lead changes. The sort of game that kept their attention to the end. Bailey was grateful. The close game meant she didn't have to think about Tim or talk to him or wonder about her frustrations toward him.

Clear Creek pulled out a seven-point win in the last quarter with Bailey and her family and the other fans on their feet. The whole time Cody was completely engaged in the action. He was either consulting urgently with Coach Taylor or intently talking to one of the players, motioning toward the field and giving constant instruction. Bailey tried not to stare. She couldn't help but see the similarities between Cody and her father. She'd spent her whole life watching her daddy coach, and now—watching Cody help guide Clear Creek to a victory was as wonderful as summer itself.

At the end, only Tim wasn't cheering with them. He'd gotten a phone call and he was standing off to the side on his cell. Bailey tried to pretend he wasn't here. He didn't care about football, anyway, so she wasn't sure why he'd come.

The phone call turned out to be the photographer who had taken Tim's headshots. Everyone was going to Bortolomi's Pizza after the game, but Tim begged off. "I guess she loves what she got, but she wants to do a few shots over. She's only in town today." His hands were in his pockets and he looked anxious to leave. He chuckled nervously and his eyes sparkled, not quite arrogant but clearly proud of himself. "She said I could model if the Broadway thing doesn't work out."

"That's great." Bailey tried to feel something, but the only pressing emotion stirring inside her was the urgency to congratulate her brothers and Cody. She gave him a happy shrug that said their time was clearly up. "I guess you better go."

He hugged her, but she pulled away quickly. Before he left he grinned. "I had fun with you today."

"Thanks." She took another step back. "Me too." She moved to walk away, but Tim caught her hand.

"Hey, tell me about Andi ... what've you heard?"

Everyone was headed toward the field and Bailey wanted to join them. "Uh ... I talked to her mom the other day. She's worried about her. I think we all agree Taz wasn't good for her."

"Definitely not." Tim frowned. "I was reading my Bible this morning and Andi came to mind. This whole change in her, the way she's been so down ... it just shows that God's Word is true. There are consequences for sin—and Andi's living proof."

Bailey felt her shoulders sink. "We're all living proof."

"Right." Tim seemed taken aback. "That's what I mean. Hey, meet me for lunch tomorrow. At the Campus Café? One o'clock?"

"Sure," Bailey backed up. "Hey, I gotta go." She started toward the field, waving back at him. "Call me." She couldn't run off fast enough, and once she left she didn't look back to see if he was leaving or still standing there. She didn't care. If she stayed around Tim another five minutes she would say something she might regret. She tried to shake off the conversation with him as she caught up to her mom and brothers.

"Where's Tim?" Her mom kept her voice low, as if the others might not notice he wasn't with them any longer.

"Places to go." She smiled, more because they were approaching the field than because of anything about Tim. Bailey gave her mom a side glance. "I'll tell you more later." Ahead, the players and coaches milled about with the fans, accepting congratulations and celebrating the game. Her dad was already out there, standing next to Coach Taylor and Cody.

Bailey made a point of finding her brothers first, hugging them and posing for a phone picture with them. "Three Flanigan boys on one team!" she beamed at them. Shawn and Justin had each scored a touchdown, and Connor's interception set up the winning drive. "I can't wait for the season."

Her mom agreed. "We've looked forward to this for so long." She hugged each of the boys too. "You three were wonderful."

Finally Bailey looked around and spotted Cody, still standing with Bailey's dad and Coach Taylor. She walked up and looped her arm around her father's waist while they were mid-conversation about the Clear Creek pass defense. Bailey listened for a few minutes, understanding most of what they talked about as only a coach's daughter could.

"We can't run the prevent," Coach Taylor was saying. "The quarterbacks in our league will nickel and dime us to death."

"Exactly." Her dad was still passionate about seeing Clear Creek play well. "We need man coverage, and we need to watch the tight ends. If they shoot straight through, it's a pass every time."

Cody wasn't adding much, so Bailey tried to catch his attention—something that usually was as natural as breathing. But not today. She might as well have been invisible for how little he seemed to notice her.

Bailey's dad kissed the top of her head. "The fans liked it, right?"

"It was great." She grinned at Coach Taylor and then at Cody. Again Cody only looked at her long enough to not seem rude. "Best Cross-Town Scrimmage ever."

The guys talked another few minutes, and then Cody gathered his gear bag from the ground a few feet away. "Gotta go, guys." He waved at Coach Taylor. "Thanks for letting me be out here."

"You added a lot today." Coach pointed at him. "We need you, Coleman. See you at practice."

Bailey drew back from her dad and followed Cody as he waved and turned toward the parking lot.

"Hey," she kept her tone light. The other guys were still in earshot, and she didn't want to make a scene. She caught up with Cody and walked alongside him. "You're leaving?"

"Yeah." He kept up his pace, and shot her a quick glance as he looked briefly back to the bleachers. "Where's Tim?"

Bailey wanted to scream. "Cody." She fought to keep her tone even. "Can you stop? Please."

He was more than halfway to the parking lot now, and they were by themselves, the rest of her family and the others still back on the field talking to the players. Cody took another few steps and stopped. He didn't act put out, but his body language made the implication anyway. He cocked his head, his eyes never really making contact with hers. "What?"

"You're mad at me." She took a step closer but kept her distance. She had a feeling if she came too close he'd back up. "I know you are."

"We've been over this." He sucked in a frustrated breath and released it in a hurry, his eyes searching the air between them as if the answers might be written in the summer breeze. "You've got Tim. The way he treated me the other day … I don't know. I didn't feel like I mattered that much to you." He smiled, clearly working to keep things light. "No big deal. You've got your life, and I've got mine." He gave her the lightest pat on her shoulder. "See you, Bailey."

"Cody … wait. I can explain." She wanted to run after him, but that would create more drama than either of them needed. Especially here with sixty football players who respected him as a coach.

"Nothing to explain." He waved once, the smile still firmly in place. "Don't worry about it."

And with that he was gone, jogging toward his car, every bit the athlete he'd been back when he'd worn the Clear Creek Uniform. Bailey stood in place and watched as he reached his car, climbed in, and drove off.

Angry tears burned her eyes and she blinked them back. Nothing was turning out like she wanted it to. Wherever Cody was going, he seemed in a hurry to get there. She turned and walked slowly back to her family, but along the way she kept replaying Tim's actions, his words. Why was she still dating him? She was going to break up with him a month ago, right? She slowed, still bitterly disappointed at the way the afternoon had turned out. *What am I doing, God?*

No loud and clear answer came to her, but she suddenly could hear her dad's voice talking to Coach Taylor above the others ten yards away. "Never be passive. Victories happen when you take charge of a game. You can't win by playing not to lose."

Her dad had told that to his players as long as Bailey could remember, but here—with Cody driving off to who knew where and Tim lost in his own world, it was like she was hearing his words for the first time. How self-centered she'd been, staying with Tim because of convenience, because it was easier than breaking up with him. Of course she was frustrated. She'd been as mean and thoughtless to Tim as Tim had been to Cody. She should've ended it with Tim when the thought first hit her. That would've been the fair thing—maybe for all of them.

So what if Cody didn't want to date her? She didn't need a boyfriend. She needed time with God, time praying about the plans He had for her. She thought about Tim's comment earlier, about the consequences of sin. By being passive, she was getting what she deserved. She was ashamed of herself because she'd been wrong in how she'd acted toward Tim, how she'd been playing not to lose. Certainly God wanted more from her than that. With His help, it was time to recognize her faults and take action.

The way she should have a month ago.

Nineteen

CODY DIDN'T SPEED. THE LAST THING he needed was a ticket on his way to see his mother. She had left a strange message on his cell phone, half crying, half talking and asking him to come as soon as he could. Between that and the scene with Bailey, the day hadn't exactly turned out the way he'd hoped it would.

The game was the single bright light. On the sidelines, helping the guys read the defense and run the offense, Cody felt vibrantly alive. Like he'd been born to do this. The only time he lost focus was once when he scanned the bleachers looking for Bailey. He expected to see her sitting with her mom and brothers, but for some crazy reason he hadn't expected to see Tim beside her. Tim dressed for success in his preppy shorts and Buckle T-shirt, already looking like a part of the Flanigan family. Or at least the way anyone would expect Bailey Flanigan's boyfriend to look.

Cody wanted to be Bailey's friend, really he did. But lately the idea felt like a colossal exercise in futility, because every time they were together, all he could think was that he didn't want to be her friend. He wanted to hold her hand and run along the shores of Lake Monroe with her. He wanted to take walks in the summer moonlight and sit on her porch swing poring over the truths in Scripture, dreaming about their future together. He wanted to take a wild and dangerous jump and fall madly and marvelously in love with her, and the fact was this: He was tired of pretending otherwise.

He wasn't jealous of Tim Reed. Every time Bailey talked about him—every single time—her tone was lukewarm. She liked him, yes. He was kind and they shared common interests, but she wasn't sure if he was the guy ... wasn't sure if this was forever. The story was as repetitive as Mondays, but still Bailey stayed. And now that Tim had taken to talking down to him, Cody couldn't think of a reason why he should make an effort to be Bailey's friend. She was young and immature at love. They could be distant friends, yes. Acquaintances, of course. But he had to help his heart move on; otherwise he wouldn't know the right girl when she walked through the door.

His mother's message flashed in his mind again and he felt a rush of nervous energy work through his veins. What was she doing, calling him like that, her words sounding all slurred? Was this about Benny? Or had she jumped off the wagon on her own? He clenched his teeth and gripped the steering wheel harder than before. *God, help me get through this next hour.* He relaxed his grip and sank back against the seat. The last time she called, she hadn't been drunk or drugged. Just sick with a fever. Maybe that was all it was this time too. But he'd found more beer bottles at her house, and he worried about her constantly. *I'm not mad at her, God. I want her to succeed. If she falls again I could lose her.*

It was a familiar prayer where his mother was concerned. That was the problem, really. All of his life felt like a series of familiar prayers. Praying about Bailey, praying about his mother, praying about God's direction for his life. Cody wondered how long a person could feel stuck at the starting line.

He pulled into his mother's driveway, and even before he reached her front door he had a feeling something was very wrong. A stillness in the air, or the lack of sounds from inside the house. Something about the moment made his skin crawl, and by the time he'd knocked on the door twice, he pulled out his key and hurried inside.

"Mom!" The living room was empty, but there were sofa pillows on the floor and the bookcase was half empty, the contents of its shelves scattered about in hurried disarray. A quick look toward the kitchen and Cody saw a dozen broken plates shattered across the linoleum. His heart thudded against the walls of his chest as he rushed toward the hallway. "Mom! Where are you?"

No answer. He pushed his way past a chair that was smashed against the bathroom door. If Benny had done this, he might still be here. Cody hoped so. He'd love the chance to level the guy, chuck him out onto the street. Still, he had to be careful. Benny could easily be armed, hiding around any wall, behind any door. Cody tore around a corner and into his mother's room. She was there, passed out on the bed. Passed out or—

"Mom!" He raced to her side, grabbed her wrist, and felt for a pulse. It was slow and weak, but she was still alive. He surveyed her, the black eye and ripped shirt, the scratches on her arms. A few smears of blood on the bedspread told him her head was bleeding from somewhere. He gave her a firm shake. "Mom, wake up!"

A low moan came from her and she turned her head slightly, before going still again. Cody glanced frantically around the room. Was she knocked out from being hit, or had she taken something? He moved to her nightstand, and there in the top drawer was all he needed to see. A pipe and an amber-colored vile, a small mirror, a half straw, and a razor blade. He stepped on something and looked down to see an empty Jack Daniels bottle.

"Mom, why?" He shouted the words, furious and terrified all at the same time. He went to her again and took hold of her shoulder. "Wake up!"

He waited, trembling, and that's when he heard it. The rattle in her chest, the strange uneven breathing. Whatever she was suffering from, she wasn't okay. She wouldn't want him to call an ambulance, but he had no choice. He wasn't going to stand here and watch her die. Cody grabbed the phone by her bed and dialed 9-1-1. His heart was racing so hard and fast he could barely think.

"Nine-one-one, what's your emergency?"

"My mom's unconscious. She's not breathing right." His words spilled out one on top of the other. "Please hurry ... she's in a lot of trouble. Someone broke into her house. Everything's a mess."

"You're with her, is that right?"

"Yes, ma'am." Cody sat on the bed, his hand on his mother's head. *Please, God ... don't let her die like this. Please.*

"Are the perpetrators still in the house or are you alone with her?"

"I'm ... I'm not sure."

"Fine, we'll send police as well." The operator talked quickly and efficiently. "She's breathing, and she has a pulse?"

"Yes, but it's not good. Not strong."

"Okay, someone's on the way." The operator asked Cody's name and the address, to make sure it matched with their records. "Are you able to perform CPR if the need arises?"

"Yes, ma'am." He felt suddenly dizzy, fear and anger dancing at a frenzied pace across his heart. "I'll stay with her."

The call ended and Cody stared at his mother. Her skin looked gray; it was cooler than usual and clammy. What had happened to her? Had she and Benny gotten in a fight or had someone broken in and robbed her? And what about the drugs? Was she high when the assault happened, or the other way around? He pulled his cell phone from his pocket and checked the time on her voicemail. Guilt hit him like a bullet, shattering what remained of his composure. Her call had come almost an hour ago. What if he'd found a quiet place and taken her message right when it came in? Would he have caught the jerk who'd torn up her house and beat her up? And would she have avoided the drug bash—whatever she'd taken?

"Mom?" His voice was softer now, and he leaned in close to her face. "Mom, can you hear me?"

There was no response. Just her raspy, shallow breathing—which sounded worse now than it had a couple minutes ago. He was taking her pulse again when he heard squealing tires outside. He'd expected sirens, but sometimes they didn't use them when they reached a residential location like this.

He heard the door fly open and he stood, one hand still on his mother's shoulder. "We're in here!"

"Baby!" A string of cuss words rang through the house. "Baby ... I'm coming!" The voice was hardly the professional one of a paramedic or emergency worker.

Cody felt his anger explode into rage as Benny barreled into the room. "What the—"

"Oh, you're back?" Cody was on his feet, grabbing Benny by the shoulders and shoving him against the wall. The biker was heavier than Cody, but that didn't stop him. His military training kicked in and Cody could only see red. Blood red. He shoved the guy again. "What? Did you come back to finish her off?"

"Back up!" Benny jerked Cody, and he bounced against the edge of his mother's bed. "I didn't do this! I was out riding when she—"

Heavy footsteps sounded in the hall, and in a matter of seconds two officers burst through the doorway. "Police. Freeze!"

Cody and Benny slowly raised their hands, and Cody gulped. *This was crazy. How had everything gotten so out of hand? God, help me ... help my mom. Please.* "Officer, I made the 9-1-1 call." He still had his hands up. "My mom needs help."

Sirens pulled up outside as the police officer and his partner turned to Benny. "Who are you?"

"Benjamin Roth." He blinked, clearly petrified. "I'm her boyfriend, but I ..." he gestured toward Cody's mother and the disarray on the floor. "I didn't do this." He ran his tongue across his lip, his eyes wide. "But I might ... I might know who did."

"Keep your hands up." The police officer patted Benny down

and directed the other officer to do the same to Cody. When they were satisfied that neither of them were armed, the officers tried to lead them into the living room.

"I need to stay!" Cody couldn't believe what was happening. The police were treating him like a criminal when his mom was lying there dying on the bed. "Please ... let me stay with her."

The officers exchanged a look and the second one nodded. "We'll need to talk to you once they take her."

"Yes, sir." Cody nodded, barely breathing. As the police led Benny out of the room, the paramedics rushed in.

One of them was Landon Blake—who had just been at the football game. He was at Cody's mother's side immediately, checking her pulse, her breathing. "Cody ... what's going on here?"

"I'm not sure." Cody felt a burst of panic again. "She left me a message and I came to check on her. The house is a mess and she's been beaten up pretty bad."

Landon nodded. "What about the other guy?"

"Her boyfriend." Rage flooded him again. "The guy's not good for her. I'm not sure if he did this." Cody tried to think clearly. "He just showed up ... before the police."

Another two paramedics were working on his mom now, and Cody stepped back against the wall, watching. *Please, God ... not like this.* To think his mom would spend most of his childhood in prison for drugs, and then die like this—just when she was starting to live ... the idea was devastating, and it consumed him. *Please, God ... help her.*

Landon and the other guys were moving quickly, starting an IV and getting her on a gurney.

"I think she's on something." Cody pointed to the open drawer on the nightstand. "I found that."

"Is she a user?"

Was she a user? The question felt like a dagger, slashing every dream and hope he'd ever held out for his mother. There was only one answer, no matter how long she'd been clean. Before she was a woman, before she was his mother, before she was anything else she might've been or become, she was definitely a user.

Landon was collecting the drugs and drug paraphernalia, putting them in a large Ziploc bag. He looked back at Cody, still waiting for an answer. "She's done this before?"

"Yes," Cody's vision blurred with angry tears. Because his mother had done this to him since he was a little boy, and because unless something drastic changed, she was going to do this to him as long as she lived. Choosing drugs over a healthy life, over living for God or loving her son. Real life, real love, was never enough for her, and the truth hurt like crazy. "She's been clean for a while, but she's fallen before."

Landon must've caught the pain in his tone, because he reached back and took firm hold of Cody's shoulder. "We're gonna get her help, Cody. We are."

He nodded, biting his lip, his eyes locked on his mother's face. He wanted her to wake up and tell them all it was a joke, a trick. She would never in a million years go back to the drugs that had cost her the chance to raise her son, drugs that had kept her in prison through Cody's high school years and stopped her from seeing him play even a single football game. But she didn't move or speak, and in a blur of motion the paramedics wheeled her from the room.

Landon trailed the gurney, and he looked back at Cody as they left. "We're taking her to Bloomington Community Hospital. Meet us there when you're finished with the police."

The police. Cody nodded, his mind racing. What were they learning from Benny, and how would they figure out who had torn apart his mother's house. He moved down the hall behind Landon. "Is she … is she going to be okay?"

"We have to figure out what she took." The compassion in

his eyes brought the first peace to the moment. "Her vitals aren't great, but they're steady." He hesitated briefly, still moving with the gurney. "Still, I'd get to the hospital."

"I will." He watched them go, and he moved to the corner of the living room where the police were still talking to Benny.

The first officer looked at Cody. All accusation from earlier was gone from his eyes. "Benny says he wasn't here earlier, but he knows who was."

His mother's boyfriend shot him an indignant look. "I would never hurt her." He crossed his meaty arms. His tattoos twisted around his biceps. "She's been getting back into drugs. Sometimes when I'm here, sometimes not." He seemed to measure his words, especially since the officer to his right was taking notes. "I told her she was getting in too deep, but she wouldn't listen."

That much rang true, but there was something about the guy that made Cody doubt his story. Something in his eyes.

The second officer looked up from his notes. "And you say she told you she was having a drug dealer over to the house?"

"Yes. She wanted crack, and she'd made a few phone calls."

Cody felt his heart split in half. How could she do this? When she knew where it would lead? She'd told him so herself, that if she used again she'd leave in an ambulance, a hearse, or a squad car. And she'd been right.

"So you knew she'd invited a crack dealer here?"

"Just for a quick purchase." He waved his hand at the torn-up room. "Something must've gone wrong, because this ... this is how I found the place."

"Something definitely went wrong." Cody glared at him.

"What're you, the doting son? Why don't you shut the—" Benny cussed and the police officer closest to him grabbed his arm.

"Quit it." The officer released Benny with a slight shove. He glanced back at Cody. "Work out your differences later."

They asked Benny a few more questions and then released him. Before he left he looked back once at Cody, and this time he didn't glare or cuss or make a single threat. But the look in his eyes was chilling, a sneer almost. As if he'd just gotten away with murder and he was happy about the fact.

When he was gone, Cody had another couple minutes with the officers. "I'm still worried about that guy. He could be the dealer for all we know."

"We're on it." The first officer looked grim. "We have no reason to detain him, but his record has us suspicious." They stood and the other officer slipped his notepad into his pocket. "We'll be in touch. You can go ahead to the hospital."

The three of them left at the same time. It wasn't until Cody reached his car and started off to the hospital that his tears came in earnest. Angry, defeated tears because this was his life—the son of a single mom who was engaged in a lifelong battle with drugs. She'd missed whole sections of his life—his grade school years when he lived with his grandparents because she was in prison, and his middle school days when she was in and out of rehab. By the time he graduated from eighth grade, she'd been arrested again for dealing and using, and her prison sentence kept her locked away while he had his first day of high school and his first homecoming game, his first prom and his final summers of being a kid.

By then his grandparents had both died, Cody was caught up in his own alcoholism, and the Flanigans were his only hope.

He took rough swipes at his wet cheeks and forced himself to gain control. But the thought of the Flanigans only made him more aware of his reality. Whether Bailey stayed with Tim Reed forever didn't really matter. Cody wasn't the right guy for her. Look at him. He was a recovering alcoholic with a prosthetic lower left leg, no family support, and none of the easy money people like Bailey and Tim took for granted. He was the son of a drug addict. No matter how he felt when he was with Bailey or how he sometimes wanted to believe she had feelings for him, the answer was painfully obvious.

Bailey deserved better.

Twenty

THE COUNSELING APPOINTMENT TURNED OUT TO be the best thing Andi could've done, even though she felt terrible pretending the session had helped. Still, Andi was grateful for the reprieve from her parents. They were convinced she was on the road to becoming her old self, able to think a little more clearly and committed to finding her way back to God again.

Once the counseling session was behind them, her parents made it very clear that Andi simply couldn't spend the summer in Indianapolis—even if she found a job and paid for the experience herself. She needed help, counseling, and time with her family. Andi didn't fight them ... She had no idea what the future held, but there was no point arguing with her mom and dad now. Otherwise they wouldn't want her going to the city for even a few days. And she desperately needed to go.

"Maybe you can take classes in Indianapolis next summer," her mom had told her last night. "When you're feeling better."

Andi listened politely, nodding and smiling at the appropriate times. She had no intention of taking art classes in Indianapolis this summer or next. If she stayed with her friends, it would only be for her abortion, and to clear her head so she could figure out what to do next.

But for now she couldn't think about her future past this afternoon at four o'clock.

She'd found an abortion clinic in Indianapolis, and a week ago she'd made an appointment for the last appointment today. The abortion wouldn't take more than an hour, they'd told her.

Once she had the appointment in hand, Andi had called her friend Sherry who had already moved to the city for the summer. She asked if she could come on Friday for a visit.

"Definitely. Stay with us." The girl was very open-minded, and now she didn't hesitate. "We have room on the couch. You need a week or what?"

"Just through the weekend." Andi had planned it this way. Have the abortion on a Friday, stay with Sherry and the girls through the weekend, and head home Monday. Her parents would never suspect a thing that way. Her stomach hurt from the planning, from the fact that she refused to think about what she was about to do. "Oh, and Sherry ... I have another favor to ask."

Andi explained that she was pregnant and that she'd scheduled an abortion for that afternoon. "I need someone to drive me there and back. They said it won't take long."

"Oh, honey. I'm sorry." Sherry was immediately sympathetic and glad to help. Andi had met Sherry on the mall during rush week last fall. She stood for everything contrary to Andi's beliefs and upbringing, but Andi found her funny and refreshing. Then Sherry turned up in two of Andi's classes and they became friends, studying for tests a few times and having coffee together once in a while. Sherry liked Taz—at least at first—and thought the experience was good for Andi. Even the heartbreak at the end.

"We learn the most through pain," she'd told Andi back then, and she reiterated the mantra on the recent phone call.

Andi wasn't sure she agreed, but this time the pain was inevitable. Because she wouldn't embarrass her parents, wouldn't do anything to ruin all the good they'd accomplished. The last thing they needed now was a scandal—especially a public one. People would think Jeremiah Productions was a joke.

Now, with the plan set, Andi packed a small roller suitcase and tried to keep from panicking. Was she really doing this, heading out to Indianapolis for an abortion? What about her baby? It wasn't his or her fault, right? She glanced at the piece of paper on her bookcase. She'd jotted down the name of the abortion clinic and her appointment time, as well as the clinic phone number. All the details she needed. Next she pulled out her cell phone and copied the information into her phone's address book.

Tossing the paper in the trash, Andi stuffed her thoughts back to the basement of her soul and pulled her suitcase down the hallway. She found her parents at the computer in their new office. They were reading a review on *The Last Letter*—Andi could see that much on the screen. Her dad turned and grinned at her. "The critics love it! The whole world's going to know about this movie!"

Andi tried to look enthusiastic, but she didn't have even the slightest interest in what the review said. "I'm leaving. The girls are expecting me in the city."

"Honey, I don't know." Her mom stood and came to her, pressing the back of her hand to Andi's forehead. "Are you feeling up to it? I mean, it was just a week ago that you were sleeping all day."

"I'm fine." She was touched by her mom's concern, but she struggled to make eye contact. *Mom, if you only knew ...* Again she pushed back her fear and found a quick smile. "It's a short drive. Just an hour and hardly any heavy traffic until the end."

Her mom hesitated, and her dad turned and looked at her from his computer chair. His eyes clouded with doubt. "Are you sure, honey?"

"Yes." She ignored the strange rhythm of her heart. "I really need this."

Her dad stood and gave her a tender hug. "Please be careful."

"Oh, I don't think we told you." Her mom's expression suddenly changed. "Brandon Paul's coming Sunday. He'll be here for a few nights."

Andi was glad she was still holding onto her suitcase handle.

Otherwise she might've fallen flat onto the floor. Brandon Paul? "*The* Brandon Paul?"

"Right." Her dad chuckled. "He's meeting with Dayne and me, so most of the day will be business." He hesitated. "Brandon's an interesting kid. He's not much older than you. A few years, maybe. I think he wants to know the Lord, wants to do right. Maybe that's why he's drawn to work with us in *Unlocked*. But he still has a wild side ... I'm not sure he understands the scope of the battle he's in."

Andi was sure her father was right. Even she hadn't understood the scope of the battle until she imagined what her pregnancy might do to her father's reputation. A megastar like Brandon Paul? Of course he didn't understand it. "He's staying here?"

"Actually at Dayne's house. We're meeting there." Her dad angled his head, as if he was processing the possibilities. "Anyway, maybe you can come by. Take him around campus and give him a breather that afternoon. It might be fun ..."

"And good for him." Her mom nodded. "Not because he's Brandon Paul ... but because we want him to have good, solid people around him."

"If he gives his life to God during the filming of *Unlocked*, think of our country—the millions of kids that could be affected."

And if she moved home unwed and pregnant, imagine what that would do? She doubled her determination to make it to her appointment this afternoon.

"Anyway, just think about it." Her dad hugged her one last time. "Drive safely, honey."

Her mom hugged her, too, and after another round of promises that she'd be safe and that she'd call later that night, Andi was behind the wheel of her four-door, headed to Indianapolis. Her mind stayed ten miles ahead of her the whole ride. Brandon Paul was coming to Bloomington? How different might this weekend be if she hadn't gone with Taz? If she hadn't let him have his way with her? Her parents clearly still thought she'd be a good influence on the nation's top celebrity. The idea was ludicrous, and now the last thing Andi wanted was to spend time with Brandon. She would still be aching from an abortion. Her world had no room for frivolous afternoons with movie stars — not anymore.

She would stay in Indianapolis a few days longer and miss his visit altogether. He wouldn't be interested in her anyway. She looked ragged and worn out, and her stomach would be swollen from the procedure. No, there would be no meeting with Brandon Paul.

As that thought lifted, the more pressing one filled her mind. After a lifetime of believing God's Word, of holding tight to the value of life, she was only hours away from killing her baby. It wasn't a thought she allowed very often. Ever since she'd made up her mind, she'd acknowledged it only as a procedure or an abortion — the way the woman at the Indianapolis clinic called it. But here — driving into the city — she couldn't stop the truth from consuming her.

The closer she got to the city, the more she became convinced she was making a mistake. If she went through with the abortion she would carry the secret to her grave. But she would also carry the guilt. She allowed her mind to race, imagining other options. She couldn't tell her parents or ask for their support. Not without ruining her dad's reputation, his credibility with the public. She could hardly call Taz and ask him to step up and help raise their child. Every option seemed wrought with terrible implications.

As she passed the city limits sign, tears began to choke her. They streamed down her face and compromised her ability to see the road. She needed to call Taz. She hadn't gotten through to him last time she tried, and now he needed to know. The baby was his, too, and he deserved the chance to give her advice or offer his help. He wasn't a terrible person, really; he had simply moved on to another love. But back when the two of them were an item he had always been kind, his words flattering, his actions gentle.

She pulled off the freeway at the next exit and turned into a gas station parking lot. Her hands shook as she snagged her cell phone from the seat beside her and found his number in her address book. She hit Send and waited while it rang. Just when it seemed his voicemail might come on, she heard him. He sounded groggy and distracted. "Hey ..."

Andi felt another wave of panic, as she searched in a hurry for the right words. "Taz ... it's me. Andi."

"What?" He made a sound like he was yawning. "Sorry, I didn't hear you. Who?"

"Andi." Frustration raised the level of her voice. "Andi Ellison, Taz. Remember me?"

"Oh, Andi." He laughed lightly. "Sorry sweetheart, I was half asleep. Long night."

"It's three in the afternoon."

"I know." Most of the humor faded from his tone. "It's summer, okay?"

This was a terrible start. Andi covered her face with her free hand and pressed the phone to her ear. There was no easy way to say this. "Taz ... I'm pregnant."

For a long time he said nothing, and she wondered if he'd hung up. "You're ... pregnant? Do you ... do you know who the father is?"

If he'd been sitting across from her she would've gladly slapped his face. "I've never been with anyone but you."

Another silence. "I see." He exhaled loudly, slowly. As if the truth were finally hitting him. "What're you gonna do?"

"I scheduled an abortion for today. But," her voice broke, "I'm struggling. It isn't fair to the baby."

"There is no baby." His voice took on an authoritative voice, the one that mixed passion and charisma with absolute power.

The voice he'd used when he was directing her in his film. "You know better than that, Andi. You're what—three months along?"

"Not yet."

"Then it's not a baby." His easy laughter was back. "You had me worried there. I don't want to be a father. No way."

She felt sick, and she couldn't tell if the ache was in her heart or her stomach. She clutched her middle. "God says it's a baby, Taz. I don't care what you think. If I have the abortion, I kill our baby."

He cussed under his breath. "God says you shouldn't have slept with me, isn't that right?" His voice had become a menacing hiss. "Do what you have to do to get rid of it. No one's forcing me to be a father."

Andi was still thinking what to say in response when she realized he'd hung up on her. How dare he talk to her that way? Throwing it in her face that she'd slept with him, when he was the one who had talked her into it. She began to shiver, disgusted with herself for losing her virginity to someone so manipulative, so hateful. She pounded on the steering wheel and hung her head. What had she done? How could she be trapped in this nightmare? For five minutes she sat there, weeping and occasionally hitting her fist against the wheel or her own leg.

What about Rachel? Her friend wouldn't recognize her now. No one who had known her back in high school would see anything in this Andi that was familiar to the one they'd known. She was a terrible person, cheap and used and without a hope in the world. If she drove her car off a cliff, everyone would be better off. Her parents would be sad, of course, but they would get over the loss. That way they'd never have to know that she'd slept with Taz, or that she'd had an abortion.

But gradually a thought began to dawn on her. Maybe when the baby was conceived under such horrific conditions, abortion was the only answer. Certainly she didn't want to be linked to Taz the rest of her life. And what were her other options? For a split instant she could hear Ashley Baxter Blake at the crisis pregnancy clinic telling her about adoption—how beautiful it could be to give her child the gift of life with a family praying for a baby.

Pregnant with Taz's baby for nine months? Facing her parents and their circle of Hollywood friends and investors? Having the whole entertainment world know that Keith Ellison—Christian producer—had a daughter dealing with an unwanted pregnancy? The picture was too horrific to imagine. She needed to get into the city, call Sherry, and find her way to her friend's house. By tonight it would be over, the agonizing behind her. Andi wiped her tears and pulled her car back onto the road, back up the on-ramp onto the freeway. Traffic had built up and she inched her way into the slow lane.

She had forty minutes before her appointment, and she couldn't be late.

LISA ELLISON FELT UNEASY FROM THE moment her daughter drove away earlier that afternoon. Something wasn't right. Yes, in the year that Andi had been living on her own at Indiana University she was bound to have gotten used to a certain sense of freedom, and of course she had made friends that Lisa and Keith knew nothing about.

But the two of them had just landed in Bloomington. They weren't even unpacked, and with the meetings and busyness ahead, Andi might not get another chance to spend this sort of time with them. So why the sudden rush to head to the city? Keith was caught up in phone calls back to LA, and discussions with Dayne about the theatrical release for *The Last Letter*, so Lisa was forced to keep her fears to herself.

Her daughter might have changed considerably. She might be suffering from depression and unsure of her faith. But Lisa still knew her, and something about this trip to Indianapolis simply didn't add up. By three that afternoon, Lisa wandered back to Andi's bedroom and sat on the corner of her mattress. *Dear God, my daughter's in trouble. I can feel it. But there's nothing I can do to reach her, Lord.* Lisa put her hand on the familiar bedspread and ran her fingers over the soft cotton. None of this would've happened if Rachel hadn't died. The girl's death had rocked Andi's world and opened possibilities she hadn't considered before. Doubts about God she hadn't dared imagine.

Lisa stood and wandered slowly around the room. Andi had moved her things from the dorm and already she'd unpacked her belongings. The photo of Rachel that Andi loved so dearly stood on her small bookcase in the corner of her room. Lisa went to it and picked up the picture. Sweet Rachel. Such a good influence on Andi after they'd returned from Indonesia. Andi had come back to the States looking for life, for adventures she hadn't experienced on the mission field. But Rachel had kept her grounded, convincing her that the best adventures were those taken with the Lord.

Sunlight streamed through the window revealing a layer of dust along the top of the bookcase. Lisa absently used the arm of her sweatshirt to remove the dust. The layer came off easily, the way she wished it would with Andi's heart.

She glanced around and her eyes fell on a few pieces of notebook paper in the nearby trash can. She recognized Andi's handwriting on them, and she bent down, lifting them from the container. A few scribblings, dates and addresses. Nothing important. She stacked the notes on Andi's bedside table and returned to the window again. With every breath she could feel it. *Something's wrong with her, God, something very bad.* The ache in her soul was absolute proof, a heaviness that wouldn't be relieved until she bathed her daughter in prayer.

Slowly, and with all the love she could muster, she dropped to her knees and covered her face with her hands. Then, for the next thirty minutes, she prayed for Andi as if both their lives depended on it. She begged God to protect Andi and guard her, to grant her peace and clarity and to remind her of the truth. "Put your angels around her, Father. Whatever's taking her to the city, meet her there." She begged God over and over again, barely aware of her tears. "If she's pregnant, convince her to tell us." Lisa wasn't sure what else she could do on that topic. The counselor had asked Andi point-blank—and Andi had denied being pregnant.

So what was this terrible hurt in Lisa's heart, the awful certainty that something terrible was about to happen to Andi even at this very moment? She kept praying, committing Andi to the Lord, and beseeching Him for His protection over her daughter. When she was finally finished, when she pulled herself wearily to her feet and looked out the window again at some far-off place in the clear summer sky, Lisa was no closer to knowing what her daughter was doing in Indianapolis, or what sort of trouble she might be in. But she was sure of this much: No matter how much she and Keith loved Andi, God loved her more. So much more. And this afternoon—whatever Andi was doing—God would be with her.

For now, that would have to be enough.

Twenty-One

TRAFFIC GREW WORSE AS ANDI NEARED the city, and she chided herself for not being more mindful of the possible delays. Of course there'd be traffic on a Friday afternoon. Andi had just hoped most of the traffic would be heading out of the city, not into it. Twenty minutes passed, and finally Andi was at the turn-off for Sherry's rented house and the IU Indianapolis campus. According to the directions from Google, the clinic was only a few miles away. She drove off the freeway at the next exit and pulled into the parking lot of a place called Megan's Diner. It looked fairly upscale, the neighborhood one of the nicer ones on the outer edges of the city. But time was ticking away, and she silently willed Sherry to answer as she called her friend's cell number.

Instead, there was no answer, so Andi tried again. *Come on, Sherry ... don't let me down.* The phone rang and rang, but again the call went to her friend's voicemail. Thick walls of anxiety closed in around Andi. She hadn't counted on this. In her wallet was a debit card with access to barely enough money to pay for the abortion, and a ten-dollar bill. She didn't have money for a cab or a hotel room. Frantically, she hit Redial four more times, but Sherry never answered her phone.

Andi locked her car doors and leaned her head against her steering wheel. She had no address for Sherry, no land line, and none of the other girls' cell numbers. No way to reach her except the way she'd been trying—and that wasn't working. Something must've come up, but that wouldn't help Andi now. She checked the time on her phone. A quarter till four. Fifteen minutes and she was supposed to be walking through the doors of the clinic. Even if she reached Sherry this moment she wouldn't have time to get to the clinic by four. And she couldn't go by herself.

Her heartbeat jumped around, from slow and erratic to speeding fast. What was she supposed to do now? Turn around and go home? And if so, what would she tell her parents? They would be completely suspicious if she tried to explain how her friends didn't answer, and how they must not have been expecting her. They'd definitely be wary if she explained she was going again next Friday.

For as terrible as the past hour had been, Andi realized she was hungry. She hadn't eaten since breakfast, and then only a couple scrambled eggs. She had no choice but to go into the diner and find something cheap on the menu—a salad, maybe. Then she could keep trying Sherry, and eventually her friend would answer. They would laugh about the miscommunication, and Andi could stay the night with her and the girls. When the weekend was over, she would reschedule the abortion for Monday afternoon. Yes, that's what she'd have to do. Besides, she wanted to stay in Indianapolis to avoid the Brandon Paul visit anyway.

She climbed out, locked her car, and headed into the restaurant. Inside, she was seated at a table near the back—adjacent to a pretty woman and her three children. All of them were very attractive, and Andi noticed they spoke with a strong accent. Something European, maybe.

Andi checked the menu. She had enough money for an order of cheese sticks, a side salad, and water. Nothing more. If the bill was too high, she'd have to use her debit card and then she wouldn't have enough money for the abortion. She'd earned the money working part-time jobs for a photo shop near campus in Bloomington. Between that and the hundred dollars a month her parents gave her, she had saved up enough for the clinic.

Her cell phone was still in her hand. *Come on. Answer the*

phone. She hit Redial again, but still Sherry didn't pick up. Three more times she tried before the waitress walked up. The girl wasn't much older than she was, and after Andi placed her order the waitress hesitated. "Hey ... are you okay?"

Her tears came despite the fact that she tried everything in her power to stop them. "Y-y-yes." She dabbed at her cheeks with her fingertips. "Just a long day."

The waitress looked uncomfortable, like she wanted to help but she had no idea what to do. Finally she backed up some. "Okay, well ... if you need anything, let me know."

Andi nodded, refusing to look up. If she needed anything? She didn't know where to begin. With shaking fingers she lifted her cell phone once more and tried three final times to reach Sherry. The last time she left a message. "Hey, Sherry," her voice gave away the fact that she was crying. "I missed my appointment. If you could ... if you could call me back ... that'd be great."

Her tears kept coming, even though she wasn't sobbing or making any noise. It was like her heart had sprung a leak and nothing was going to stop it from breaking right there in Megan's Diner. She forced herself to stay quiet, praying that no one besides the waitress would see her meltdown. What was she supposed to do now? Drive home and find a clinic in Bloomington? Tell her parents the truth? Every possibility only made the walls close in a little tighter around her, until she was sure she would suffocate before her dinner arrived.

But even with tears falling onto her lap, Andi couldn't help but hear the conversation at the table beside her.

"We're starting a band, did I tell you?" The voice belonged to a boy in his mid teens, maybe.

Andi blinked back her tears and dabbed her eyes with her napkin. As she did she stole a look at the family. The boy talking was tall and blond, maybe sixteen or seventeen. "Nathalie's going to sing and Kenny'll play the piano."

"Really?" Their mother was a pretty dark-haired woman, her

eyes full of life and something Andi inherently knew was a strong faith in Christ. The same eyes her parents had. The eyes she'd had before this year at college. Their mom's expression brightened. "What about you, Mr. Marco?"

The oldest teenage boy stuck out his chest. "I'm bass guitar and drums."

"Both?" Their mom was teasing now. "People will pay to see that."

"Not at the same time." The middle boy's eyes were wide with possibility. "Some songs I'll do the guitar and he'll do the drums."

"Actually, I might have to do the drums most of the time." Marco swapped a look with his brother and sister. "Kenny, you'll play guitar or piano. Depending on the song."

"Right. That's a better plan." Kenny grinned at Marco and then at their mother. "What? You don't think we can do it?"

"Oh, yes. With your faith and determination, you can do anything you want. Just like your father."

"He's meeting us, right?" The little girl was darling, beautiful and blonde, with striking blue eyes. The family clearly wasn't from the United States.

"Yes, honey. But he can't stay long. He has a meeting tonight."

The girl put her elbows on the table and frowned. "Another meeting."

"We knew it would be like this when we agreed to a year abroad." She smiled at the kids, and then without warning she turned her eyes to Andi. With a slight nod of her head, she seemed to express a sympathy and caring that Andi desperately needed.

Andi could only imagine how she must've looked. Tear-streaked and swollen-eyed. But something told her she didn't have to worry about this woman judging her, so she found the slightest smile and returned the nod. Then she looked immediately back at her lap. The woman's children didn't seem to notice Andi, or the silent greeting from their mother in her direction.

They chattered on about their pending band, and how they were going to sing at churches all over America, and how they couldn't book any dates during soccer season.

"I might be a pro soccer player." The middle boy, Kenny, sounded happy and confident. "When the band's not playing."

Andi recognized young Kenny's tone, because once a lifetime ago that had been her — ready to take on the world, certain that success would find her wherever she turned, trusting on God's grace and goodness to take her into a life of happiness and joy. She was still listening to the family's happy banter when the children's father hurried up and hugged and kissed each of them.

Again Andi couldn't help but discretely watch.

"Felix, you smell wonderful." His wife looked totally in love as she snuggled up next to her handsome husband. "Hard to believe you've put in a day at the office."

"It's all so new and amazing. So much to take back to Switzerland."

So that was it. The family was here for a year from Switzerland. Andi couldn't help but feel jealous of the joy they had together. This was how she'd pictured her life, right? Successful and faith-filled, like Katy and Dayne Matthews. Happy and adventurous like the family a few feet away. She dabbed at her eyes again and willed herself to be invisible.

The waitress brought food for the family, and then for her, and like the woman had warned, her husband didn't stay long. When he left it was with promises of watching a movie together when he got home. "Friday's movie night," he grinned at them. Then he was off and running. Once he was gone, the kids finished picking at their plates, still talking about their band and the songs they'd write together. They paid their bill, and Andi did the same.

She was trying to decide what to do next, whether she should sit in her car waiting for Sherry to call back, or drive home and hope for some sane-sounding explanation for her parents. As she sorted through the fragmented thoughts clouding her mind, Andi looked up. The woman at the next table was looking straight at her, sympathy marking her expression. Andi wanted to wave off the attention, explain that she wasn't worth the woman interrupting her meal and her joyous time with her family. But just then, the woman whispered something to her kids. She stood and approached Andi. "Can I talk to you?"

There was no way Andi could reject the woman's offer. To do so would've caused more of a scene than she'd clearly already made. Andi nodded and turned her back slightly to the woman's children. She waited, not wanting to let the woman see her eyes.

"I've been watching you." Her voice was soft, rich with understanding and a willingness to help. "You're very upset."

"Yes." What could she say? The woman was a stranger … she wouldn't want to get involved in Andi's messy life. "I'm … sorry. You were having a nice time together."

"You didn't bother us." She leaned in a little closer. "Are you hurt? Is someone threatening you?"

"No." Andi looked up, and she realized how desperately she needed help. Even from a stranger. "I … I live in Bloomington, but … I had a doctor's appointment today. My friend was supposed to meet me here, but she didn't answer her phone and I missed the appointment, and now I'm not sure what to do. I was supposed to stay with my friend, but now I don't know where to stay." Andi couldn't believe she was spilling her entire story. Something about the woman's patient way of listening encouraged her to continue. "I can't afford a hotel, but now my appointment will have to be Monday, so I really need to stay. If only I could get hold of my friend."

"My name's Lucia Kunzmann." She held out her hand and patted Andi's fingers. "What's your name, dear?"

"Andi. Andi Ellison." She wanted to add that she came from a great family, and she wasn't a crazy person. But maybe the woman could already tell that somehow.

"My husband, Felix, and I are in the US for a year because of his work. He's an international banker. But in our hearts we're missionaries." She smiled and it warmed the space between them. "We pray for God to bring people into our lives who need help." She paused, her smile never wavering. "You can stay with us tonight, if you'd like. We live just a few blocks from here."

Andi could hardly believe what she was hearing. Was the woman serious? Would she really take in a stranger like this? She studied the woman, her trusting eyes. "You're a Christian, aren't you?"

"I am. We've been involved in youth ministry and counseling all our lives. We love Jesus very much." Lucia gave Andi's hand a quick, tender squeeze. "You too?"

"Yes." She thought about the choices she'd made the last year, the ways she'd compromised her faith and taken on viewpoints contrary to God's Word. She thought about the abortion she should've already had by now. She looked down at her hands. "At least ... I was."

"I thought so." Lucia ignored Andi's doubt. "God told me you were a believer." She stood and waited for Andi to look up again. "So you'll come? Be our guest tonight?"

The woman seemed sent straight from the Lord, exactly what she needed at this moment. She gathered her purse and stood, feeling desperately awkward. "It would just be for one night. If you really don't mind."

"We'd love it." Lucia put her arm around Andi's shoulders and walked her the few steps to her own table. "Kids, this is Andi. She's staying with us tonight." She introduced Marco, Kenny, and Nathalie. The kids seemed completely at ease with the idea that their mother had just invited a complete stranger to spend the night with them. The only explanation was the one Lucia had already given. The family lived out their days looking for people to help, looking for opportunities to be missionaries where God had placed them. In the year away from her parents, it was a concept Andi had almost forgotten. And as she and the Kunzmann family walked out to the parking lot, Andi had a sudden and certain thought.

Somewhere in Bloomington her parents must be praying for her.

IN A PERFECT WORLD, NO ONE would ever have to know that Cody's mother had been taken by ambulance to Bloomington Hospital, or that after they ran tests the truth was painfully clear. Yes, she'd been beat up, but that wasn't why she nearly died that day. The reason was the drugs. If Cody could've hidden the fact from all of Bloomington, he would've. But Landon Blake was one of the paramedics, and John Baxter was a doctor in the area. People would see Cody here—the families of football players, teachers at Clear Creek High visiting a relative. Bloomington was a small town. People were bound to find out.

After pumping her stomach and giving her medication to offset the way her organs were starting to fail, his mother was alive. But Cody could barely bring himself to talk to her. He was sitting by her bedside now, and she was sleeping, stable after hours of critical care. Bailey would be out tonight with Tim, no doubt, or home with her family—doing everything Cody would've loved to have been doing right now. Anything but wrestling with the blaring realization that his mother was using again.

He wasn't sure how long he sat there, but eventually his thoughts took him back to Iraq—when he'd been a prisoner of war. No matter how bad things got back then he believed he'd find a way out. He prayed and trusted God and determined that one day he would be free—and when the day came, he was ready.

But drugs? Watching his mother slowly kill herself? There was no escaping this prison, no way around the fact that he was the only one who could care for her. And even then, any day, at any minute she could take a fatal dose or wind up crossing paths with the wrong drug dealer. She could be arrested or killed or die in a scene like the one he'd found earlier today.

It was a life of guilt and shame and regret, and Cody couldn't free himself from it no matter what. He loved his mom, so he would stay. He would see her through the ups and downs to the end—whenever that came. He would pray and he would believe she could be set free if she chose Jesus over her addiction. The way he had done so many years ago. He would never give up, but he would never be free either. And that realization made him miss Bailey and her family until his body physically hurt from the pain.

Finally when he couldn't take another minute watching his mom sleep off the effects of the drugs, when he wasn't sure he could draw a breath without hearing Bailey's voice, Cody stepped out of the room and called her number. It was late by then, almost ten o'clock, and he was pretty sure he'd be interrupting some sort of date night she'd be having with Tim. But he didn't care. He wouldn't take up much of her time.

She answered on the fourth ring, just when he was about to hang up.

"Hello?" Her voice was soft, and she sounded sleepy. "Cody?"

"Hi." Tears scratched at his eyes and made his throat too tight to talk. He coughed quietly. He didn't want to wake up his mother. Not now. "Am I … are you with Tim?"

"No." She yawned. "I'm in bed. The boys are going fishing early with my dad. We turned in early."

He wanted to ask if she'd seen Tim that night, but he had no right. His jealousy over the guy was getting out of hand. He massaged his brow and closed his eyes. "Bailey, I … I was wrong earlier. How I treated you." He pictured the way she'd looked—at the football field—begging him to stay and talk to her. Her long brown hair blowing softly alongside her beautiful face, her blue eyes piercing his. Her long dancer legs and slight frame—no longer the kid she'd been when he had lived with them. She was so irresistible he'd had no choice but to leave. Otherwise she would've seen what had to be obvious to anyone.

He was in love with her.

"It's okay." She sounded more awake now, and a depth filled her tone. "I wanted you to know I'm done struggling. With Tim ... with being his girlfriend." She sighed, long and slow. "I hate how he treated you at the cafeteria, and I don't know. Everything. I was gonna ask you to pray for me."

"I will." He savored her voice, the goodness of her. He held on as if by doing so he could will her here beside him. "I always pray for you. I told you that."

"But today ... you didn't want to talk to me." Her tone told him how hurt she'd been by his actions. "You've never been like that before."

"I know. I'm sorry." How could he explain that he could feel her slipping away? That a chasm lay between the reality of her life and the reality of his, and it was growing all the time? *God ... if You'd only give me a chance with her ... I'd love her with every breath, the rest of my days.* But even as he uttered the silent prayer, he knew it could never happen. Their worlds were simply too different. He clutched the phone more tightly, pressed it to his ear. "I'll let you get back to sleep." He wanted to say it, tell her how much he loved her. But it wouldn't be fair to either of them. No matter what troubles she was having with Tim, he was better for her. Cody had known that since the day he returned from Iraq.

"Okay, well ..." Bailey paused, as if she didn't want to get off the phone. "Maybe you should get some sleep too."

"Yeah." He looked back at the hospital bed, at his mother still passed out from the effects of her drug binge. He turned away. "Sleep would be good." He wanted to tell Bailey, wanted to pour out his heart and beg her to come down to the hospital with him. Just so he could hold her hand and believe somehow everything was going to get better. But he could never tell her what had happened that afternoon. The truth would only put more distance between them. No, hearing her voice, feeling her against his heart this way, would have to be enough.

"Hey, you were amazing today." Her words were a caress against his wounded soul. "My dad talked about you all the way home. He says you're very talented."

"Thanks." The compliment opened a window to a future that must have still existed outside the prison of the hospital room, the prison of his mother's addiction. "I thought I'd love it, but it's more than that. Really, Bailey. Like I was born to do this."

"I'm not surprised." She laughed lightly, keeping their conversation quiet since everyone else was asleep. "I mean, think about it, Cody. All those boring film sessions with my dad? Sitting there all those hours? We all should've known you'd be a coach one day. It was God's destiny for you." A softness filled her voice. "And look how good you are."

"Hmm." This was the best he'd felt all day. "That means a lot. Thanks."

Again he had the sense Bailey wanted to talk longer, but there was nothing to say. He had no right to let the conversation go longer, and she must've sensed his desire to keep the call brief. "I'm glad you called."

"Me too." He held onto these final seconds, the way her words felt as close as breath against his skin. "I needed to hear your voice." As soon as he said that, he wondered if he'd gone too far, let her see too much of how he was feeling.

But she didn't act upset or taken aback. "Same here. Because now I know you're not mad at me anymore."

"I never was." Again he longed to tell her everything he was feeling. But it was time to go. "Good night, Bailey."

"Good night."

He clicked the End button on his phone and slipped it back into his jeans pocket. Then he stepped into his mother's room and fell back against the first wall he came to. He closed his eyes and willed himself to remember Bailey's voice, her words. The nearness of her. If there was a way, he would run from the hospital room, from everything about his past and his mother's past, and he wouldn't stop until he had Bailey Flanigan in his arms.

But that could never happen. It was wrong to think of Bailey breaking up with Tim, no matter what she said. Wrong to think about her dating a recovering alcoholic whose mother was in the throes of drug addiction. Bailey wasn't the girl for him, though she would forever set the standard for everything good about love. But that was just it—Bailey was too good. He'd known it for a long time, and the sooner he acknowledged that to his heart the better.

Somewhere out there, Cody had to believe God had a girl for him—a young woman who would love him despite his past, and who together with him would raise the sort of family he still believed in. A family who laughed and prayed together, cried and played together. The sort of family he believed in because once—for a short season—he'd been a part of a family like that. A family he would love forever.

The Flanigan family.

Twenty-Two

In about twelve hours, Brandon Paul would be in Bloomington, Indiana, meeting with the producers of *Unlocked*. Which meant tonight was the absolute last night he could party this hard for a long time. A week at least.

"Around back!" The music in the custom Escalade was loud, the way Brandon liked it. Beyoncé singing about her halo. Brandon crooned along with her. "Baby I can see your halo ..."

His driver whipped the SUV to the back door of Club 21—the hottest new spot in Los Angeles. The paparazzi were waiting, but Brandon didn't care. It wasn't going in that got him in trouble. It was coming out. For that he'd have to be a little more careful.

Brandon gave the cameras a quick grin and ducked inside. Part of his entourage was already waiting—a couple guys he'd known back in his middle school football-playing days, and a new round of girls. Always a new round. The club was dark and loud and packed, the music pulsing.

"You're finally here!" TJ, one of his friends, slapped him on the back. "We got a whole cheerleading team in the private room."

"Really?" Brandon felt the thrill of all that lay ahead.

"Nah." TJ laughed a little too hard, too loud. He was probably already on something—cocaine, maybe. "But a couple of the girls are hot. Come on ... they got a sick spread back there."

Brandon followed his friend toward the private room, and he realized he should've done something to disguise himself. A hat or dark glasses. Something. His arrival was causing too much commotion. People were pressing in, shoving paper at him, shouting for an autograph. Screaming his name.

"Let us through!" TJ held up his hand and pushed back, creating space.

For a moment, panic rose in Brandon's heart. He had no bodyguards here, no one to stop the crowd. If they didn't back off, Brandon and TJ could be crushed. That was the reality. TJ shouted again, and another minute of finagling and they were through to the private room.

Brandon looked around. TJ had greatly exaggerated. The room held a few of their buddies and a handful of girls. The night would be calmer than he expected. He stretched, still shaking off the sensation of being suffocated. As he did, a girl walked up — a brunette he'd never seen before. Her eyes were red and puffy, and she couldn't walk straight.

Higher than a kite, he thought. *Just the way I like 'em*. "Hey, sweetheart, what's your name?" Brandon met her partway across the room, leaving almost no space between them. The music wasn't as loud in here, but the lights were dim. Brandon squinted at her, trying to make out her face. "Tell me your name."

The girl did, but Brandon forgot it almost instantly. Names didn't matter. He downed a couple of whiskey shots and felt himself loosen up. The girl was telling him about her modeling career, something about a runway job she had next weekend, when her friend walked up.

"Brandon Paul ... what's this I hear about you doing a Christian film?"

Heat filled his face and he chuckled, buying time. "You must have the wrong guy."

"No. I read it in the paper." She eyed him, obviously doubting that he would be aligned with anything Christian. "'Brandon Paul to star in *Unlocked*.' That's what it said."

He laughed again, like this was the funniest thing he'd heard in a long time. "*Unlocked* was a national bestseller." He grabbed another shot from a passing tray and downed it. "The author's a Christian, but don't worry, baby." He walked up to the new girl and kissed her full on the mouth. Really kissed her. It lasted half a minute before he pulled back. "There. That ease your doubts?" He grinned at the girl and her friend, and he took a few steps toward a table where people were doing coke. "Don't think I'm turning Christian any time soon."

He laughed then and he laughed as he set about doing blow with the guys. No one mentioned anything Christian the rest of the night, so he'd done what he wanted to do. He'd stopped anyone talking about him like that. Craziest thing, right? Brandon Paul doing a Christian film. He laughed at the idea the rest of the night. Never happen, not in a million years.

But no matter how often Brandon laughed about the comment, the scene haunted him. His words stayed with him while he was doing lines and later when he and some of the guys downed a few more shots. He skipped the girls. Couldn't concentrate long enough to care. By the time TJ helped him back to his ride, he was wasted and even then the sound of his own voice screamed at him.

Don't think I'm turning Christian any time soon ... any time soon ... any time soon.

Was that really how he felt? Could he make jokes about a faith he'd run from all his life? He collapsed in the backseat of the empty SUV and closed his eyes. Dimly he could hear the sound of cameras outside the vehicle, but he didn't care. TJ wouldn't let them get a clear shot of him like this, and with the tinted windows, he was safe from the paparazzi.

But was he safe from God?

Fear whispered in his ear and blew hot breath in his face. He thought about *Unlocked* and everything it stood for. Why was he compelled to do a picture like that when everything the girl had said was true? The book *was* written by a Christian novelist, and the producers were definitely Christians. Even Dayne Matthews—whose reputation was once bigger than Brandon's. He put his hands over his ears and tried to block out the noise in his head.

This was crazy. He was Brandon Paul. Top star of NTM Studios. Heartthrob for teenage girls across the country. Every producer wanted him in one of their movies, right? So why choose a film like *Unlocked*? He felt sick to his stomach, scared about his flippant words. What had his mother told him once? The voices from a dozen conversations that night ran through his head, but he could hear his mother's above the rest. *Being a big star doesn't mean anything to God, Brandon ... one day you'll have to stop running. I only hope it's not too late.*

Not too late ... not too late...

"Stop it!" His words slurred together.

"'Sup, man?" The driver looked over his shoulder. "You chill, B?"

"Chill. Way chill." He slumped back against the seat. "Get me home."

But even that didn't help, because once he was alone in his palatial hillside house, the voices only got louder. His own most of all. *Don't think I'm turning Christian any time soon ...*

The last thing he thought about before he crashed was his little co-star. Sweetheart Annie Sullivan. Innocent and wide-eyed. When they met for the first time, Annie peered up at him with those pretty blue eyes and said, "Do you love Jesus, Brandon? Because you should."

He hadn't even answered her. Just playfully flicked one of her braids and grinned. "You ask a lot of questions, little Annie."

And that was that.

But now he couldn't get the child's face out of his mind. Annie Sullivan. So untainted by everything Hollywood, everything fame and fortune could someday do to her. Brandon put the pillow over his head and breathed through the crack. But that didn't stop the voices. He had all the money in the world, but he couldn't buy the one thing he wanted. The thing Annie Sullivan still had. The thing that eluded him every night, whether he was home alone or out getting wasted.

Peace of mind.

Especially tonight, with his own words keeping him awake, preventing sleep from getting a word in edgewise. Had he really said that about not being a Christian? Who was he like? Some Bible guy, some jerk who announced to the crowd something about not knowing Jesus, right? Brandon tried to remember the story from his childhood Sunday school days. Was it Paul … He rolled onto his other side, hating the dizziness, wanting the drugs and drink gone from his body now. No, it wasn't Paul. He thought back, picturing himself as he'd once been. Just like Annie Sullivan.

But now he was just like … like …

He opened his eyes wide, the pillow still smashed to his head. "Peter!" he muttered. That was it; he was like Peter. Denying Jesus. He thought about the scene back at the club and he knew—for absolute certain—that if the girl asked the same question again, he'd answer it exactly the same. *Don't think I'm turning Christian any time soon …* The words smothered him and spat at him, strangled him and mocked him. When he finally fell asleep he was sure of one thing. Fear was watching him, and it would be there waiting for him in the morning. Because he had lied to the girl at the club. The truth was something the world didn't know about Brandon Paul.

He had given his life to Jesus a long time ago.

KEITH PULLED INTO DAYNE'S LONG DRIVEWAY and parked his car near the front door. He hadn't been to Dayne and Katy's lake house, and though the place was bound to be nice any time of the year, here in June it was breathtaking. The views stretched out across the entire lake and the foliage around the house looked like something from a movie.

Appropriate, Keith told himself as he walked up to the door. He stopped before he knocked and he looked out, savoring the view. *God ... I've been looking forward to this meeting for a year. Please be with us today ... let us see whether Brandon's a right fit for this film.* He paused, his heart and mind torn. As much as he wanted to be here, he agreed with Lisa. Something was wrong with Andi, and if he had his way, he'd be driving to Indianapolis, finding her and bringing her home where she belonged. Since she'd been gone, she'd sent only a few text messages. Every time they tried to call her, she didn't answer her phone. Both he and Lisa were frustrated at themselves for not getting more information about the place where she was staying. They didn't know the girls' names or where they lived in the city.

In her last text, Andi had said she was fine, and she'd be home Tuesday. *Sorry I haven't been around when you call. God's with me here. Please don't worry.* And that was that. Lisa texted back right away, telling Andi they were going to call, asking her to answer her phone this time. But Andi neither replied with another text nor picked up her phone. Andi wasn't missing; she wasn't in danger—at least as far as they could tell. They could drive around Indianapolis all day and night and still not be any closer to finding her.

Which meant there was nothing Keith and Lisa could do but wait.

Keith knocked on the door and heard Dayne's voice inviting him in. He made his way to the back den where the meeting was set to take place, and there they were—two of America's most recognizable faces. Dayne Matthews and Brandon Paul. The table was round and solid mahogany. Dayne and Brandon sat opposite each other, and after a round of greetings, Keith took the seat between them.

Dayne's demeanor was easygoing, light-hearted. If anyone in the world could relate to Brandon Paul, it was Dayne. Keith decided to take a more passive role in the conversation, observe Brandon's actions and personality, analyze his motives for wanting to star in *Unlocked*.

"So how's the party scene?" Dayne leaned back, his pose casually confident, like something a magazine would run on the cover page.

Keith watched Dayne, amazed. This wasn't anything like Dayne had acted any other time the two of them had been together. Dayne was humble and funny, a family man through and through. But clearly he still knew how to play the Hollywood role. Not only that, but his acting was still top-notch. Only by coming across as relatable to Brandon Paul would either of them catch a glimpse of the young star with his guard down. Already his method seemed to be working.

Brandon linked his hands behind his head and grinned at Dayne. "You remember the days."

"Things were crazy." Dayne stopped short of giving off any sense of approval. But he raised his brow and let out a low whistle. "I mean so crazy."

"It's worse now. All the private rooms at the clubs." He laughed, and then just as quickly he seemed to remember where he was and who he was talking to. He eased himself into a straighter, more business-like position. "But we're here to talk about *Unlocked*, right?"

"It's a great story."

"Love it." Brandon looked more serious now. No question he truly liked the story. "Read it three times. Really, man." He looked at Keith. "You've read it, obviously."

"I have. It's phenomenal." Keith leaned his forearms on the

table and looked straight at Brandon in a way that was just short of intimidating. "The fact that it was inspired by the author's sister makes it even more amazing. It's a great responsibility to develop a film on a project this special."

Brandon nodded, but his attention seemed to have slipped. He reached for the can of Coke sitting in front of him, popped the top, and took a long sip. "Which reminds me. I haven't read the latest version of the script, but there's gotta be a love scene, right?"

Dayne glanced at Keith, deferring the answer. As much as Dayne had done to get up to speed, he hadn't read *Unlocked* yet. The screenplay, yes. But not the novel. Keith cleared his throat and tried not to sound too intense. "For your character?"

The surprise on Brandon's face told them he was surprised by the question. "Yeah, of course." He looked from Keith to Dayne. "My audience will expect that, don't you think?"

A warning light flashed in Keith's mind. "The guy's autistic. He has friendships and tender moments." Keith hesitated. He couldn't believe they were having this conversation. "But a love scene?"

"It's not a deal breaker." Brandon shrugged, as if to say he wasn't going to make any demands on the topic. "Just think it'd help at the box office if I get a make-out scene or two." He flashed his famous grin. "The girls love that sort of thing."

Enough time had been spent on the issue. Keith shook his head. "No love scenes. No kissing, no sex. It's not that sort of picture." He didn't let his frustration show but kept his tone matter-of-fact. "It's great we're talking about this. That way we won't have any surprises later."

The conversation shifted to the supporting cast and Brandon's favorite choices for his co-star, the peer who introduces him to the arts. "I want someone fresh, someone new." Brandon pulled a sheet of paper from his bag. "Here's a few ideas from my agent, but the girl can't be all Hollywood weird, you know?"

Something in Dayne's eyes softened, and Keith figured he was thinking about his own past, how he'd come to know his wife, Katy. He'd seen her once at a Bloomington Christian Kids Theater performance, and he'd been struck by the fact that the girls in Hollywood lacked her small-town charm, her innocence. He'd done everything in his power to cast Katy in his next film—the impact she'd made on him in a single evening was that powerful.

Now here was Brandon feeling the same way, that only a girl with true innocence could play opposite him in a film as powerful as *Unlocked*. Keith jotted down Brandon's preference. "We'll take a look at your agent's suggestions."

"I mean, seriously, you probably have girls around here who would do a better job with the part than the girls lining up around the block at LA casting calls."

"She's out there," Dayne grinned at Brandon. "Keith and I are asking God to put together the perfect cast for this film. It'll happen; I can feel it."

Keith wasn't sure, but he thought Brandon reacted negatively to the mention of God. Nothing overt, just a downward glance and a slight change in his mood. Again he couldn't let the moment pass. "What are your thoughts on God, Brandon?" Keith didn't want to come across pushy, but they had to discuss this. "You understand this film will have a strong faith message, right?"

Seconds passed while Brandon struggled with the question. He leaned back in his seat and squirmed in a way that showed he was beyond uncomfortable. "Well," he raised his hands and let them fall back down to the table. "It's not a Christian film. I mean, there won't be a lot of preaching in it or anything. That's my understanding."

"The faith message will be authentic, integrated into the story the way it is in the book," Keith wanted to tackle this part of the discussion, because he was the producer with the reputation for bringing faith to Hollywood. "But the message will be there." Keith looked at his notes and then back at Brandon. "Some things to think about ... you'll be asked about why you chose this film. People will want to know your stance on Christianity and faith. Are you ready for that?"

Again Brandon seemed troubled by the question. He shifted his body, clearly antsy. "I'm an actor." He let loose a nervous laugh. "I'd like to avoid the topic of faith and defer to the character. The character's faith experience, the character's view on Jesus, that sort of thing." He raised an eyebrow toward Dayne. "That'll work, right?"

"Probably." Dayne was still playing the role of fellow actor, and not so much the businessman probing Brandon Paul for proof of his commitment. But his eyes told them he took this part of the meeting very seriously. "It's less important what you say than how you live. A film like this, people will be watching. More closely than ever."

Brandon laughed again, more in disbelief. "So, you're saying I have to be perfect? Clean up my image?"

"Your image is actually pretty clean." Dayne wasn't laughing. "I think it's important to keep it that way. Stay low on the paparazzi radar. Do your best to honor the faith of the character—even if you can't relate to him on a personal level."

In some ways this was nothing new. Producers often met with their key actors to lay out what was expected of them based on the character. A male lead in a story about the devastating effects of alcoholism could hardly be caught drunk in the clubs during the filming of the movie without damage to the project. "It's like any picture." Keith searched Brandon's eyes for even a hint of rebellion. "The off-camera choices of the actors always affect the film."

Brandon nodded slowly, and the professionalism that had

been wavering for the last couple minutes returned. "I understand that." He glanced at Dayne and then Keith. "I'll lay low, guys. I won't let you down. This is a big movie for me. My agent thinks it's a chance to win a couple awards, even." He grinned. "A year from now we could be talking Oscars."

Keith wanted to say that first they needed to talk about committing to the current script. But he chose his words carefully. "Okay, then ... I'm sure we'll have ongoing talks about the faith element in the movie. And as for the script, I've got a copy of the latest draft. You can get into it tonight and we can talk about it tomorrow."

The meeting went another hour before they broke for dinner. Lisa and Dayne's wife, Katy, were back at the Ellison house unpacking, so Keith offered to drive the fifteen minutes back into town for sandwiches. Even if their wives had been available to bring in a meal, Keith would've jumped at the chance to be alone for a while, sort through the implications of the first couple hours with Brandon Paul.

He flipped on his radio—a Christian talk station—and stared at the pretty drive ahead. A pastor was talking about living for God. His voice was passionate. "That means you take a hard look at what drives you. If it's your wife and kids, you're out of alignment with God ... if it's your promotion at the office, you're off base. If it's the climb to get ahead of the pack, your priorities are askew." He paused. "Folks, hear me on this. Living for God means waking every day with the same question in mind: How can I get through the next twelve hours in God's power, accomplishing His purposes, and concerned only about pleasing Him?"

Keith agreed with every word, but he turned down the volume. The reminder troubled his usually calm soul. Brandon Paul wasn't sold out to God. By the sounds of it, he wasn't willing to admit to having even the slightest faith. He definitely didn't want to be aligned with Christianity.

So why were they having the meeting with the kid at all? Was it that important that Brandon Paul star in their movie? Even Brandon wanted an innocent, untainted girl as his co-star. Isn't that what the world would want in Brandon if he took the leading role, if he played an autistic teenager whose world was unlocked by the power of God through the arts?

They had two days with the young actor, but it wasn't like they could change their minds. Contracts had already been signed. This was the only chance they had to discern any threat Brandon might be to the message of the film, the power of it to change lives for Christ. The only chance to coach him on how to act and what to say during the process. And what they'd heard so far was beyond troubling. Brandon had alluded to his partying ways, joking that he kept things in control. He'd expressed a desire for a make out scene in a film where one would absolutely not be appropriate, and he'd flinched when they brought up faith. There were enough notes of concern on Keith's pad of paper that he was going to run out of space before the day was through.

For one thing, if Brandon wanted a make-out scene or a full-on sex scene, once they got into production, once a studio had agreed to fund half the picture, Keith and Dayne would struggle to keep it from happening. Brandon could add it on the spot, and if the cameras caught it and the studio liked it — the scene would appear in the film. He thought hard. It was a problem they could solve if they tackled it up front. They'd have to get with Luke Baxter quickly to make sure the final contracts were very clear about what would and wouldn't be allowed in the last edit.

But even then, Brandon was a wild card, a loose cannon who could destroy the reputation of the film and Jeremiah Productions in a single night on the town. Yes, having him in the film meant more people would see it. But was the risk worth the reward? Keith heard a text come into his phone. He picked it up and glanced at the message. It was from Andi.

Tell Mom I'm fine. Just didn't want you to worry. I'll call soon.

Keith tossed the phone back on the console. He didn't believe a word she said at this point. The old Andi would've called a few times a day, shared details of her time in Indianapolis, and talked about when she'd be home. Something was clearly wrong, and Keith felt sick that he couldn't do anything to help her. He remembered Brandon's request—that they find someone new and innocent to play his co-star. A year ago he would've thought of Andi before anyone else. She could've at least read for the part. But now she'd changed her looks and her love for God. She was distant and moody with brooding eyes where once she had shone brighter than the sun.

Andi could hardly play the part now. But if she wasn't suitable as the music student who helps unlock the world of Brandon's autistic character, then how was Brandon suitable? The only answer, the one Keith hated to admit, was that Brandon was a bigger box office draw. Period. By having him star in the film, Jeremiah Productions would become one of the most powerful moviemakers in the business.

Keith sighed and focused again on the beauty around him. *God ... give us the answers. As sunny as the day is, my heart has nothing but clouds and rain ... please guide us.*

He turned up the radio again. The preacher was just finishing, reciting a verse from Matthew 16. "Remember, friends. What good will it be for a man if he—gains the whole world, yet forfeits his soul. Live for God. Start today."

Keith couldn't have said it any better. Maybe if he'd been more involved in Andi's life this past year she wouldn't be fighting whatever she was fighting. Which meant just one question remained. If they didn't control Brandon Paul, if they gained the whole world's attention, the whole world's box office receipts, the whole world's praise and cheers ...

What exactly might they lose in the process?

Twenty-Three

ACTING LESSONS HADN'T BEEN BAILEY'S IDEA.

But after the Cross-Town Scrimmage, she talked with her mom about what the summer would hold. She had pictured lazy days by their backyard pool, swimming with her brothers, and having game nights as often as they were all together. Helping out with CKT summer camps and heading off to New York at summer's end for the audition.

Bailey's mom was always sympathetic to whatever was on her heart. But she was honest too. It was what kept them so close. That afternoon she took her time responding, but when she did, her opinion surprised Bailey. "Maybe Tim's approach to the audition is right, honey. This audition is one of the biggest breaks either of you have ever had." She gave a slight shrug. "I think it's okay that he's consumed. Passion is important when it comes to using the talents God gives us. We've always taught you kids that, right?"

Her answer was right on, and the rest of the morning Bailey wrestled with her feelings. In the end she realized it wasn't that she had a problem with Tim's passion. She had a problem with Tim. The one God had clearly pointed out earlier that day. When Katy Hart Matthews called that morning, the timing couldn't have been more perfect.

"I have an idea." Katy's voice was as cheerful as it was familiar. She went on to explain how Dayne had signed on as co-producer of Jeremiah Productions, working with Andi's dad. CKT was thriving with several directors running the shows so Katy could spend most of her time with little Sophie. "But I miss teaching." Her smile rang through in her voice. "Or maybe I just miss the Flanigans."

Katy's idea was perfect. She would bring Sophie over a few times a week. If Bailey's mom was willing to watch her, Katy would give Bailey acting lessons. And Katy was willing to start right away. It was midday Saturday and they'd already had their first lesson. Bailey was practically buzzing with excitement. They rejoined Bailey's mom and Sophie in the kitchen, and Bailey couldn't stop talking about the past hour. "Katy's so good." Bailey poured water for all of them. "It takes me back to when I was in CKT." She grinned at Katy. "We all knew you were talented, but I mean, you're so gifted. Everything you told me today ... I feel like after just one lesson I'm way more ready for the audition."

"You're a joy to work with." Katy took Sophie in her arms and cooed at her daughter. "You're a joy, too, isn't that right, Soph?" The blonde little girl giggled at Katy and tried to reach for her earring. Katy laughed and settled Sophie on her hip. "Everything in the mouth ... I know how you teethers are." She turned her attention to Bailey again. "You, you're very good, Bailey. I always saw that in you, but after today ..." Her eyes lit up a little more. "It'll be interesting to see how the audition goes. God's given you a gift, Bailey. No question about that."

They talked a while longer about Tim and his preparations for August, but Katy seemed to sense that Bailey didn't want to linger on the topic. The conversation moved around to Katy's help that morning over at the Ellison house and how Lisa Ellison was deeply worried about Andi.

"She won't return my calls," Bailey said. She took a long drink of water, picturing her roommate. "Something's very wrong with her. I've been asking God to show me how I can help."

Katy agreed that for now prayer was what Andi needed most. She shifted the talk to Jeremiah Productions and Brandon Paul's part in it. "He's in town, you know. They're meeting at our house today."

"Brandon Paul?" Bailey gasped. "Brandon Paul's at your house?" She jumped to her feet. "We should've had today's lesson in your living room."

Katy laughed. "The guys need this time." She looked at Jenny, then Bailey. "Just to make sure he's clear on what they expect."

The thought was sobering, and Bailey let her initial exuberance fade a little. "He isn't a Christian, is he?"

"Not that I know of. He doesn't have to be, but his off-screen actions will affect the film. The guys are aware of that. You can pray for them to have wisdom."

"On the other hand," Jenny raised an eyebrow, "imagine if Brandon Paul works with Dayne and Keith, and in the process he gives his life to Jesus."

"Yeah," Bailey tried to imagine the impact. "That would be something."

"Exactly." Katy didn't look in a hurry to leave. "That's why they need this time."

They caught up on the Baxter family next, how John and Elaine were coming up on their anniversary—both of them in great health and enjoying their respective families. "The biggest news is Luke and Reagan. They're looking to adopt again, so we're all praying for them. Asking that God bring about the right baby in His time. They're thinking they want a boy."

"The new little guy better be tough." Bailey gave a mock look of exhaustion. "That Tommy's a little terror."

Katy laughed. "He's getting better. Becoming a little more like Ashley's Cole. But his imagination is still stronger than all the other grandkids put together."

Next Jenny talked about summer football and how great Cody was working out as a coach for Clear Creek. At the mention of his name, a curiosity tugged at Bailey's heart. Why had he really called her last night? He'd sounded so sincere, so much more like the Cody she'd known when he lived here. All day she'd thought about texting or calling him and asking what had triggered the call.

A half hour passed quickly, and Katy and Sophie needed to leave — too soon for Bailey. She loved this, the chance to catch up with Katy again. They saw each other once in a while of course, but not like when she had lived with them, back when she and Dayne first met. It was one more reason Bailey was grateful Katy had come up with the idea. They made a plan to meet every Saturday, Monday, and Wednesday until the audition in August, and then Katy and Sophie headed home.

Bailey checked the time on the microwave and her breath caught in her throat. "Oh, no." She raced her glass to the dishwasher and hurried toward the stairs.

Her mom was pulling cans of tuna from the cupboard. Football practice was earlier today, and she had promised the boys a platter of tuna salad sandwiches after practice. She watched Bailey run past. "What's the rush?"

"Tim. I forgot about him." She groaned as she reached the stairs. "I'm so bad. We were supposed to meet for lunch at one."

Bailey flew to her room, fixed her hair, and grabbed her purse and was pulling out of the driveway in five minutes. Even then she pulled up at the restaurant fifteen minutes late. She grumbled at herself. "So rude ... he's probably gone by now."

She ran across the parking lot and burst through the back door of the diner, breathless. Tim was still there, sitting by himself in a booth by the windows. He was on his cell phone, and he looked relaxed. Bailey smoothed out her pale pink T-shirt and caught her breath. Then she calmly crossed the restaurant and took her place opposite him. She'd texted Tim earlier about the lesson with Katy, so he probably figured she was late because the lesson ran over.

"Hi," he mouthed. He pointed at the phone and held up his finger, letting her know he was almost finished. Then he turned his attention back to the call. "Well, hey ... I'm glad I got hold of you. We've been worried, Andi."

Bailey sat back against the vinyl booth and stared at him. Andi Ellison? He'd called Andi and she'd actually answered? Bailey was torn between feeling grateful someone had gotten hold of her and wondering why she had taken Tim's call but not hers.

The call ended and Tim made a point of looking long and hard at the time on his phone before setting it on the table beside him. "Lose track of the day?" His smile told her he wasn't too mad. "I mean, I figured the lesson would get intense. Katy's a great teacher."

He figured the lesson would get intense? Bailey wrinkled her brow. What was that supposed to mean? She thought about asking but changed her mind. If she became angry every time they were together, there wouldn't be any point. "So ... that was Andi?"

"I called her." He winked. "Figured it would give me something to do while I waited."

Bailey nodded, anxious to get past the issue of her lateness. "How is she? Her mom and dad are worried sick about her."

"She sounded okay, a little confused maybe. She's hanging out with friends in Indianapolis for a few days. She told me she wants to get back into acting." Tim picked up the menu and absently looked at it. "I told her she definitely should." His eyes met Bailey's over the top of the menu. "She's a natural."

His words settled in Bailey's gut like a mouthful of thistle weeds. Again, she refused to react. "Definitely. Andi's amazing."

"What I didn't tell her," he set the menu down again, "was that God could hardly bless her now. Not without a complete change of heart."

Bailey was losing her appetite. "Because of Taz, you mean."

"Of course. You give yourself to a guy like that and what do you expect? Taz is the Cody Coleman of Indiana University—leaving a trail of used girls in his path."

A seething anger bubbled quickly and completely to the surface of Bailey's heart. "Cody's not like that."

"He was in high school." Tim acted like he had every right to defend the comparison. "That's what I meant. Guys like that, I mean, what do girls expect?"

Beneath the table, Bailey started tapping her foot. Her heart seemed to shout at her to leave the restaurant, find any other way to spend her afternoon. She exhaled, gathering what remained of her control. "Actually," she lifted her napkin from her lap and set it on the table in front of her, "I have housework to catch up on back home." She inched toward the edge of the seat. "Sorry I was late. I just ... I don't have time for this."

If Tim had been trying to push her, trying to punish her for being late, in that moment the instant remorse in his eyes told her he was sorry. Clearly he'd gone too far. "Hey, Bailey ... I was wrong. I shouldn't have said that."

"No, it's fine." She studied him, searching her heart for any sort of feelings. Anything that would keep her here another hour. She remembered the conviction she'd felt the other day, that she'd let God down by not acting on how she truly felt about Tim. "You're right." She couldn't defend Cody's past. It was what it was. "Cody wasn't a great guy back then."

"Yeah, but I shouldn't have said anything." Here, in his apology, was a little of the guy he'd once been, the one Bailey had fallen for so long ago. "I'm sorry, really."

Bailey forced herself to calm down, not to bolt from the restaurant and never talk to Tim again. She was still his girlfriend, after all. He deserved to know how she was feeling. She exhaled, knowing there was only one thing to do. "Tim ... I think we need a break."

Tim's expression went completely blank. "A break?" He blinked twice. "What sort of a break?"

"You know ... a break. Time apart." Her eyes were dry, and she realized how wrong she'd been not to have this talk with Tim a long time ago. A modicum of compassion eased her anger. Tim clearly hadn't seen this coming. "We both have a lot going on this summer. Maybe time apart would give us ... I don't know, a better sense of direction."

"So, you mean like break up?" He set down his menu and leaned back, dazed. "That's what you want?"

"I guess." She'd never done this before, and it was harder than she thought. "It doesn't have to be like some awful thing where we never talk. And maybe things will work out between us later. When we're older."

Tim slouched forward and shaded his eyes with his hand. When he looked at her again, his eyes weren't damp, but they were hurting. "So you're serious? You want to break up?"

"Yes." She bit her lip, trying to feel appropriately brokenhearted. But even as she did, a hint of brilliant joy splashed light across the awkward moment. Suddenly Bailey knew this was what she desperately wanted. She needed a closer walk with the Lord, not with Tim Reed. "I think it's best. For both of us."

"Is that why you agreed to meet today? To break up with me?" He allowed a weak laugh, as if he were dizzy and trying to remember which way was up. "Without even talking about it first?"

There was nothing to talk about, but Bailey couldn't say so. She didn't want to come across heartless. *Make my words kind, God ... I don't want to hurt him.* She breathed the silent prayer and drew a steadying breath. "I wanted to be your girlfriend for a long time." She smiled, hoping he could see that she truly cared for him. "Way before you ever saw me that way."

"But I do see you that way." He let his hands fall to the table. "I still do. We have so much ahead."

"Maybe." She was anxious to leave. "Right now I need to think about my life, the future. I want my faith to be stronger so I can tell where God's leading me. Staying together now would only hurt our chances of a future. Don't you see that?"

The realization of what had just happened was hitting Tim harder, and the shock was wearing off. He was sad now, more sad than he'd ever looked before. "What about the audition? We're supposed to go to New York together."

"We'll still go." She thought about reaching across the table and taking hold of his hand, just to show she still cared. But she didn't want to confuse him. "We were friends before we dated ... there's no reason we can't have fun in New York City."

He stared out the window, quiet for a long time. Finally he turned to her and shrugged one shoulder. "I guess this is it, then."

"No." She gave him a sad smile. "Don't say that, Cody, not when—" her hand flew to her mouth and she felt the color leave her face.

"*Cody?*" The sorrow in Tim's eyes was instantly replaced by a deeper hurt.

"Tim, it was an accident ... I'm nervous, that's all." Her mouth was acting on its own, because her heart was still too horrified to believe she'd just done the unthinkable. She'd actually called him Cody.

"That's what this is really about, right? The undying love you have for Cody Coleman." He glared at her, but after a few seconds, his anger faded. In its place was a forced indifference. He stood and dropped his napkin on the table near hers. "You and Cody have a good summer. I'll find my own way to New York."

"Tim ..." she stood and grabbed her purse, working to keep up with him. They walked out the back door together and in the parking lot she took gentle hold of his arm. "Stop ... don't do this."

"Do what?" He groaned and crossed his arms, staring at her. "You're not the only one who's felt it, Bailey. Something's been missing between us for a while. I know that. But I figured we just needed more time together, more chances to laugh and play at the lake. See a movie together."

"That would've helped."

"No." He shook his head. His tone took on a deeper understanding. "You've never given me your heart. You've kept me at a distance. Even in the best times."

Bailey could hardly argue. She deserved some of the blame for why they weren't closer, more connected. God had shown her that. But she wasn't willing to argue with Tim. He deserved a better ending. "Can I say something?"

He stared at the ground for a long while, and when he looked up the fight was gone for him too. "What?"

"Thank you." She put her hand on his shoulder. "You respected me, you treated me with honor." It was partly why she'd stayed with him so long. "I'll always love that about you."

The compliment hit him square in the heart, Bailey could tell. It softened the tension in the moment. "I care about you." He wrapped her in a long hug, and when he released her his eyes were damp for the first time. "I'll always care."

"See?" She smiled at him, remembering a hundred good times. "That's why we have to stay close. We both care too much to walk away forever."

He searched her eyes a final time. "I'll be in touch then? Before New York?"

"Yes." She gave him one last quick hug. "And you're coming with us. We already have your ticket."

There was no need for him to respond, no need to do anything but slowly step back and go their own ways. As they did, they both waved, and then in a blur Bailey was back in her car headed home. Her emotions scattered wildly across the surface of her heart. She ached for Tim and the loss he was feeling. Clearly he hadn't been expecting a break-up. But the truth was, Tim would be fine. He would have more time for his family and his lessons, more time to focus on his audition.

But as sad as she felt for Tim, as final as it felt to be broken up after two years, Bailey couldn't deny the greater joy bursting through her. Because this was a freedom unlike anything she'd ever felt. Her mom had asked if she felt tied down, and she'd said no. Just a week ago she'd said that. But she must've felt that way, and she must've been missing God's leading in her life, because now she felt free and amazing! She didn't have to think about Tim or worry about their relationship or wonder why she didn't want to spend time with him. She was free! Free to be herself and free to be open to whatever future God had for her.

She sang along to the radio as she drove, Five for Fighting's song "100 Years," about how short life was, with only a hundred years to live. Such a finite number of days. She couldn't spend one more moment in mediocrity, not in love or life or any part of her future. She would never settle again, the way she'd settled these last months with Tim. Yes, he was a great guy, a strong Christian. And yes, he'd respected her. She would always be grateful to him for that. But he didn't love her—no matter when he'd toyed with the word before. Even today he couldn't quite say it. Just that he cared for her, nothing more.

And that was fine. She cared for him too. But that didn't mean they should be dating. Bailey felt lighter than she had in a year. Sure, she would have days when she would feel lonely, when the reality of what she'd just done would hit her hard. But it was the right choice—Bailey had no doubt. As she pulled into the driveway, she remembered her horrible slip-up. How could she have called him Cody? And at a time like that? The question hung in the early afternoon breeze as Bailey parked her car, and suddenly the answer was obvious.

She pictured dozens of times when she and her brothers had said something they shouldn't have said. A criticism or unkind word. And other times when the opposite was true, and one of them would compliment someone in the family, saying something that made the other person walk away smiling, his head higher. Always their parents would remind them of a Bible verse from Matthew 12—"Out of the overflow of the heart the mouth speaks." With that truth in mind, Bailey wasn't surprised she'd called her first boyfriend Cody. Bailey knew what was in her heart, the feelings for Cody she'd carried for so long. Based on that, it wasn't a question of why she'd slipped and said his name. It was a question of how she'd kept from saying it sooner.

As she walked into the house, she felt the finality of the breakup with Tim. She couldn't imagine getting back together with him, though only time would tell. For now it felt like a chapter in her life had ended—and for that reason she was more subdued as she found her mom in the kitchen, as she told her what happened, and as the two of them hugged.

"God knows the plans He has for you, sweetheart." Her mom still held her hand. "I've told you that since you were a little girl."

"I believe that." Bailey frowned. "I'm not sad the way I thought I'd be. But I feel bad. God wanted me to do this sooner, and I didn't listen." She hesitated. "I feel bad about that."

"Well, you did the right thing now."

"Yes." She gave her mom a crooked smile. "I'll miss him."

"Mmm." Her mom nodded, keeping the moment unrushed. "I'm sorry."

Bailey made a face. "I didn't tell you the worst part."

"Worse than breaking up?" Her mom waited, listening with her whole heart.

Bailey told her about calling Tim the wrong name. "I wanted to take it back as soon as it was out of my mouth ... but it was too late."

"Ooooh." Her mom bit her lip. "That must've been awkward."

"It was awful."

Again her mom waited, studying Bailey. "You know what I think?"

"What?" Bailey still felt terrible. She hoped Tim wasn't home reliving the moment the way she was.

"I have a feeling next time around," her mom pulled her close again, "if you find yourself calling your boyfriend by that same name—it won't be awkward at all."

Bailey took a few seconds to realize what her mom was saying. Then, despite her conflicting emotions, she laughed just a little and hugged her mom tight. Her heart felt lighter than it had all day. Because one thing she'd learned and come to count on being close to her mom all these years.

Her mom was usually right.

Twenty-Four

ANDI'S WEEKEND HAD BEEN LIKE SOMETHING from a dream. That first night she'd gone home with the Kunzmanns, and since then they'd insisted that she stay. Lucia knew about Andi's doctor appointment, and the fact that Sherry had let her down, never called her back. Of course, Andi hadn't explained exactly what type of doctor appointment she'd missed.

"You were planning to stay in the city for the weekend," Lucia told her at breakfast that morning. "Now you'll stay with us."

"Yeah, and we're better!" Young Nathalie beamed a bright smile in her direction. The girl was so sweet and full of life—so much like Andi had been at that age.

Everything about the Kunzmann family felt like Andi had stepped into another world, like the nightmare of her own life didn't even exist. She loved the way the Kunzmanns did everything as a family, the meals and clean-up, their homework and reading time. And even though they didn't know her, they included her like she'd been a part of them forever.

Andi appreciated their welcome hearts, but she kept her distance, watching them, studying them. This was the sort of life she'd always wanted, and there were times with the Kunzmanns when she actually thought it was possible. She would go home and find her faith again, put God first and make her way back to innocence. But that's when the reality of her situation would hit.

She was pregnant, about to have an abortion Monday morning. She could never find her way back to innocence.

A couple times since she'd come home with them, Lucia

would find a private moment with her and try to learn more about her situation. Once she even asked about her doctor's appointment. "You aren't sick, are you?"

"No." Andi's answer was quick. "Nothing like that."

"What about your parents? Where are they?"

Andi explained that they were in Bloomington, and that they knew she was okay. She had a feeling Lucia could see house-size holes in her story, but not once did Lucia push for details. Andi knew her parents were worrying, so she tried to text them more often. But she couldn't talk to them, otherwise she'd break down. She'd made up her mind — now she had to follow through.

On Saturday night they ate roasted chicken, and after dinner, Felix — Lucia's husband — poured himself a second towering glass of milk. "Best drink ever," he raised his glass. He nodded to the jug of milk. "You want some?"

It'd be good for the baby, she thought. Then she dismissed the thought in horror. What did it matter? Her baby would be dead in a few days. "No," she looked down, certain he could see the guilt in her eyes. "No thank you."

Felix and Lucia talked to her about school, her major, and her interests. Watching them was a lot like watching her parents. The two of them were clearly in love, sharing a chemistry and private sort of love that time had only made stronger. Later, Andi watched the way Felix related to his kids, getting down on the floor to wrestle with them, or hovering over his oldest son's algebra homework. The sort of dad Taz never would've been. It was another reason to go through with the abortion. Why should her baby have anything less than what the Kunzmann kids had?

Andi learned quickly that the Kunzmanns loved playing board games — more than any family Andi had ever known. It was Apples to Apples Friday night when their movie ended, and Pictionary on Saturday night. Sunday they played Catch Phrase, and everyone was glad for Andi because her presence meant the teams were even. "Finally," Lucia announced as they settled in to play, "Felix has no excuse if he loses!"

The family laughed, and Nathalie giggled so hard she spilled her milk. The ordeal sent everyone into action, helping clean the mess. The whole time Andi could only watch them and long for what they shared. Long for it and mourn it at the same time. She'd made her choice. She'd walked away from the chance at having what the Kunzmanns had. She resolved to enjoy the time there while she could.

Monday was coming soon enough.

LISA FELT LIKE SHE WAS GOING crazy. Andi wouldn't answer her phone, and her text messages were so brief they felt cryptic. She and Keith had been praying all weekend, and now that it was Sunday, Keith could barely focus on the meetings with Brandon Paul. This morning they'd all gone to church, and Brandon had stayed at the Matthews' house—reading the newest script.

"I might have you hang out with him the rest of the day." Keith told him as they left the service.

Dayne nodded. He had Sophie in his arms, and he reached for Katy's hand. "He might open up more to me if you weren't there right now."

"Exactly." Keith put his arm around Lisa. "I couldn't concentrate anyway. We're worried sick about Andi."

Lisa worked to keep from crying. "We both feel the situation's dire—but we can't do anything to help until she comes home." Lisa shared a look with Katy. Her new friend already knew how grave Lisa's concern was for Andi. "I'm afraid if we wait till she comes home it'll be too late."

She didn't have to explain that she was worried Andi was pregnant. But after days of praying for their daughter, that's what she and Keith had come to believe. If she was pregnant, then she might be in Indianapolis for an abortion, or worse ... because she no longer believed she had a reason to live. The idea made Lisa sick to her stomach, and she'd begged God all day for a sign, a clue. A way to reach her before it was too late.

With Brandon taken care of, Keith talked the whole way home about what they might do to find her. They could talk to her other friends—starting with Bailey—and find phone numbers of Andi's classmates. Anyone. Eventually they might come across someone who would know the names and whereabouts of the girls Andi was staying with. Another plan was to call the phone company and see if her phone had a GPS finder built into it. Maybe then they could pinpoint exactly where she was and be at her side in an hour.

They decided on that plan, and Lisa had the phone company on the line minutes after they walked through the door.

"We need to find our daughter. She has her phone, but we don't know where she is."

"Yes, ma'am. How old is your daughter?" His tone suggested he'd been through this before.

"She's nineteen."

"She's an adult, ma'am. We can't give out the whereabouts of the cell phone of an adult unless there's reason to suspect foul play. When's the last time you heard from her?"

Lisa wanted to lie, but she couldn't. "She's been texting us off and on." She pushed her fingers through her hair and stared helplessly at Keith. God was aware of their problem. If doing things His way meant missing out on this information, then He would have another plan.

"Ma'am, if you're hearing from her and she's an adult, I'm afraid there's nothing I can do. She has a right to her privacy."

Lisa tried once more. "She isn't acting like herself. If you could just tell us—"

"I'm sorry, ma'am." And with that the man hung up.

She dropped the phone on the kitchen counter and moved into Keith's arms. "What are we supposed to do?"

For a long time neither of them said anything, but then Keith stepped free and studied her. "What about her room? You sure there was nothing? No sign, nothing she might've written down?"

Lisa sucked in a quick breath. "Yes!" How could she not have thought about this sooner? She hurried down the hallway to Andi's room, with Keith behind her.

"What is it?"

"Notes. Papers I found in the trash." She rushed through the doorway and grabbed the stack of papers, the ones she herself had collected from the can and set there on Friday afternoon. Why hadn't she thought to look at them sooner? If something happened to Andi, if she did something she would regret, Lisa could never forgive herself. She sat on the edge of Andi's bed, and Keith sat beside her.

"What are these?"

"I'm not sure. They have to be recent. She hasn't been home long enough to have anything old in the trash." Her hands shook as she sorted through the papers, scrutinizing the scribble marks and bits of writing. Suddenly one of them practically screamed at her. "Look at this." She held it out for Keith to see. In Andi's printing was this notation: Indianapolis Family Planning Center. The words were followed by an address and a phone number.

Lisa felt the floor give way. She lowered the paper and looked at Keith. No matter how often they'd mentioned the possibility, Lisa had never really believed it until now. There could be only one reason Andi had written down the name and address of a family planning center.

"You think ..." Keith's face was ashen.

"She must be." Lisa hung her head as the reality shot shrapnel across her heart. Their precious daughter—the one who had taught countless village women about Jesus and His plan for their lives — was pregnant. Worse, she was clearly considering an abortion. That's what family planning centers did.

Lisa sat up straighter. She couldn't afford to break down now, not when Andi clearly needed her. There were other notations, scribbles on the pieces of paper, and after a few seconds she made sense of something else. Written at the bottom of one page were the words, *Sarah's House — Crisis Pregnancy Center. Bloomington.* Surrounding it were a dozen question marks, each of them heavily doodled over. Not far from that were the words *free ultrasound* and more question marks.

Suddenly Lisa's heart leaped with hope. "Sarah's House is here in town, remember?"

A dawning came across Keith's expression. "Dayne's talked about it. His sisters run it."

Lisa couldn't move fast enough. "Come on, we have to hurry." She and Keith ran back to the kitchen and Lisa handed him the phone. "Call Dayne."

As fast as his fingers could move, Keith did as she asked. Three minutes later he had Ashley Baxter Blake's phone number. "Dayne told me she might not be able to talk about it. Confidentiality rules."

"I'll call her." Lisa felt like a mother bear, ready to tear doors off walls if it meant getting to her daughter. She dialed the number and waited until Ashley picked up.

"Hello?"

"Hi, Ashley. This is Lisa Ellison. Keith's wife." She worked to keep her tears from taking over. It was important that she sound calm and clear-minded. "We have reason to believe our daughter Andi is pregnant. She's in Indianapolis and she won't answer our calls. Did she come to your clinic?"

There was a long pause on the other end. "Mrs. Ellison ... Lisa ... our clients trust us with their confidentiality. I'm not sure how much I can — "

"Your center, it's there to save lives—isn't that right?"

Another long beat. "Of course."

"I have the name of a family planning center in Indianapolis, and if I'm right about this, I think Andi might be planning to have an abortion. "Please ... tell me if she's been to see you."

Another long pause across the line. "I've seen her. Yes." Ashley hesitated. "Andi's in trouble, Mrs. Ellison. I'm sorry ... I can't say much more. She only came in once."

"So she's ... she's pregnant?"

Ashley's silence clearly conveyed the truth.

Lisa closed her eyes and grabbed for Keith's arm. "Dear God ... why didn't she tell us?"

"We give all of our clients information about raising their babies or releasing them for adoption." Ashley sounded broken by the situation.

For a split moment, Lisa wanted to be angry with Ashley. If she'd known about Andi, why hadn't she come to them? Told them about their daughter's pregnancy before this weekend? Then they wouldn't be in this situation.

Ashley seemed to read her mind, because she explained again that the reason pregnant girls came in for a pregnancy test was because they believed the results would be private. "Have you talked to Bailey? She might know something, a way you could reach her."

"We'll try that next." Lisa's anger dissolved, and all that remained was gratitude. "Thank you, Ashley. If we have to go camp outside the abortion clinic Andi wrote about, we will. At least we know what she's up against." Lisa thanked her again and the call ended.

Keith looked despondent. The news was overwhelming, and Lisa felt practically paralyzed by it. First, their daughter was definitely pregnant. And second, she clearly planned to end the life of her baby. At least that. There was no telling what else was going through her mind while she was in Indianapolis this weekend.

"What next?" Keith took the phone from Lisa and set it back on the base.

There was only one answer, one way to get another step closer to Andi so they could help her. Lisa grabbed her purse from the kitchen counter. "We need to go see Bailey."

They reached the Flanigan house in ten minutes. Much to Lisa's relief, Bailey answered the front door and invited them in. They must've both looked crazy with worry, because Bailey froze in place. "Is this ... about Andi?"

"Yes." Again Lisa fought to keep control. "She's in a lot of trouble. We'd like to talk, if you have a minute."

Bailey called her parents to join them, and the group went into the Flanigans' living room. It was the first day in a week that hadn't been brilliantly sunny, and Lisa found it fitting. The clouds cast dark shadows through the wall of windows, and even though it was late June, Lisa began to shiver as she sat down. Keith took the spot beside her, the two of them opposite Jim and Jenny Flanigan. Bailey sat in the closest chair.

"You've heard something from Andi?" Jenny started the conversation.

"Not really." The mere fact that this kind woman knew even that much—that Andi was out of town and not communicating much—was proof that Bailey told her everything. The way Andi used to tell Lisa everything. She focused her thoughts, as she squeezed her husband's hand. "We found out today. Andi's pregnant."

Bailey groaned and gripped the arms of the chair, her eyes downcast. "I was afraid of this."

"Us too." Keith sat rigid beside her. His posture told Lisa he wasn't willing to give up. "She's in the city, and she's texted us now and then. But she won't answer our calls. We think she's scheduled an abortion there. We found the name of an Indianapolis clinic."

They were quiet for a few seconds, each of them grasping what Andi might've already done, what she might be going through this very moment. And how they could possibly reach her.

"Wait!" Bailey looked up. "Tim talked to her yesterday afternoon. He called her around noon. She told him she was staying with friends, thinking of taking classes there."

"Same thing she told us." Lisa frowned. "We're here because we hoped you might know these girls, the friends she's staying with."

"No." Bailey frowned. "I have an idea who they are. One's a girl named Sherry. She's involved in theater."

"Do you know her last name?"

"No."

Lisa's mind raced. "There has to be someone who would know. Maybe if we talk to Tim."

"Absolutely. He might not have told me everything." Bailey rattled off Tim's number and Lisa dialed it.

But after a brief conversation, the call ended. "He doesn't know anything. Just that she sounded upbeat."

"Which maybe does tell us something." Jim had been thinking. He put his arm around Jenny and looked from her to the others. "If she just had an abortion, I doubt she'd be taking a call from Tim Reed."

"True." This was helping. Even if no one had any exact answers, they were getting somewhere.

"You're pretty sure you know which clinic she's been in contact with?" Jenny's tone was grave.

"We found the name and an address written on a piece of paper in her room." Had the expectations they'd placed on her really been so hard to live up to? So much that she couldn't face them in her greatest hour of need?

Please God ... we need an answer, some sort of direction. We're getting nowhere, and Andi needs us. "Maybe ... maybe if we pray for her."

They all agreed, and for the next several minutes they took turns asking God to protect Andi, to prompt her to call home. And they asked Him for a sign, some sort of direction so that if Andi was resistant to their help, they could find her.

The prayer ended and Lisa was about to thank the Flanigans for their time when her phone vibrated. It was still in her hand from the call to Tim, and Lisa saw that a text message had come in from Andi. "It's her!" She tapped a few buttons and there it was, Andi's latest message.

She took a quick breath and read it out loud. "It says, '*Hi Mom … I know you're mad at me, and I'm sorry. I'm really okay. But it looks like I won't be coming home until Tuesday evening.*'" Lisa paused, distraught at this latest news. "'*The girls and I are having fun, and we want a few days to look around the campus here. Thanks for understanding.*'" She shrugged. "That's all she said." In the old days, she never would've texted Lisa without saying she loved her. But now … she must've been so racked with guilt and shame she couldn't even think clearly.

"You know what that means …" Jenny looked at Lisa.

"Her appointment—if she has an appointment—must be Monday morning."

"Exactly." Bailey hadn't said much. She still looked pale and shocked—worried sick about her friend. "Someone has to be there."

Jim clasped his hands hard, his knuckles white. "If she were my daughter, I'd be waiting at the clinic for her tomorrow morning."

"Absolutely." The idea was the most natural answer of all. Lisa's heart lifted for the first time since they'd heard the news about Andi's pregnancy. "We can see if the clinic has a website. Find out their hours and be there first thing in the morning."

"We could wait in the parking lot and pray for her." Keith

looked relieved. "Just in case. I mean, the text coming when it did. We have to believe that's a sign, that God's leading us to her."

They talked for a few more minutes, and the Flanigans promised to keep praying. Before they left, Bailey hugged Lisa. "When you see her, tell her I love her. I'm here for her."

"I will." Lisa couldn't express how much Bailey's comment meant.

With that, Lisa and Keith hurried home again. On the way, Lisa texted Andi, asking if she'd please call. But there was no response. They tried several more attempts at reaching her, but she didn't answer, and no more text messages came the rest of the evening. They found a website for the Indianapolis Family Planning Center, and they learned that the clinic opened at nine the next day. After that there was nothing to do but pray and wait.

They'd be on the road to Indianapolis first thing in the morning.

Twenty-Five

Luke Baxter had been on the road far more often than usual, and he was grateful for a weekend at home. Even still he'd be back in Los Angeles by tomorrow night for one more round of meetings. He'd talked to Dayne, and for now at least it looked like Jeremiah Productions was ready to finalize the deal with Brandon Paul.

"We have our reservations, but that's where you come in," Dayne told him. "The contract has to be a steel trap. No loopholes, brother." Dayne laughed. "Of course, that's why we have you. You're the best."

Already Luke was hammering out a first draft of the contract. Money wouldn't be an issue. Any studio in town would take on the movie and pay Brandon's considerable salary for a chance to have a picture with him. It was the other details that concerned Dayne and Keith—the morality clauses, that if broken, could destroy the movie.

Luke loved the challenge as much as he loved the personnel changes at Jeremiah Productions. Chase would be missed, of course. But he needed to be home with his family, and now Luke could work more closely with Dayne, his brother. After a lifetime of missing out on having a brother, these days were golden—getting to work with Dayne, being close to him.

The only downside lately was the time he'd spent away from home. Now it was Sunday night and he'd tucked Tommy in four times already. Tommy was still telling people he was a Tommysaurus Rex—the meanest dinosaur of all. If his behavior at bedtime was any indication, Luke could only believe him. But on the last round of good nights, Luke had used a more serious voice. "This is it, buddy. Don't get up again."

A repentant look came over Tommy and he settled down on his pillow. "Okay, Daddy." He waved his fingers, meek-like. "Sorry."

"It's fine. Just don't get up."

"Okay." One more quick wave. "Wuv you."

"Love you too." Luke stifled a grin as he left his son's room. Malin was already asleep down the hall, so finally he could go find Reagan. He'd told her to take the night off, curl up with a book while he managed the bedtime routine. It was the least he could do since he'd been gone so much lately. He tiptoed down the stairs, past the place where Tommy had gotten his head stuck in the spindles when they first moved into the house. He found Reagan in a T-shirt and comfy-looking sweats, reading *Unlocked* next to an open window.

She smiled up at him. "The breeze is amazing. I can smell the jasmine you planted last summer."

He sat beside her and breathed in. "It's great."

"See?" She leaned close and kissed him. "I knew you'd like it."

"I believed you." He nuzzled up against her. "I always believe you."

"Mmm." Reagan looked straight at him, past the lighthearted banter between them. "Like about the adoption?"

"Exactly." He grinned and crooked his finger beneath her chin, kissing her more slowly this time. "But that one didn't take any convincing. I'd love another baby."

"You don't care — girl or boy?"

"Nope. Whatever baby God brings us is fine with me." He felt relaxed and content. Being with Reagan filled his senses, and the smell of jasmine only heightened the moment. Like the peacefulness of the night would go on forever. He leaned back, watching her. "Our paperwork's in, right?"

"Everything's done. The agency called last week. It's just a matter of a birth mother choosing us, finding the right match."

It was the first time they'd done a domestic adoption, and Luke was a little nervous about the fact. International adoptions like Malin's carried virtually no risk of a birth mother showing up after so many years with a lawyer in tow. But this time around they were willing to consider a more open adoption. Children were on loan anyway. That's what his mother had always said. "God's probably picking a baby for us right now."

"I've been thinking about her lately." Reagan pressed her head into the sofa cushion, a dreamy look on her face.

"So now it's a girl?" Luke was teasing her, enjoying the easy way they had with each other. Their marriage had only gotten stronger this last year, and now that they were dreaming about a third child, Luke felt like God was blessing them beyond anything he could've imagined.

"Not the baby, silly." Reagan's expression deepened. "The girl, the birth mother. She's out there somewhere. Maybe already pregnant. Trying to decide what to do with a pregnancy she didn't plan for."

"Hmm." Luke angled his head, imagining the same thing. "I haven't thought about that."

"I think God put the idea on my heart. We pray for the baby all the time, of course."

"For years." Luke was serious. They'd known from the beginning that Reagan couldn't have more biological children after Tommy. Which meant whenever they prayed about their family, they prayed for the children yet to come, the boys or girls only God knew about.

"So maybe it's time we pray for the girl, our baby's birth mother."

"What if she's in her forties—and this baby just doesn't fit in her plans?"

Reagan giggled. "Girl, woman. Whatever." Her laughter faded. "I'm serious. We should pray for her, don't you think?"

Luke was quiet, thinking about the troubled mother somewhere out there in the city of Indianapolis, maybe just getting news of an unwanted pregnancy or worse—thinking about whether to release the baby for adoption or abort. A shudder ran through him and he sat up straighter. "You're right. Let's pray for her."

"Right now?" Reagan leaned forward too. Her face close to Luke's.

A sense of urgency filled Luke's heart, robbing him of some of the serenity from just a few minutes ago. He pictured this woman—young or old—one more time. The woman who might even this moment be carrying their next child. "Yeah, baby. I think so. Right now." Then he took Reagan's hands in his and prayed with an intensity that surprised him—that God would know exactly who the birth mother of their baby was, and that even this very night he would surround her with his angels and protect her and the baby. That God would grant her peace in her decision, and finally one last thing.

That he'd grant her baby life.

ANDI WANTED TO GET THERE EARLY.

Her appointment was for nine that morning, but the woman she'd talked to said they opened the doors half an hour early. So their clients could avoid the protestors who sometimes gathered near the front of the clinic during business hours. The last thing Andi wanted was to run into a protestor—someone who would scream threats in her face and call her names for killing her baby.

She wanted to slip in unnoticed, and slip back into life the same way. The problem gone, no one the wiser for what she'd done. No one but her and God. Of course, she hadn't planned on thinking much about God this day, but all that changed at the Kunzmann house. Their family lived and breathed God's presence. His Word and truth, His ways and peace were a part of everything the Kunzmann family said and did. There was no getting around it.

Before she left this morning, Lucia pulled her aside. "Your appointment is this morning, right?"

"Yes." Andi couldn't make eye contact with the woman. She didn't deserve the woman's kindness, and she felt ashamed for what she was about to do. As if by looking into Lucia's eyes, the woman would know exactly where she was headed.

"Before you go, let's pray. Whatever's wrong with you, Andi, God knows. He will meet you there."

Praying before an abortion? Andi's heart pounded in her throat, but she couldn't escape. Before she knew what was happening, Lucia had hold of her hands and she was praying, asking the Holy Spirit to be Andi's constant companion in the coming hours, and asking that Andi hear His voice whatever lay ahead. It was like Lucia already knew her plans. Like God Himself had told her.

Andi pulled into a bank parking lot across the street from the clinic and slumped behind the steering wheel. *What're you worried about?* she asked herself. *No one knows you're here*. For a full minute she surveyed the clinic across the street, making sure there were no protestors, no one to interfere with her quick and certain entrance. She placed her hand on her stomach and wondered if her baby would feel what was about to happen. As soon as the question hit her, she banished it. The woman at the clinic had promised her there was no baby. The only thing her body contained right now was tissue. Tissue that would become a baby.

Ashley Baxter's face came to mind, telling her that people at abortion clinics would lie to her. The ultrasound told the real story. Growing inside her was a very tiny baby and a very tiny heart.

She felt sick to her stomach, and finally she'd had enough. She jolted from the car and ran lightly across the street. But just as she was about to cross into the clinic parking lot, a man stepped in front of her.

"Hello." He was older, white hair and a neatly trimmed white beard. His eyes were so piercing blue, they almost looked otherworldly. "I'm Clarence." He checked his watch. "I thought you'd be early, Andi."

A slice of terror cut at Andi and she took a few frantic steps back. How did he know her name? "Don't ... please don't hurt me."

The man stepped aside, but even though her path to the clinic was wide open, Andi had the sense she couldn't get by the gentleman, no matter what she tried. His voice was soft as he tried again. "I'm not here to harm you. I bring you truth. Please ..." he held a pamphlet to her. "Take this. Your appointment's not until nine o'clock."

"How do you ... I don't have an appointment. I'm just ... I'm looking into it."

He watched her, kind and gentle. "I've prayed for you and your baby ... I've prayed all morning." He was still holding out the brochure. "Please take this. Go back to your car and read it." What was it about his eyes? He smiled at her, and his tenderness touched her much the way she felt when she was around her father. She made a quick grab of the pamphlet and looked around, hoping no one else could see them.

"You'll read it? For your baby?"

"There's no ba—"

He held up one hand and nodded at her. "Read it. I'll be praying."

She still had the sensation she couldn't get past the older gentleman, even if she made a run for it. So instead she turned around and ran the other way. Halfway to her car she turned back to see which way the man went, where he'd come from. But he was gone. Her heart thudded in her neck, making it hard to breathe. Where was he? Clarence, right? Wasn't that his name? He was too old to race off, and there was no other car or doorway in sight. Could he be hiding in the bushes? Was that how he handed his material to unsuspecting girls like her? And how had he known her name?

Shaking from fear and the adrenaline coursing through her, Andi ran as fast as she could back to her car. She didn't want to stay here. What if the man turned up by her car somehow? She set the pamphlet down on her passenger seat, started her engine, and pulled out of the bank parking lot as fast as she could. Halfway down the block she saw a public library, and she turned her car quickly into the parking lot. It was empty, so she could be alone—without wondering whether the man with the strange eyes was watching her.

Her forehead was damp with sweat, and her heart still sped along at double speed inside her chest. What sort of crazy thing had just happened to her? She'd scanned the parking lot and made sure no one—absolutely no one—was lurking anywhere near the clinic. She'd been walking toward the parking lot, her eyes fixed on the clinic door, and he was suddenly there. From out of nowhere.

She made sure her doors were locked, and she leaned her head against the seat rest. *Breathe,* she told herself. *This is insane. Go back, and get inside before more protestors show up.* But the man's words filled her mind, consumed her soul. He thought she'd be early? Like he knew her? Another series of shivers ran down her arms. Then without wanting to, she reached for the brochure and looked at the cover. It was a picture of an unborn baby, very little. Probably about the age of her own baby. The title read, "Give Life a Chance."

Her heart pounded harder in response. She couldn't give life a chance. If she did, she'd have to tell her parents and have the baby and then what? Embarrass her father ... mar his chances at making movies with a Christian message? Or spend a lifetime raising Taz's child alone? Or somehow find a way to put the baby into the arms of another family? None of the answers felt even remotely possible. But as if some supernatural force was compelling her, she opened the pamphlet and read the entire thing, every word. The minutes ticked away, and still Andi sat there.

One of the lines from inside the brochure jumped out at her. For every abortion, two lives are destroyed. Most women will spend a lifetime seeking healing and forgiveness from this one single choice.

Could that be true? Was the brochure right, that she'd spend a lifetime regretting this? Her mind was so full of conflicting thoughts she could barely think or see straight. Even so she started her car again and pulled back onto the busy street. She drove without thinking, first toward the clinic and then after a quick U-turn she drove away. Suddenly, without knowing how or why, she pulled into another parking lot and looked at the building near the back. The blood drained from her face as she read the sign.

Bethany Christian Services—an Adoption Agency.

This couldn't be happening. She couldn't have driven aimlessly into the parking lot of an adoption agency. Maybe she was dreaming. The whole strange situation with the man and his unforgettable eyes, the way he'd come from nowhere and disappeared as soon as she turned around. Now this. She shut her eyes as tightly as she could. Yes, she was dreaming. That had to be it. But then why was her heart pounding, and how come she couldn't catch her breath? She opened her eyes slowly, hoping she would find herself in the guestroom of the Kunzmann house, the morning not yet begun.

But she was exactly where she'd been a minute ago. A Christian adoption agency staring her straight in the face.

Suddenly... like scales from her eyes, the truth began to dawn on her. Nothing that morning had been strange or coincidental. God was reaching down from heaven to spare her life and the life of her baby. First the Kunzmann family—and Lucia's prayer that the Holy Spirit stay with her over the next few hours ... then the strange, kind-eyed man.

Andi thought about her family's time in Indonesia. The supernatural was more accepted there, and believers regularly experienced encounters with beings they believed to be angels. She thought about the man, pictured his unusual blue eyes and his way of speaking straight to her. Maybe he was an angel. It was possible. How else could he possibly have known her name? Hebrews 13 talked about being careful to entertain strangers, for in doing so some had entertained angels without knowing it, right?

Another set of shivers ran through her. The man had been aware that she'd be early, and he'd known private details about her appointment, her name. Even what it would take to change her mind. There could be no other answer. She covered her stomach tenderly with her hands. "Little one, I'm sorry... I'm so sorry."

Her tears came like they hadn't since she first found out she was pregnant. How had she lied to herself these past few weeks, refusing to think of her baby, but only of the abortion? The brochure was right. She would've hated herself forever if she'd gone through with it. She stepped out of her car and walked slowly to the front door of the adoption agency. Stuck to the window was a list of hours, same as those of the abortion clinic down the street. Fitting, Andi thought. Life or death, a few blocks apart.

She tapped the agency's number into her phone's address book and walked slowly back to her car. A new sense of hope filled her heart. Her baby was going to live! She wasn't going through the doors of the abortion clinic, not today and not ever. It had been her choice to sleep with Taz, to believe him that in some twisted way, breaking her vow to God would be art. The lie was flat-out diabolical. Breaking a promise to God, going against what Scripture taught, could only be called one thing.

Sin.

Yes, Andi had sinned against God and her parents. Even against herself and the plans God had for her life. But Andi hadn't lost all her Bible knowledge in one year. She remembered a verse her parents had referenced often. Romans 8:28 — all things work to the good for those who love the Lord.

And she did love Him. She'd put Him off and walked away, but the truth was now as clear as the sky overhead. She loved God and she wanted to live for Him again — the way she hadn't lived for Him since she'd set foot on the IU campus. Andi started her car one more time to head back to the Kunzmann house. Lucia would be the first person she would tell about this decision. But before she drove very far, she realized something. She had to go back to the clinic and look for Clarence. She wanted to hug him and thank him and tell him what a difference he'd made. Let him know his prayers had been answered. She was choosing life.

One last time she turned her car around, and as she drove she suddenly pictured her sweet friend, Rachel. Something dawned on her, the way it hadn't for an entire year. Rachel would finally recognize her. And somewhere in heaven she had a feeling Rachel was celebrating with the angels.

Maybe even a blue-eyed old gentleman named Clarence.

Twenty-Six

KEITH AND LISA SAT IN SILENCE, their car parked in a lot across the street from the clinic. They'd been here since 8:35, but still they hadn't seen Andi. A few protestors were gathered outside the clinic, talking amongst themselves. Keith watched as three of them circled on the sidewalk and bowed their heads, clearly praying for the work ahead of them.

"Interesting." Lisa was as nervous as him, but she seemed struck by the protestors. "I've always seen them portrayed as violent, screaming and waving signs."

"A few extreme people probably are like that." Keith narrowed his eyes, watching the group as they continued to pray. "But this doesn't surprise me. There's a mission field here—if it's handled right, anyway."

Lisa sighed and glanced around. "You think she's coming."

"I do." Keith felt a peace in his heart, a certainty. "I can't explain it. I just think she'll be here."

They had prayed together for almost an hour that morning—most of the drive here. The goal, of course, was to tell Andi they'd help her, to change her mind about the abortion. But beyond that they'd talked about what might come next. Whether Andi would raise her child, or give the baby up for adoption. They both agreed that they would welcome Andi home, and help her parent the child if that's what she wanted to do. No matter what circumstances led to this life—the life mattered. This was their first grandchild, after all.

Also, early this morning Keith had called Chase. They might've parted ways, but no one knew him better. No one besides Lisa would hurt for his Andi more than Chase and Kelly. The friends who had watched her grow up, the two who knew how great Andi's love for the Lord had once been, and how drastic the changes in her this past year.

Chase promised to tell Kelly, and even now Keith knew his friends were praying. God was hearing from the people who loved their Andi, and Keith believed this was where they'd find her. God had led them here, after all. He took hold of Lisa's hand. "She'll be here."

He'd no sooner said the words, when a car pulled up a few spots away and parked facing the clinic.

"Andi!" Lisa practically shrieked her name. "Dear God, it's her …"

"Thank You, Lord … thank you." Keith's eyes blurred with tears, and he held his wife's hand more tightly. "Don't rush. There's no hurry now."

They stepped out at the same time, and as they did, Andi spotted them. From the moment Keith saw his daughter's eyes, he knew something had changed. They shone almost as if she'd seen a vision. She jumped out of her little sedan and rushed into their arms, the three of them hugging and rocking and not ever wanting to let go.

"Mom … Dad … I'm sorry." She spoke the words against Keith's chest, and he clung to her. His precious daughter. His baby girl. As he did, he realized that this was how the father in *Unlocked* must've felt. Holding his child and knowing that in this moment a miracle had happened.

Because here and now he had his Andi back.

"You know," she looked up at them, tears spilling from her eyes. "You must know, right?"

"We do." Lisa pulled a piece of paper from her pocket. "We found this in your trash can. When we didn't hear from you we figured we'd come here and wait."

"I made the worst mistake of my life." The guilt that seemed to consume her was almost a physical presence. "I knew better, but I wanted to do things my way. I'm so sorry."

Lisa pulled a tissue from her pocket and handed it to Andi. "It's okay now, baby. Everything's going to be okay."

"I know." The guilt lifted, and the newfound light shone in her eyes once again. She told them a rambling story about some family named Kunzmann who took her in over the weekend and how they lived out their faith, and that the woman prayed with her this very morning, and how an older man named Clarence stopped her from going into the clinic, and how God—only God—could've led her to the adoption agency down the street.

"Wait!" Keith searched his daughter's eyes. "You drove down the street and randomly came across an adoption agency?"

"Yes!" Unbridled laughter came from Andi, and she tipped her head back for a moment. "Isn't God so good? He led me there, Dad. I'll show you."

Keith felt a slight sadness, one that he had to acknowledge. Andi had apparently made up her mind—she was giving the baby up for adoption. It was the best decision by far, and Keith would spend the next months applauding his daughter for having the courage and compassion to give her baby to a Christian family, parents ready for a child.

But in this single moment, he marked the loss—Andi's firstborn, their grandchild. A little boy or girl none of them would ever know.

Andi linked arms with her parents and walked across the street. Boldly and with great joy she talked to the protestors and thanked them for the work they were doing. Then she asked about Clarence.

A woman in her forties shook her head, glancing at the others. "I've been coming here every day for two years. For a few hours each morning." She looked back at Andi. "I've never met a Clarence."

The others agreed. There was no one named Clarence working this clinic, helping girls know the mistake they were about to make, trying to compassionately lead them to choose life. Andi nodded, and thanked them again. Keith had never been more proud of her in all his life.

"You get it, right, Dad?" The shine in her eyes made her look alive again. "He must've been an angel. What other explanation is there?"

Keith could only agree. God was answering every prayer they'd breathed this past weekend. Why wouldn't He send an angel for Andi? They caravanned together to the adoption agency a few blocks down — Lisa riding with Andi. Once there, they went inside and Andi took the lead.

"My name's Andi. I'm pregnant, but I'm not ready to be a mother," she told the woman at the desk. "And God led me here." She looked at her parents on either side. "I'd like to give my baby up for adoption to a Christian family."

The woman must've dealt with scenes like this one every day, but listening to Andi — her joy and certainty — brought tears to the woman's eyes. She blinked a few times and handed Andi a packet. "Why don't you have a seat in the lobby. Look this over. Someone will be out to talk to you in a few minutes."

Keith could hardly believe the morning was playing out this way. They'd jumped major hurdles all in less than an hour — and now Andi — her childlike faith once more a driving force in her life — was ready to tackle what would inevitably be the hardest decision of her life. They looked through a book of families ready to adopt, but the counselor told Andi she didn't need to make a decision yet. That could come in time. She'd have several more counseling appointments — one a month, tied in with her checkups. The agency worked with a doctor a few minutes away. All medical expenses were covered by the agency.

Throughout the hour, Andi never wavered in her decision.

She was happy and talkative, and when she looked at the pictures of families she dabbed quietly at her eyes. With Lisa's help, Andi filled out the paperwork while Keith mostly took in the scene. A life had been saved today. He was too awestruck to do more than think on that single fact. Besides, between the Kunzmann family and Clarence and the time here at the adoption agency, Keith didn't need to say much, really.

They were all three on hallowed ground.

ANDI COULDN'T BELIEVE HOW GREAT SHE felt. How had she gotten through the last year without her faith? God had never given up on her, that much she knew for sure. But she'd chosen to walk through her days without His constant presence, His perfect friendship. And she'd made a mess of things as a result.

But God had opened her eyes, and in the light of His mercy and grace she could breathe again. She wouldn't ever again turn her back on the truths she'd been raised with, never again listen to the lies of the enemy. There was no truth but God's alone, no other way to eternity. The miracles of this morning were more proof than she deserved. She would live with her parents until the baby was born, and then she'd say good-bye to her firstborn. Maybe if the adoptive family was willing, she'd stay in touch here and there. Send letters and pictures. That way her baby would know how she felt right now. That she loved this child with a love she'd forgotten existed. A love that was God's alone. Yes, she had mixed feelings about the adoption, but definitely no doubts.

As they left the adoption agency, she stopped and looked intently into her father's eyes. "I'm sorry, Daddy. If this embarrasses you. If it hurts Jeremiah Productions."

Her father looked shocked by her apology. "Is that what you thought? That this would embarrass me?"

She nodded, ashamed again. "It'll look terrible."

"I don't care about any of that. If the media wants to write about this, I'll defend you to anyone, sweetheart." He hugged her, caring for her. "You're doing the right thing."

Andi's heart soared, lifted by his love and acceptance. Why hadn't she believed they'd respond this way? She could've avoided the heartache of the weekend, but then she might not have heard God calling her back to Him. Now she had a plan, and after the baby, she couldn't wait to get back on campus and start up once more with Cru. If they'd let her, she wanted to be a group leader. No one could help the girls on campus avoid the lies that surrounded them more than she could. She couldn't wait to build her relationship with her parents and get back to church. And she couldn't wait to talk to Bailey.

Before they left Indianapolis, Andi wanted them to make one more stop—to the Kunzmann home. Again her mom rode with her, and Andi tried to explain how God had placed her in their home for His purposes. "It was a miracle, Mom. I'm serious."

Her mom could only smile and listen. Andi was grateful she didn't lecture her about not calling or about making them worry. She'd been blinded just hours ago. Now that she could see, she only wanted her parents to love her and forgive her. The way they were doing.

They pulled up in front of a large home, and Andi led her parents up the walk. Lucia answered, and Andi made the introductions. Then without another moment's hesitation, she flew into Lucia's arms and hugged her close. "How did you know? You prayed like you knew."

Lucia laughed, her eyes filled with joy. As she stepped back she looked at the trio on her porch. "About the baby?"

Andi felt the chills across her arms again. "Yes. See … how did you know?"

"Honestly? God told me. I knew from the moment I saw you crying at Megan's Diner." She smiled at Andi's parents. "I figured if she were my daughter, I'd want someone to step in. Sometimes mission work happens when you least expect it."

Lucia invited them in and they stayed half an hour, eating lunch with her and the kids — all of whom were homeschooled. When they left, Andi promised to stay in touch. And her mother hugged Lucia for a long time. "You were my answer to prayer."

"That's our job as believers," Lucia smiled at Andi's mother. "To be an answer to someone's prayer — every day ... as long as we live."

The whole day was one miracle after another, and on the way home Andi let her mom drive. She was exhausted, certain she would be asleep before they hit the open road. But even as she nodded off, she acknowledged one more miracle — something she hadn't shared with her parents. She'd found the adoptive family for her baby. The counselor had been clear, she didn't need to decide yet.

But as she looked through the book, one family stood out.

Andi wasn't sure exactly what struck her about the family. Maybe because the dad looked a lot like a young Dayne Matthews, and his wife — with her blonde hair — looked a little like Dayne's wife Katy. Andi had memorized the page, the way the family looked, the description of them. They lived in Indianapolis, and the mom stayed at home with the kids. They loved Jesus and each other, and they were praying for a special birth mother — that she would choose to bring their baby into the world. The book didn't give last names, but Andi had memorized their first names. She was that certain about her choice.

Luke, Reagan, Tommy, and Malin.

Her baby's family.

Twenty-Seven

THE REST OF JUNE SLIPPED THROUGH Bailey's fingers, in a blur of long talks with her mom and Andi and acting lessons with Katy. Andi had apologized for the way she'd treated Bailey, and the girls had found the beginning of a friendship that had escaped them all last year. Bailey apologized too. For not trying harder, for in some ways writing Andi off once she started dating Taz.

Somehow July had snuck in unannounced and now suddenly it was the Fourth already. Andi and her parents had flown to Los Angeles for the holiday—time to be alone together, just the three of them. But Bailey and her family were joining the Baxters in their annual barbecue. It was a nice break from the usual all-day backyard party her parents threw most years.

Humidity filled the air, and the sun was already warming the fields surrounding Bloomington. Bailey had wanted to do something different with her hair, something so she'd look as young and free as she felt. So that morning she'd asked her mom to braid it. Two braids framing her face, from beneath a red American Eagle baseball cap. It matched her red T-shirt and navy capris. They were minutes from leaving so she darted back upstairs to her closet and picked out a pair of shoes she hadn't worn all winter—her white Jack Purcells. While she was slipping them on, her eye caught the same framed picture of her and Tim from last winter—the one when they were in *Scrooge*.

They'd been broken up for more than a week, so that was long enough, right? She sprang across the room, took the picture, and slipped it into one of her desk drawers. *Never liked the photo anyway*, she told herself. She plopped down on the edge of her mattress and finished tying her shoes. She hadn't heard from Tim, and she figured that was best. They both needed time to sort through their feelings about the breakup. Besides, by the time Tim gave the situation any real thought, he was bound to see it the way she did. They hadn't been more than friends for a long time anyway.

Somewhere some girl would meet Tim and fall in love with him, and Tim would look back and thank her for setting him free.

Wherever Tim's future took him, Bailey would never settle for a passive life again. Never play not to lose, but only to win. Seizing every day, the way God wanted her to live. Love needed to be so much more. She wanted someone who felt alive beside her, a guy who dreamed about her when she was away and hung on her every word when they were together. Someone who in time would make it difficult to know where she ended and he began. A love so bright and beautiful a hundred years would never be enough time together.

Bailey bounced down the stairs to the kitchen and found her mom finishing up a bowl of homemade potato salad. "Grab the pepper, will you, Bailey?"

"What about paper towels?" Bailey grinned as she reached for the pepper and handed it to her mom. "Look at you. You've got potatoes halfway to your elbows."

"That's what makes it so amazing." She was using two spoons, digging them deep in the salad and tossing the pieces of potatoes. "You can't get this kind of touch from a supermarket carton." Her mom peered at her and blew her hair off her face. "You look adorable, Bailey. Very all-American."

"Thanks." She leaned in and helped her mom tuck a strand of hair off her face and behind her ear. "I feel that way. Glad to be alive, grateful to be an American, happy that we can still worship

God and that most everyone I know still loves Him. Happy to have a reason to celebrate." She leaned against the kitchen counter and watched as her dad and brothers filed into the kitchen. Their conversations were loud, their laughter contagious. Bailey helped her mom get to the sink without dropping blobs of potato salad on the floor. They laughed while Bailey handed her a dishrag and her mom pumped a handful of soap into her hands.

While they were wrapping the bowl with tinfoil, Bailey reminded herself again to soak in these precious moments—all of them still at home, her brothers excited about a day at the lake. An Independence Day to celebrate. These were the times of their lives—moments they would always remember.

"You're so happy today." Her mom gave her a knowing look. "I don't remember you being this excited last Fourth."

"Mom ... I'm hurt." Bailey could feel her eyes begin to dance. "I love all holidays."

"But this time ... maybe a little more." She dried her hands and arms on a dish towel. "What time will Cody be there anyway?"

Bailey felt her cheeks grow hot. Her mom knew her so well—there was no hiding that Cody was one of the main reasons she was so happy, the reason she'd been singing all morning. "Three o'clock. Same as us."

Her mom held her gaze for a special few seconds, time where they needed no words to know what the other was thinking. "I'm praying for you. Don't get ahead of yourself."

"I won't. Cody doesn't even know about Tim and me." She took hold of the potato salad and grinned. "It's just a great day, that's all."

Her dad caught the fact that the women were ready. He raised his hand and made a sweeping motion toward the garage. "Okay, guys, everyone into the Suburban! The Baxter family barbecue can't start without us!"

Bailey had done everything in her power not to dwell on the

fact that Cody was coming to the barbecue. They'd talked last night—the first time since that strange call the night of the football scrimmage. When he'd seemed like he had so much more to tell her than he was actually saying. When he didn't call for a week, Bailey finally decided she could call him. Her brothers had said he'd been quieter lately—and that worried Bailey. Had something happened to his mom, or had he met someone who had turned his head?

Either way, it felt wonderful talking to him last night. She asked him about his plans for the Fourth, and he had nothing. He wanted to drop by the cemetery and put flowers on the graves of a couple fallen soldiers he knew. But he was doing that in the morning.

"Meet us at Lake Monroe!" Bailey couldn't hide her enthusiasm. "Remember when you went that one time with us?"

"The famous ankle-twisting." Cody chuckled, but the sound dropped off. "I don't know … Tim doesn't like me being around your family."

"Tim isn't coming." She wanted to tell him about the breakup face-to-face, so she kept her tone even. "Meet us there, please Cody. Come on—we need a day of fun, you and me."

In the end he agreed, and promised to bring a bag of hotdog buns for the barbecue. Bailey conveyed the information to Elaine Baxter, and everything was set. Now, though, she could hardly wait to see him. She wondered a dozen times if she'd dressed too young or if he'd think she was being too forward for inviting him. She tried to remember her mother's advice—take it slowly. She'd known Cody since she was in middle school, and he'd made it clear he only wanted to be her friend—both then and now. There was nothing to rush, so her mom didn't need to worry. Even still the time couldn't go fast enough.

They reached the lake and hauled their coolers and picnic baskets down the hill to the place where the Baxters were set up.

Bailey was struck by how much the crowd had grown over the years. Everyone was there—most of them having arrived hours earlier to set up. A quick scan of the sandy beach and she saw all the Baxter kids and their spouses, their children. Too many to count, anymore. She spotted Dayne and Luke playing with their kids near the water's edge. Every one of the kids wore matching life jackets, and as Bailey came closer she could make out the words stitched in white across the back of each one. "Baxter Baby," they read.

Bailey had a feeling they were Dayne's doing. It was at the annual Fourth of July picnic that he'd first found his family, after all. The event held more meaning for the Baxters than anyone outside the circle could ever know.

"Flanigans!" John Baxter raised his hand and motioned to a table adjacent to the trees and not far from the water. "We saved that one for you. So glad you could join us!"

They were setting up their table, she and Connor spreading out the checkered plastic tablecloth when she felt someone behind her. Before she could turn around, Ricky and Justin came running up from the water. "Cody!" They shouted his name at the same time.

Bailey turned and saw that he was only a few feet from her, his eyes on hers. He didn't make the moment awkward, or let his eyes linger on hers. Nothing that could be construed as anything out of the ordinary for a couple of old friends. He hugged her quickly and turned to the boys. "Hey, guys! I brought a football!"

He and the boys helped get the rest of the things down the hill from the Flanigans' SUV, and then, with a quick look back at her, Cody followed the boys to the water. They played football for a long time, splashing through the water and knocking each other into the gentle waves lapping at the water's edge.

Bailey met up with Katy and the two of them talked about the progress with Jeremiah Productions—how the guys felt good about Luke Baxter's contract. "Brandon Paul can't change the movie," Katy seemed satisfied. "Now we're all praying the movie changes him."

With everything in her, Bailey tried to stay focused. She believed in Jeremiah Productions, and she most certainly would pray for Dayne and Keith. But she was grateful for her dark sunglasses, because she kept being distracted by Cody. At times, she couldn't take her eyes off him. He was tan from being outdoors every day with football, and his white tank top only emphasized the fact. He was tall and muscled and supremely athletic. His hair was cut short, the way Bailey loved it—accenting the handsome ruggedness of his face.

She had to remind herself again and again not to stare.

Finally, when she'd been social enough and helped all she could help, Bailey kicked off her Jack Purcells and joined the boys near the water.

"She's on your team!" The announcement came from Ricky.

Bailey put her hands on her hips and made a face at him. "You'll be sorry."

"You will." Connor grinned at her. "She can throw the ball, little brother."

"So whose team am I on?"

Cody ran close for a pass and caught it inches from her. He stopped, his chest heaving, his breath minty against her face. "Mine." He took a few steps and flung the ball back to BJ, then he glanced back at her. "Okay? Just follow my lead."

Her knees felt weak, and she silently yelled at herself. *Get a grip, Bailey Flanigan. This is Cody who you've known forever. Cody who only wants to be your friend.* Even so she wanted to tell him that wouldn't be a problem. She'd follow him anywhere.

He was going on about the rules. "It's a passing game. Sort of football and volleyball mixed. Main thing is don't drop the ball."

"Okay." She was ready. She really could throw the ball and she wouldn't mind getting splashed a little. It was easily the hottest day so far that summer.

"Better take off the hat." Connor backed up, his feet in the sand, body in position.

"It's fine. I won't be getting that crazy."

But just at that moment Ricky winged the ball in their direction. Bailey ran forward to catch it just as Cody shuffled sideways, neither of them more than a little aware of the other. In a rush the two of them collided and fell together into the knee-deep water.

As hot as the day was, the cool lake water made Bailey catch her breath. She was soaked as she wiped sand from her eyes and propped herself up on her knees. Her cute hat was still somewhere in the water. "It's freezing."

"Yep." Cody was drenched too. He started laughing, and the sound of it was contagious. He held up his hand for Bailey to help him up. "I'm stuck in the sand. Seriously."

She was laughing too, now, and she helped him to his knees. Side by side, he put his arm around her waist and the two of them struggled to their feet. Cody snatched her hat from just beneath the surface and handed it to her—drenched and covered with slimy pieces of lake grass. "I forgot to tell you … the most important part."

"What's that?" Gradually they tried to trudge toward the shore, but Bailey tripped on something. She fell against Cody and knocked them both back into the water. Now Bailey was laughing so hard she wasn't sure she could do anything but sit back and let the moment have its way with her.

"The most important part is …" Cody was barely able to catch his breath, laughing at least as hard as she was, "you have to call it."

"Call it?" Bailey was sitting in waist deep water, alongside Cody, and as soon as she could talk through her laughter she looked at him, at a piece of lake grass strung across his face. She picked it off, falling into another wave of laughter too strong to fight. When she could finally talk, she put her sorry-looking hat back on her head and looked right at him, her eyes bleary. "Call it?"

"Yes." He splashed her a little. "You have to call it."

"Okay, fine." She laughed again. "Call it what? It's a football."

That was all Cody needed to hear. Now he let himself fall completely back into the water. As he did, he intentionally pulled her with him, splashing her and teasing her. "You told me you could play!"

A crowd of Baxters and Flanigans had gathered along the near shore, laughing and enjoying the moment. "Way to go, honey," her dad called out. "Way to use everything I taught you."

They were on their feet now, more careful to watch their steps so they would actually make it to shore. Somehow, Bailey still had her hat, though she could only imagine how they looked together. The moment they reached the shore, Connor stepped up and snapped their picture, arms around each other's waists, lake grass hanging from their clothes and hair. And smiles wider than the lake behind them.

Bailey had a feeling it was a picture they'd remember forever.

Once the commotion died down, she found her sunglasses, and she and Cody took their towels down the beach a stretch and spread them out next to each other. Bailey was glad she'd worn her hair in braids. Once she'd brushed herself off, and after she dried, she'd be good as new. A little rumpled, but that didn't matter. Rumpled worked for a Fourth of July picnic.

"I thought you were one of the boys trying to tackle me," Cody said as he settled onto his towel. He sat up and leaned back on his hands. "It was a pretty good bit of contact."

"I know." Bailey rubbed her shoulder. She, too, leaned back on her hands. Their shoulders were close, though nowhere near touching, but still Bailey felt like she was dreaming. She and Cody so close together, laughing and sharing a day like this. Bailey reminded herself to breathe. She laughed lightly, and turned her face to the sun. "I remember thinking, 'Wait ... you're supposed to be on my team.'"

He chuckled a few times and shook his head. "See what I mean ... I'm always laughing around you."

She made a funny face and peered at him warily. "I don't give you much choice."

"Ah, that's okay." He nudged his elbow against hers. "I love laughing, Bailey. You should know that."

Neither of them needed to talk, and still Bailey felt close to him. It was that way now as they let the sun dry them, their faces turned upward. Cody broke the silence first. "Tim had something with his family? That why he didn't come?"

Funny how long she'd waited to tell him her news. When she first broke up with Tim, she'd thought about calling Cody constantly. But the timing had never seemed right.

Until now.

She turned slightly, studying him, still unable to believe that he was here beside her and that she was free to enjoy the fact. She drew a steady breath. "I wanted to tell you in person."

He looked at her, and she could see his eyes through his sunglasses, the way they locked on hers. "Tell me what?" Cody knew her so well, he must've sensed the subtle change in her tone.

"Tim and I ... we broke up."

Slowly Cody turned to face her, searching her eyes and her face. He wasn't smiling or rejoicing, just wanting to hear every detail. "Like ... a serious breakup?"

"Yes." It would be inappropriate for her to smile, so she bit her lip and looked down at the sand between them. "Ten days ago. But I told you, Cody ..." she lifted her eyes to his. "It was coming for a long time."

"So you're ..." he looked like he wasn't sure if he should hug her or offer words of comfort. "You're okay?"

This time she couldn't help but smile just a little. "It was my idea." She winced, sensing the laughter in her voice again. "The whole breakup scene didn't go that well."

"It didn't?" He was still maintaining his respect toward Bailey's two years with Tim, but even then she watched the corners of his lips lift a little. "What happened? You didn't push him in a lake, did you?"

She covered her mouth, trying to stop from losing herself to a laughing attack when she was supposed to be upset over her break-up. "No." She returned the elbow nudge and shook her head. "I didn't push him in a lake." Again she made a nervous face. "Worse than that."

"Worse?" Cody raised his brow, as he fanned his still soaking wet tank top. "What could be worse?"

"I called him the wrong name."

"What?" Cody sat up straight, his eyes wide. "You did not."

"I did." She had a feeling Cody was trying not to laugh, same as her. "I felt terrible. Seriously."

Cody started to laugh, and he quickly lost control. He let himself fall back on his towel and Bailey did the same on hers. They lay there on the sand, their bodies a foot apart, laughing until they had to stop to catch their breath. "Sorry ... it's really not funny."

"I know." Bailey dabbed at her eyes. "I guess it's just ... I keep seeing Tim the way he talked to you that day."

"I wasn't going to say so." Cody chuckled again, little bursts that threatened to consume him once more. "But the wrong name? During a breakup?"

They fell silent then, needing a moment to regroup from the laughter and the lake water and this new reality between them. The reality that Bailey no longer had a boyfriend. Every minute or so one of them would start to laugh again, and for the next hour and even after they were dry and back with the group eating dinner, Bailey caught Cody's shoulders shaking a few times, silent laughter racking his body. He sat across from her, and when she had taken a full drink of iced tea, he mouthed the words, "The wrong name?"

Her tea came spewing out on her plate, soaking her burger. But she didn't care. A hamburger had never tasted better. Not until after the picnic, after Landon and John Baxter had staged their annual fishing derby and again John had won, did Cody find her and pull her aside. This time his eyes lingered, and she loved the feeling. "Wanna take a walk?"

"Sure." She checked in with her mom and the two of them set off for the path that led through the woods and around the perimeter of the lake. It was already dusk, so Bailey was sure the walk wouldn't take long. There would be fireworks over the lake tonight, and all of them wanted to get lined up on blankets, shoulder-to-shoulder, so they could take in the display.

They walked slowly, closer together than they'd been since their lake fiasco. Bailey's clothes were dry, but the air had cooled considerably. That or Bailey couldn't fight the constant chill she felt in his presence. Either way, she was grateful for Cody's warmth beside her.

"Seriously," he grinned at her, but he was in control now. No bursts of laughter threatening his composure. "You're doing okay? About Tim?"

"I should've done it sooner." Her eyes locked on his, and gradually they slowed to a stop. "He never had my heart." She leaned against a tree at the edge of the path, and he faced her.

"No?" He looked mesmerized, lost in the moment. The same way she felt.

"No." Bailey wanted to capture this, slow it down and freeze it. But already everything seemed to be happening in slow motion. What was happening to them? The feeling consuming her was too great to fight.

"I have a question." He ran his finger along the side of her face, his voice deep with emotions neither of them were ready to admit. Not yet, anyway. In the distance they could hear the laughter and voices from the picnic, but they had walked far enough that they were alone.

They were definitely alone.

"Ask it." She lowered her chin, a new shyness coming over her. Could he finally see how she felt about him? How long she'd wanted to be lost in a moment like this? "Go ahead," her tone fell to a whisper. "You can ask me anything."

Cody came a step closer. They wore no sunglasses, so the raw emotion in their eyes was there for both of them, capturing them, intoxicating them. He searched her face, and for a brief second fear tried to edge in on the moment. Like he was afraid of asking the question, even if he couldn't help himself. "When you and Tim broke up ... when you called him the wrong name ..."

She knew where he was going, knew exactly what he wanted to know, but she waited for him to say it anyway.

Cody took her hand, eased his fingers between hers, his eyes never once looking away. "What name did you call him?"

As long as she lived, Bailey would remember this moment with Cody, the anticipation of her answer, the answer she knew he wanted to hear. He didn't want to be her friend; he was in love with her. Finally she knew for sure. His eyes told her that without saying a single word. Their faces were only a breath apart now, and Bailey knew ... she just knew what was about to happen. Night was falling, and the waning moon shone light off the water and onto the pathway.

"Tell me." He was still waiting, motionless, the rest of the world lost to the incredible beauty of all they were feeling. "What name?"

As naturally as the beat of her heart, she reached up and put her hand alongside his face. "Yours, Cody. Who else?"

In a dance as old as time, he came to her and took her face tenderly in his hands. "Bailey ..." Then, like she'd wanted him to do for so very long, he touched his lips to hers and kissed her—slow and with years of love that had never been expressed until now. The sort of kiss a princess would wait a lifetime for. The way Bailey had waited.

Cody was careful—the kiss was over before it had time to become something more. And that was a very real possibility. Bailey had never felt this way in all her life. She didn't know feelings this intense even existed. A ripple of laughter tugged at her, and this time she kissed him. Slowly and with so much love and meaning she thought her heart would burst. "Why," she said as she eased back, "Why did we wait so long for this?"

His expression grew more serious, his smile fading. "Because you deserve better than—"

"Shhh." She put her finger to his lips. "Not today. Don't talk like that. Please, Cody."

He hesitated, then he kissed her one last time, and he grinned at her. That slow, lazy grin that had turned her head so many years ago. He stepped back, the private moment over for now. "If I'm not mistaken ... someone has a footrace to finish."

"What?" She was still dizzy from his kiss, from the newness of feelings she'd never felt with anyone but Cody Coleman. "That was years ago."

"We never finished it." He put his hands in his pockets and let his eyes melt into hers again.

"You're crazy." Bailey laughed again, and the sensation felt wonderful.

"Come on." He pretended to strike a racing pose. "And ... set, go!"

"Fine." Bailey set off, light on her feet, careful of the path ahead of her as she ran. "Try and catch me."

He let her have the lead, and she could feel him just behind her, hear him laughing like she was laughing. Just before they reached the open beach, he gently caught her hand and pulled her into another hug, one that felt more desperate than before. "You win," he whispered into her hair. Then he drew back far enough to look to the places in her heart that had long been reserved only for him. "This is really happening." His voice was still a whisper, his breath warm against her face. "Tell me it's really happening."

They wouldn't have the freedom later, so she allowed herself one more kiss, savoring the sensation. "It's really happening!" She stepped back and then impulsively hugged him again.

His hands found hers, his fingers melting between hers. His eyes sparkled, teasing her. "Can I say something?"

"Go ahead." She was already giggling.

"Finally!" They both laughed and headed down the last section of the path toward the others. Bailey had never felt anything as wonderful as his fingers wrapped around hers. They were almost to the clearing when they heard a whistling sound and through the trees they saw a distant explosion of light.

"Fireworks." She smiled up at him.

Again he held her eyes. "Not like the ones back there."

Bailey was glad he couldn't see the heat in her cheeks. She wasn't sure anyone would notice they were holding hands as they joined the group, but she didn't care. They found an open spot and Cody wrapped his blanket around their shoulders as they took a spot near her parents. The display across the sky over Lake Monroe was beautiful, each firework more stunning than the last. Bailey rested her head on Cody's shoulder, and tried to believe this was really happening. She and Cody, together the way she'd dreamed about practically forever. She smiled, dizzy from the feel of him beside her, from the way she felt protected with his arm around her.

She wasn't sure what would come next. There remained a

hundred unanswered questions, and neither of them could possibly have those answers. Not yet. One thing was sure. After tonight they could no longer lie to themselves about how they felt, about the crazy intensity of their feelings for each other. But Bailey was confident of one thing—they would take this slowly, because they had to. God would come first, or they would have nothing. Because she could see in Cody's eyes that neither of them would do anything to risk what they'd found here tonight. On Lake Monroe, in each other's arms ... on a Fourth of July they would remember as long as they lived. She thought about what Cody had said about all this. The one word that truly summed it all up:

Finally.

CODY LOOKED AT HER, AND HE could feel his eyes shining in the light of the fireworks. The intensity of emotions filling him was more than he was willing to share right now. She still didn't know about his mother, how she was taking part in an intense rehab, and how Cody still worried every day that she might relapse again.

Logic still told him Bailey was out of his league. But here, now, there was only this moment together. He relaxed a little and a quiet laugh hit him. "You know what?" he whispered.

"What?" Her eyes danced, and he felt himself getting lost in them.

He held her eyes, memorizing the way he felt. "It's just like football on the beach." He didn't look away, and neither did she. Both of them lost in the way it felt to be together like this.

"Like football on the beach?" she whispered. She looked like she, too, wanted this time to last forever. "The two of us ... finally finding this ... that's like football?"

"Yes." He smiled at her. "Someone has to call it."

A Note from Karen

Dear Reader Friends,

Thanks again for traveling with me through the pages of *Take Three*. This time, telling the story felt like a sprint—a flat-out run. I always outline my books, and *Take Three* was no exception. But this time the characters kept getting ahead of me. I know, I know. For people who never live in imaginary worlds, the idea of the characters taking charge sounds a little crazy. Like maybe I need more time with people who breathe. But that's seriously what happened this time. Major events happened in *Take Three* that simply weren't on my outline. I'd get to the next chapter, and the characters would basically refuse to cooperate. Which, of course, was fine for me because it was fun. It was a full-out, fast-paced run through a story I came to love deeply—as differently as it turned out.

Here's the most exciting part—now that we've gotten to this point, *Take Four* will be a blast to write. New events and crazy changes are definitely going to happen because some of what happened here was supposed to happen there. One example? Bailey's breakup with Tim. That girl was supposed to take a break, only. Find a little space away from Tim. But I was sitting with her at that restaurant table, listening to Tim trash talk Cody Coleman, and that girl absolutely demanded a complete breakup. I could only agree, and so it was.

Another surprise move—bringing Dayne in as one of the producers. It made sense that Chase would go home with his family, because he missed his girls, and he wasn't sure if he could take another year away from them. But Dayne was a huge surprise. It just happened that as Chase wanted to be home again, Dayne was missing movies. This time around, he wanted to see a different side of Hollywood—the side that believes a faith-based film is exactly what the market wants. And he wanted to work with his brother, Luke Baxter. Anyway, the whole process was a thrill ride. I hope you thought so too. Of course, it was hard going through Andi's part of the journey, but I loved how God met her at every turn in the road. She still has a lot to walk through, but it was wonderful to see her come back to her family and make the first step in turning back to Jesus.

By the end of *Take Three*, I could hardly wait to get the book into your hands, and I was struck by an exciting realization: There would now be much more to write about in *Take Four*! In the final book of the Above the Line Series, Bailey will take part in an adventure that I never imagined until I finished *Take Three*. That's what happens when the characters take over the storytelling!

And guess what my next stand-alone book is? That's right—*Unlocked*! The story has pressed in and around my heart for a few years, and I believe it will be one of my strongest ever. God gave me the complete outline on a recent cross-country flight from Dulles Airport to Portland. Twenty-four pages of handwritten notes in a spiral-bound notebook. When I was finished, I was quietly crying—the story that real and rich in my heart. I could only thank God because the outline, the story, felt like such a complete gift. And maybe one day a real-life Dayne Matthews will want to turn it into a movie. Only God knows!

Also, I have a big surprise for you at the end of this series. My next series is already coming to life, and it will involve many of your favorite characters! Stay tuned, and know that I pray for God to continue to lead me as these stories fill my heart. As always, I look forward to hearing your feedback on *Take Three*. Take a minute and visit my website at www.KarenKingsbury.com, where you can find my contact information and my guestbook.

Feel free to write me a private letter or post a public guestbook entry about how God is using these books in your life.

On my website you can check out my upcoming events page in case I'll be speaking somewhere near you. At my events we'll have the chance to meet and share a hug and a picture together. Also on my website, you can get to know other readers and become part of a community that agrees there is life-changing power in something as simple as a story. You can post prayer requests or read those already posted and pray for those in need. You can send in a photo of your loved one serving our country, or let us know of a fallen soldier we can honor on our Fallen Heroes page.

My website also tells you about my ongoing contests including "Shared a Book," which encourages you to tell me when you've shared one of my books with someone. Each time you email me about this, you're entered for the chance to spend a summer weekend with my family. In addition, everyone signed up for my monthly newsletter is automatically entered into an ongoing once-a-month drawing for a free, signed copy of my latest novel.

There are links on my website that will help you with matters that are important to you — faith and family, adoption, and ways to reach out to others. Of course, on my site you can also find out a little more about me and my family, my Facebook and YouTube channel, and my Karen's Movie Monday — where I release occasional Monday YouTube clips dealing with some aspect of my family and faith, and the wonderful world of Life-Changing Fiction™.

Another way to stay in touch is to follow me on Twitter. I will be giving a free cruise passage to two of my Twitter friends this fall — so join up. It's free and fun, and much less time-consuming than Facebook.

Finally, if you gave your life over to God during the reading of this book, or if you found your way back to a faith you'd let grow cold, send me a letter at Office@KarenKingsbury.com and write "New Life" in the subject line. I would encourage you to connect with a Bible-believing church in your area and get hold of a Bible. But if you can't get hold of one, can't afford one, or don't already have one, write "Bible" in the subject line. Tell me how God used this book to change your life, and then include your address in your email. My wonderful publisher Zondervan has supplied me with free copies of the New Testament, so that if you are unable to find a Bible any other way, I can send you one. I'll pay for shipping.

One more thing. I've started a program where I will donate a book to any high school or middle school librarian who makes a request. Check out my website for details. Again, thanks for journeying with me through the pages of this book. I can't wait to see you next time for *Take Four*, the final installment in the Above the Line Series. *Take Four* will answer a lot of questions you might have about Bailey and Cody and the future for the producers.

Until then, my friends, keep your eyes on the cross, and don't forget to look for angels.

In His light and love,
Karen Kingsbury

www.KarenKingsbury.com

READER STUDY GUIDE

1. In the early part of *Take Three*, Chase Ryan feels concerned about his ability to handle the pressures of producing. Have you or someone you know ever been in a job or a season of life when these feelings were an issue? Explain.
2. Chase's pastor asked him to consider becoming the church's new youth pastor at a time when the idea seemed crazy to Chase. The pastor's explanation was an easy one—he had prayed about the position, and Chase's name came to the top of the list. Have you or someone you know ever had God present a change in careers or locations that at the time seemed crazy, but that turned out to be God working in mysterious ways? Describe.
3. How did Chase come to see that the change in careers was God's plan for his life? How did that scene with Chase's wife and daughters in the backyard of their home make you feel?
4. How did Keith feel when he realized he might be losing his co-producer? Give an example of a time when you felt as if God had forgotten you. How did that situation turn out?
5. What was Dayne Matthews' last experience with Hollywood? Why do you think he'd choose to come back to the entertainment field at this time?
6. Describe your thoughts on the recent increase of faith-based films. What do you think this area of filmmaking should strive for, and how do you see it affecting today's culture?
7. The book mentions that Andi Ellison cut her hair and dyed it dark. Why do you think she did this? Have you or someone you love ever attempted to change something on the outside when the real change needed to come from within? Describe.

8. Through most of the book, Andi is determined to have an abortion. What do you think led to this decision?
9. How could Keith and Lisa have done a better job with Andi through her freshman year at Indiana University? What is a mistake some parents make in raising Christian kids toward adulthood, and how can this mistake be avoided?
10. Tim and Bailey are in their second year of dating through most of this book. What did you like about their relationship? How was it lacking?
11. Who do you like better for Bailey—Tim or Cody? Explain why.
12. When Bailey and Cody go on the retreat to Lake Monroe, what in their conversation shows that Cody has matured from the guy he once was? Do you think it's possible for single young women to have friendships with single young guys? Why or why not?
13. Bailey's family often spends time together—like the time they all went to the summer scrimmage football game. Why is this important for the Flanigan family? Tell about a time when you or someone you know made an effort at creating family together times.
14. Keith and Lisa make an attempt to help Andi by taking her to a Christian counselor. How have you seen Christian counseling be beneficial in your life or in the life of someone you know? Explain.
15. Andi makes a decision to lie to her parents about her pregnancy, and about her trip to Indianapolis. The Bible calls the devil "the father of lies." How is this evident in the lies Andi tells? How does lying about her situation nearly destroy Andi?
16. Tell about a time when lying nearly destroyed you or someone you know. How did you or that person finally come around to the truth? What was the outcome?

17. Andi runs into the Kunzmann family, and their intervention makes a dramatic impact on her. Describe a time when you or someone you know was affected by a stranger who came along just at the right moment.
18. Andi plans to arrive at the abortion clinic earlier than it opens to avoid protestors. What do you know of people who protest outside abortion clinics? What do you think about them and their mission to save lives of unborn babies? Which of their methods are effective? Why or why not?
19. On her way into the clinic, Andi is approached by Clarence. What is his role in her life? Explain whether you think he might've been an angel. The Bible says in Hebrews, chapter 13, "Do not forget to entertain strangers, for by doing so some people have entertained angels without knowing it." What does this verse mean to you?
20. Tell about a time when you or someone you know experienced what might've been an angel encounter.

Read an excerpt from the next book in the Above the Line Series: *Take Four*

The audition was more strenuous than anything Bailey imagined. If she'd known how many hours of dancing they'd do, and how they'd be expected to sing without any sign of exertion throughout, she would've practiced more for the opportunity. But even so, she did her best.

One thing was certain. The casting director from *West Side Story* was right about the numbers. There had to be a thousand college kids lined up around the block looking for a shot at only a couple of ensemble spots. The slight flicker of hope was that the audition had grown into a combined talent search for not just the spots open on *West Side Story*, but also a few ensemble jobs with *Wicked* and *Mary Poppins*.

Bailey would've been thrilled with a part in any of those shows.

She moved to the side of the room and wiped her forehead with a towel from her bag. At the same time, she pulled a water bottle from among her things and downed it in three long swigs. Her mom had given each of them two bottles, which was a good thing. Already the audition had gone for five hours. Cuts had been made every hour or so, probably based on looks more than anything. So far, she and Tim were still in the running.

"Okay, everyone. Take five." Sebastian was running this part of the audition and the next. He gestured to them to go their own ways, and throughout the gymnasium-sized room the dancers fell into groups of two or three and moved to the side walls. Bailey wanted to talk to Tim, but she needed to get word to her mom about what was happening.

She turned her cell phone on and moved into the hallway. Her mom answered almost instantly. "Did they make their decisions yet?"

"Not hardly." She tried to keep the weariness from her voice, but it was impossible. She was ready to lie down and take a nap right there in the hallway. "It'll be at least another two hours by the looks of it."

"How's Tim doing?"

"We're both doing about the same. I think the directors like us, but the place is filled with so many dancers. It's overwhelming."

Her mom had hired a car for the day, and after breakfast the driver had dropped Bailey and Tim off. Now Bailey's mom was making her way down the shops along Fifth Avenue, killing time until the audition was finally over. "Okay." She sounded upbeat, her enthusiasm contagious. "Go give it your best, sweetheart. I'll pray."

Bailey's heart melted at her mother's words. In the last few years her mom had admitted only a couple times that she wasn't looking forward to the day when Bailey moved to New York City. She and Cody had talked about it too. He made her promise she wouldn't think about the two of them, their future. Not this weekend, with her dreams on the line. Even so, she thought about him constantly.

The break ended much too quickly, even before Bailey could connect with Tim. The next set started off with just the guys. There were maybe a hundred left by now, and Sebastian placed Tim in the front row. "Okay, follow me and pay attention. I won't repeat myself. Once we're all up to speed, I'll walk the aisles. If I tap you, you're finished for the day. Thank you for coming out. If you remain untapped, stay here. You've made it to the next round."

Sebastian launched into a difficult series of eight-counts, all set to a ridiculously fast beat. Bailey wasn't sure what show the dance represented, but she doubted the ensemble would perform it at this speed. Probably just one more way the director could make cuts. Dancers who couldn't keep up were eliminated. End of story.

The teaching session lasted only ten minutes at the most, and then the guys were on their own, running over the series of eight-counts again and again while Sebastian and three of his assistants walked between the rows and tapped the shoulder of one guy after another. When they'd passed by every guy in the room, only eight dancers remained.

Tim was one of them.

She wanted to stand up and clap for him, but it wasn't the moment. She hoped he could feel how proud she was, how glad that the dreams he had were coming true right before their eyes. Enough time had passed since their breakup that they really had found their friendship again. A friendship void of desire for something more.

Sebastian gave the guys a ten-minute break and then ordered them back in the room to watch the girls. He barked out orders to the female dancers, forming them in rows similar to the guys. "Same thing, ladies. I'll teach you the dance and you'll perform it over and over until I've walked past every one of you. Same drill as the guys. If I tap you, thank you for coming out. If not, please stay for the next round."

Bailey felt exhausted as she walked out to her place on the floor. She was in a back row, and she wondered as she took her spot whether that was a problem. Was her placement a sign of things to come? She stretched her legs behind her, one at a time, and wished again that she'd done more to prepare for this moment. She was so tired she wasn't sure she could learn a single eight-count, let alone a series of them.

Sebastian clapped his hands, fast and intense. "This is the beat, girls. Stay with me."

Then he launched into a dance harder than anything Bailey had ever done. All her life she figured she was ready for an audition like this, ready to leap and twirl and soar across a Broadway stage. After all, she'd done this for CKT a hundred times. But it took all her physical and mental energy to grasp the dance, and in what felt like no time, Sebastian shouted out the order. "Ready ladies, uh five, six, seven, eight."

With that, the pulsing music began and one row of dancers after another burst into action, performing as if their lives depended on their next move. Sebastian seemed to know exactly what he was looking for. He walked the rows tapping on the shoulder of nearly every girl he passed by. Bailey wanted to pray or hold her breath, but all she could do was dance.

Finally it was her turn, and she could picture it, feel him walking past her, avoiding her shoulder, giving her the privilege of making it to the next round. They sort of knew each other, really. So maybe he'd have pity on her and ...

She kept dancing, pushing herself, but just then Sebastian hesitated near her and gave her a sad look and a quick raise of his brow, as if to say she should've worked harder. Then without giving her another few seconds to prove herself, he tapped her shoulder.

And that was that.

When the music stopped, Bailey did everything she could not to cry. She walked with the group of girls who were being let go, and she found her bag along the wall. *God ... why? The prayer came instantly, silently. I asked for Your will, and this is what happens?*

But even as her ungrateful words overflowed into the most selfish of prayers, she had a realization. She wasn't the only one who had prayed for God's will here at this Broadway audition. Also praying were her parents and brothers, and Cody. Every one of them had asked God for His perfect will, which could only mean one thing.

It wasn't God's will that she get a job on Broadway. Not now anyway.

The realization grew into more of a tremendous relief, and very quickly her silent prayer changed to one of gratitude. What had she told Cody at their Lake Monroe retreat? She wasn't sure if she wanted to live in the city, right? Wasn't that how she'd been feeling? And now here she was, after being given a fair shot at a legitimate role, and God had closed the door.

Which meant she would return home for the rest of the summer and see Cody as often as she wanted. She would be home for college another year, and there for every fall football game at Clear Creek High. The longer she thought about the gift she'd been given, the more it felt like one.

She could hardly wait to call Cody.

But first she wanted to watch Tim, this last and final stage of his audition. She slid to the floor and sat next to her bag. The other girls were gone, and she wasn't sure if she was allowed to stay. But she wanted to be there, because what if ... what if Tim was chosen? How weird would that be? Him living here and performing without her? Her heart pounded in her chest, Tim's next year being decided in the next few minutes by strangers in an oversized New York City dance hall. She dragged the towel over her forehead again and opened another water bottle. *Your will, God ... let Tim receive Your will ...*

Sebastian paired up the eight remaining girls with the eight remaining guys. This time Bailey had no doubt where the dance came from. It was the ensemble number from "Dancing through

Life," one of the biggest numbers in the musical *Wicked*. The dance was one any musical theater kid would've loved to learn.

Again Sebastian wasted no time. He taught them half the dance, and then counted down as the music began. Tim was paired up with a small Asian girl, a beautiful dancer whose stage presence made up for what she lacked in height. Bailey watched them, and she couldn't blink, couldn't look away. When had Tim gotten so strong, so good at commanding the stage?

The decision was made quickly that four pairs would remain. They wouldn't be cast as pairs unless the directors made that call, but altogether they were only looking for eight dancers. "If I call your number, you may sit down. If not, please get your things and leave. Again, thank you for your time." He read from a list without fanfare or build-up. A minute later, half the dancers were leaving, and the other half—including Tim—were sitting down on the floor, their eyes on Sebastian.

"Congratulations. We saw more than twelve hundred dancers today, and you eight have won the jobs. You'll each be given a minimum six-month contract and connected with a housing director. Your minimum pay will be two thousand dollars a week," he grinned at them, "which should be plenty—especially if some of you share apartments, the way our housing director will suggest."

Bailey put her hand over her mouth. Two thousand dollars a week? For a minimum of twenty-six weeks? That was over fifty thousand dollars! Bailey had no idea ensemble Broadway actors made that kind of money. Tim didn't dare turn around until Sebastian released them, but then he dashed across the floor to Bailey and swung her around in two full circles. "I did it! I can't believe it, Bailey, it's really happening."

He seemed to remember that she hadn't made it, and he brought his excitement down several notches. "They should've picked you, Bailey. You were amazing."

She blinked back tears, her smile firmly in place. "It wasn't God's will." She squeezed his shoulder. "But, hey … congratulations. I'm so proud of you. When will you know what show you're in?"

"Didn't you hear him? At the end there he pointed to each of us and told us where we'd be working." His face was all lit up again. "I'll be part of *Wicked*. I can't even believe this is happening."

Wicked? The top show on Broadway? She was suddenly nothing but thrilled for Tim. If he could win a role in the ensemble for that show, this first six-month contract would only be the beginning. She was grateful they'd broken up nearly two months ago. Otherwise they might've been confused by this good-bye — since the separation here was out of their hands. But Bailey had long since let Tim go — long before their breakup. Now she was truly happy for him and his future here in New York City.

Bailey phoned her mom, and five minutes later the car pulled up. Jenny gave each of them a quick hug. "Okay, I'm dying. What happened?"

Bailey took the lead. She smiled, even as another layer of tears built in her eyes. "Tim got a job with *Wicked*. He was one of four guys chosen. You should've seen him. He was easily the best out there."

Her mom's immediate response was to congratulate Tim, but at the same time she reached out and took hold of Bailey's knee, squeezing it as a way of saying she hadn't missed the obvious. If the news was about Tim, then that meant Bailey hadn't been chosen. But she also knew Bailey well enough to know this wasn't the time or place for sympathy. It was Tim's shining moment, and he deserved their excitement. Not until later in their hotel room, when the door was finally shut and they were alone, did Bailey explain how she was feeling. "I'm okay. Really. I asked for God's will."

"I know, honey. I did too." Her mom hugged her. "You can try out again next summer. Don't forget that."

Bailey still wanted to act, and she had a feeling God was about to open doors for her in film. Just something that had been on her heart lately. She had talked with Cody about it just before her trip to Manhattan. As for New York, she felt pretty sure that her feelings had changed. And that by next year at this time, she might not want to audition at all.

Now, in her mother's arms, Bailey didn't say anything. Ever since the audition ended, she'd found herself practically desperate to get back to Bloomington. To her friendship with Andi and her classes at IU, to her family and the coming football season, and to her role as a leader with Campus Crusade. Back to a guy who had finally told her how he felt.

And to a future the two of them just might have together.

ABOVE THE LINE SERIES

Take One

Karen Kingsbury,
New York Times *Bestselling Author*

Could they change the world—before the world changes them?

Filmmakers Chase Ryan and Keith Ellison left the mission field of Indonesia for the mission field of Hollywood with a dream bigger than both of them. Now they have done the impossible: raised enough money to produce a feature film with a message that could change the world.

But as Chase and Keith begin shooting, their well-laid plans begin to unravel. With millions of dollars on the line, they make a desperate attempt to keep the film from falling apart—even as a temperamental actress, a botched production schedule, and their own insecurities leave little room for the creative and spiritual passion that once motivated them. Was God really behind this movie after all? A chance meeting and friendship with John Baxter could bring the encouragement they need to stay on mission and produce a movie that will actually change people's lives.

In the midst of the questions and the cameras, is it possible to keep things above the line and make a movie unlike anything done before—or is the risk too great for everyone?

Available in stores and online!

ABOVE THE LINE SERIES

Take Two

Karen Kingsbury,
New York Times *Bestselling Author*

Filmmakers Chase Ryan and Keith Ellison have completed their first feature film, and Hollywood is buzzing with the news. In the wake of that excitement, the producers acquire rights to a novel that has all the ingredients they want for their next project. At the same time they cross paths with a well-connected player who introduces them to the right people, and suddenly every studio in town wants to talk to Chase and Keith. The producers' dreams are on the verge of coming true, but Chase's marriage is strained and Keith's daughter – Andi Ellison – is making questionable choices in her quest for stardom. The producers are gaining respect and are on the verge of truly changing culture through the power of film – but is the change worth the cost?

Available in stores and online!

Beyond Tuesday Morning

Karen Kingsbury

Winner of the Silver Medallion Book Award

Determined to find meaning in her grief three years after the terrorist attacks on New York City, FDNY widow Jamie Bryan pours her life into volunteer work at a small memorial chapel across from where the Twin Towers once stood. There, unsure and feeling somehow guilty, Jamie opens herself to the possibility of love again.

But in the face of a staggering revelation, only the persistence of a tenacious man, the questions from Jamie's curious young daughter, and the words from her dead husband's journal can move Jamie beyond one Tuesday morning ... toward life.

Even Now

Karen Kingsbury

Sometimes hope for the future is found in the ashes of yesterday.

A young woman seeking answers to her heart's deepest questions. A man and woman driven apart by lies and years of separation ... who have never forgotten each other.

With hallmark tenderness and power, Karen Kingsbury weaves a tapestry of lives, losses, love, and faith—and the miracle of resurrection.

Available in stores and online!

Share Your Thoughts

With the Author: Your comments will be forwarded to the author when you send them to *zauthor@zondervan.com*.

With Zondervan: Submit your review of this book by writing to *zreview@zondervan.com*.

Free Online Resources at www.zondervan.com

Zondervan AuthorTracker: Be notified whenever your favorite authors publish new books, go on tour, or post an update about what's happening in their lives at www.zondervan.com/authortracker.

Daily Bible Verses and Devotions: Enrich your life with daily Bible verses or devotions that help you start every morning focused on God. Visit www.zondervan.com/newsletters.

Free Email Publications: Sign up for newsletters on Christian living, academic resources, church ministry, fiction, children's resources, and more. Visit www.zondervan.com/newsletters.

Zondervan Bible Search: Find and compare Bible passages in a variety of translations at www.zondervanbiblesearch.com.

Other Benefits: Register yourself to receive online benefits like coupons and special offers, or to participate in research.